PENGUIN BOOKS

THE CRYING BABY

Sheila Kitzinger is known world-wide as a writer about child-birth, the experience of being a mother and female sexuality, and as an advocate for women's rights in health care. She is a social anthropologist and birth educator who read social anthropology at Oxford University, did postgraduate research into race relations, and went on to teach and do research at the University of Edinburgh.

With her 'psychosexual' approach to birth she has helped thousands of women, in many different countries, towards self-awareness and self-confidence. She has studied childbirth and motherhood in cultures as varied as those of the Caribbean, the United States, South Africa and Japan. She is a Consultant to the International Childbirth Education Association, an Adviser to the National Childbirth Trust and on the Board of Management of the Midwifery Resources and Information Centre. She lectures widely in North and South America, Israel, Japan, Australia and many European countries and was awarded the MBE in recognition of her services to education for childbirth.

Sheila Kitzinger's other books include *Being Born* (a book for children), *Giving Birth: How it Really Feels*, *Birth Over Thirty*, *The Midwife Challenge*, *Pregnancy and Childbirth*, *The Experience of Childbirth*, *The Experience of Breastfeeding*, *Woman's Experience of Sex* and *Freedom and Choice in Childbirth* (the last five are published by Penguin).

SHEILA KITZINGER

The Crying Baby

Illustrations by Heather Spears

PENGUIN BOOKS

PENGUIN BOOKS

Published by the Penguin Group
27 Wrights Lane, London W8 5TZ, England
Viking Penguin Inc., 40 West 23rd Street, New York, New York 10010, USA
Penguin Books Australia Ltd, Ringwood, Victoria, Australia
Penguin Books Canada Ltd, 2801 John Street, Markham, Ontario, Canada L3R 1B4
Penguin Books (NZ) Ltd, 182–190 Wairau Road, Auckland 10, New Zealand

Penguin Books Ltd, Registered Offices: Harmondsworth, Middlesex, England

First published by Viking 1989
Published in Penguin Books 1990
1 3 5 7 9 10 8 6 4 2

Text copyright © Sheila Kitzinger, 1989
Illustrations copyright © Heather Spears, 1989
All rights reserved

Printed and bound in Great Britain by
Richard Clay Ltd, Bungay, Suffolk

To all those who are worrying about
a restless, fussy or inconsolably crying baby –
a baby who needs constant attention –
a baby who seems to be at the breast non-stop –
a baby who has taken over a woman's life so completely
that she feels she is disappearing –
a baby whose needs override all others, so that
the couple feel their partnership is being eroded –
to all those women who are exhausted, drained, and feel
they haven't the strength to go on
this book is dedicated

Contents

Preface

This book isn't so much about babies as about mothers. The babies are there, of course, yelling their way through the pages. But my focus is on the woman and everything that is happening to her as she struggles with a crying baby and tries to make sense of, and to cope rationally with, the confidence-shattering, mind-numbing, overwhelming experience of having a baby who cries inconsolably.

Acknowledgements

I want to thank all the women who made this book possible – the mothers of crying and wide-awake babies who shared their experiences, their knowledge and their insight with me.

Wendy Rose-Neil of *Parents* magazine in Britain and Carol Fallows, editor of *Parents* in Australia, were an enormous help in agreeing to print the original questionnaires, and in producing computer analyses of the statistical data that formed the basis for the rest of the research.

Jenny Kitzinger made a perceptive psychological analysis of women's patterns of thinking about crying babies, which was of great help.

I am also very grateful to Dr Berry Brazelton for all the work he has done on this subject and the way in which he has stimulated my thinking and pointed me to relevant research material.

Penny Simkin worked through the chapter on drugs given to crying babies with great skill so that the drugs to which I refer are quite clear to American and Australian readers, and the patent names that apply to medications in different countries are included.

Judith Schroeder, my secretary, has brought her commitment, care and lively interest in the subject to every page, and I thank her for being in such a good working partnership with me.

Why I Wrote This Book

The sound of a crying baby – one that goes on and on, rising in crescendo, falling only to swell again to a shrill clamour that seems to pierce the eardrums with its urgency – is just about the most disturbing, demanding, shattering noise we can hear. In a baby's cry there is no future or past – only now. There is no appeasement, no negotiation possible, no *reasonableness*.

This is why I wanted to do some research into the effects on women of having a crying baby – on their images of themselves and their relationships with other people: their partners, family members, doctors and other health workers, friends, colleagues and casual acquaintances; for having a crying baby has far-reaching effects. It somehow changes not only self-perception, but your entire view of the world, how you perceive other people and how they see you.

One of the things I wanted to find out was what kinds of support are best and who can give them. There seemed to me to be a good deal that masqueraded as support but was really not helpful at all. And what happens when support is lacking and a woman feels isolated and alone? Only women who have gone through the experience of having a crying baby can enable us to understand what the ordeal is like and what can help.

I decided to trace back the whole series of events and processes in the life of a woman with a crying baby to see if there were any factors in the immediate post-partum days, the kind of delivery she had and the birth experience, and even in pregnancy, that were associated with babies' excessive crying. What combination of factors make it more likely that a baby will cry? What changes ought to take place in the care given to women in pregnancy and during childbirth if we want to have more contented babies and if women are to be freed from the anxiety and depression that many of them experience?

So I asked two magazines for mothers to help me, one in Britain and one in Australia. Each is called *Parents* and has a wide readership of women from different social classes and backgrounds whose children are, on the whole, under the age of five. A questionnaire in two slightly different versions was published in these magazines. The questionnaires are in the Appendices. Fourteen hundred women responded and in many cases not only answered the questions but provided me with a great deal of extra information and detailed descriptions of their lives and feelings. This book has grown out of everything I have learned from them. Not only did the questionnaire material provide the basis for my further research, but I am glad that the preliminary British data was also of use to some other writers on the subject, in particular Pat Gray of Cry-sis.[1]

After I had analysed responses from all the women who answered the questionnaire, I turned my attention to the 100 babies who cried most (more than six hours a day) and compared what their mothers told me with the 100 accounts from women whose babies cried least (less than two hours a day). Some exciting results came from this part of the research, and highly significant statistical associations emerged between some aspects of these mothers' and babies' lives and events that had occurred since the beginning of pregnancy.

I went on from there to interview, usually on the telephone, one in twenty of those who lived in Britain, and those women who seemed especially stressed. Some of the latter were at the end of their tether and desperately needed someone with whom to talk. It is not surprising that many had hostile and violent thoughts about their babies at times and that some had lost control and physically assaulted them. I was able to spend extra time listening to what they had to tell me and put them in touch with other people on the spot who could help them.

Another important element in my research was discovering how to cope with a crying baby, the things that help most – either because, though the baby goes on crying, a woman feels better about herself and the baby or because crying is actually reduced.

Why I Wrote This Book

There is a great store of female knowledge about babies in the Third World and traditional cultures, as well as in the industrial West, which often does not find its way into books of advice written by experts. If women can share their experiences and what they have learned from their babies, a new mother may no longer feel so isolated and desperate, and may discover some way of handling her baby that results in less crying. So, although this book does not aim to be a kind of recipe book for stopping babies crying, it is full of ideas from women about what works best for them.

A Note to the Reader

You will notice as you read that some words and phrases are repeated in other forms within brackets. This is because this edition is intended for US and British readers, so I have put in both American and British terms in order to clarify the text. In some cases, where American usage is familar to British readers, I have simply used the US term.

CHAPTER I

The Impact of a Crying Baby

The cry of the baby is music! When it is still,
especially in the night, one longs
for this primitive expression of the little being,
and is consoled, enraptured when
the helpless creature breaks into loud wails, and says to us:
'I live, give me what I need!'
Oh, cry of the baby in the night,
nightingale song for mother and father!

From Semming, *A Father's Diary*, quoted in Milicent Washburn Shinn,
The Biography of a Baby, 1900

Most of us don't have this romantic view of crying. Another father, John Todd, writing in 1829, recorded in his journal that Mary, his 4-month-old daughter, 'cries more than any child that we ever saw, sometimes there is not an hour in the night that we are not disturbed, and do not have to get up to still her. We asked the advice of four different physicians, but nothing that we have ever tried has done any good. We sometimes get quite discouraged, and almost worn out with her.'[1] At 16 months she still 'never wants to sleep . . . It seems as if we shall never have a night's rest, or ever be free from headache or fatigue.'[2]

We are biologically programmed to respond to the alarm signal of a baby's cry. It does not just give a logical message, 'I need you' or 'I'm hungry', but conveys a host of other signals to which we react emotionally and, if we are mothers, with every fibre of our being. These feelings we have are *physical*: the knot in the stomach, the choking throat, the straining to understand, which produces tense muscles, held breath, quickened heart rate – and sometimes, too, our own tears.

Mothers are expected to cope. They are supposed to know

1

instinctively what to do with babies, and their own feelings are secondary to the task of being a good mother. They are expected to know immediately after delivery how to hold and suckle a baby. In some hospitals staff watch for this as evidence of effective 'bonding'. If a woman does not understand immediately how to respond to her baby appropriately, she may be put on a secret 'at risk' list of women in danger of neglecting or maltreating their children. From the very beginning we are expected to put on a good performance, and it is this sense of being 'on show' that can add to the desperation felt by the mother of a crying baby.

In fact, mothering skills do not flow in our blood. Knowing how to get a baby latched on to the breast, feeling comfortable about holding a new-born baby, being able to bath and change a squalling infant, understanding how to respond to the pre-verbal

2

language that is the only one a baby knows – all this comes from learning and from experience. And this learning takes place best in the context of support from other people who help you grow in self-confidence.

My research as a social anthropologist has brought me in close contact with mothers and babies, both crying and non-crying. I have always been struck by how little babies cry in peasant communities and by the many ways in which babies are cared for not only by their mothers, but also by other women and older children. Reading about babies and motherhood, some of it cross-cultural, some within the sociological, psychological and pediatric literature of our own culture, also led me to focus my thinking on the relations between mothers and babies, and on what mothers know about how to prevent and deal with crying. I wanted to draw on all their female knowledge.

The first thing I discovered from the responses to questionnaires made by mothers in Australia and Britain was that the degree to which babies cry, and women's ideas as to how much a baby can be expected to cry, varies enormously. Some babies cry only less than one hour in the twenty-four, though this seems a long time to their mothers. Others cry for hours on end – sometimes for six hours out of the twenty-four.

Another thing I learned is that however much advice you are given, and however effective different methods are for other people's babies, getting your own baby to settle and feeling happier about life in general are part of a process of learning to know and understand your baby, and of an unfolding relationship in which you gain insight about yourself as well as the baby.

The aspects of women's lives that I explore in this book concern all women, not only mothers; for they are part of the female condition in our society, the culturally imposed template from which it is very difficult to escape. The mother trapped at home with a crying baby and feeling depressed and desperate epitomizes all those women who are unable to define and give voice to their own condition, who often cannot even understand why they are so miserable, and all those who realize well enough what is happening but who dare not, or cannot, break the mould lest they are punished for it, and all those who can't just walk out of the trap in which they find themselves.

A man who does not make a success of being a father can still be proud of other achievements, those that in men's lives count for much more – their jobs, sport or politics, for instance. It is usually not so for a woman. When she feels that she is failing as a wife and mother, she comes to believe that she must be failing as a woman. This is one reason why a crying baby seems to strike at the roots of our being.

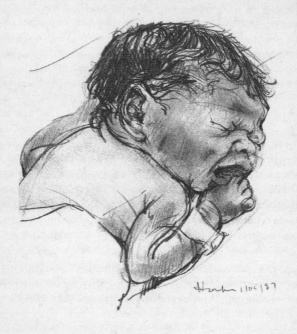

I hope that by hearing about other women's experiences the woman with a crying baby who reads this book will realize that she is not alone, for isolation and loneliness is one of the most obvious elements in the suffering a woman endures when she has an inconsolably crying baby. She feels completely cut off from everything that has happened in her life before and from other people who are not sharing the experience. She often feels isolated from a partner, too, who can escape into the world of work outside the home and may not really comprehend what she is going through.

As I listened to and read women's accounts, I was no longer surprised that they were sometimes violent towards their crying babies. I was more surprised that many control themselves so well that they do *not* hit out, especially when they are isolated from contact with other adults and are without any help or emotional support for many hours at a time. Thirty-eight per cent of all these mothers were alone for between eight and twelve hours on weekdays, and a further 34 per cent for four to eight hours each day. So nearly three-quarters of them were stranded with their crying babies for much of the day, having to cope alone, bearing full responsibility and often desperately trying one thing after another to soothe them for just a few minutes at a time. They said things like:

> I was depressed, frightened and all alone. I lost all confidence.

> There was a constant feeling of weariness and anxiety over the baby. I felt that I would be tied to him for ever – never have my own life or be free again. I wanted to leave him outside Sainsbury's [a supermarket] or get in the car and drive a 100 miles away from him. I did not want him or love him, and felt that I was a terrible mother and should never have had a child.

The phrases kept recurring: 'I felt so trapped', 'I couldn't get away from her', 'I felt completely useless', 'very guilty', 'exhausted', 'inadequate', 'bewildered'. And over and over again they said they were depressed.

Eighty per cent of those with babies who cried most talked about depression, compared with 33 per cent of those whose babies cried least. They also expressed a desperate need to escape from the baby: 57 per cent of those whose babies cried most, but also 22 per cent of those who cried least. Many were near the edge of violence and admitted that they were itching to smack the baby – 50 per cent of them, and even 20 per cent of those whose babies cried least. Some described with horror occasions on which they had broken down and smacked or shaken the baby, or thrown it on the floor.

Many were in a very stressful relationship with a sexual partner.

A third of the mothers of crying babies made negative comments about their partners, compared with only 4 per cent of those whose babies were not crying very much. A partner who is difficult to live with obviously imposes extra stress when a woman is struggling to cope with the tremendously challenging task of trying to get to know and understand her baby. A baby's crying often exacerbated conflicts in a couple's relationship. When the baby cried, the man blamed the woman for not being able to control the child and often resented being deprived of her services. The woman was striving to

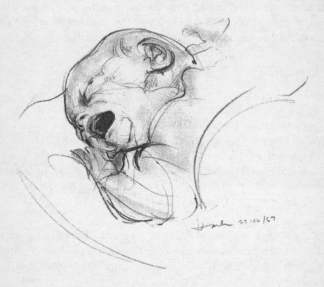

gain control over the baby's behaviour in order to placate her man – so there were *two* people she was trying to keep quiet and to satisfy. Many were desperately striving to fill the role of the good wife while at the same time meeting the baby's needs: 'I was still losing blood, so my husband sulked because he thought I should be back to normal by then, so he made me feel even less happy.'

Fathers' tolerance levels were often rather low. When a baby didn't stop crying, they either handed the child back (36 per cent), escaped from the scene (27 per cent) or started shouting (12 per cent). There seems to be a long way to go if we are really to have shared parenting in our society and if boys are to be brought up knowing how to care for small babies and feeling that it is a masculine thing to do.

But before we explore exactly how these women felt, it may be wise to ask a basic question: what is the meaning of a baby's inconsolable crying? And what about the explanations that are usually given for almost non-stop crying?

CHAPTER 2

Why Do Babies Cry?

Crying is the most powerful way a baby can summon attention. The more disturbing the cry, the more it seems to pierce our eardrums and screw up our gut. Berry Brazelton describes how he was once on a jet plane when a baby in his mother's arms started to cry lustily. 'The door to the cockpit was open and the pilot obviously could hear the sound over the noise of the engines, for after a short while he sent word to the stewardess that either she quiet the baby or shut his door, because, he said, he was afraid he might lose control of the plane.' [1]

The poetic phrase 'no language but a cry' is sometimes quoted as sufficient explanation for a baby's crying. This is not quite true. Babies do have other ways of communicating and of getting us to respond. They open their eyes wide, fix their gaze and engage in early pre-verbal conversations with an adult who is attentive. With their mothers or anyone else who is feeding them, they pause during sucking and elicit a response on the part of the adult, which usually consists of jiggling and/or verbal encouragement to continue feeding. When they are bored or over-stimulated, or simply want a break in the conversation, they turn their heads away. When they are drowsy, they become relaxed and floppy. We know from the feel of the baby's body and the little head nestling into the adult's arms or against the shoulder that he is about to drop off to sleep. A mother in close physical contact with her baby quickly learns from her baby's restlessness that in a short time he will empty his bowels. When the baby is replete and satisfied after a good feed and there is no physical urgency to do anything at all but relax and enjoy life, he conveys through reduced muscle tone and a contented Buddha-like expression that is almost a smile the message that all is well with the world.

Parents learn a hundred things about what their babies want and what feels uncomfortable or good without their having to cry. In fact, some mothers pick up their babies' messages so quickly that there is little need for them to cry. Some of these mothers tell me that they too would have crying babies, but they do not *let* them cry and give them immediate attention. They say they have 'fussy', 'jumpy', 'irritable' or 'highly stimulated' babies, but do not think of them as crying babies, though they need regular attention at certain, often prolonged, periods within the twenty-four hours – and would become very distressed if they did not get it.

Nevertheless, for most babies much of the time, and for all babies at least some of the time, crying is a way of summoning help. As Berry Brazelton says, it is 'a rich language. A cry can mean, for example, hunger, pain, anger, being wet, "pick me up", or just "leave me alone".' [2] It is an extremely effective signalling system for a creature who is new to the world and who has not yet learned our adult language.

Yet prolonged, inconsolable crying – the kind of crying that continues for two hours or more and that, though it may stop for a while when you talk to or pick up the baby, starts again within a few minutes and persists when you have done everything you can possibly think of to make the baby feel comfortable, well-fed and secure – is quite another matter.

When a baby is in a frenzy of crying, it often seems that everyone except the mother knows why the baby is distressed. Other adults come up with all sorts of explanations for the crying, many of which sound absolutely logical, and as a result the mother makes frantic attempts to change her behaviour and the way she handles the baby, her diet, the living conditions, the timing of her day, and even her psychology. Usually none of these things works, or they appear to work, but only for a limited period and then the baby's crying starts again. Occasionally, whatever has been changed occurs at the same time that the baby happens to come to the end of a crying spell or grows out of the crying. Then it is seen as the solution. Many of the explanations readily given for crying have only the flimsiest foundations. Let us look at a selection of the most common explanations of crying and what psychologists and pediatricians have to say about them. Knowing that no evidence has been produced to support some pet theories about crying may be very useful if you have a doctor who tells you that you are making the baby cry because you are so tense, or that if you switch from breast to bottle or introduce solids the baby will stop crying, or that you are not burping the baby correctly, or you are overfeeding or 'spoiling' the baby.

Fictions and fables

A baby does not cry inconsolably simply because a woman is anxious about mothering. To criticize a woman whose baby is crying almost non-stop, to say that it is her fault because she has allowed herself to get edgy and overwrought, or that she must have deep psychological problems, which are at the root of the baby's crying, is to blame the victim. It does nothing to alleviate her distress or to stop the crying. No wonder she becomes anxious when her baby cries inconsolably! Her anxiety is the result, not the cause, of the crying. This is one way in which new mothers are often made to feel guilty and why many end up believing that *nothing* they do can be right. The mother is criticized for picking up the crying baby, for leaving the baby alone, for being 'uptight' and inhibited, for being too emotional, for being passive, for being domineering, for rejecting or suffocating the child with 'smother love' and, as if all this were not enough, for being inconsistent! Whatever she does, she feels guilty. A mother's place is in the wrong!

There is no evidence to support the claim that babies cry inconsolably for hours on end simply because their mothers are the kind of people who are tense or worried about dealing with them. Back in the 1960s a study was done between crying and personality disorders, including anxiety, 'rejection of the female or maternal role' (whatever that is), depression and so on. The women who scored highest and lowest on the scale had equal numbers of crying and non-crying babies. The conclusion was that there is 'no relationship to maternal emotional factors, whether estimated clinically or measured by a standardized psychological test' and that colic is not the result of 'an unfavourable emotional climate created by an inexperienced, anxious, hostile, or unmotherly mother.' [3]

Subsequent research using different personality tests revealed that mothers of crying babies were no more likely to be neurotic than those whose babies were contented.[4] It seems that babies have their own personalities and do not merely reflect their mothers' moods.

Though some babies start crying from birth, inconsolable crying usually does not begin until the second or third week of life. If babies cry because their mothers are over-excited, anxious or lacking in confidence, you would expect them to start before this. A new mother tends to be all these things just after having a baby. Winnicott called it 'primary maternal preoccupation'. If anyone else behaved like this, it would be considered distinctly odd. But for new mothers that mixture of intense concentration on the baby, excitement, worry and self-doubt is quite normal.[5]

A pediatrician compared women whose babies had colic with others whose babies did not cry. He measured how much the mother touched her baby and her responsiveness to his cues – even her sense of humour and 'sense of success as a wife' (shades of the patriarchy again!).[6] He could discover no personality differences. What he did find, however, was that crying disturbed the relationship between mother and baby and that women quickly lost confidence and felt less warmly about their babies by the time they were 3 months old. He tested the women again when the babies were 6 months old and by that time, with the crying over, the differences had disappeared.

When babies cry a lot, there is more likely to be tension in the family. That is hardly surprising. To a large extent it is the consequence rather than the cause of the crying. Parents would have to be terribly thick-skinned to avoid getting tense when a baby cannot be consoled. I shall come back to this topic later when we discuss psychological stresses and interaction between the parents in Chapters 7 and 8.

Then there are the physical explanations. Inconsolable crying like this is not caused by air bubbles in the stomach and intestines, though people claim that it is. When babies cry a lot and gasp, they inhale air and as a result get bubbles, which are expelled as burps or farts. But this is the result of prolonged crying, not its cause. Tests

11

have been performed with barium enemas and X-rays to see if gastro-intestinal malfunction could be the reason for their crying. It is not: the stomach and intestines of contented babies look just like those of crying babies.[7]

Yet when a baby cries inconsolably and a mother can hear ominous sounds from inside the baby's tummy, with bubbles seeming to come from everywhere, this doesn't seem to make sense. When she jiggles or bounces her baby up and down in attempts at soothing her, she hears noises in the baby's stomach rather as if she were shaking a half-filled hot-water bottle, and may feel sure that this is what must be causing the crying. This is what I thought when one of my own babies cried in the evenings. But I did a little experiment. I drank three cups of tea and then jumped up and down and listened. The result was that I could hear exactly the same sloshing sound, and it was not causing *me* any discomfort. Yet it often looks as if the baby has an awful tummy-ache because he draws up his knees as we would do if we had severe stomach pains. One suggestion may be that inconsolable crying like this is caused by constipation or diarrhoea. But research has shown that this is not the case.[8]

Some babies seem to be much more comfortable if they are placed with their tummies over a hot-water bottle. Since that works with menstrual pain too, we infer that the cause of crying must be rather similar. But the fact is that a vigorously crying baby usually bends up his knees, whatever the cause – when the baby is frightened or has an injection the reaction is just the same. Babies don't just weep, they *double up* with crying. As Brazelton observes, 'When a baby is crying desperately the whole organism – gastro-intestinal, autonomic, motor – is involved.'[9]

Inconsolable crying is not caused by overfeeding either. Babies do not drink more milk than they want. It is difficult, if not impossible, to overfeed a baby, provided that the milk is breast milk or a humanized artificial milk – formula – reconstituted in the correct proportions.[10]

Nor is inconsolable crying the result of underfeeding. Of course babies cry when they are hungry. But when they are fed, or fed again, they stop. Then they may cry for other reasons – because they want to be held close or suck something or be held up so that they can see what is going on.

A breast-fed baby needs feeding more often than an artificially-fed one because the solute concentration of human milk is less than that of artificial milk. In fact, compared with other mammals, women have one of the most dilute milks of all. Deer and antelope, for example, suckle only once or twice a day. Human babies are often more like bear cubs, who suckle almost non-stop.

When babies cry, they get fed more often. Crying is an effective biological survival mechanism. In a study in the 1950s Illingworth compared fifty 'colicky' babies with fifty babies who did not cry, and followed their progress for six months. The crying babies put on more weight on average than those who did not have a crying problem.[11] In fact, a badly underfed baby usually becomes very quiet and passive, whimpering rather than crying. Even so, if you have a crying baby, people are bound to say, 'That baby is hungry' and urge you to try extra food of one kind or another. You, too, may feel that it must be hunger, especially if you are breast-feeding, because this requires a great deal of self-confidence. Mothers of crying babies often put the baby to the breast every half-hour or so during the worst crying periods. The baby grabs the nipple as if famished, only to pull away again after a few minutes and start crying again bitterly. For a mother who is trying everything she knows to soothe her baby and is giving her own body as a peace-offering, this seems like the ultimate rejection and she feels sure that she has not enough milk or that it is upsetting her baby.

If a baby is latched onto the breast correctly, with a good mouthful of areola (the dark circle surrounding the nipple) as well as the nipple drawn deep against the soft palate, and is able to suckle whenever he wants, it is very unlikely that the mother has an inadequate milk supply. And every woman can be assured that the quality and nutritional constituents of her milk are perfectly adapted to her baby's needs, whether the child is pre-term or especially large, a boy or a girl, frail or bouncing with health.

When a baby is bottle-fed, the mother is often recommended to switch to a different brand. She tries one kind of infant food after another in a frantic search to find something that suits her baby. Sometimes the baby stops just after she has introduced a new brand, so she thinks the previous formula must have 'disagreed' with the baby. But research has shown that if the baby is given an artificial milk made up in the correct proportions there is no connection between the kind of formula the baby is fed and this kind of crying. So, in theory at least, switching brands does not help. On the other hand, sometimes it is valuable occupational therapy for the woman because she feels that at least she is doing *something* to try to change the situation. Without that, she may just feel helpless and completely at the mercy of events.[12]

Digestive disturbance as a result of drinking cow's milk, even when modified for infant feeding, is another matter, however, and evidence is building that some babies are not only unable to cope with cow's milk in their diets, but are also upset by breast milk if their mothers drink a great deal of milk or have milk products in their own diets. There is more about this on page 20.

Breast-fed babies who feed 'on demand' do not cry any more, or less, than bottle-fed babies. In my own study there were equal numbers of artificially-fed and breast-fed babies in the groups who cried most and least. An Australian study came up with the same result.[13] So it is not a good idea to change from breast to bottle in an attempt to stop the crying, though many mothers do – and are advised to by friends, families, family doctors, pediatricians and the health professionals who ought to know better.

There is no connection between crying and the mother's age.[14] The first baby is not more likely to cry than other children, though mothers are often told that first babies cry more, the implication being that it is their own lack of experience that is contributing to the crying. This tends to make a woman feel even more self-conscious and awkward than she did before.[15] Boys do not cry more than girls, though mothers are often told that they do. Gender stereotypes often lead adults to think that boys must be more vigorous, angry, naughty and stubborn than girls.[16] Crying is unrelated to the occupation of the father or the mother's IQ or educational level.[17] It is not due to the mother having smoked or drunk a great deal of coffee during pregnancy. A baby is not more likely to cry when there is a family history of allergies or when other babies in the family have cried.[18]

In a study in Chicago a pediatrician examined a wide spectrum of possible associations between crying and other elements in babies' lives. He looked particularly at things the mother did or did not do that might affect her baby's crying to see if it was the consequence of a mother not knowing how to handle her baby correctly. He discovered that the crying does not occur because a mother is trying to get the baby to sleep at times when he is not ready to settle down, nor because she is not willing to let the baby have a 'good cry' before going to sleep, nor because she behaves inconsistently when the baby cries at night, nor because she does not react promptly when the baby cries.[19]

Babies don't cry because they are 'spoiled' either. As Illingworth says, 'It is difficult to understand why inconsolable crying should be ascribed to over-permissiveness. Any parent who has possessed a child with colic knows that it is the most worrying and disturbing complaint, and that a baby with obvious pain has to be picked up and cuddled.'[20]

Having ruled out all these causes of inconsolable crying, where can we go from here? In the end we are forced away from all the generalizations and have instead to look more closely at the baby and try to understand what it *feels* like to be a baby.

The one overwhelming fact about a baby as it emerges from the uterus is its energy. Indeed, even before it is born the mother has often been amazed by its energy as it kicked, jumped, swerved, rolled, jabbed, dipped, bounced, turned and somersaulted inside her. A normal baby is power-packed from the first moments of life. The mother looks down and sees this amazing creature who already has motor and communication skills that enable it to attract her attention and, once it is close against her body, to cling like a limpet. The baby can cry, turn its head, gaze at her with wide-open eyes, grasp and come homing onto the breast. The jaw snaps shut, and he starts to suck and swallow with a lively tongue and an incredible pressure coming from a mouth that, though it may look like a rose-bud, is actually a highly efficient nutritional machine. When the baby feeds, its whole body is involved in the act, the entire length of the back and the toes quivering with concentration. The new-born baby's tight grip is one evidence of an ancestral past in which the new-born being was equipped to hang onto its mother's fur or hair without losing hold as she ran from predators or foraged for food. Those little clenched fists represent survival against all odds.

And then there is the baby's cry: sharper and more intense than that of new-born lambs on the hillside, more arresting than almost any other sound that can be imagined, as it pierces the night air with a compelling message – feed me!

A baby – any baby – presents us with a fundamental paradox. From one point of view, the one depicted in advertisements in most magazine articles about babies, a baby is soft and pliable, to be held, carried, stroked and kissed. From another point of view it is a miniature dynamo of seemingly boundless energy that squirms, kicks, becomes rigid in our arms, arches its back, screams and makes impossible demands on us.

Frustrated babies

It cannot be easy for a healthy, vigorous baby to let out all the power packed inside its little body. There is not yet sufficient neuro-muscle coordination to enable movements to be successful in reaching a goal – to grasp a rattle or touch the sunbeams on the wall or the branch of a tree outside the window. As you watch a baby it is obvious that she does not accept these limited capacities. She is always striving beyond them to know, to touch, taste, see, hear more keenly and to incorporate the experiences into her own being, to make them *hers*. A baby's life seems to be a relentless striving for that which is out of reach and impossible of attainment.

It is not only that the baby is born already full of energy; from the moment of birth, too, babies are confronted by adults' ideas about them and our attempts to control them. Sometimes care-givers are fairly relaxed and allow the baby to do more or less as he pleases. In some Third World cultures adults accept small babies just as they are, without trying to mould their behaviour, on the grounds that they are not yet ready to be taught anything. This may continue for several years, until the decision is made that now the child is capable of learning, and from that point on the child's behaviour is moulded according to cultural pattern.

When I was working in Jamaica I was struck by the very relaxed attitudes adults had towards babies. Peasant mothers did not try to make them conform to pre-set schedules and they could feed whenever they liked. If a baby started to empty its bladder when sitting on the mother's lap, she casually parted her legs and let the urine stream to the ground. Her dress would soon dry out in the sun. When the baby grunted and made the little noises that told her that it was having a bowel motion, she strolled outside her hut and held her baby out over the dried mud a little way from the homestead. There was no attempt at bowel and bladder training until the child could toddle outside on its own. Babies were greatly indulged

17

by everyone in the family and no one would think of deliberately frustrating a baby in order to teach it anything.

In our northern industrial culture it is very different. From the earliest weeks we tend to be concerned to mould the child into an acceptable member of society. Mothers want their babies to have

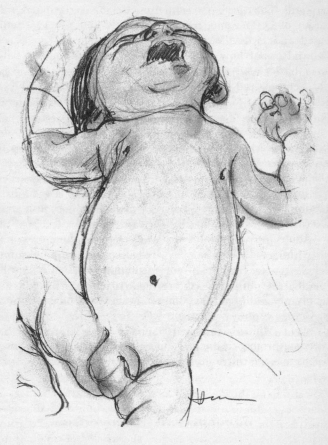

regular habits, eat and sleep at certain intervals, and – even though we try to be more casual about this than our own mothers and grand-mothers – be potty-trained and socialized at the earliest possible age.

We don't want little wild animals in our homes. We expect them to adapt to our life-styles and our divisions of night and day and times for feeding and sleeping. So we try to train and domesticate them.

They are put to bed, isolated from human contact and expected to go to sleep. They are fed and expected to settle contentedly afterwards. They are bathed and dressed and taken out and paraded in front of visitors and expected to smile and coo and make us pleased and proud. We read books and articles about parenting skills and about how long the baby should sleep. The baby, of course, hasn't read these books and magazines and goes on just as before, empowered by its own inner biological drives. Babies must often be intensely frustrated by our attempts to mould their behaviour and to acculturate them.

When babies don't do things we planned for them to do, we ask ourselves whether we are doing something wrong or whether there is something wrong with the baby. So then we try coaxing her to behave differently, make more complicated plans, and become more than ever determined to succeed. The battle is on! Thus both the baby's immaturity and our attempts to condition and train the child cause frustration and pent-up inner tension.

Adults have all sorts of ways of discharging inner tension when we are frustrated. We watch TV, listen to music, jog, smoke or drink alcohol or pour energy into making things, whether it is a 'do-it-yourself' project, or another form of creative activity. For a baby the only way of discharging this intolerable build-up of tension is to cry. Crying enables the tension to be released. It is sometimes the only way in which babies can free themselves both from the tension that comes from being immature and relatively helpless and from tensions that are culturally imposed. And the baby feels better afterwards.

Some parents' discoveries

Sometimes parents feel there must be a physical problem that, once in the open and dealt with, would stop the crying from then on. For most of us there is no easy solution like this, and the crying is caused

19

by the tension and discomfort that come from a variety of stimuli, no single one of which is responsible, but which together make the baby distressed.

On the other hand, some parents do discover a physiological key to crying and are able to change the way they handle the baby or to provide an appropriate treatment that ends the crying. In the next few pages I want to explore some solutions that other parents have found after doing concentrated detective work and following every tiny clue until a cause was revealed.

Cow's milk intolerance

Some babies cannot digest cow's milk, artificial milk derived from it or any cow's milk product. They may be sensitive to cow's milk protein or unable to digest lactose. Most so-called 'baby milks' are based on cow's milk. Babies are most likely to be miserable as a result of intolerance to cow's milk when bottle-fed. Babies who would become quite ill if fed artificially on baby milk can usually cope well with the small amount of cow's milk protein they receive in their mothers' milk. Some babies, however, are also sensitive to cow's milk proteins in breast milk after their mothers have been drinking milk or eating cheese.

A Swedish study revealed a high correlation between colic in breast-fed babies and their mothers' consumption of cow's milk.[21] One-third of breast-fed babies who cried with what was diagnosed as colic stopped crying when their mothers excluded cow's milk from their diets. A few years later two other studies were done in Britain to examine the effect of maternal dietary exclusion of cow's milk, together with eggs, on breast-fed babies with eczema.[22] Some of the babies got better when their mothers omitted milk and egg from their own diets. Not only did their eczema disappear when the mothers avoided egg and milk, but it got worse again when these foods were reintroduced. Some of the babies also had gastric upsets after their mothers had these foods. If your breast-fed baby is crying a great deal, it is worth experimenting by eliminating cow's milk from your diet. But the authors of these studies warn that only if exclusion of these foods results in an obvious improvement, and if the baby's condition deteriorates when they are reintroduced, should a woman have such a restricted diet, 'and then it should be with dietetic help to ensure nutritional adequacy'.[23] The problem is that if this is seen as a cure-all for crying, a great many mothers may be inadequately fed themselves. A diet from which all dairy foods are omitted should be embarked on with caution.

The symptoms of cow's milk intolerance are crying after and between feeds, a swollen, tender stomach, wind (gas), vomiting, bowel motions that are frothy and green, poor weight gain, a sore bottom, skin rashes or eczema and a runny nose. Bottle-fed babies have loose motions, often with undigested curds. (A breast-fed baby may have very soft, even liquid motions because nutrients in breast milk are so completely digested, so if you are feeding your baby yourself, loose motions are not a sign that anything is wrong.) Sometimes the baby's breathing is affected and you can hear wheezing or a crackle or rasp as the baby breathes. This may be the precursor of asthma or bronchitis. A baby who is sensitive to the lactose or proteins in cow's milk fails to thrive and has little resistance to infection. He often gets one cold after another and has ear infections, one sign of which is that the baby scratches or rubs his ear. Some older babies become anaemic because of inflammation and bleeding in the intestines. Very rarely, a completely breast-fed baby who is suddenly given cow's milk goes into anaphylactic shock. He becomes limp, pale and damp with sweat, he breathes with difficulty, has a fast pulse and, most frightening of all, may sink into a coma. None of these symptoms can in themselves give a sure diagnosis of sensitivity to cow's milk, but in combination they offer a strong clue that this is the cause of the trouble.

Babies who are sensitive to cow's milk are often switched to soya or goat's milk. Unpasteurized goat's milk can be dangerous. If you are using diluted fresh goat's milk, it is vital to ensure that the goat is healthy and kept under ideal conditions. Babies can also be allergic to goat's milk and to soya milk and soya products, so you need to watch the baby's reaction very carefully.

Most babies who cannot digest cow's milk become able to do so some time during their second year. Some are happier if kept on a cow's-milk-free diet right through childhood. This is especially likely to be the case with children of Chinese origin. In the Far East and in parts of Africa some people have a genetic inability to digest cow's milk.

In the production of breast milk many chemicals and food proteins are filtered out. They either do not reach the baby at all or do so in minute quantities. Yet some babies are sensitive to even these tiny amounts. Mothers have discovered that their babies cry less when they either reduce or exclude entirely all foods containing milk, including yoghurt, butter, cheese, sauces based on milk, cakes and puddings, dairy ice cream, bread and rolls, milk chocolate and confectionery. It takes three or four days after omitting cow's milk from your diet before you can see any effect on the baby's behaviour. Then the results may be dramatic.

I have heard people say that the notion that something a breast-feeding mother eats could upset her baby is simply an 'old wives' tale'. Since the mid-1970s there has been good scientific evidence that babies can react adversely to substances in breast milk that are derived from things their mothers have eaten. The 'old wives' were right all along! Some women have noticed that when they drink coffee or carbonated cola drinks their babies cry a great deal. The baby appears to be reacting to the presence of caffeine in the breast milk. Women who had found solutions to their babies crying cited, in addition to cow's milk, eggs, chocolate, nuts, strawberries, sugar, wheat and wheat products, grapes, oranges, all other citrus fruit, onions, peas and beans, certain spices, alcohol, coffee and tea. A woman told me, for example, that her little boy 'cried more if I had red wine about six to eight hours previously, and grapes had the same effect'. Another said of her daughter, 'Chocolate, coffee and alcohol always seemed to make her worse.'

If you suspect that a particular food or drink is having an effect on your baby, it is worth excluding it for a week or two. If crying is reduced, see what happens once the substance is reintroduced. If you do not experiment in this way you will never know for certain whether this food was the cause of the baby's irritability. Since most babies start to cry less some time between 10 and 16 weeks anyway – and this is often a sudden change – you may conclude wrongly that merely a chance association was cause and effect. At the risk of a couple of disturbed days, it is probably worth testing your hypothesis so as to be sure, for the baby who is sensitive to certain foods in breast milk does not necessarily continue to be sensitive to them months later. Babies grow out of food intolerance. A woman who told me her baby 'cried worse than usual when I ate eggs or cheese', said that she reintroduced these cautiously, and rather apprehensively, when he was nearly 10 months old and found that by this age he was able to tolerate them.

Other food sensitivities

A baby often starts crying inconsolably for the first time when solid foods are introduced. It may be significant that the babies who cried most in my study were more than twice as likely as the babies who cried least to have been put on solids before they were 2 months old. We know that babies under 3 months tend to have difficulty in digesting foods other than milk. A woman often decided to try solids (perhaps under pressure from other people) *because* her baby cried so much. Yet they did not reduce the crying and probably made the baby still more uncomfortable.

Some babies also react to additives in processed and packaged food, and to the presence of these additives in their mother's breast milk. These include natural products (such as annato, a red dye extracted from the bark of a tree), chemical food colourings, antioxidants and other preservatives. In Britain the Royal College of Physicians has set up a food intolerance databank that can provide doctors with details of substances in manufactured foods and lists of similar foods that do not contain these ingredients. So it is worth consulting your doctor to get expert help if you want to cut out certain foods because your baby seems to be reacting to them in your milk or when an older baby who is on solids is thought to have a food sensitivity. Wherever you live, if you think that your baby may be reacting to additives, it is worth consulting the labels on all products and keeping a note of any suspect foods.

Babies are often sensitive to the protein in eggs and to wheat. It is best to introduce a rice cereal before wheat and to try solid foods only *after* the age of 6 months, when a baby is better able to tolerate them. Give a tiny quantity at a time – one teaspoonful is ample;

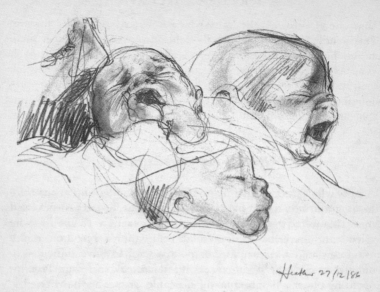

Heather 27/12/86

introduce only one new food so that you can watch for any reaction, and allow a week before trying any other new tastes.

If you have allergies yourself or are aware that there is asthma, eczema, hay fever or migraine in your or your partner's family, breast-feed as long as you and the baby are happy with it. Do not be tempted by remarks made by other people, or the blandishments of the baby-food manufacturers, to wean on to cow's milk or a mixed diet until the baby is in the second half of the first year.

Advertisements that promote a wide variety of canned and packaged foods for babies and describe them as 'real food' as compared with breast milk may offer a recipe for disaster. One baby-food advertisement, for example, contains a drawing of a baby of about 4 months, and offers a menu of fish in cheese sauce and fruit salad for lunch. It then goes on: 'Meal-time comes round. Decisions, decisions. Cauliflower cheese, vegetable and bacon risotto or maybe spaghetti bolognaise. I've had something new and delicious to try almost every day for the past two months.' This is irresponsible advertising.

If you are working outside the home it is possible to express your milk with a breast pump and store it in the refrigerator so that someone else can give it in a bottle. You can freeze extra for any emergency. Many women, too, find they can continue breast-feeding by giving feeds before and after they return from work, though it used to be claimed that it was impossible to keep up a good milk supply under these conditions. Whatever the theory, women have found that it works in practice. It is good to be able to come in from a hectic day at work and put your feet up to feed the baby.

Breathing difficulties

A baby who has difficulty breathing often finds it hard to synchronize sucking and breathing. Feeds take a long time, are exhausting and miserable for both of you because the baby can suck only in short spurts, and if you try to put the baby down after fifteen or twenty minutes, she then cries from hunger. Some babies can breathe easily only when upright. They stop crying when held over your shoulder or sitting on your lap, but cry inconsolably when lying down.

A mother knows there is something wrong, but may find it difficult to convince a doctor that this is more than just irritable crying. She realizes she is being labelled as 'over-anxious', may be told to shut the door and let the baby 'cry it out' and, because she is obviously worn out and distressed, is often prescribed tranquillizers.

One woman whose baby cried from birth told me she was made to feel it was all her fault because she was letting herself get overwrought. Breast-feeding was unsuccessful because the baby could never get a good latch. She took so long over feeds, both day and night, that the mother's whole existence became a non-stop feeding session, punctuated only by brief forays to eat and snatched sleep. Feeding became slightly easier when the baby was switched to artificial milk, since she was able to get the feed faster. But the crying persisted, she brought back feeds and coughed a lot. Because the baby was distressed when lying down, the mother learned that she either had to prop her up or hold her in her arms all the time. So she slept sitting up against a pile of pillows with the baby leaning against her.

She asked her doctor to refer her to a specialist, but was told that the baby was perfectly normal and she was making a fuss about nothing. The doctor suggested that she must be communicating anxiety to the baby and this was causing the crying. He wrote prescriptions for tranquillizers for her and a variety of different medicines for the baby, including a cough suppressant. After being dosed with this, the baby went into respiratory distress and was rushed to the hospital, where her breathing had to be assisted. After prolonged investigations and repeated breathing crises that resulted in emergency treatment and a hospital stay every third or fourth week, the pediatrician diagnosed asthma.

Infections

Some women discovered that their baby's crying was due to an infection. They described how at last an ear or a urinary tract infection was diagnosed and treated and the crying stopped. Or how when a baby's oral thrush (candida, a yeast infection) was cleared up by medication there was a dramatic reduction in crying. Thrush looks like little white scales in the baby's mouth. It should not be confused with milk curds, which are often present too. Since thrush can infect the mother's nipple and then, in turn, reinfect the baby, both the baby and the mother's breasts need to be treated. When a baby has an ear infection, her face is sometimes red on one side and she may pull on or scratch her ear, sometimes drawing blood, and it is this that may alert you to the cause. The only obvious symptom of a bladder infection may be the crying itself, though you may notice that the urine has a very strong odour and that it seems to hurt the baby when it is passed.[24] Babies with a urinary tract infection often scream intermittently when urine is being passed because it stings and burns.

Dislocated hip

Some babies are born with a dislocated hip. It may occur after a breech or Caesarean birth. Sometimes the condition has occurred already in the family and is inherited. It is usually possible to identify it at birth, so all new-born babies are screened for it. This is done by testing the stability of the hip joints and feeling for 'clicking' as the hips are moved.[25] The doctor or midwife bends the baby's legs up and spreads them wide like a frog. Yet of every ten babies who have this problem, at least one or two are missed. And other babies are treated for dislocation of the hip when they need not have been. Since treatment entails splinting (or sometimes braces or a harness) for up to twelve weeks, which can make the mother very anxious and cause difficulties in breast-feeding, it has been suggested that ultrasound should be used to give a more accurate diagnosis, and that this would result in fewer babies being splinted unnecessarily.[26] We do not know for certain that ultrasound has no adverse long-term effects. It is impossible to say that it is absolutely safe until some fifty years have passed. It appears to be harmless and certainly has no immediate obvious effects, but the question remains whether it is wise to use a powerful screening technique on all babies when only a minority benefit from it.

Some of the women who told me about their babies' inconsolable crying found that, often after the baby had been in distress for weeks, the cause of the problem was a dislocated hip. These mothers could not understand why, when they tried to comfort their babies by rocking and patting them, changing their position or jiggling them up and down, they cried more and more. It was as if the baby did not want to be comforted and whenever he was touched or moved seemed to be in pain.

One woman, who had been told that her baby had colic, and who spent ages lifting her over her shoulder, patting her on the back, rocking and bouncing her, noticed that she could not bear any movements that affected the lower part of her body. They seemed to cause pain, which was localized around her pelvis. The woman took her baby to the doctor and was insistent about her findings. The cause of the crying turned out to be 'one dislocated hip and the other clicky . . . The splints she had fitted worked like a charm – and we had a much more contented baby immediately.'

Hernia

Another physical condition that can cause a baby pain and result in inconsolable crying is a hernia, the protrusion of part of any internal

27

organ because the muscle enclosing it is weak or has torn. An inguinal hernia occurs when a piece of the intestinal tract sticks out of the inguinal canal. The result is a lump in the groin. This can exist at birth and is much more common in boys than girls.

Whooping cough vaccine

Two babies started crying after being vaccinated against whooping cough. One woman said she had already found that her breast-fed baby was allergic to salicylates and cried after he had drunk orange juice. 'He then reacted to the whooping cough vaccine and cried almost continuously for six weeks. After nagging from my health visitor my doctor referred us to Great Ormond Street Hospital, and there it was confirmed that Peter had reacted to it and they advised against any more of the vaccine for him or any other of our children.'

CHAPTER 3

Is It Hunger?

He was less a complex organism than . . .
a long tract from mouth to anus for whose
maintenance I was responsible.
Roberta Israeloff, *Coming to Terms*

Every woman with a crying baby wonders whether her baby is hungry. Surely no baby could go on crying like this unless it were starving? For the breast-feeding mother, who cannot see and measure the amount of milk a baby is taking unless she goes in for tedious test-weighing over a twenty-four-hour period, the question looms still larger: do I have enough milk? *Can* I produce enough milk? As one woman told me, 'It's that I can't *see* how much milk the baby is taking, so I never know if she's had enough and am left wondering if I'm underfeeding her. If she's grizzling [whimpering] and I put her back to the breast half an hour after a feed, she'll always suck, so I keep feeling I must be starving her.'

Babies enjoy sucking so much that they will often suck when offered the bottle or breast even when they are not hungry. Because your baby eagerly comes to the breast an hour, or even half an hour, after the last feed does not mean that she is underfed. One whose tummy is already full sucks a minute or so, then drops asleep, either releasing the nipple or holding it in the mouth, and wakes when you try to remove it and sucks enthusiastically again. Though these babies come to the breast as if to an oasis in the desert, they don't want to feed for long, and even if they continue sucking off and on, they avoid swallowing. They are not starving.

Your breast gives comfort, not only nourishment. Adults can feel comforted by seeing that someone they love is in the room or by holding hands. This isn't so for a 3-month-old baby. To feel

29

completely secure the baby needs a closer clasp, more intimate contact, and to learn through the feel of the breast drawn into her mouth that all is well with the world.

A baby's eyes explore the environment as she reaches out to discover more about the great adventure of living. The mouth, which is especially sensitive in a new-born baby, is also questing and seeks to draw in and make the breast the child's own. This is why a baby will grasp the breast as if utterly famished when she is not hungry, suck a little and then fall asleep. But it is the lightest of sleeps. If the mother attempts to withdraw the nipple, the baby rises, like a trout snapping a fly, to seize the nipple and fix more firmly on the breast again.

The hungry baby of 3 to 4 months stops crying and gasps with excitement on seeing that you are about to give the breast or are preparing a bottle, and if either is slow to appear the crying is resumed with renewed force. Once the teat or breast is given, the baby sucks vigorously and passionately. After a few minutes of intense sucking like this, as hunger is satisfied, the baby slows down a bit, gets interested in the mother's hair or sweater, or pauses and smiles – even perhaps sliding off the nipple as if teasing, only to draw it into his mouth again with renewed relish and to continue sucking. As hunger becomes more completely satisfied, the baby shows increasing interest in his surroundings and is more easily distracted by things going on around him.

At this age babies often play with the nipple when they are full, grabbing it in their mouths, pushing it out with the tongue, nibbling the end of it and then snapping at it again and sucking greedily for a few seconds, only to spit it out again and so on. When you put them down, they scream. They are not hungry either. They like to play with the breast.

Babies cry from thirst as well as from hunger. The baby who has become overheated needs extra fluids. The first milk let down in the breasts is lower in fat content than that at the end of a feed, so it is particularly thirst-quenching. In hot weather your baby needs to suck more often than usual, but because low-fat milk satisfies thirst best, may not require long feeds. The same thing happens in winter if the baby is in too hot a room or is over-clothed. She falls into a very heavy sleep but wakes up with hair damp and crying miserably, needing to be put to the breast immediately or, if artificially fed, to be given plain boiled water from a bottle or teaspoon. This is a thirsty baby, not a hungry baby.

Overheating a baby can be dangerous: he not only gets fretful, but may become dehydrated, breathe with difficulty and even have fits and become desperately ill with heat-stroke.[1] Small babies sweat very little, so can't cool themselves down in this way as adults can, and modern synthetic coverings may insulate them as if they were tucked into thermal bags. No wonder they are uncomfortable! There has been so much emphasis on the risks of hypothermia that this cause of crying is often forgotten.

The physical signs of a well-nourished baby are firm flesh, vitality and alertness, six or more wet nappies (diapers) in the twenty-four hours, bright eyes and a definite weight gain over a three-week period. Since babies often put on weight in leaps and bounds, with plateaux in between, don't expect a weight gain every week. It may be one ounce (28 g) one week and six ounces (170 g) the next, or nothing one week and eight ounces (226 g) the following one. Even if there are weeks when the weight is stable, a baby who gains one pound (450 g) every four or five weeks is well nourished.

If you want to weigh your baby, do so on the same scales at the same time of day once a week *at most*. Unless there is a special reason to worry about a baby not gaining enough weight, restrict weighing to every four weeks. Babies thrive – and do so all over the world – without ever being weighed at all.

From 2 weeks to 3 months of age the average weekly gain is six to eight ounces (170–226 g). Because that is an average it means that some babies put on less, some more. They don't start doing this until they have regained their birthweight at around 10 days of age. Not all babies lose weight in those first days, but most do. Light-weight babies at birth often put on weight at a faster rate than babies already of a good weight.

Don't expect your baby to keep up that kind of weight gain after she is 3 months. It is usually only five ounces (140 g) or so from then till she is 6 months old and perhaps as little as two ounces (56 g) a week, on average, from then until the end of the first year. A reduced weight gain as the baby gets older does not mean that you have lost your milk or that you are not satisfying your baby. If she is crying, yet is progressively putting on weight, look for other reasons for her crying. Nor should you think that because your breasts are no longer as full as they were two or three weeks after the birth that your milk supply is dwindling.

As a rule of thumb, babies usually need approximately three fluid ounces (85 ml) of milk per pound (450 g) of their weight in the twenty-four hours. So a 6-pound (2·7-kg) baby takes 18 ounces (510 ml) and an 8-pound (3·6-kg) baby, 24 ounces (680 ml). But, like adults, they don't want equal amounts at every meal, so sometimes your baby will have had enough after a short feed and at others – usually when you are in a rush or trying to hurry a feed so that you can get out – the baby is ready for a long, leisurely feed in banquet-style with course following on course. If you stop short of the equivalent of the port and nuts, your baby may scream as if deprived of life's basic necessities. The cry sounds like one of hunger all right, but there is no question of starving the baby. He just likes being at the breast and could go on – and on – and on.

You may find that though your baby usually has a definite feeding rhythm and is fairly contented, some days this is lost and she wants to suck all the time and cries when not at the breast. Occasionally this is a sign that your baby is fighting an infection and needs extra comfort. Sometimes it is an expression of insecurity and unease, and she needs to be in your arms and to suck non-stop for psychological reasons of which you are not aware. Most often it is a sign that your baby is about to have a growth spurt and requires an increased milk supply. More frequent feeds will stimulate the production of milk. This often happens at about 6 weeks, some time between 8 and 14 weeks, and again at 6 months. The crying does not mean that you are starving your baby. It is a way of ensuring that supply is increased by making demand irresistible.

It usually takes several days for a woman who is breast-feeding to build up the milk supply to meet her baby's increased demands. Those days can be very difficult and if you try to resist the demand, the baby cries and you are likely to feel very tense. The answer is to anticipate that there will be periods like these when your baby is about 6 weeks and 3 months old and be flexible, to adjust your day so that you can cuddle and feed ad lib or, if you have returned to work outside the home, have extra supplies of frozen breast milk for these occasions.

Giving the baby artificial milk and solid food when this happens will *reduce* your milk supply and you will discover that you cannot keep pace with the demands of your growing baby.

Milk doesn't just 'dry up'. If you are tense or upset, it may not flow. But that is a matter of the milk-ejection reflex not being triggered. Milk is there, but is not accessible to the baby. Some women told me about incidents when their babies cried desperately and they discovered that their milk had 'disappeared'. Chrissie, for instance, said that when her healthy, well-nourished little son was 13 weeks old he cried one night the whole night through. She rang the doctor in the morning and her health visitor came and went with her to the local hospital to use their electric breast pump. Hardly any milk was produced. She was told she had lost her milk and should change to bottle-feeding. She accepted this verdict and gave up breast-feeding.

What Chrissie didn't know was that since she had breast-fed her son for three months and he was thriving, she could still make milk. She was not like a well that had dried up. Her baby was about to have a growth spurt and needed extra feeds for this. When he cried that night she worried that there was something wrong with

him, and her anxiety caused physical tension, which inhibited her milk-ejection reflex – the hot 'buzzing', sexy sensation as milk flows to the nipple, as if a warm fountain has been suddenly switched on inside both breasts. She just couldn't relax and let milk flow. The case for bottle-feeding seemed to be clinched when the breast pump produced only a very little milk. Yet an electric machine is not like a baby and does not stimulate the warm, 'giving' feeling in response to your baby's sucking. In this case, too, the pump was being used to test and examine her ability to make milk, rather like a ducking stool for a witch. No wonder that, exposed to such judgement by machine, Chrissie couldn't give milk.

Many women make the decision, or feel it is forced on them, to switch their babies to the bottle when they need more milk because they are about to have a growth spurt. Some mothers are very disappointed and feel they have failed. They may even get angry with mothers who extol the virtues of breast-feeding, or for whom breast-feeding is no hassle, because of this sense of failure and the guilt that goes along with it. 'It makes me sick, the fuss about breast-feeding,' one woman told me. 'Women who are successful at breast-feeding delight in making those who can't, feel guilty. I'm fed up with all the breast-feeding "hype". My baby's doing perfectly well on the bottle.'

No woman should have to feel under pressure either to breast-feed or to give her baby artificial milk. But between the baby-food manufacturers, health professionals, baby-care books, other mothers and her partner, most women are under this pressure. As a result some feel torn apart because they are bottle-feeding when they 'should' be breast-feeding, others because they are struggling to breast-feed without getting the support and help they need.

If you feel like this, look at the pressures you are under, see if there is help you need and what kind of help would be best – and ask for it. This is your baby, your breasts, your life, so it is a matter for you, not for the doctor, a multinational company manufacturing baby formula, your mother, baby 'experts' or anyone else.

If you think that your baby's crying – or perhaps part of it – is due to hunger, give more milk. One woman found her baby stopped crying when she followed her grandmother's advice: 'Gran said I should "feed like a gypsy" and not pay any attention to clocks.' Offering solids before 6 months can upset the baby's digestion and cut down the amount of milk she takes. Since milk contains all the essential nutrients and is the ideal food for a baby through the first year of life, it is a pity to do anything that reduces milk intake, and solid foods are best kept as interesting tastes and extras.

For a bottle-feeding mother this is a matter of making up more formula. Do not add an extra scoop to make a more concentrated feed. That is dangerous because it loads the baby's system with superfluous salts, which can cause diarrhoea and dehydration. Stick to the manufacturer's instructions and use the scoop provided. If your baby cries during feeds, starting to suck but then jerking away from the teat (bottle nipple) as if she had been hit, make sure that the holes in the teat are not too small. They can be enlarged with a hot needle.

If you are breast-feeding, you will want to increase your milk supply. The first thing to ensure is that your baby has a good grasp of your breast. Some babies get excited when they realize they are about to be given the breast, but then start to fight it. It feels terrible to be trying to force-feed a baby who doesn't want you and is acting as if you were offering poison. When this happens it is often a sign of a delayed milk-ejection reflex, and the baby is getting only drops of foremilk. The hungry, impatient baby becomes rigid with frustration because milk is not yet flowing. Being anxious that you may not have enough milk can itself result in a delayed milk-ejection reflex. When the baby behaves like this it makes you still more anxious.

If you think your own tension may be interfering with your flow of milk, you may find that practising the relaxation you learned in childbirth classes is very useful, especially if you focus on releasing your shoulders. It may also help to play music and to create an especially restful background for feeding whenever possible. (I realize that it's easier said than done.)

Nipple-nibbling

One reason for a delayed milk-ejection reflex is that the baby is not firmly fixed on the breast. This happens because when the baby can get only the nipple in her mouth, like a cherry on its stalk, she cannot stimulate the whole milk production process deep inside the breast. As a result you get no sensation of the milk-ejection reflex and the baby, though working hard to get milk, is getting only drips, or, at best, a succession of small snacks – never a satisfying meal. Because of the position of the baby's mouth on the nipple 'stalk', you are also likely to get sore, bleeding nipples and this makes feeding even more traumatic. The answer is to make sure that every time the baby comes to the breast the nipple *and the surrounding tissues* are deep inside the baby's mouth.

Some babies have to learn how to suckle correctly. You have to show them the correct position at the breast. To do this effectively you have to be confident yourself about what you are teaching the baby. Though it may seem odd that anything so natural as suckling should be learned behaviour, other mammal babies, too, do not always get the knack immediately and need help. When an elephant has her first calf, experienced cows gather round her and nudge the baby to the correct position. When a dolphin gives birth, other mothers gather round her, act as midwives and may guide her in

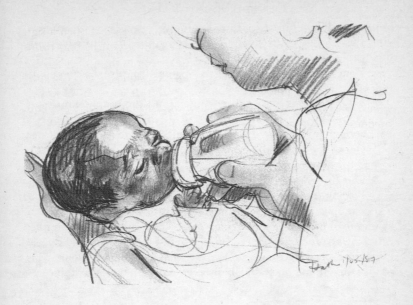

suckling her young. A baby needs to suck at the *breast*, not just the nipple. In order to ensure a good flow of milk she has to have a satisfying mouthful, drawing the tip of the nipple deep into her mouth where the hard and soft palates join. The action of pressing the milk out with the jaws, using muscles above the ears, is quite different from the way we suck a soft drink through a straw. If the baby is presented with the nipple only, her attempts to get milk are likely to make it sore, and she may succeed in taking only the foremilk and none of the rich milk deep in the breast. As a result, this baby may be put to the breast often but never be fully satisfied, getting that lovely feeling of a full tummy and a rosy glow, and drifting into a deep, idyllic sleep.

Even if a woman has abundant milk in the first few weeks after birth, when feeds consist merely of nipple-nibbling, her milk supply is quickly reduced, since the baby is giving insufficient stimulus to make more milk.

The art of getting the baby fixed onto the breast, mouth wide open and the lower hemisphere of the areola (the darker circle around the nipple) inside her mouth, is probably the single most important skill in breast-feeding. Yet many women never learn how vital this is, and many nurses don't know how to help women in their care to get the knack of it.

Your baby may find it especially difficult to draw a good portion of breast into his mouth if:

- Your breast is hard and engorged, and the nipple has disappeared in the surrounding tissue. If this is the case, express enough milk by hand to make the nipple more accessible before you pick up the baby for a feed.
- Your nipples are very large.
- One or both nipples are flat.

Placing the baby correctly at the breast is especially important if your nipples are not easy for the baby to grasp. Your baby needs a chance to mould your nipples into a shape that makes sucking simple. A baby who is not completely 'on' the breast tends to cry and grizzle (fret), and needs feeding as often as every hour or half-hour. This wears you out and makes the baby even more tired and irritable.

Getting a good latch

- Uncover your breast, not just the nipple area.
- Bring the baby to the breast, not the nipple to the baby.
- Drop your shoulders, breathe out and relax.
- Wait till the baby is nuzzling excitedly and getting impatient. Then with a firm, definite movement draw the baby towards your breast so that her cheek is pressed against it, snatch a moment when her mouth is wide open and put her on the breast so that both the nipple and much of the areola are crammed inside her mouth.
- Watch what happens. Babies aren't finicky about eating. They don't have polite restaurant manners. They guzzle and stuff themselves. A good breast-feed is a positively orgiastic experience for a hungry baby. Babies who are well latched on get down to each feed with a basic, elemental gusto. Their ears wiggle with their enthusiastic chomping, their toes curl and uncurl with bliss, and until hunger has been satisfied all their concentration is directed on one satisfying, milk-giving breast.

- If your baby's mouth isn't filled with breast like this and there is only a bit of polite sucking going on, with lip movements rather than jaw movements, slip your finger into her mouth and take her off and try again. You may have to do this several times before you get it just right. But it is much better to start again than to have the baby lip-sucking. That is bound to lead to frustration for you both.

The second important strategy is to increase your milk supply by producing more stimulus to your breast to make milk. This you can do in twenty-four hours with my Peak Production Plan. It is described fully in my *Experience of Breastfeeding*[2] – along with a great deal of other information about breast-feeding – but here is the gist of it:

- You put the baby to the breast in response to every sign that she is ready to suck over a twelve-hour daytime period and whenever she wakes and cries during the night.
- The aim is to create a sanctuary in which you can get in tune with your baby and enjoy a one-to-one relationship without having to give energy to anything else. The best place for this may be your bedroom. Whatever you have available, it should be a protected environment, even if it has to be a corner of the living-room with a screen or other 'marker' to indicate that this is the special territory for you and your baby.
- It will help if you discuss how you are going to do all this in advance with someone who can be your support person – your partner, a woman friend, family member or paid help. This person may have to shield you from intrusions and other calls on your time and energy by looking after a toddler (it can help if older children are taken out for a treat, for example) and doing shopping, cooking, washing and cleaning.
- You will feel thirsty and need lots to drink, though it is counter-productive to force fluids down you. Aim simply to satisfy thirst. A jug of fresh lemonade or iced water on a table beside you is a good idea, and your helper should offer pots of tea, milk drinks and, if you feel rather tense, perhaps an occasional glass of wine or beer.
- Besides being of practical help, your support person should be someone who gives you strong encouragement and who has confidence in breast-feeding. He or she needs to know when to

stand back and let you get on with it without intruding, and to be sensitive enough to know when you would welcome help. Some women feel the need of a *doula* – a Greek word that means a woman who can mother the mother.[3] Still others don't want a mother figure and feel happier with a woman of about their own age who can give sister-to-sister support. Others feel that the most understanding person is the baby's father. Whoever you choose to support you, it should be someone who does not need to be emotionally dependent on *you*, either by trying to unload his or her own problems or by wanting to have you in a state of continuing dependence on his or her help and advice. So choose carefully!

● A copy of my book *The Experience of Breastfeeding* may increase your self-confidence as you put into action the Twenty-Four-Hour Peak Production Plan, and I hope that in its pages you will find extra support and help with particular problems.

● There are only two things you need remember: *demand creates supply* and *you can do it!*

CHAPTER 4

Stress in Pregnancy

A baby is more likely to cry a great deal when the pregnancy has been very stressful. That is one important thing I discovered from my research. Women whose babies cry tend to have had pregnancies in which they felt under terrific pressure from one crisis after another or were in a continuous state of anxiety because of events that they were unable to control.

Having a baby is innately stressful.[1] However gladly pregnancy is welcomed, it entails facing up to a major life change, and a transformation in the woman's social role as she becomes a mother. A pregnancy does not have to be unwanted or the woman living under dreadful social conditions for it to involve stress. Positive emotions, too – joy, excitement and eager anticipation – bring their own stresses as she sees the world through changed eyes and is confronted by the challenge of a profound adjustment in her life.

Not only is having a baby itself a life upheaval, but it often brings with it other crises and transitions that are in themselves disturbing and stressful. Many couples, for example, move to a new home when they are expecting a baby or shortly after the birth. This is often to a new area where they have no friends and are far from their families. One study revealed that 40 per cent of women moved during pregnancy or within six weeks of the baby's birth, or were still in the throes of major alterations at the time the baby was born.[2] Men switch jobs so that they earn more in order to take on the financial responsibility of a child. The same study showed that 32 per cent of male partners changed employment during pregnancy. Relationships are either sealed in the institution of marriage – 13 per cent of couples married or began living together during the

41

pregnancy – or broken as the couple separate when faced with what the man sees as the threat of the coming baby. Women give up paid work and become full-time housewives, sometimes for the first time in their lives. In the study already cited 32 per cent of women gave up a job entirely as a consequence of pregnancy. Other life crises, unrelated to the pregnancy, may also impinge on it. The same study disclosed that 22 per cent of women suffered the death of a close family member during pregnancy.

During this stressful process of having a baby the support a woman receives from other people can make all the difference between her being able to cope or being shattered by the experience.[3] Yet when she is pregnant a woman often becomes socially isolated and deprived of her usual support network. At the same time she is suddenly confronted by a new set of people – doctors, midwives, nurses and others – who oversee the pregnancy and to whom she has to relate. Twenty or thirty years ago a woman continued to see her family doctor during pregnancy. Very few women today have complete family doctor or midwife care. Instead, there are usually mandatory excursions to a hospital, often far away from their home, where they have to cope with cattle-market conditions, are screened, scanned, prodded and poked by members of staff whom they never get to know, and who don't know them, and where they have to wait, sometimes for hours on end. Thus not only is pregnancy inherently stressful, but it is made more stressful by other major life changes incurred by becoming pregnant and by the institutional organization of maternity care.

It has been known for some time that stress in pregnancy can result in premature birth. An English research project explored the hypothesis that there was a relation between premature births and major life events that resulted in severe psychosocial stress.[4] Factors listed as major life events included death of one's partner or a serious illness in the family, separation or divorce, the woman's serious physical illness or injury requiring hospital treatment, physical abuse or mental cruelty from a partner, being made homeless, unemployment, decrease in income of 25 per cent or more, severe financial worries and friction in the family. Eighty-four per cent of women whose babies were *very* premature had pregnancies in which major life events of this kind occurred. Sixty-seven per cent of those who went into pre-term labour and 43 per cent of those whose pregnancies went to term experienced these stressful life events. The more premature the labour was, the higher was the level of psychosocial stress.

Severe stress interferes with the baby's nutrition in the uterus, resulting in growth retardation before birth. Richard Newton, the pediatric neurologist who did this study on psychosocial stress and prematurity, subsequently did research on stress and low birthweight.[5] He found that low birthweight was also significantly associated with major life events. Neither prematurity nor low birthweights were associated with 'state anxiety'. What this means is that premature births or low-birthweight babies are not the consequence of a woman being an anxious kind of person, but that external events have triggered in her an intolerable degree of stress.

We do not really know all the mechanisms by which stress and the anxiety that it produces are communicated to the fetus. But stress causes a biophysical response that results in a rush of adrenalin to the bloodstream, contracted muscles, trembling, sweating, breathlessness, over-breathing and hyperventilation – which reduces the oxygen to the baby – gastro-intestinal disturbances, shunting of blood away from the uterus towards the peripheral areas, palpitations, hypertension, difficulty in sleeping, unexplained pain, which may occur in many different parts of the body and of which the most common is headache, and interference with the immune system so that the body is more vulnerable to infection.

When the mother's blood pressure goes up to 140/90 or higher, the flow of blood through the placenta is reduced. The placenta is the 'tree of life' for the baby: it depends on effective placental functioning for nutrition, oxygen and the discharge of waste products. When placental function is impeded, fetal growth is hindered. If it is severe enough, the baby may die in the uterus.

Stress also raises levels of catecholamines (stress hormones) in the woman's blood, and this in turn interferes with the flow of blood through the placenta and may constrict blood vessels in the uterine muscle – which further reduces the oxygen available. High catecholamine levels in both the mother and the fetus are associated with pre-eclampsia and make a baby more likely to have abnormal heart rate patterns during labour and breathing problems at birth.[6]

There may well be other subtle effects when the placenta is not working well and when catecholamine levels are high that result in changes in the baby's behaviour after birth. One outcome may be that traumatic pregnancy experiences tend to affect a baby's central nervous system, making it more difficult to discharge accumulated tension.

My own research revealed that 60 per cent of women whose babies cried excessively (more than six hours in the twenty-four) had a stressful pregnancy complicated by major life events, compared with 40 per cent of those whose babies cried least (less than two hours in the twenty-four). Now, of course, a mother who is under stress from a crying baby may be more inclined to look back on her pregnancy as stressful than one whose baby does not cry so much. It may also be that when she has been made very anxious during pregnancy, she tends to be more anxious in her interaction with the baby, too, and readily assumes that the baby's crying is evidence of her failure in mothering. As we shall see in Chapter 6 this leads to increased tension for both mother and baby, each acting on the other to trigger further frustration. But the significant thing is not just that these women were anxious, but that the anxiety they experienced was fuelled by external events that anyone else would acknowledge as stressful, too.

A woman who owned her own business, for example, learned when she was four months pregnant that the premises had been destroyed in an explosion: 'I had to keep the business operating under very difficult conditions for the rest of my pregnancy.' When one woman was eight months pregnant a close friend was killed in a car crash. The last weeks of her pregnancy were spent in a state of shock and grieving, and with a sense of imminent disaster, which was focused on the baby, whom she felt sure would die. Another woman was desperately worried about her mother's alcoholism right through her pregnancy.

Mothers of babies who cried inconsolably were more likely to tell of highly stressful relationships with a partner, parent or someone else in the family while they were pregnant, or to have had a close relationship shattered by death, severe illness or separation during pregnancy. Many had run the gauntlet of psychological and physical abuse from a male partner while they were pregnant. Problems like this were often exacerbated by poverty and by the man becoming unemployed during the pregnancy: 'I was under a tremendous amount of stress as we lived in two run-down insect-infested rooms and I got very depressed. My husband couldn't cope with my feelings and our conditions, so he used to go out and get drunk.'

As well as housing difficulties that led to doubling-up with parents and in-laws, and resulting stressed relationships in the family, women gave accounts of eviction – and sometimes destitution. They often did not know of allowances to which they were entitled and there were long delays in the payment of other money owing to them. One woman described how when she was several months pregnant she and her toddler had nothing but potatoes to eat for five days. Another, who attempted suicide when five months pregnant after being evicted from her home, spent the last four months of her pregnancy in sordid welfare accommodation.

Other women had no partners: they were single, unsupported mothers enduring social disapproval and isolation. Women who conceived accidentally and were not in a stable partnership tended to be under pressure to marry the father of the baby: 'I was under stress

from my family because I didn't know whether I wanted to get married or not, and they threatened to disown me if I was not married.'

The issue of abortion cropped up over and over again. Sometimes the woman herself sought abortion and then changed her mind or couldn't get one. Sometimes it was her parents or the father of her child who subjected her to pressure to have one: 'When I told my parents of the pregnancy they told me to have an abortion. Then, when I didn't, to have the baby adopted'; 'My mother wouldn't accept that I was going to have a baby . . . she turned the other way . . . she tried to blackmail me by saying that if I would only have an abortion for her sake, not mine, then she would come to my wedding.'

One woman, who described having nausea and vomiting all day and every evening, told me: 'I really hadn't wanted to be pregnant. It was a big shock . . . I was devastated and went to pieces completely – long hours crying and totally unable to concentrate on anything.'

Her husband suggested an abortion: 'I longed to say yes but just couldn't. It took me many months, if not all of my pregnancy, to come to terms with "why me?" I didn't want my baby but couldn't face an abortion – couldn't live with the guilt.'

It turned out that *none* of the women whose babies cried very little described social pressures of this kind in their pregnancies, whereas nearly half – 48 per cent – of those whose babies cried more than six hours a day experienced severe psychosocial stress. Here are some of their stories.

One couple had constant quarrels, often resulting in his being violent towards her, until they separated when she was six and a half months pregnant. They tried living together again one month later, but he continued to assault her. They already had three children, were living in poverty and had run up massive debts.

A woman who had understood that when she became pregnant her lover would at last leave his wife discovered that when it actually happened he was unwilling to make that decision.

One, whose father had cancer of the larynx, was told he would probably live only until the month her baby was due. Another, whose father was diagnosed as having lung cancer when she was ten weeks into her pregnancy, explained: 'I am a nurse and looked after him at home. He died when I was eight months pregnant.'

When she was two months pregnant, a woman was sacked on the grounds that her job was unsuitable for a pregnant woman. The couple were very short of money and were living with his parents, who strongly disapproved of her. There was constant conflict. 'This was very depressing,' she told me. 'I stayed in my room most of the time. I was at my wits' end.' It wasn't until she was eight months pregnant that they found their own accommodation.

One woman had been treated for chronic alcoholism three years before the pregnancy. When she became pregnant, she told me,

a social worker threatened to have the baby removed

immediately after it was born. All the way through my pregnancy she was never off my back. She tried to persuade me to have the baby adopted after I left his father, but I considered carefully what a baby needs most: love, security, food, warmth and being wanted. I *knew* I could give my baby all those things and refused to have him adopted.

A woman who was not sure her husband was the father of the baby said: 'One day he would say he loved and wanted the baby. Another day he hoped it would be born deformed. He left me at four months pregnant, but he was still upset and came and rowed [argued] with me at every opportunity.' She says he pursued her and became violent on many occasions, until in the end she obtained an injunction. She added: 'I was addicted to tranquillizers. I was determined to give them up and did so, very gradually, but suffered severe withdrawal symptoms the remaining two months of my pregnancy.'

Other women described enforced separation from partners because of their jobs. Some husbands were in the armed forces and were sent to the Falklands at the time of the Falklands War. Couples were also split when firms closed down and men were out of jobs. In one case, for example, the husband got a new job that entailed working away from home all week, and the woman lived with her parents, her furniture and clothing in storage. She said: 'I had to trail down from West Yorkshire to London at weekends to start looking for another house.'

Not only did women whose babies cried most describe severe stress during their pregnancies, but they reported *multiple* stress. They were nearly twice as likely as the mothers of babies who cried least to report multiple stress. Here are some typical accounts of what they went through.

One woman's partner left her when she was four months pregnant: 'I was shattered. My family doctor placed me on the sick [declared me unfit for work] for three weeks.' When she returned to work, she was under further strain because the father was working in the same place, but she stuck it out. Then in the seventh month of pregnancy her mother died unexpectedly. She says: 'It left me feeling very empty, this being the reason that I could not react when a

friend in his twenties also died suddenly five days after my mother.'
Others told me:

My husband was on a very poor wage and then was
unemployed twice during the pregnancy. My child was
born a few weeks early because my dad died and he was
born on my dad's funeral.

My baby is mixed race [the father is Arab], so I knew I
could expect racial problems, too. I left my 'husband' –
we have an Islamic marriage, which is not legal in England – because of his attitude towards my pregnancy. He
was terribly angry that I told my family of the expected
baby, which is not done in his culture, but I am not of his
culture and was so proud of having his child that I wanted
people to know. During a spell in hospital, when I was ill
in pregnancy, he and my 'best friend' had a short-lived
affair and she was then pregnant by him. [That child was
adopted.] I left him. He made no offers of help to provide
anything for my baby.

My Nana [grandmother] died at the beginning of my
pregnancy. I was very close to her and cried for three to
four hours at a time. Then my uncle died when I was
eight months pregnant.

My husband was out of work and we were under
financial stress with a third baby arriving. There was also
stress from my mother-in-law, with constant rows.

For single, unsupported mothers the pregnancy entailed a series
of crises. A teenager, for example, said that when her father found
out about her pregnancy and she would not agree to an abortion, he
disowned her. She was also under great pressure from her boyfriend's
parents to terminate it. At night she lay awake worrying: 'I had been
taking the Pill and acting as normal and I was worried about damage
done [to the baby] and because I have a mentally handicapped
brother.'
Another thing that made pregnancy stressful for many women

was a series of obstetric screening procedures, many of which did not come up with any conclusive results, but left them worrying. Though the association between this and having a crying baby was less significant than between crying and difficult or shattered personal relationships, those whose babies cried most tended to have had more special investigations in pregnancy, to have been treated as 'high risk' and to have had false positive diagnoses of conditions such as placenta praevia (a condition in which the placenta is lying in front of the baby's head, which could result in massive bleeding) and intra-uterine growth retardation. One woman, for example, spent

three separate weeks in hospital with enforced bed rest because she was told that her baby was 'small for dates' (not growing properly in the uterus), but delivered a baby weighing 8 lb 4 oz (3·7 kg). These investigations often took place because the women were already in a high-risk category as the result of a previous stillbirth or a series of miscarriages. They described pressures created by the medical system and by the kind of care they were given.

Alpha-feto-protein (AFP) testing (screening blood for substances that suggest possible fetal abnormality) and amniocentesis (testing the amniotic fluid for signs of fetal abnormality) caused a great deal of stress. Women told of the torture of weeks of waiting for amniocentesis results that were delayed and of elaborate screening procedures that resulted in further screening but failed to produce a definite diagnosis. One woman who had a routine blood test that showed a high level of AFP said: 'I was summoned back from holiday [vacation] to have another test. This also produced a high level. I was told I could be carrying a spina bifida baby.' She had a scan, which revealed no abnormality, 'but my doctor wasn't satisfied, so I had to have an amniocentesis. By this time I was seven months pregnant and there would have been nothing they could do anyway.' No abnormality was detected from amniocentesis, 'but I was told there could still be something wrong with him. So right up until I gave birth I was in a terrible state. I never stopped worrying and kept getting very bad migraine headaches.'

Women who had some bleeding in early pregnancy often remained anxious until the baby was born, as did the woman who said: 'I was worried throughout pregnancy that perhaps the baby would not be normal after losing so much blood.' Advice given by doctors often contributed to their anxiety. A woman who conceived again three weeks after a miscarriage, had some bleeding in early pregnancy and was very worried that, with a demanding job, she was bound to lose this baby, too, or go into pre-term labour. Her doctor told her to rest – but it was impossible to follow this advice, as she would have lost her job and she and her partner needed the money desperately. Some women who felt under a lot of pressure and were smoking were warned sternly by their doctors to stop smoking. This contributed to tension, which led to their smoking still more. Some of the women who were waiting for amniocentesis results described how they resumed smoking, which they had stopped when they knew they were pregnant, or found themselves smoking more than usual.

Diet also often became a source of anxiety. Many women were told that they were not putting on enough weight and that they must eat more. They tried to stuff themselves with nutritious food, and for some eating became a penance. At each antenatal clinic visit they were reprimanded and made to feel still worse about it. Nearly as large a proportion of women were told that they were gaining *too much* weight and must start to diet. They became miserable and anxious too. For some, life seemed to revolve around the food they were supposed to be eating or to avoid and they were frightened that they were harming their babies.

This fear that things they had done or omitted to do could damage the baby was a recurring theme:

> I felt guilty about continuing smoking, even though I got nowhere near giving it up (and still haven't). My baby appears very healthy, but I still worry if I've harmed him in some way.

> At the time of conception I contracted German measles. I went to the hospital for a blood test. It came back positive. My husband and I were absolutely devastated. We desperately wanted the baby. At ten weeks we told the doctor that we would continue the pregnancy. We were told that there would be a 20 per cent chance of the baby being born infected [sic] with a handicap of eyes or ears. We went through hell. I was under terrible strain. Not many days went by without crying either in the loos [toilets] at work or at night in bed. I lost blood at twenty-eight weeks – again more strain. I was convinced things were going wrong. I will never know how my husband and I survived those everlasting forty weeks of pregnancy. The stress never left either of us. The terrible feeling of worry will never leave us.

Some women spent the larger part of pregnancy trying to get the kind of care they wanted while confronting opposition all along the way. Sometimes this was a home birth. Sometimes it was the certainty that they could have an epidural (anaesthesia from the waist down) or an active (moving around freely) or drug-free birth: 'I was treated like a schoolgirl, in a very condescending way,' said one woman who wanted a natural birth. In desperation she changed her obstetrician shortly before the baby was due and only then was able to relax.

Sometimes, of course, problems that cause stress in pregnancy persist after the baby is born. Any woman trapped in an unhappy relationship, or a single, unsupported mother trying to cope alone, is likely to suffer the same or similar stresses after having the baby as during the pregnancy. Ongoing stress obviously has an effect on the present and may play a part in causing crying. But the important thing that emerges from these accounts is that, *even when problems have been resolved*, stress in pregnancy can affect the baby's behaviour.

The experiences these women went through could not account for and explain all babies' crying. But it seems to have been one important precursor to crying for many babies who cried most. It certainly meant that these women were anxious and tense through most or all of pregnancy. The romantic image of a pregnant woman knitting in the lamplight, radiant with the knowledge that a baby is growing within her, is very far removed from the nine months of torture these women endured.

None of us can expect to have a completely stress-free pregnancy. Maybe it would not be such a good thing, either, for stress is a stimulant. The right amount of stress, neither too little nor too much, nudges us towards psychological change and growth, infuses excitement into life and introduces goals to strive for and problems to be triumphantly overcome. But when stress is so great that we feel we lose complete control of what is happening to us, it becomes pathological. The evidence from these women's accounts is that this is exactly what happened to them. They felt 'shocked', 'scared', 'unable to cope', 'panic-stricken', 'anxious', 'distressed', 'petrified', 'depressed', 'helpless' and 'out of control'.

Taking action

What can you do if you know that you had a stressed pregnancy and think this may be an element in your baby's persistent crying? The first thing is to acknowledge the stress you felt. This is sometimes easier said than done because women are trained not to express anger. We are supposed to leave that to men. Anyone who has been through the kind of experience that these women described to me is justified in feeling angry, even when there is no clear object for her anger. When anger is not acknowledged and is internalized, it becomes depression. So it helps to bring the anger out into the open

53

and see if you can accept it. Instead of trying to push these dreadful experiences behind you and forget that they happened, get in touch with your feelings and acknowledge the emotions that were aroused.

It may also help if you write down what happened and your feelings about it. People who write about problems facing them and express their pent-up emotions in a daily journal visit the doctor less and six months later are in better health than those who do not write about their feelings.[7] If you want to look back on your pregnancy in this way, it will entail making a retrospective journal of the events that proved stressful, describing in detail what occurred and how you remember your feelings at the time. It could be a way in which you begin to come to terms with things that happened to you, which were beyond your control at the time. Though it is unlikely to have any direct effect on your baby's crying, this can help you accept the strength of your emotions, acknowledge your right to feel this way and thus increase self-confidence, reinforce the sense of your own identity and indirectly have a positive effect on the way you relate to your crying baby.

When you realize that things that happened even before your baby was born – circumstances you could not change, although you very much wanted to – may have affected the baby, and understand that these were the same things that caused you distress in pregnancy, you will no longer feel responsible for and guilty about the crying. It is not faulty mothering that is making your baby cry; instead, it is the outpouring of response to a stress you both shared.

Your lives were mingled and you were in partnership together long before birth. You cannot change the past. What you can do is to contain your baby's distress, hold and make it safe by acknowledging and accepting the pain without trying to blot it out. It is not a question of rushing around trying one stratagem after another to make the baby stop crying. That can lead only to further frustration for you both. When you felt most under stress, if anyone had told you not to worry or to stop being depressed, or to be quiet and not cry, this, far from doing anything to help you, would have made you feel worse. In the same way, it does not help to struggle to stop the baby crying.

You may have to be very patient in waiting for the baby to discharge tension through crying. You may need ways of releasing your own tension that is built up in sympathy with your baby – by punching pillows, kneading bread, going for a run or singing at the top of your voice, for instance. But you are together, sharing in and working through an experience triggered by the same stress. Your baby's crying is not accusing you of being a bad mother. It holds this other message – that you have shared experience together since long before the birth.

CHAPTER 5

The Birth

Mothers of babies who cry a great deal – six hours or more in the twenty-four hours – are significantly more likely to have had a birth in which there was obstetric intervention and in which they had little choice about what happened to them than those whose babies cry far less (under two hours). Labour was often induced or accelerated with an intravenous drip to stimulate contractions. This happened to 64 per cent of those with first babies and 35 per cent of those with second or subsequent babies.

And they are also significantly less happy with the care given them during labour (37 per cent said they were 'very happy' with the care they received compared with 60 per cent of those whose babies did not cry much). Many had distressing birth stories. I thought at first it must be that babies cry more after complicated deliveries – forceps deliveries and Caesarean sections, for example. They do, but that in itself has less marked an effect than the mother's *feelings* about what happened. What turns out to be significant is that the mothers of babies who cry most look back on their labours as experiences in which other people wielded power over them and they felt powerless.

From the obstetric point of view many of these labours were uncomplicated. They fall into the category of births that doctors describe as 'uneventful'. But *in terms of the woman's own experience* birth was difficult and left her emotionally traumatized, with her confidence shattered. Women spoke of being 'shocked', 'confused', 'angry', 'helpless', 'cheated' and 'depressed'.

Twenty-two per cent of babies cried from birth onwards and another 34 per cent started before the sixth week of life. Some started when the mother returned home from hospital, either immediately or when whatever help she had after the birth was withdrawn or phased out. For many women there suddenly came a time when they felt terribly alone and were frightened by the daunting responsibility they had taken on, and this coincided with the start of crying.

The first post-partum weeks are a period of major physical and emotional adjustment for many women, and, since doctors divide pregnancy into three trimesters, it might be called the 'fourth trimester'. What happens during that time is profoundly affected by what has gone before – the kind of birth a woman has experienced and her feelings of competence or disability.

The baby, of course, is also affected by events surrounding birth. Labour may have resulted in shortage of oxygen, for example, and things done immediately after birth – like having a naso-gastric tube stuck inside or being in a brightly lit, noisy nursery – may have caused distress, too. Some women whose babies have been delivered by forceps comment that they behave as though they have a headache. Some say that every little noise and change in the environment makes them jump and they seem to want just to be left alone.

It is already known that babies who have had a difficult birth or whose mothers have had pre-eclampsia in pregnancy tend to have sleep problems.[1] Those delivered by Caesarean section or whose mothers had a great deal of pain-relieving drugs in childbirth and those who were short of oxygen during labour or had breathing problems immediately following birth are all more likely to be disturbed – and this for many months. In fact, reduction in the oxygen flowing to the baby may subtly change the way the brain works and hinder the smooth functioning of the central nervous system for weeks, months and sometimes years.[2]

Pain-killing drugs and their effect on the baby

So many drugs are used today in childbirth that most babies start off life with a variety of chemicals in their bloodstream. Much of this obstetric medication consists of pain-killing drugs: anaesthetics (which take away the pain) and analgesics (which reduce pain).

Other substances are also often introduced into the mother's bloodstream: beta-mimetic drugs to suppress uterine activity, prostaglandin pessaries (which have occasionally been absorbed through the baby's mouth and led to breathing problems), oxytocin to induce or accelerate labour, sedatives and tranquillizers to calm the woman, drugs to reduce or raise her blood pressure, antibiotics, and syntometrine to contract muscles in the third stage of labour. Some of these are known to have an adverse effect on the baby's behaviour after birth. But it is difficult to conduct research on this subject because very few women receive no drugs at all in childbirth, so no unmedicated control group is available.

Researchers face another difficulty. It is often hard to trace the effects of drugs because a baby who is drowsy in the first few days when still in hospital may turn out to be quite different – especially irritable and jumpy – later. Just about the time when the mother returns home from hospital the baby wakes up and starts to cry inconsolably.

The effect of drugs is often subtle, too, and it is impossible to know whether a baby's behaviour is a direct consequence of obstetric medication or of a variety of other factors. Psychologists are interested now in the effect that these drugs can have on communication between the parents and child. As Rudolph Schaffer expresses it:

Both parents and child operate within a system of mutuality where the behaviour of one produces effects on the other that in turn modify the behaviour of the first. One has to consider the whole network of interacting influences . . . A mother's task is . . . not to create something out of nothing but rather to dovetail her behaviour to that of the infant . . . Mothering can, after all, only be understood in relation to the kind of being that is to be mothered.[3]

It is worth examining results of research on the effect of drugs on neonatal behaviour since, if your baby has received drugs through your bloodstream, it can help you understand behaviour that can otherwise be inexplicable and that you may think is the result of your mishandling of the baby.

Most studies of the effect of drugs in labour follow babies only over the first three days of life. Some follow them up to seven or ten days. Few go beyond this. A normal, healthy new-born baby is skilled at adjusting to the environment and communicating needs, actively interacts with those caring for her, and influences and changes adult behaviour. A mother can enjoy caring for a baby who is bright and responsive, and her interaction with the child enables her to develop confidence and self-esteem. If, on the other hand, a baby is unresponsive, it is hard for the mother to develop the same self-assurance, and child care is unrewarding. Drugs used in labour can interfere with this synchronization of behaviour and with the intricate balance created mutually between the mother and her baby.

After general anaesthesia, for example, babies may be very sleepy and difficult to feed in the first days of life, and need a lot of stimulation if they are to wake up.[4] When pethidine (demerol) is given within a period of four hours before delivery, the baby tends to have breathing difficulties at birth, is sleepy and slow to suck, and does not orient so skilfully to the human voice.[5] All analgesics and tranquillizers are associated with early feeding difficulties and the mother may have to work hard to keep her baby interested in sucking.[6]

It is often claimed that epidural anaesthesia does not affect the baby. In fact, when women ask, doctors often reassure them that bupivicaine – the drug most often used – does not reach the baby since it is an injection only into the epidural space and does not cross the placenta. This is not true. Bupivicaine, especially in large doses and over a long period of time has been shown to reduce a baby's alertness and may modify the ability to orient to visual and auditory stimuli for as long as six weeks after birth.[7] This in turn affects the developing relationship between the mother and her baby. A baby who does not interact with the mother in a lively way is cared for differently from one who is alert and responsive. One study suggests that interaction between the mother and child can be affected for many years, and that, following an epidural birth, even after five years the child's cognitive development is slightly slower.[8]

Though some studies have shown no differences in orientation skills (the baby's ability to turn in the direction of stimulating sounds or sights) following epidurals, mothers themselves believe otherwise.

When women were asked about their babies' behaviour, only 45 per cent of epidural mothers said they thought their babies' orientation skills were exceptional, whereas 85 per cent of those in the control group of women who had not had epidurals believed their babies oriented themselves extraordinarily well.[9]

When oxytocin has been used to stimulate the uterus in order to induce or accelerate labour and the mother has also had an epidural, the baby is more likely to be drowsy and emotionally 'flat' in the first week of life. The same thing happens if the mother's blood pressure has been low during labour – one effect of an epidural. Women who have had an epidural may have to persevere at stimulating and tempting their babies to suck throughout the first month.[10] When women kept diaries of their baby's behaviour, those whose labours had been stimulated with oxytocin and who had also had an epidural revealed that their babies were so sleepy that they had fewer feeds than babies of mothers who had not had these interventions. But after some weeks there was often a marked change and then babies suddenly became much more demanding. It can be a great shock when a woman has had to coax her baby to wake, suddenly to discover once she is past that phase that the baby seems to have a totally different personality and cries inconsolably.

Babies vary in the extent to which they can self-regulate their states of consciousness. Some are slow to learn self-soothing skills – sucking their fingers, for instance. They vary, too, in the degree to which they will receive help in being comforted – relaxing when they are being cuddled and moulding themselves to the arms of the person holding them. When a woman has had many drugs in childbirth her baby tends to be less 'cuddly' at first. Babies of women who have had analgesics in labour are not so easily comforted on the third post-partum day. And they may continue like this for as long as a month.[11] Studies have shown that following epidurals babies are less skilled at soothing themselves on days 3, 10, 28 and 42.[12]

Like other analgesic and anaesthetic drugs, bupivicaine may affect the interaction between mothers and babies. One study found that epidural mothers had to stimulate their babies more both at 5 days and 1 month in order to keep them sucking.[13] They tended to handle their babies less affectionately and there was less eye contact during feeds.

There are all sorts of methodological problems in doing research like this and many of the results are conflicting, so it is clear that follow-up studies are needed. It is also important to discover what kind of support women can best be given when their babies' behaviour is disrupted by the effects of drugs used in childbirth. For there is a good deal of evidence now to indicate that analgesics like pethidine, tranquillizers, drugs used to stimulate the uterus and epidural anaesthesia can all give rise to difficulties in the early relationship between mother and baby – difficulties that can make the early months of parenthood an obstacle course.

Power and powerlessness

A birth that is difficult for the baby is also likely to have been hard on the mother, both physically and emotionally, and this is likely to affect the way she handles her baby. Her emotional state after childbirth, whether she feels triumphant and powerful or powerless and a failure, are important elements in her confidence in herself as a mother and her pleasure in mothering.

An overwhelming emotion experienced by a woman with a constantly crying baby is the feeling of being trapped. There seems to be no solution to the baby's distress and she cannot escape from it. She is unable to decide what to do because there are no choices. She can only suffer and endure it.

For more than half the women who say their babies cry a great deal this sense of being unable to exercise choice was a marked characteristic of the birth, too. They could not share in decisions made about their bodies. They felt at the receiving end of care rather than being in charge themselves. Many of them also said this feeling started even before the baby was born – and was a psychological characteristic of pregnancy.

Care in labour was often kind but autocratic. Many women told of their fear, bewilderment and anger over incidents about which they were not consulted or informed, and described interventions to which they did not give their consent. In spite of this, when asked if they were happy with the way they were treated by hospital staff, most make positive remarks about the care they were given. Even though awful things were done to them, they are grateful. They feel bewilderment, frustration, helplessness, anger, and at the same time, relief and gratitude. They are caught in a double-bind.

Power over the woman in childbirth can be exercised in many different ways. An especially important one is restriction on physical movement and position. Women are often not allowed to move around and change position as they like and are expected to adopt particular postures – sometimes more or less flat on their backs – for pelvic examinations, electronic fetal monitoring and delivery. Only 17 per cent of the women whose babies cry most say they were allowed to give birth in a position they chose. There is a striking difference between them and the women whose babies cried least, 40 per cent of whom could choose the position in which they gave birth.

The helplessness and frustration women felt during childbirth extends beyond delivery and threatens their relationship with their babies. One woman said: 'I felt suicidal! The baby was an undiagnosed breech and after being in labour for about twenty hours I had to have a Caesarean birth. I produced no breast milk at all and the baby had to be bottle-fed, something I still feel very unhappy about. I felt I couldn't give birth normally and then couldn't even feed him.' Another woman who wanted to avoid episiotomy but nevertheless received one, said she felt angry, helpless and 'mutilated'.

This frustration is often accompanied by post-partum physical symptoms that make the women feel weak, exhausted and incompetent. A woman told me, for example, that she was depressed and could not bond with her baby at all during the first weeks because 'my primary concern was for myself'. She had a failed epidural with *two* spinal taps, which resulted in severe headaches that forced her to lie flat for the first week. Another said:

> I felt very depressed, because I had a difficult birth which resulted in an epidural and forceps. I had a lot of stitches and was very sore. I was put in a side ward and felt very alone. I resented the baby crying at all, as it was so uncomfortable to get in and out of bed. I was breast-feeding and couldn't get comfortable in any position. In my pregnancy I had felt very fit and active and then suddenly I was reduced to a hunchback, shuffling wreck.

Another woman said she felt 'shocked at feeling so ill and because I could not look after my baby myself. I felt a failure.'

Women who feel helpless and taken over in childbirth are more likely to have had labour induced or to have had a Caesarean section. Some had both: 'I was induced and had a hard twenty-hour labour with an epidural, which I didn't want and was forced to have and which did not kill the pain on one side.' Staff told her several times while she was in labour that the baby was in distress and she was very afraid. A Caesarean section was then carried out under general anaesthetic. After the birth she felt on an emotional switchback: 'depressed because I could not do much for the baby and he cried a lot. It took a few days to feel he belonged to me and not to anyone else.' Another woman, who had her second emergency Caesarean section when her uterus ruptured after nine hours on an oxytocin drip, said her dominant emotion was one of failure: 'They told me I was lucky to be alive and to have a healthy baby – which didn't help.'

A typical example of the kind of birth experience that is later followed by a baby's inconsolable crying is that of the woman who said she had 'a terrible birth, which started with an induction I did not want; being monitored, which I did not want; and having to stay in bed, which I also did not want – but succumbed to because I was told it was best for me and the baby.' The baby was face to pubis and got stuck,

so they kept speeding things up and the pain was incredible, so I also had pethidine, which I did not want. I had to have a huge episiotomy and forceps and then the

placenta had to be evacuated manually. I had to have blood transfusions. I was in a daze, confused and scared, and for some reason kept thinking of the baby as me. I wanted to cry and cry, to sob everything out, but I didn't even have the strength for that. I never got the elated feeling. I was more scared for her than anything.

In retrospect, the mothers of babies who cry most are often surprised that they allowed professionals to make decisions for them and turn them into compliant patients, and protest that they are normally not like this at all. They talked about their jobs, for instance, and were shocked by how difficult it was to be assertive in childbirth. One woman in her late thirties described how she taught a class of often unruly 14- and 15-year-olds and considered herself a good disciplinarian. She could hold her own in difficult situations in which less confident teachers panicked. Yet in childbirth she found it impossible to be assertive and felt sucked onto a conveyor belt that she could not stop.

What these women are all saying, in fact, is that they feel alienated from their own bodies, out of control and helpless. This learned helplessness persists after birth and contributes to their feeling helpless when faced with the astonishing strength of the baby's crying.

The reality of the power and passion with which a new baby can communicate often comes as a shock – especially to a woman having her first baby. As one said: 'I felt completely lost and very naive, as my son was the first baby that I've ever held.' When he 'yelled solidly during the day', she reacted by withdrawing emotionally into a protective shell and describes her feelings about him as 'very little, either negative or positive'.

A woman needs to be self-confident and strong to cope with the violence of feeling expressed by the baby – and with the violence of her own emotional reaction to such stark need. She may manage to keep her equilibrium by withdrawing, as this woman did, and shutting out the messages the baby is giving by distancing herself from her child. When this happens, women often say they felt 'numb', 'confused', 'detached from reality' or that they 'felt nothing for the baby except sorry that it had me as a mother'. 'There was no maternal instinct,' one woman told me, 'and I felt towards him what I might have felt towards any small animal in my care.'

Instead of clamping down on their feelings, other women cannot help being emotionally sucked into the baby's rage and shattered by it. Then the woman becomes almost like a child herself, shaken and at the mercy of the emotional distress aroused by the baby.

Any woman whose confidence is shaken by a bad birth experience in which she felt helpless in the power of the medical system starts out on her relationship with the baby already handicapped. Many hospitals have changed their routine practices following delivery as a result of the publication of Klaus and Kennel's work demonstrating that the time immediately following birth is a sensitive one in which the mother usually becomes emotionally attached to her baby, and that when she is deprived of contact with the baby, she may have difficulty in bonding.[14] As a result they have instituted a mandatory 'bonding' time following delivery.[15] The mother is allowed, or perhaps helped, to hold the baby for a period of ten minutes or longer and can put it to the breast. Sometimes couples are left alone with their babies so that they can get to know each other. There have also been changes on the post-partum ward. In some countries, such as Britain, mothers and babies are now kept together routinely throughout the daylight hours, and in some hospitals at night too. This has been a marked step forward in recognizing that babies need their mothers, and that mothers need their babies. Yet it is disturbing that women were not permitted to have close contact with their babies, in spite of asking for it, until pediatricians demonstrated in a scholarly work that some babies could be neglected or abused if this were not done. Mothers' wishes could be dismissed; pediatric research and the invention of a special word for mother love – 'bonding' – endorsed that love and validated it so that at last it has become respectable.

There can be problems with 'bonding' when it becomes an institutionalized routine. Professional enthusiasm for it is often imposed on women without sensitivity to their individual needs. Despite exhaustion, a Caesarean wound or a painful episiotomy, women are expected to look after their babies throughout the twenty-four hours. Some are more or less forced to breast-feed, and criticized if they appear reluctant.[16] There is evidence to show that women's feelings about their babies are affected more by the environment in which they give birth, and by whether or not they have an opportunity to control what is done to them, than by the hospital practice of 'bonding'. Women express more affection for their babies in hospitals where mother-baby contact is *facilitated*, than in one where staff are enthusiastic about bonding but require mothers to be passive patients.[17] A woman should be able to decide what *she* wants, and not have bonding thrust upon her.

The woman in childbirth who is treated as if she were an irresponsible child may either struggle against this or may submit and become a 'good patient'. Either way, her self-image is assailed. Motherhood is far from being a passive condition. It entails constant decision-making, the setting of limits, the exercise of power, active learning from the baby and acceptance of the frightening responsibility for the life of another human being. After a high-tech, obstetrically managed birth experience a woman has suddenly to transform herself, in the space of a few hours, from child-patient to adult-mother.

For many women it is difficult to leap that chasm. This is not because there is anything inadequate in their personalities. It is because they have been conditioned by the medical system to accept a passive role or, if they have resisted, been forced into stressful conflict.

Some resolve this conflict by discharging themselves from the hospital at the earliest possible moment. They breathe a sigh of relief when they get home with their babies and, once they can do things *their way*, swiftly make the transformation into motherhood. Others find the going more difficult. Then everything that should have occurred spontaneously is subject to conscious direction and agonized over. They feel they have to prove themselves, to show they can be good mothers – to demonstrate competence in the face of the evidence. They have to provide proof to their own mothers, their partners, their doctors, friends and family – to themselves – and, most of all, to the baby. One consequence is that a tussle develops between mother and baby. As one woman says: 'Once I was home things changed. My daughter wouldn't sleep at nights, which was my fault as I let her sleep too much during the day. I felt very tired and depressed. I soon realized how parents could hurt their babies.'

Other women – those who have been effectively reduced to an infantile status by the way they were treated in the hospital – become fixed in the role of a child. Like the woman quoted earlier who said that she was in a daze and kept on thinking that the baby was herself, they find great difficulty in making the transition to motherhood. When the baby cries, they feel as if it is *themselves* crying. They can do little or nothing to soothe or comfort, since it is they who are weeping, they who need comfort. 'I cried virtually all day,' one woman said. 'I didn't really believe that the baby was mine. One day after I had fed him four times in two hours I felt I wanted to give him away and forget that I had him.' For a woman who is also in a weakened physical state and in pain from stitches, her own needs become even more paramount. The baby becomes tyrant and enemy.

From women's descriptions of their post-partum experiences it seems that going home proves most difficult for those who have become dependent on nurses and doctors in the hospital. Their reversion to 'the little girl' state makes them good patients, but anxious and bewildered mothers. A recurring theme in these women's accounts is a longing to be cared for, yet over and over again confronting the reality that the baby must take precedence over their needs and wishes. 'I kept wondering when my maternal instincts would take over,' one woman told me. 'Actually, I didn't like my daughter very much. All I felt was tired – like a tatty [shabby] drinks machine – and really washed out. Breast-feeding was a chore and I found myself wishing my daughter's life away to a time when she'd start giving me something in return.' Another woman said that depression hit her 'rock bottom' when her husband forgot to buy her cigarettes: 'Usually I was a between five to ten fags a day person, but after I had the baby and my depression mounted, I was smoking anything up to twenty a day.'

A partner's pleasure in the baby may reinforce this sense of being abandoned: 'I felt jealous of the attention my husband gave to her'; 'I felt my partner loved the baby more than me.' A hunger to be cherished may be so great that she more or less ignores the baby. As one woman put it, who felt this yearning to be cared for when she was still in hospital, but was on a ward where new mothers were urged to start coping as soon as possible: 'I don't think I fully realized that he was mine. All I wanted to do was go home with my husband and leave the baby in the hospital.'

While still in hospital, however, many women are protected
from this sense of loss. Sometimes the post-natal ward offers 'a sanctuary' or 'cocoon' (though, as we shall see, the realities of life on a
post-natal ward make that difficult). Most women feel clever at having
had a baby: 'I felt very proud and motherly almost straight away
and very happy about the baby and for once I had the attention I so
much needed,' one woman told me. It was when she went home and
had to cope alone that she felt lost and entered a state of black
depression, while the baby cried and cried.

When a woman has been deprived of autonomy in childbirth
there is no way of going back and making the birth different. Yet
many women relive such birth experiences like an old film being
played over and over again in their heads. They struggle to sort out
the sequence and timing of events, who said and did what, and to
understand why. There is rarely anyone willing to tell them exactly
what happened. A partner who was present during labour may
have understood even less than the woman herself. A man sometimes
accepts the obstetrician's view of events and, without realizing it,
tends to discount and trivialize the woman's experience. Hospital
staff are reluctant to give full explanations or acknowledge mistakes,

often because they are anxious about possible litigation. Even when this does not enter the picture, they rarely know how to deal positively with complaints and tend to become defensive and hostile. The woman is treated as a 'difficult patient' – even a 'neurotic' one – who must be handled cautiously. So when she tries to talk about the birth, she encounters bland reassurance. She is told she should be grateful that the baby is alive and healthy, and it is usually implied that everything is for the best in the best of all possible worlds.

Yet to deal with her birth experience, to make sense of what happened and incorporate it into the continuous flow and pattern of her life, a woman needs to talk it through and to piece together events, processes and emotions that have been fragmented. She needs to be able to discuss what happened with someone who understands, who is accepting and does not grudge the time. Such coordination of experience – the patterning of any experience in life in which we have felt deprived of adult identity – is vital for a woman who is starting out on the most quintessentially adult role of all, that of parenthood.

Every new mother needs somebody to talk to who is non-judgemental, who is genuinely interested in what she is saying and who acknowledges and can reflect back to her the whole range of emotions she expresses about the major life transformation of childbirth. For the mother of a baby who cries inconsolably it may save her sanity – and sometimes the baby's life. Yet, as we shall see in Chapter 6, after having a baby many women are socially isolated and more alone than they have ever been in their lives before.

Taking action

If you are finding it difficult to come to terms with a bad birth experience, it is a good idea to seek out someone who is willing to listen and talk it through with you. That might be your childbirth teacher, a close woman friend, your mother or a sister, or a sympathetic midwife, doctor or health visitor. Or you may feel your partner is the right person. Consider asking someone you do not already know well, so that you do not feel that you have to live up to any expectations the other person has of you. If he or she seeks to reassure you or tell you it was not like that or give advice, let them know that this is not what you want. You need to be able to express your grief and anger without feeling it is crazy or dangerous, or that you are a failure, or that being open about your feelings can harm you or anyone else. You would like the other person to give you the security in which you can do this.

You owe it to yourself to refuse to dismiss the birth and your emotions about it as an insignificant event in your life. You have every right to feelings of disappointment, anger or bitterness. But do not cling to them. Do not let them fester in your mind. Talk about them and, if there is a chance, join with other women in a childbirth or women's group to work out different strategies in the future, in other medical encounters – especially if you are ever going to have a subsequent baby – taking the strength of your feelings as a stimulus to doing something to create a more positive experience next time, and for other women who come after you.

CHAPTER 6

Down from the Mountain

I felt I should never have had a baby.
If anyone had told me what it would be like, I might
have saved my life in time. Who was
this immensely powerful person screaming unintelligibly,
sucking my breast until I was
in a state of fatigue the likes of which I had never known?
Who was he and by what authority
had he claimed the right to my life? I would never
be a good mother. The experts were right,
I thought. Babies are born to be placid, contented creatures.
It is only the bad mother repressing
her unfair resentment, holding the baby too tightly,
too loosely, too often, too rarely,
letting him cry, picking him up too soon, feeding him too much,
too little, suffocating him with her love
or not loving him enough – it is only the bad
mother who is to blame.
Jane Lazarre, *Mother Knot*

After giving birth a woman usually feels she has done something very special and is often astonished that she has managed to deliver a real baby. Many women feel something close to ecstasy. It is as if they have given birth to themselves and they feel more radiantly, splendidly, gloriously alive.

Following a vaginal birth in which they felt in control and in which, though intervention may have been employed, they were able to make informed choices between alternatives, they describe feelings of triumph and fulfilment. It is as though they have scaled a mountain and stand at the top, triumphant: 'I was overwhelmed with happiness that my husband and I had produced such a perfect little person'; '. . . euphoric, excited, pleased with myself – and much

72

closer to my husband'; 'I felt a complete woman, rather smug and very elated'; 'I was ecstatic. I felt very clever for producing the most wonderful little thing in the whole world.'

Though there may be a temporary drop from this emotional high some time in the first week – the 'fourth day blues' or 'the weeps' – this rarely lasts longer than twenty-four hours. The honeymoon with the new-born baby continues until he starts to cry inconsolably some time after three weeks. Then this euphoria is cracked wide open.

The contrast between the sense of achievement a woman experiences shortly after giving birth and her feelings when her baby cries and will not be comforted is dramatic. It is as if she has been on a mountain summit and is now swept down to the bottom – and often further and further down, into a chasm of despair. 'It was the worst time in my life,' one woman told me, 'and I have never felt so completely alone. No one understood. I was totally isolated.' 'I give him his 10 p.m. feed, sleep until midnight and then walk with him non-stop until his 6 a.m. feed, when I hand him over to his father,' another said. And another remarked, 'Although I have never done him any physical harm – I am too weak from lack of sleep – I am sorely tempted. Every night is a nightmare.'

When a baby cries inconsolably the mother's whole life is as if sucked into a vortex and she feels that she loses herself in the process. 'Down, down, down – utterly down' until there is nothing of her left. There is only the sound of the baby's ceaseless crying. This sense that you have lost identity is one of the most frightening aspects of having a crying baby.[1]

Such a violation of selfhood can be made more severe if a woman has a baby when she is still very young and before she knows who she is, what she wants to become or what her choices are. She may then feel trapped in her role as a mother with a totally unrewarding baby. Many women having their first baby who have been brought up in the small nuclear family typical of a northern industrial society have started out on motherhood with little idea of the realities of life with a baby. They are subjected to heavy social pressure to become mothers and it is assumed, from their own early childhood on, that when this happens it will bring a fulfilment and satisfaction that equals nothing else in a woman's life. To men, fatherhood is incidental. Masculinity is not defined in terms of fathering. For women, motherhood, or potential fertility, is seen as a basic element of femininity.

A woman of 26 who had her uterus removed when she was 22 because of pelvic infection was reported in the press as being a highly successful model and explained how this had come about: 'I thought, now I'm not going to be able to do normal things like having a baby, I'm going to have to get myself a good career.'[2] It is still considered 'normal' for a woman to have babies. Anything else is an aberration and she has to justify her conduct. Under social pressures like these, women are forced into motherhood unable to make a realistic appraisal of what it entails in terms of their own identity. It often means that, even if they would want to have a baby at some stage of their lives, they become pregnant long before they are ready.

When I interviewed older mothers of crying babies, I discovered that they were often able to cope better emotionally than those in their teens and early twenties.[3] Because they were more self-assured and confident, the crying proved less of an attack on their identity. In practical terms they suffered from the crying in much the same way as younger mothers, and it wasn't any less awful, but they were still *themselves*.

A dominant emotion experienced by the mother of a crying baby is the sense of being out of control. Women describe feeling flustered, overwhelmed and in a state of panic: 'I lost all confidence ... I cried almost as much as the baby'; 'The dogs were nervous wrecks because I screamed at them all day'; 'I was near to tears all the time as my emotions were so mixed'; 'I couldn't give a true account of my feelings as they were in turmoil!' One woman told how she and her husband paced the house at night with their screaming baby 'like demented bag-pipers'. It is clear that women were distressed at having been turned into something very different from their usual rational selves and that some felt on the edge of insanity.

Many also told how they felt rejected by the baby: 'He cried every time I tried to cuddle him'; 'I felt as if I had failed to win his love'; 'I found it very difficult to love him as he cried so much. There was almost no feedback at all from him.' This was accompanied by overwhelming feelings of guilt. As one woman said: 'I feel as though I must be an awful mother. Why do my children cry? Is there something that I don't do properly? When they are older I shall be apologizing to them for being such an awful mother.' Others said: 'I felt an utter failure'; 'I thought everyone was talking behind my back saying I couldn't cope as a mother'; 'I felt guilty because I could not breast-feed or even settle my daughter'; 'I felt I was a terrible mother and should never have had a child'; 'I thought it was because of me that she was so unhappy and disturbed'; 'I felt useless because I couldn't console my baby.'

Because women are expected to fit a severely restricted role as housewives and mothers and are judged socially in terms of their dutiful fulfilment of these expectations, women who did not get time to keep the house clean and tidy felt dismal failures. They said things like: 'Housework was not done. I was very ashamed of my home'; 'I couldn't cope with the house at all'; 'I worried about not having time for my husband, not keeping the house tidy, and guilty because I felt that I should be the one doing the housework and having a meal ready for him when he came home from work. Instead of which he was doing the bulk of the housework and finishing off the dinner while I coped with the baby.'

Any woman with a crying baby is likely to suffer from chronic exhaustion: 'I was absolutely tired out all the time'; 'I was overworked, overtired and often wondered how I was going to last the day'; 'I would go to the baby and find myself asleep on our bedroom floor not knowing if I had seen to her or not'; 'I felt I had nothing left to give.' Many women were acutely aware that this was also affecting their relationship with their partners and were frightened about it: 'When she was crying a lot I felt anger towards my husband'; 'We had lots of rows [arguments]'; 'The baby was wrecking my marriage.'

Sex

It is hardly surprising that under these conditions women don't want sex and that if a man insists on intercourse, it becomes either something with which a woman complies wearily so as to please him or an act of rape. Women said: 'We had a very bad year. I didn't ever want another baby, so sex was out! I was too tired most of the time and there were too many stresses'; 'Absolute exhaustion is preventing us from trying to improve our sex life. We have talked about sex but we're too tired to get down to it'; 'I went off sex, as I felt I needed every ounce of energy just to cope with the baby. I wanted affection and support, not sex'; 'I was overweight, overtired, lifeless. I felt a physical and emotional wreck, going bananas with the "goo gah" baby talk. Physical contact with my husband was abhorrent. I always felt too tired. Nevertheless he persisted. I felt, "get on, and for God's sake hurry up and let's get it over!" I tended to make love dutifully, if I'm honest, for about six months after Henry was born'; 'I used to enjoy sex, but now I almost never want to make love or enjoy it when we do.'

When at last a couple do get together and the woman becomes aroused, there are other hazards. The baby starts to cry! Many women told me that their babies seemed to have a sixth sense and know exactly when attention was diverted from them, so that love-making was interrupted regularly by the crying.

Some women said that they could not enjoy sexual sensations because they felt out of control of their bodies and themselves all the time the baby was going through this crying phase. 'Body felt soft, leaky, tired. Relationship with husband terrible. Babies [she had twins] crying, me crying, husband hitting me.' Even when they had loving partners, women often felt they were unable to control *anything* – not the baby, nor their emotions, their own bodies, their relationships, or anything they did during the twenty-four hours. They were completely used up in service to the baby and had no strength for anything else: 'I felt depressed and exhausted and I didn't feel as if it was my own body. I didn't feel in control – just sort of went from one day to the next. I was worn out and very tense all the time. Our love-making was rather strained. It all felt mechanical and I found myself deliberately avoiding sex.'

Women felt sorry for their partners, but often also very resentful that, however much they might help with the baby, *they* could always choose to escape from the trap. The mother had no such choice. With the birth of a first baby, the man and woman went into parenthood as if they were free and equal individuals. But now the truth was out: a woman bears the responsibility for her baby. A man helps when he can. As we shall see in the next chapter, it does not always work out as well as this in practice: many men give little or no help, some are a definite hindrance and some, like the man described above, resort to physical violence. As a result an inner rage builds up

in the unsupported mother who, to all intents and purposes, has male support, but who in fact is struggling to cope alone. The anger she dare not express towards her partner is directed instead towards the baby. Ashamed about these intense emotions and anxious to protect her baby, the hostility is redirected against herself. When hatred is turned inwards like this, it becomes depression.

Depression

There's something we call post-partum depression . . .
Oh you've heard of it? . . . A satisfaction
settled in his eyes, and he seemed unaware that
he had accepted the descriptive term as
an explanation. The words are like a chant of absolution
and cover a multitude of sins.

Charlotte Painter, *Who Made the Lamb*

Fifty-eight per cent of the women who described how they felt six weeks after the birth said they were depressed. Many others used terms and phrases that suggested that they were depressed, too, though they did not use the word. They said they felt 'numb', that everything was 'unreal', and that 'every little act seemed a mammoth task'. One woman encapsulated the experience of many others when she said: 'I just went inside myself and couldn't communicate at all, even to my close friends. At the time they seemed to me to be different.' A common theme was the difficulty in feeling any attachment to the baby: 'I had negative feelings about my much wanted baby daughter'; 'I felt very cut off from the child, as if I had bought him from a shop. I wondered if the baby wasn't mine and he'd got mixed up in the hospital' and 'I didn't want to hurt her but I had no interest in her at all.' In one woman's words: 'I had always prepared myself for the worst, but it was worse than that.'

The state of depression into which a woman drops in these first months after childbirth sometimes drags on so long that it becomes an integral part of her personality. Some women are put on a steady diet of tranquillizers by family doctors who feel helpless to do anything else for them. Some see psychiatrists and are prescribed antidepressants. Many others get by somehow, drained of energy, under constant pressure to satisfy the demands made on them by other people and with no opportunity to meet their own needs. They feel trapped in motherhood and convinced that they are complete failures not only as mothers, but as human beings too. No one realizes they are depressed because no one has seen them *not* depressed for months on end. They rarely find their way into the statistics of mental illness.

Only a very small proportion of women who suffer with depression after childbirth have psychiatric treatment – probably not more than 10 per cent.[4] Some psychoanalysts and psychologists claim that post-natal emotional problems result from a woman's failure to accept her 'femininity', and have constructed a variety of scales in order to demonstrate this.[5] What this usually amounts to is an observation that a woman who is depressed no longer functions effectively in servicing her husband and family. She is, in one psychiatrist's words,

> unable to stand her husband or home. They are now felt burdensome and distasteful, dirty and demanding. Cooking, cleaning and other wifely or maternal functions are now not pleasurable but exhausting – to be undertaken with suffering and anxiety. . . Unable to look after home, husband, or child, she seeks instead to be looked after, to be fed, sheltered . . .[6]

It may come as no surprise to know that this is a man talking – one who himself expects to be 'looked after, to be fed, sheltered' by a woman. But even if it were not written by a man, the argument puts the cart before the horse. Feeling that housework is distasteful, demanding and exhausting is not a symptom of mental illness. Women become emotionally distressed because they are trapped in their role as housewives, mothers and carers. If men were expected to do these difficult and low-grade jobs, they might also become depressed. Women psychoanalysts, too, sometimes make the same sort of judgements based on patriarchal attitudes. One female analyst, for example, has described how in 'pathological' women 'ego functioning was so seriously disrupted that they were unable to carry on their household chores' and 'care for their family'. 'Pathological' women are hostile towards others and express their anger. 'Normal' women direct hostility towards themselves and are 'masochistically oriented', deriving gratification from a 'passive-submissive position' and from the self-sacrifice and service that motherhood demands. Women suffer post-natal mental illness because of flaws in their femininity.[7] In a research study on post-natal care a midwife faces the issue squarely when she comments: 'One wonders what the reaction might be if it were suggested that depression occurring in men following trauma was due to some default in their masculinity.'[8]

In spite of such theories about femininity, women are often criticized by professional health-carers for investing emotional energy in those female life processes that offer potential fulfilment – childbirth and breast-feeding among them – and for grieving when they feel they have failed to live through these experiences in a satisfying way. The woman who had a prolonged labour terminated by Caesarean section and who mourns the loss of her fantasy birth, and the one who is persuaded to switch to artificial feeding because of difficulties with breast-feeding but who feels she has failed in a basic maternal function, may both be labelled as 'natural childbirthers' and 'cranks' who cannot come to terms with reality. Another element in post-natal depression for many women is this grieving over unfulfilled hopes and dreams. This tends to be trivialized, dismissed as ludicrous or treated with open hostility. Women are supposed to knuckle down to it and take whatever comes, and not to hope for or want anything from these major life experiences. In the long run it seems that it is not femininity that is demanded, but sheer passivity.

To ascribe depression after birth to hormonal disturbance or to pathological elements in the female psyche is to miss the point. Instead we ought to be looking at society's failure to give adequate social support to mothers. Studies of mental illness reveal consistently higher levels in women than men – particularly in women who are living with men.[9] Married women suffer from more mental illness than single women. Depression is especially high among women in low-income groups in urban areas, who are three times more likely to suffer from depression than women working in the professions.[10]

When she has a baby, a woman is exposed to added socio-economic stress. In the early 1980s, 30 per cent of the poorest fifth of the population in Britain consisted of families with children (compared with 22 per cent ten years previously).[11]

Yet however well off she is, a new mother often finds herself having to cope alone, without anything or anyone to make her feel good about herself, unable to get proper sleep for weeks or months on end and ashamed at the often violent feelings she has about the baby who got her into this trap and who is constantly crying at her and seems to be telling her what a bad mother she is. There must be thousands of women who say, 'I've got a lovely husband, a lovely house, a lovely baby and I know I ought to be happy, but . . .'

Few of us are prepared for the resentment, the sense of inadequacy, the guilt, anger and murderous feelings we have as mothers. There is delighted discovery and joy and sometimes sheer ecstasy too, and that makes it all worth while. But the trouble is that the image of motherhood is romanticized. Before we are plunged into motherhood we learn little or nothing about how we are going to feel when woken by a crying baby for the third time between 3 and 5 a.m., and what it is like to be alone in the house with complete responsibility for a child for eight to ten hours a day.

The baby can seem like a tyrant, demanding more than a woman can possibly give. Jane Price, a psychotherapist, told me about her own experience: 'I thought children came with an "off" knob and that you could turn them off at six in the evening. The baby cried and I wondered how anything so small could have so much energy. I was ten times as big as him but he had more energy.'[12]

Our society puts motherhood on a pedestal while disparaging and degrading mothers in practice. And because women have been taught to protect others and deny their own feelings and needs, when they crack under the strain they are told to pull themselves together and be grateful they have such a beautiful baby. Their distress is trivialized. A British Medical Association booklet for mothers says that if you find yourself 'crying bitterly without any real reason for it', it 'is of no importance, so don't worry.'

Uncontrollable weeping may be sparked off by hormone changes, but the feelings that are expressed are real: a woman's anxiety that she has no maternal 'instincts', panic about taking on the burden of responsibility for a new life and above all, fear that she has lost herself.

Post-natal depression cannot be dismissed as a woman's personal failure to adapt or as a problem that will disappear if only the right drugs are prescribed. Though tranquillizers and antidepressants may be useful, all too often they merely dull the pain, stifle emotions and make the intolerable just bearable. The woman puts on a façade of coping, nobody else is threatened and the treatment suppresses a crisis that can be creative.

When a new mother becomes depressed she is the victim of a social system that fails to value women as mothers and does not consider housework or child care real 'work'. It is a system in which she is cut off from the sources of self-esteem that all of us usually depend on and from the support that in traditional societies comes from other women in the extended family and the neighbourhood. When a woman cracks under stress, the system labels her as 'sick', offers her drugs to keep her going and implicitly blames her for her failure to adjust.

A real mother

Child-rearing books are all about how to be a perfect parent and produce the perfect child who is super-intelligent, kind and caring, secure, ambitious without stress, cooperative, who develops its full potential – and is a credit to you.

Before the curtain rises on this motherhood performance, you read, study, meditate, share and carefully learn the script. You offer Leboyer birth, underwater or in darkness, a gentle birth breathing the baby out like a holy rite. Then you hold, draw to the breast, and of course the baby never leaves you, is in skin-to-skin contact and assured of your love.

You will nurse two or three years, do this task properly, create a new, radiant creature, a work of art and love and patience.

In all your ways you are consistent, tender, reasonable, liberal, you never say no, are never rejecting, offer all that is fair and sweet.

Then what are these ugly feelings like the slug on the lettuce, the slimy trail of ego, the dog-shit suddenly underfoot? Why is your gut twisted, hot anger scalding, thick rage rising like scum on boiling jam, sobs choking like vomit? Why do you want to escape from your child or to wring its neck?

You are grateful to have husband, home, lilac flowering by the window. Everything's all set for the future. But this hate curdles kindness, snuffs all hope. The pastoral idyll, making babies who shine with trust and a high IQ, your lovely Eden with wing-sprouting cherubs in a clean, new world, is shattered.

And you have smashed it.

Guilt wraps round like a tired old coat, the sky turns black. And women say, each one in her own prison, her own isolation and despair, 'It must be all my fault. I should never have had a child. I don't deserve one . . . Why can't I be happy like other women?'

Post-natal depression is not a woman's private problem. It is a political issue, ultimately something that can be changed only when there is social change.

Practical aspects

The point of my writing like this about the crises that occur for many women around six weeks is not to cast gloom and despondency, but to enable any woman who is going through this ordeal to realize that she is not alone. There are thousands of other women who feel like this too, and many more who have survived it at some time in their lives. Only when women come together to share what they know can we develop strength and the understanding to change the system so that women need not suffer all this in isolation, but can look to each other for support and help. It is through such experiences that women have set up peer support groups to help each other through these difficult and challenging months. The addresses of some of these organizations are listed on pages 251–76.

It is important to talk about the psychological impact of a crying baby and the frightening fragmentation of identity it entails for the woman for another reason: because those close to her need to understand what she is going through. A woman who is suffering from depression may not herself realize that this dreadful numbness she is feeling, as if cut off from other people by plate glass, is a sign of depression. Friends and family often become alerted to her needs only when a medical name can be given to her condition and she is ascribed the status of a sick person. Even then, often all that is done is to prescribe mood-changing drugs, advise her to stop breast-feeding and tell her husband to take her out for a meal occasionally.

In closely-knit traditional communities where women share child care and where more experienced mothers help the new mother over the often difficult bridge into motherhood, this sense of alienation is rare. To have one's first baby is to enter a society of women with special status and a vigorous multifaceted life of its own. Even in cities, support networks like this exist among immigrant communities and within certain religious groups. Women of the Orthodox Jewish community in London, for example, support each other in effective, practical ways and have set up a scheme in which other women offer to new mothers a helpful and sympathetic ear, help with older children at supper time, to take and fetch older children to and from school or nursery, and to deliver to the door ready-cooked meals.[13] Once mothers are up and about, they meet with their babies in a relaxed and informal atmosphere at special mother and toddler/baby centres. Perhaps this kind of support group is easiest to organize and runs most effectively when women share ideals and values so that they do not just come together as strangers meeting. But it should be possible for any group of women friends, a neighbourhood group or one based on a woman's health centre, to set up a similar support network once the need is recognized, and simple, reliable ways of giving practical help can be worked out together.

There are other things you may be able to do, too.

● Practise a little self-affirmation. As you struggle through a day in which everything seems to have gone wrong, think back to just *one thing* you did right. Acknowledge it. Say to yourself: 'I did that well!' It may have been a matter of only half an hour out of twelve that were a mess, but recognizing that for those thirty minutes you were doing well lifts your self-esteem and helps to build self-confidence.

● Ask your partner or a close friend to give you a massage. Get some pleasantly scented oil or lotion, warm it, make yourself comfortable on a big towel or old soft rug, propped up with pillows where you need them, and have the tensions massaged away from your back, shoulders, the back of your neck and your feet.

● If you have an understanding family doctor, talk to him or her about how you feel. Many doctors set aside time each week to see patients who need a chance to explore their feelings. Even half an hour can make all the difference. Your doctor may refer you to a psychotherapist, who can give more specialized help with these problems. You can ask for this if you feel it would be of benefit.

● There is a list of organizations on pages 251–76 that may be able to help you.

● Women's health centres and well-women clinics may also provide a counselling service or put you in touch with other people who offer individual or group counselling.

You will find further ideas – things that other women discovered helped them – in Chapter 13.

A baby's inconsolable crying should not be dismissed as the result of either faulty management or personality defects in the mother. It is frequently the consequence of psychosocial stress and is linked to the powerlessness women experience in living in a society that is ill-adapted to the needs of mothers and babies. When women in our northern industrial culture become mothers they often also become socially isolated and lose any emotional support they could get from other women.

Yet it is not only a question of isolation and loneliness. All over the world the primary role of mothers is to be cleaners of dirt and disposers of waste products. In many countries women are engaged in endless toil with sweeping brush and besom, soap and scouring cloth, boiling soda and bleach, mangle and iron, carrying water and wood for fires, searching heads for lice, brushing away flies, and protecting food from mice, rats and a horde of insects. It is a constant battle against dirt and an attempt to keep children's energy within bounds, to prevent it intruding on men's lives in a disturbing way. In shanty towns clinging like suppurating sores to hillsides around great cities in Latin America and the Middle East, in village hovels with mud floors in Asia, in shacks made of packing cases and old car bodies on the wasteland around harbours, in refugee camps, even in modern homes where there are vacuum cleaners, washing machines and dishwashers – the struggle continues, day in, day out.

From an anthropological perspective, a baby's crying, like the products of bowels and bladder, and nasal mucus and vomit, can be seen as 'matter out of place'.[14] Women as wives and mothers spend most of their lives dealing with matter out of place in the form of dirt, faeces, urine, blood and other body products, dust, stains, clutter, the left-overs of food and waste matter from the preparation of the meals and all the spill-over of children's vitality in the form of noise and movement – ensuring that it is restricted to culturally imposed forms.

Women's tasks are centred on the place where nature meets culture and they are expected to contain, canalize and mould nature to fit a culture that serves the needs of men. When a baby cries inconsolably, it is a powerful signal to everyone that the mother is failing in what she is taught is her most basic task. If she is occupied with a crying baby, she is also criticized because she cannot perform satisfactorily the duties of eliminating dirt and other matter out of place – and becomes anxious herself that she is a bad housewife.

It is not only that women's work in the home is undervalued or that our own hopes and wishes must be systematically subordinated to the requirements of men. The repetitive and back-breaking toil in which women are engaged in the service of their families has gone largely unrecorded and unpraised over thousands of years. Yet without it no culture could exist. Civilizations have flourished and empires have been built on women's unpaid labour and on the nurturing skills that are taken for granted as an inherent characteristic of being female.

CHAPTER 7

The Father of the Crying Baby

A partner who shares equally in child care, who gets up in the middle of the night to see to a crying baby, who deals with nappy (diaper) changes, clears up the bathroom, knows the right temperature cycles for stretchsuits and knitted coats, who notices when essential supplies of liners, soap, toilet paper and baby necessities are running low and sees that they are replenished, who can whip up a delicious meal quickly and without fuss and leaves the kitchen spotless, and who will spend hours rocking, cuddling and soothing a fussy baby – and all this without being asked . . . Someone who does not ask for praise or gratitude but takes it for granted that he should be doing these things . . . A person who is sensitive, understanding and tender, and who values human relationships above achievement . . . That is one image of the new man. It is one that few mothers of crying babies recognize in their male partners.

For the reality is different. Fathers help off and on but, on the whole, they think it is the woman's job to look after the baby. Two-thirds of fathers of crying babies give a hand when they can, as assistants rather than main care-givers. They do this so that the woman can perform other household chores. They hold the baby or give a bottle while she prepares the meal, for example. More concentrated baby-care – really taking over – is restricted to those times when they realize that the woman is at the end of her tether because she is crying or in a state of physical collapse. Even then, some men manage never to notice that a woman is desperately in need of help.

This happens at all social class levels. It is sometimes assumed that middle-class men share in parenting more than men in low-income groups. For the fathers of crying babies this is not so. In fact, middle-class fathers' work often spills over into off-duty time in a way that restricts the time available for child care. Wives of professional men, especially, refer to their commitments over and above official working hours. These fathers are often concerned about the deprivation of personal space caused by a crying baby and women are anxious and guilty when the man gets irritated or is not able to get his full ration of sleep at night.

The middle-class mother is also more likely to breast-feed – and to breast-feed for longer.[1] This, too, limits the help that middle-class fathers provide. Breast-feeding mothers often say that since the most obvious form of comforting is to put the baby to the breast, there is no way they can take a break from a constantly crying baby.

In most families, whatever the social class, women whose babies cry long into the night say they worry that the man has to work in the morning, so they deal with the baby during broken nights, ignoring the fact that they have to work in the morning too. This reflects the priority given to paid over unpaid work. The family's livelihood depends on one partner being able to keep the money coming in – usually the man. It also has to do with the presentation of a 'public face' in the workplace. The one who has to present himself to other people has priority over the woman whose work is at home and who can, if necessary, slop around all day in a dressing gown or a dirty sweater and jeans. Women go to great lengths to protect their men in the traditional male economic role and to help them preserve this public image of the man with responsibilities outside the home.

When a man is unemployed and around the house most of the day, women may be equally, or even more, concerned to shield his ego, and be hesitant about asking him to accept 'female' jobs. Though some unemployed men start to become more active fathers, and find they enjoy it, others try to preserve their dominant male role through meeting with other males in the pub (bar) and other places that are strongholds of male identity. A woman who suffered from recurring uterine infections three months after the baby's birth, and who was severely depressed all this time, told me she worried about not having enough time to give to her husband and about not keeping the house tidy enough. Her unemployed husband gave a hand for the first two weeks after the baby was born, but then said he felt 'restricted' and wanted to be 'normal' again, and drifted off for regular drinking sessions with his pals.

Women usually express astonishment and admiration that their partners help at all with housework or the baby. It is obviously not expected. They sometimes say that other people – family members and friends – comment on how wonderful the man is as a husband and father. It seems that these men receive a good deal of praise and gratitude because they are doing something not normally required of males, and over and above the standard role model of fatherhood.

The new man has been much heralded but his coming is long delayed. Most fathers cannot stand a baby's crying and tend to feel it is the mother's responsibility and that she should make it stop. They ask: 'Why don't you feed that child?' They make suggestions about things to do, which the mother has tried already. If it gets too bad, they turn up the TV. When they cannot tolerate the crying any longer, they go out of the room banging the door or leave the house because there is urgent business they have remembered elsewhere. Some men escape to a male peer group, others go home to their mothers.

Though this may seem a very negative and dated view of fathers, it is one that emerges from the descriptions women gave of men's behaviour in the home. One woman in three said that her partners did not do anything to help when the baby cried. And those who did offer help tended to opt out if crying continued. A man would often pick up and rock the baby when it first started crying, but asked the woman to take the child away when it continued to cry and he felt he could no longer cope. One man in every four escaped out of earshot and, when the crying persisted, one in ten began shouting or became physically violent.

Men often say that the reality of fatherhood came as a terrible shock to them. They should realize that motherhood is often a shock, too. It is true, though, that men have even less preparation than women for parenthood. As one man, who is the primary care-taker of his child, told me: 'There was no opportunity to attend antenatal "mothercraft" classes. The "fathers' evenings" were a brave effort, but overall I felt very much excluded from the pregnancy business. Our attempts to share the experience were constrained by the medical machine', and he says this made him 'hurt, angry and bemused'.

Not only do men have little or no practical preparation for life after a baby comes, but they are not prepared for the conflicting and often disturbing feelings they may have as fathers, and are often reluctant to discuss their hopes and fears. One man put it this way:

> When I began looking after my son, I came crashing up each day against the limits of my masculine upbringing. Nothing in my life experience, nothing I had observed in other men or in my father prepared me for doing this job ... My identity as a man, my whole life, had been organized around activities and events outside myself and my home. Everything had been about my acting on the world around me, and in doing this I had expected others to support me emotionally. Personal relationships, my emotional life, domesticity and children. I lived in a whole culture that downgraded their importance and centrality to people's lives. [2]

It is often claimed that insufficient attention is paid to the role of being a father, that psychologists and sociologists have neglected it in their studies of the family and that there is not enough published for and about fathers. I find that whenever I lecture about becoming a mother and the experiences of birth and breast-feeding, there is always someone in the audience who considers that I am neglecting fathers and wants me to focus on *their* needs. (It is usually a man.) Publishers are keen to explore the 'other' side of parenthood, there are films and situation comedies about fathers, and newspapers and magazines examine in depth how they imagine Prince Charles and well-known film and pop stars and footballers are as fathers. They eulogize those exceptional fathers – one whose wife is paraplegic, another who is a full-time house-husband, for example – who act as role models for all the more ordinary fathers.

If we look more closely at the way in which the media present accounts of fatherhood, it is evident that these stories are produced for women, not men. The mass of material about fatherhood is in women's magazines and on TV and radio programmes the main audience for which is women at home. In newspapers they appear on the women's page. The great human interest story of fatherhood is considered primarily a female concern. So at the level of popular culture and the mass media there is little to prepare a man for the changes in his life when a baby comes.

It might be thought that as there is such a lively interest in fatherhood, it must be going through a process of astonishing change. That is certainly the impression given. We are told that fathers are very different today from how their own fathers were, that they spend much more time with their children and do things for them that their fathers would never have dreamed of doing.

This is one aspect of the mythologizing of modern fatherhood. In fact, sociologists and psychologists reveal that most contemporary men make little regular commitment to child care and housework.[3] A 1986 survey of men and housework disclosed that 61 per cent said they had not used a vacuum cleaner during the previous week, only 21 per cent did any washing – and when they did it was often a question of shoving things in the washing machine – and only 19 per cent did ironing. Though just over half said they washed the dishes, men usually stick to traditional male tasks like painting and decorating, repairing appliances or tinkering with the car.[4]

Charlie Lewis, a psychologist who researched what happens when men become fathers, found that men are not so very different from their fathers. Because of the way Western society is organized, fatherhood is seen as a 'luxury' superfluous to the 'necessary' function of motherhood. 'Evidence for the "new fathers" is, in reality, hard to find.'[5] He concludes that: 'Truly participant fatherhood will not become the norm until great changes are made outside the family – in child-care arrangements and in the sexual division of labour in the workplace.'[6] The marketing of the 'new man' has been vigorous, but for the most part it advertises a purely fictional character.

During pregnancy

When men talk about the birth of their babies it is clear that for many of them pregnancy is an unsettling time. They are anxious about the responsibility they are taking on, financial problems that may lie ahead and the irrevocable change in their lives as they 'settle down'. Many are secretly afraid that they will lose the woman to the baby, or that she will be injured or even die in childbirth.

A man may be ashamed of what he is feeling. Or he may be unaware of what is going on inside him. He then retreats from the scene or behaves in a disturbed and disturbing way. One who feels rejected and is frightened that he is going to lose his partner to the baby, for example, may seek understanding and warmth from another

person who makes him feel important and wanted. It may be his mother or another woman – often someone who is close to his part- ner, a friend or even her sister – and because his wife is busy with a new baby, the relationship continues. This exacerbates the new mother's loneliness and her burden of total responsibility. She experiences the shock of being abandoned by the one person on whom she depended to be strong. If she discovers that the man is having an affair, it is the ultimate act of betrayal.

Fathers are often in a cultural double-bind. Expected to participate fully in pregnancy, birth and care of the new baby, they receive all sorts of messages telling them they are outsiders. 'I felt forgotten,' one man told me, 'pushed into the background', and he added, almost enviously, 'She was so *arrogant* with her pregnancy!' As one psychologist father explains:

> The double-bind results from the inconsistency between what fathers are told – 'please be involved' – and the unspoken afterthought – 'except for your negative feelings'. To be truly involved, a new father must get in touch with his feelings. But when he does, not all of them are positive. At times he will be as frightened, concerned, sad and angry as his wife.[7]

During this crucial transition in a couple's life, gender stereotypes are emphasized. The pregnant woman is portrayed as passive, full of half-voiced fears, timid, unable to concentrate or engage in intellectual work and emotionally unstable. The man, on the other hand, is supposed to be logical and down-to-earth. He is the protector, provides financial security and offers a strong shoulder on which she can cry. Women often don't fit this stereotype. And the truth is that men often don't fit it either.

After the birth

A new father is often overwhelmed with emotions he does not understand. He may be thrilled at first, but is soon conscious of the heavy burden of responsibility and of restrictions on what he is able to do from now on and into the future. Most men when interviewed stress this burden of responsibility and the feeling that doors have closed in their lives – that now they have a child there are going to be deprivations, things they are never going to be free to do. Other confusing emotions may crowd in, too, which a man is ashamed to admit. One who has never resolved the emotional turmoil he felt when his mother had another baby may relive this experience and be unable to cope with the violence of resentment. A man who was an only child now experiences the shock of realizing that he is not the only or the most important one. The mother and baby are centre stage.

With the birth of a first child a man also comes face to face with his own mortality. Until that time he belongs to the younger generation. He is a child to his parents. Now there is a child who will outlive him. He feels he has to achieve something in his life besides his baby. His work may become specially important. This, combined with an increased sense of financial responsibility, leads to a sense of urgency.

Life is seen as more precious and fragile. Men say they drive more carefully and do not take the risks they did before the birth of a child. The man whose life was fairly free and easy before, who felt he could act independently and take chances, feels he can no longer do this. A pall of gloom settles over him. He is expected to be happy. People are congratulating him on becoming a father. Yet he is inexplicably depressed.

A survey by the magazine *Parents* in Australia found that many fathers accept their share of baby-care in the first weeks but on realizing that the woman can do everything better, they give up. Most take to baby-care best either when they and their partners know equally little about babies or when they have attended a course of parentcraft classes together and are both well informed. Many men become frustrated and feel 'degraded' as mere nappy (diaper)-changers. Some compensate for this feeling by becoming specialists in bathing or in filling bottles with formula and find these tasks rewarding. Others never develop confidence in doing anything for their babies and are aware of their partner's anxiety that they cannot do it properly. So they retire behind the newspaper or go off for a drink and leave the woman to get on with it. The upshot is that most fathers limit their involvement 'to a bit of play in the evening, to a flirtation with a freshly changed and fed baby'.[8]

In fact, most men *assume* that the mother must be the main care-taker. They are more likely to have jobs outside the home that make it difficult for them to take on continuous responsibility for baby care. That is the way our society is organized. Any couple who want to do it differently need to have well-planned strategies, which are largely in conflict with our accepted culture of child-rearing. This comes over clearly in the comments made by women in my own study about partners who try to help:

> My husband doesn't have much patience. He usually left me to calm down the baby when he cried, as he thought it was *my* baby and I should calm him down.

> He does not seem to realize how wearing it is to have a $2\frac{1}{2}$-year-old constantly at you all day talking non-stop and then to have the baby wake in between times. Then as the first goes to bed and all could be quiet, the baby wakes for four hours while he has been quietly working at the office. This is something you cannot describe to anybody adequately to make them understand unless they have experienced it.

> My husband gave me all the support he could but it was not sufficient. He did not know what help or advice to give so if the baby was going through a difficult time, he usually went outside. He is a farmer. As he works such long hours, he never feeds, changes or baths the baby.

A woman describing her experience of a crying baby following Caesarean section said:

> I was completely unprepared for the way I would have to manage. My husband didn't understand why I didn't just revert back to normal as soon as I came home. I didn't have anyone to help me because he went back to work straight away. My partner seems to crumble when Sally screams. We inevitably end up arguing. I can handle this now [a year later] but when she was tiny I needed moral support badly.

Other women said: 'My husband has been very supportive but also found it very tiring running his own business and having to come home to a crying baby and finding me worn out, and with the thought that he'd got hours of paperwork to do with a crying baby to distract him from his pricing estimates' and 'My husband spends a lot of time on projects of his own and it is only when he has no other jobs to do that he gives support to me.'

When a man takes on a job in the home or with the baby he expects to take *over*. He is used to being in charge and to having women do things *his* way. If the woman feels she has special understanding of what her crying baby is going through or skills in nurturing that the man has not yet acquired, it makes sense for her to help him learn effective ways of handling the baby. Yet if she makes suggestions he often takes it as a challenge to his authority and expertise:

> When he was there, he wanted total control, no help. This made the baby unhappy. He'd do things to annoy the baby like taking away his bottle when he was quite happily feeding, which of course would upset him. He didn't seem to understand, didn't like to be told what to do, didn't like to see the baby go to bed or sleeping. He never understood that both myself and the baby got tired. Things got so bad that now that the baby is 8 months I have found the courage and support to get rid of my fiancé.

There are other obstacles to men acquiring skills in caring for babies. They are not accustomed to dealing with other people's body fluids and may be quickly nauseated by dirty nappies. The anthropologist Levi-Strauss makes the point that there is a vast difference between the raw and the cooked, and that they represent the natural and the cultured.[9] In most societies women process raw, untamed nature and men see only the end product – the 'cooked'. In the same way women are accustomed to coping with menstruation and the disposal of bloodstained cloths. In many societies they are also the nurturers from their own early childhood, caring for babies and smaller children and handling their waste products. Men are at one remove from all this. For them it is a new cultural task to deal with body products and also to nurture in an intimate way. As one woman told me: 'My husband never does feeding or nappy-changing, as he is very squeamish about mess of any kind, including that made by a 9-month-old baby trying to feed herself.' In fact, fathers themselves mention changing as the chore they dislike most.

A man is often totally unprepared for the enforced change in his life-style when a baby arrives and is shocked at the way everything revolves around the new baby. Getting into his own home through a narrow hallway cluttered with impedimenta, the times of his meals and their quality and variety, finding some free space on which to put anything down, the hot water supply – even the availability of the bath – peace in which to work, the opportunity to sleep when he needs sleep and his access to the woman's time and attention – all these become problematic. Mothers, too, are usually unprepared for change, but the shock is greater for men because they are accustomed to being serviced by women and tend to feel that the mother should be able to sort everything out and have a well-run home and a contented baby, with some time to spare for togetherness. When this does not happen, a man may feel he has walked into a trap: 'I needed to be able to relax on my own terms and I realized I couldn't'; 'I'd wanted to be independent. Now I felt there was no more choice. Suddenly I was stuck with this person for the rest of my life'; 'I felt these boys were latching on to me and I was never going to rid myself of them.'

Some fathers are jealous of the baby and feel the women has deserted them. Many men nowadays have experienced a divorce, either their parents' or their own divorce after a previous marriage, and this may lead to them feeling especially anxious about being replaced by a baby, even though they are often unaware of this. They feel pushed into the background and excluded from the close bond between mother and baby. No one talks about these feelings and if a man does begin to acknowledge them he tends to feel very ashamed. When the baby cries it is almost as if the child's distress gives clandestine expression to his own strong feelings and this adds to his irritation and inability to cope. Perhaps this is happening to the man who, according to his wife, 'cannot bear babies crying. I therefore must be the one who does the soothing – preferably getting the baby quiet as quickly as possible because it gets on his nerves so much. Knowing he is getting irritated makes the crying seem ten times worse and makes me feel very guilty.'

For the woman it is as if she has two babies in the house. One is the new baby, the other is the husband. Because the husband is

bigger and more powerful he is much the more threatening of the two. A woman who said her partner 'expected everything to go on as if nothing unusual had happened. He still expected cooking and household chores to be done as normal', though the baby was crying for hours on end, felt emotionally isolated and after some months of this received psychiatric treatment for depression. Another told me:

> If I had to go out without the baby, my husband got very upset at the thought of being left with him. Most times I would come home after five or ten minutes and find the baby in his cot screaming and my husband looking at himself in the mirror. He was completely helpless. Wouldn't hold the baby – even when I went to the toilet – wouldn't help with cooking and certainly wouldn't go shopping. If I asked for help, I was told that I was useless because I couldn't manage.

The baby continued to cry, she tried unsuccessfully to placate her husband and he regularly resorted to physical violence against her. The crying persisted until several days after she left her husband, when it suddenly stopped.

Historically, and in most cultures today, babies are the responsibility of women and little girls – older siblings or nursemaids – and men have little to do with them. In the West the relationship between children and their father developed, if at all, only when the boy was old enough to go fishing or play trains with him. In the rest of the world boys become herdsmen or help the men tilling the fields and gradually are initiated into adult economic activities through working alongside their fathers. Until then they are women's work. Girls work with and for their mothers and, though they are the property of the man, may have but slight personal relationship with him.

What records we have of fathers' attitudes to babies in the West suggests that for centuries they were thought of as, at best, pretty playthings to be dangled on the knee – as long as they behaved themselves. In Europe the infants of wealthy families were farmed out to wet-nurses or foster mothers until they had passed the awkward age of babyhood. In Britain this was extended for boys of the upper classes, through the public (elite private boarding) school system, to include the whole of childhood, while girls, under the tutelage of a governess, were seen and not heard until they were of marriageable age. Thus a rigid social distance was institutionalized between fathers and their children.

Lacking any familiarity with or understanding of babies, it is not surprising that some men were frightened of them. The philosopher William James, who described a baby's psychological state as one of 'booming, buzzing confusion' may have felt in this mental condition himself, for when his first child was born, he immediately left to spend the summer abroad. When the birth of the second was imminent, he disappeared for a sabbatical year on the Continent.[10] H. G. Wells went on a bicycle tour lasting ten weeks when his first child was born, writing occasional letters home but not revealing his plans or whereabouts. When the second was due, Jane got him back from a walking trip in the Alps only by pleading that though he was now a 'daddyman' she would continue to be his 'playmate'.

Many men would behave like this nowadays if they had a chance. They feel persecuted by their crying babies. Because they have an escape hatch provided by work and other commitments outside the home, one that is often not available to the woman, they can distance themselves from the problems of a crying baby. They also make social arrangements with other men that take priority over child care – and this even when they are unemployed. Some women described how out-of-work partners left them to do most of the work at home and deal with the baby, while they met their friends on street corners or in a local disco or bar, or concentrated on a home improvement project. One element in retaining masculine pride in the face of unemployment is the maintenance of traditional male-female roles in the household and a refusal to make concessions to changed circumstances.

When I asked thirty fully involved fathers who were readers of a magazine about parenting – in many ways the 'pick of the bunch' – about their feelings just after their babies were born, they described their positive emotions as being predominantly those of 'achievement', 'pride', 'importance', pleasure at having 'proved my manhood' and, if it was a son, in the acquisition of an heir. But they said they also felt a tremendous burden of responsibility, were often overwhelmed by fear that they could not cope with the baby, and were anxious about losing their freedom and at having to play 'second fiddle' to the baby.

When a baby cries and a man is helpless to do anything about it, it strikes at the root of his masculinity and he is deprived of the sense of achievement and power that was a vital element in his satisfaction in becoming a father. If the baby goes on crying for weeks or months, negative feelings take over more and more.

For a third of the men these negative emotions flooded in during the birth itself. They said they felt 'redundant and alone', 'anxiety', 'curiosity', 'resentment about being put out of a room during examinations', 'helplessness', 'guilt for causing pain to my wife', 'panic' and, though they had planned together for birth, they were sucked into a medical system in which 'all the decisions began to be made for us and technology took over'. Excited and thrilled as they were with the birth of their babies, these men, like their partners, started out on parenthood with, in the words of one of them, 'a

101

great feeling of powerlessness. Another described how after the birth a black depression came. It was deadly. I went out and collected a mate [friend] and went and got drunk.'

Though most men did not get as depressed as this, some remarked that the time following the birth was an anti-climax:

Everything had become so fixated on the birth that what followed, i.e. the baby, seemed to be rather irrelevant to it all. What were we supposed to do now? I was definitely over-prepared for birth and under-prepared for fatherhood. My wife and I would have quite happily gone home without the baby. Neither of us felt any spontaneous love for the baby.

He added that 'I can't say I felt much more than I would have done for a helpless pet.'

Parents sharing

Some men share as much as they possibly can in the care of their crying baby. They do not just help; they accept responsibility. Women who have partners like this say they do not know how they could manage without them. For the benefit of men who are reading these pages and would like to be able to support their partners better, it may be helpful to listen to what women with crying babies had to say about the men who share:

They give time: 'As my husband was unemployed, he was at home with me for the six weeks after I came home from hospital. The only way I can describe the all-round relationship involving our son and new baby was that the house had two mothers. My husband is still the same now. He's wonderful with them both.'

They empathize with their partner's feelings: 'If it had not been for the patience, support, love and understanding from my partner, I would have jumped off Chelsea Bridge.' This man does a lot of overtime as they are in great need of money, but she says: 'He was great and although he returned from work exhausted, he still helped me.'

They take responsibility for housework and baby care in a matter-of-fact and cheerful way: 'Both in the practical and emotional sense he was the person who helped me most. He never complained and if anything needed doing, either in the house or for the baby, he just got on with it. He was there to take the pressure off me, and without him I would have become completely depressed.'

They take over completely when necessary: 'He just takes over until I feel able to cope again'; 'By 8 months I could hardly bear the sight of the baby at night and had to hand the nights to my husband so that I did not hurt the child. He would take him for a walk to get him to sleep, and would sometimes collect a newspaper at 5.30 a.m. from the local shop'; 'He reassures me and spends every evening trying to calm our baby son. On several occasions he has rocked him all night so that I could sleep.'

They show their love for their partners in practical ways. These women emphasize that the man has a dual role, to comfort, cherish and protect the woman as well as caring for the baby. One woman was grateful, for example, that whenever her partner was aware that she was getting tense with the crying, he took the baby and played with her, singing or walking round the garden.

Many men started this way for a week or so but either did not keep it up when they returned to work or, in one woman's words, 'once the novelty had worn off'. A small proportion stuck at it, learned more as they went along, developed their nurturing role and shared fully in parenting. Another said: 'If it wasn't for my husband I couldn't cope, even now when she is 9 months old. He does everything that I do. That includes seeing to her if she wakes in the night, feeding, changing, walks in the park, playing. I don't have to ask. He just does it.' And this loving, caring behaviour is consistent and maintained as the child becomes older. In terms of their nurture and care of their babies, two perceptive fathers put it this way: 'At first I tried to grasp everything with logic. I would go through a mental checklist to see if the baby had everything and failed to understand why she went on crying. Then I began to try different kinds of behaviour, approaching my child with feelings and then I began to understand her'; 'Suddenly there are no more rules. What calms today may not work tomorrow. You relearn, become softer and mentally more generous. You throw away inflexible ideas out of the window.' This man says that it has resulted in his behaviour with his workmates and friends changing in quality and being more caring and perceptive, too.[11]

Renegotiating fatherhood

A woman may feel that nothing can be done to change her man. A father may feel that there is nothing he can do right. Not so! But it does require that a man is able to envisage a genuine shared parenting and has the courage to create a role of co-parent that runs counter to all his social conditioning.

So sit down together and, if you can get a word in edgeways with your baby crying, talk about the changes you both see as necessary in your day-to-day life. The best will in the world, the most tender romantic love, the greatest erotic passion does not make up for not having help with the dishes and the dirty nappies (diapers), and someone who gets up cheerfully in the night to soothe a sleepless baby and will spend the whole evening bottom-patting, rocking, singing, walking, bathing and talking the repetitive, satisfying nonsense that babies love.

Men are great at formulating plans, constructing grand schema and making rules. But what you need now is flexibility in a changing situation in which the demands being made on you tomorrow may be different from those of today. The new style fathers are going to have to be perceptive and sensitive, not rule-makers but empathizers.

In working out how you both want things to be, the woman might start by saying 'I want from you . . .' and then spend time voicing exactly what it is she would like from her partner. The man should just listen and not interrupt.

The next task is to jointly work out the practicalities and explore how the man can meet her needs. Though some of the things she wants may seem trivial, the mother of a crying baby has desperate needs – and any way he can go towards meeting them is like water in the desert.

To be able to support the woman effectively he will have to acquire new skills or develop those that he has not considered important. So another element in negotiation is devising how to increase relevant skills. That entails a learning process. He cannot be expected to perfect them overnight. Make a note of each of the skills that needs to be learned if the man is to function effectively in the sphere of what is usually considered 'woman's work'.

When you have come to some agreement about what should be done and how, write these things down. Keep a copy each. They are part of a contract. After a couple of weeks read it through to check you are sticking to it. You could even be improving on it! Or you may be ready for a further stage in which you build on what you have learned already to make an even more satisfying contract.

To any man

Reading about how some men never help in the house or with the baby, you may feel pretty pleased with yourself. You help whenever you can. You are satisfied that you take on a fair share of jobs in the house and know how to handle the baby. You are different.

Maybe.

While it is still fresh in your mind, think exactly what happened *yesterday*. On squared paper, divide the twenty-four hours into half-hour segments, indicating the time along one axis of your chart. Then invent symbols to represent work outside the home, housework, sleeping, eating, playing with the baby, doing things with the baby, shopping, making a meal and so on. List these at the bottom of your chart and then fill it in so that you can see at a glance how you spent your time.

What proportion of it was housework and looking after the baby? Are you missing out on sharing parenthood because of work brought home that gobbles up time that you could spend with your partner and child? Are you more inclined to play with the baby or to take over when s/he's sleeping or being 'good' than to take on all the work that a baby entails? If you cook, do you also plan meals, shop for them, wash dishes and clear up afterwards? Do you spend a disproportionate amount of time in the garden, doing things to your car, or tackling jobs that don't leave you time to do ordinary, humdrum, repetitive work in the house?

Make another chart in a few days' time and see if the proportions are different. Switch from weekdays to a weekend, or vice versa. Try keeping a record for a full week so that you can see the general pattern.

If you do this, you can get a more accurate idea of how much responsibility you are really taking on as a father. Your partner could do the same thing so that you can then compare your charts – a good basis for working out a strategy to be a still better father. Through practical commitment like this a man can grow in confidence and self-esteem in doing what has customarily been considered 'women's work'. Many men are anxious that if they take on child care and housework they will lose their masculinity and no longer be 'one of the boys'. In the past wage-earning work outside the home has been central to the idea of manhood, and men have evaluated themselves in terms of this very limited function – breadwinner and household head. Traditionally, they have justified their ignorance of housework and child care by claiming that they bring in the money, so the home ought to be a smooth-running support system for *them*. Accepting the challenge posed by a crying baby, learning how to be in touch with feelings, freeing himself from the compulsion to prove his masculinity through competition and the assertion of power is, in one father's words, 'to discover new ways of being men'. It will give your sons 'an alternative to the present restrictive definitions of manhood . . . It will be a real strength for a man to be able to say that he is no longer "one of the boys".'[12]

Ours is a culture that coerces and brutalizes men through the institutionalization of male power over women and children, and that oppresses and degrades women in the holy names of 'motherhood' and 'the family'. Women and children are the victims, but – paradoxically – men are also losers. For this male-dominated culture also destroys many things that could be of real value in men's lives, and tends to cut them off from awareness of their own and other people's emotions. In taking on the responsibility of shared parenthood a man has the opportunity to develop that awareness and to become a whole person.

CHAPTER 8

Target for Advice

The little one's displays of temper as indicated
by screaming or crying without cause should be regarded
as the first test of your spiritual and
pedagogical principles . . . Once you have established that
nothing is really wrong, that the child
is not ill, distressed, or in pain, then you can rest assured
that the screaming is nothing
more than an outburst of temper, a whim,
the first appearance of wilfulness. Now you should no longer simply
wait for it to pass as you did
in the beginning but should proceed in somewhat more positive way:
by quickly diverting its attention
by stern words, threatening gestures, rapping on the bed . . . or if none
of this helps, by appropriately mild
corporal admonitions repeated persistently at brief intervals until
the child quiets down or falls asleep
This procedure will be necessary only once or at most twice,
and then you will be master of the child *forever.*

quoted in Morton Schatzman, *Soul Murder*

I believe that the vast majority of mothers
truly love their children, and deprive them of the experiences
so essential to their happiness
only because they have no idea what they are causing them to suffer.
If they understood the agony of the baby
left to weep in his crib, his terrible longing and the consequences
of the suffering, the effects
of the deprivation upon his personality development and potential
for making a satisfactory life,
I do not doubt that they would fight to prevent
his being left alone for a minute.

Jean Liedloff, *The Continuum Concept*

One thing the mother of a crying baby is never short of – advice. It pours in from all sides – from her partner and other members of the family, friends and casual acquaintances, the woman at the supermarket checkout, the attendant in the department store toilets, from nurses, doctors and social workers, from books and radio and TV programmes and magazine articles.

A great deal of this advice is conflicting. Many women are reduced by it to a mental chaos in which they are no longer able to use their own common sense about their babies. As one woman put it: 'I had advice from doctors, health visitors, family and friends. I have fed baby on demand, tried to feed baby four-hourly, left baby to cry, put radio in room, left light on, rocked baby, put baby in bed with us, not let baby sleep all day, kept baby up till late – *everything!* But nothing worked.'

On the post-natal ward

This flood of freely given counsel starts while the woman is still in the hospital following the birth of the baby. It is a by-product of the system of stacking women who have just had babies all together in the same place, an alien environment where they lie row upon row as passive patients under the direction of medical professionals who are the acknowledged experts in handling this post-partum transition. Advice is given by often desperately overworked nurses, many of whom have not themselves had babies and who are concerned, at all costs, to keep ward routines running smoothly.

One woman, who found that the only solution to her baby's constant crying was to switch to artificial feeding, said the problem started in hospital:

> The baby wouldn't start sucking and the nurse's helpful comments were, to me, how did I expect her to suck at such a poor nipple as I was offering? and to the baby, 'you'll die if you don't eat'! I understood that they were busy but feel that that was the end of breast-feeding for me. My breasts became more and more painful and I know I tensed up every time the baby started sucking, knowing that it was going to hurt.

It is true that nurses on post-partum wards are often terribly overworked. Often the only members of staff who have time to sit with a mother and give emotional support rather than advice are nursing auxiliaries (aides) and cleaners – those with least power to affect routines and policies, and who come lowest in the staff hierarchy.

Previous research I have done about women's experiences of hospital care [1] shows that for many women life on a post-natal ward leaves them feeling worn out, confused and battered by conflicting advice – especially about the right way to feed the baby. Far from being havens of peace and security, most post-natal wards are a shambles. Women rarely have the rest they need, or any private, intimate space with their babies in which to get to know them and to feel competent as mothers. They are subjected to ward routines that prevent them sleeping when their babies sleep, that often start at 6.30 a.m. and that fragment the day with bed-making, medicines, blood pressure checks, doctors' rounds, meals, physiotherapy, visiting and so on. In the early morning, mid-morning and evenings many post-natal wards are like railway stations in the rush hour. Here is how one woman described her hospital day:

> 2.30–3.10 a.m. feed baby; 4.30 a.m. approx. back to sleep; 5.30 a.m. feed baby, cup of tea; 6.08 a.m. cup removed, bin [wastebasket] emptied; 6.31 drugs trolley [cart] arrived; 6.49 given tablet; 7.26 water jug removed; 7.42 breakfast; 7.52 tea; 8.10 nursing auxiliaries ask if they may make bed, I say 'no thank you'; 8.13 bed made; 8.21 asked how I am; 8.48 weigh baby; 9.05 two nurses come, laugh and go away again; 9.49 fundus measured, temperature, etc., while feeding baby; 10.02 coffee; 10.46 offered newspaper, cup removed; 11.51 post – and so on.

She said that afternoons and evenings were similar, except that visiting and bathing also had to be fitted in. She expressed breast milk and asked to be allowed to sleep through the night because she felt exhausted, but was woken to feed regardless. Some women in that hospital worked out that they were getting a total of three hours sleep in twenty-four hours. [2]

As women described their hospital experiences to me, over and over again they told of conflicting advice – even in the best hospitals and even when the senior nursing officers for midwifery had stressed in letters to me that the post-natal wards provided 'a happy and relaxed atmosphere', 'a supportive, flexible approach to care' and 'routines to suit individual needs'. Here is a typical composite report, to which more than thirty women contributed, of life on the post-natal wards of a large London teaching hospital:

> Very busy. Some women feel 'lost' and 'helpless'. Baby goes to nursery first night and most writers asked to have babies with them from then on, but some said this was

'strongly disapproved of by the night staff'. Very noisy and difficult to sleep at night. Women discharged themselves early to get sleep. TV set in ward noisy, on almost continuously and disturbing for some of us: 'A huge television dominates the ward.' Ward 'congested', 'draughty', 'uncomfortable', 'noisy'. 'My bed was in passage en route for bathroom.' 'Dirty toilets.' Some staff have not caught up with modern research on breast-feeding and, writers say, 'bully' mothers who are suckling babies as long and as often as they want, encouraging them to give boiled water. Told they will get sore nipples. Mothers falsify feeding charts to keep staff happy. 'Well-meaning but contradictory advice.' Constant pressure of people offering cups of tea, meals, pain-killers and checks of baby/stitches/-uterus. Messages from day to night staff often not passed on.

You need to be very fit to survive all of this unscathed. Most women advised that if you have help at home, it is best to leave the hospital as soon as possible in order to get some rest.

Nurses have different ideas about how a baby should be positioned at the breast, for how long it should be allowed to suck, whether prolonged sucking makes nipples sore, how often babies should feed, whether mothers should feed at night or not, whether babies should be given sugar water and complimentary artificial milk feeds – and, above all, to what extent mothers are capable of making their own decisions. Women tell of being reprimanded for 'spoiling' babies (feeding them when they cry), for letting a baby cry when they have a bath, for trying persistently to breast-feed when the going proves difficult, for *not* wanting to breast-feed, having babies in bed with them (in case they 'smother' them), taking them to the nursery so that they can have a rest, not trying to get up their wind [gas] or for trying to get it up, for cuddling and touching them 'unnecessarily', for having a baby who cries and disturbs other mothers and babies, for picking them up when they 'should' be sleeping, for walking with them in their arms (lest they drop them), undressing them to have a good look, and letting visitors hold them. Because there is no continuity of care, a mother often does not know the style of management a nurse prefers and what she is expected to be doing. One woman said: 'I was bombarded to utter confusion by each nurse giving me her ideas on feeding.' Autocratic instructions and rigid rules are sometimes masked and presented as advice that is adapted to individual needs: 'I was told, "He's a large baby so you'll not have enough for him; you'd better give a top-up [a bottle after the feed]." The woman in the next bed was told, "He's a small baby so he needs plenty of food; you'd better give a top-up."'

Enforced fragmentation of time coupled with sleep deprivation (both well-known elements in torture) and being at the receiving end of care that is insensitive to individual needs and wishes, combined with an onslaught of contradictory advice, makes many otherwise rational, capable women confused and disoriented. No more effective way could be devised to interfere with the new mother's developing relationship with her baby and to strip her of self-confidence. It is as if through the ritualized inculcation of doubt and fear women in our culture are cast into motherhood in a psychological state that introduces artificial obstacles to mothering and, for many of them, makes of this life passage a particularly hazardous journey.

At home

Once a woman is out of the hospital she discovers that still more advice comes at her from all directions. If she is a novice mother, people are especially generous with their advice; if her baby cries inconsolably, it is given with no holds barred. Most of this advice has no effect at all on the baby's crying. When I asked the mothers of crying babies if they had found advice helpful, 64 per cent said that none of the advice they received succeeded in stopping their babies crying.

Though women tended to take advice coming from friends, relatives and acquaintances with a pinch of salt, it was difficult for them to ignore it when it emanated from health professionals. It was perhaps for this reason that they found it especially disturbing when the baby continued to cry and they had to admit that the advice hadn't worked. Different advice was then offered – often by another health professional – but the baby went on crying, and the mother became increasingly confused and was convinced that there must be something wrong with *her* because she could not manage this baby.

Many mothers owed a great deal to the friendship and concern that came from their health visitors: 'My health visitor was marvellous,' one woman said, 'and talking to her was the best thing.' But others were highly critical of advice they had received from them. Health visitors came in for most praise and also for most criticism. When the health visitor gave no advice at all and tried to make some positive remark about the baby, the mother often felt she had been palmed off and thought that the health visitor was not taking the crying seriously: 'I told the health visitor that Emma seemed to scream rather than just cry and she said, "Well, it shows she's reacting well to her environment"'; 'She just said "Beautiful baby"'; 'The health visitor made sympathetic noises and said I was better off than some.'

When the health visitor *did* give advice, it was not always appropriate and since it obviously did not work, she offered further suggestions, so as not to leave the woman empty-handed, which were contradictory in themselves. This meant that the mother was exposed to a mounting avalanche of inconsistent advice, to which the doctor's advice was often also added. Some of this advice could have been harmful, and occasionally it was dangerous. This happened, for example, when a health visitor gave a woman a sample of a sugary herbal drink. Her baby liked it 'and it also helped me bring his wind [gas] up. When he started to drink more of that and hardly any milk, she sent me to the doctor and he gave me some medicine, which gave the baby constipation. After that I stopped everything and let nature take its course, and after a while the crying stopped.' Another woman was advised by her health visitor not to pick up the baby when she cried. She had not realized that this baby could usually be soothed for quite long periods when picked up, but that when she was left to cry the mother had very hostile feelings towards her, and she was at risk of being physically harmed: 'My health visitor said the baby seemed to be crying mainly for attention. She told me to let her cry. But I can't leave her too long or I lose my patience and might do something to hurt her, so I am

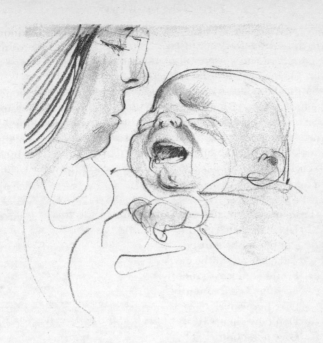

better off picking her up,' the mother apologetically explained to me.

A woman told how when her baby was about 14 weeks old, and her own health visitor was on leave, advice was given by another health visitor whom she had never met:

> Without knowing me, the baby or the situation – and by phone – she advised me to start bottle-feeding him immediately, as he was obviously hungry and I obviously wasn't producing enough milk. She even offered to rush round with a packet of formula milk. This offer I declined, but what worried me was, had this been my first baby I might have taken this advice and my breast-feeding would have failed.

Another woman said: 'One health visitor told me to feed the baby more. (I was feeding hourly.) The other told me that I was obviously overfeeding. I was very confused.'

Family doctors were also often responsible for giving bad advice. One explained to a mother whose crying baby was 6 weeks old that the baby's distress must be due to wind (gas) and she was to starve her for twenty-four hours. Fortunately she did not follow this advice because she thought it was cruel. The health visitor and doctor together were frequently at cross-purposes, as if in competition with each other to offer the advice that finally would stop this baby crying. One woman who kept a record of the advice she was given told me:

> From my doctor and my health visitor I was told:
> 'Leave her for ten minutes.'
> 'Put her in the garden.'
> 'Take her out in the car.'
> 'Feed her more frequently.'
> 'Feed her less frequently.'
> 'Give her water.'
> 'Don't give her water.'
> 'Give her a bottle.'
> 'Carry her round in a baby carrier.'
> 'Handle her less.'
> 'Handle her more.' Etc., etc., etc.

The most frequent advice of all, from both professionals and friends and relations, to the breast-feeding mother of a crying baby was to switch to artificial feeding. Mothers found it very difficult to resist this and many thought their milk must be inadequate or 'bad' for the baby. When women whose babies were gaining weight normally, but who cried inconsolably, changed from breast to bottle, their babies continued to cry, but a mother who had made this move rarely had the confidence to return to breast-feeding again. An inferior quality food had been introduced to replace human milk without any evidence that breast-feeding was the cause of crying, and the mother was left feeling that she had failed. One mother described her feelings this way: 'I felt completely useless in that I wanted so much to be the perfect mother with everything just so, but nothing worked out that way. As a home economics teacher it was very hard to accept this and I felt very guilty about not breast-feeding.'

Though some studies have shown that breast-fed babies cry more than bottle-fed ones, this is not borne out by the evidence from these mothers. Forty-six per cent were breast-feeding and 53 per cent bottle-feeding. Some babies *started* crying after they were switched from breast to bottle, often with the introduction of solid foods, too. The mother usually did this because she believed that she did not have enough milk or thought it was bad for the baby to go on breast-feeding because it was time for the introduction of 'real' food. This feeling that breast milk is nutritionally inadequate for older babies is reinforced by baby-food manufacturers in promoting the sales of 'full-strength', 'junior', 'follow-on' and 'progress' artificial milks, canned and potted solids and packaged cereals.

Crying that did not start till after 12 weeks was often associated with the introduction of modified cow's milk and solids. A baby was more than twice as likely to begin crying between 3 and 6 months of age if the mother were bottle-feeding than if she were breast-feeding. Thirty-two per cent of breast-fed babies started crying at this stage of their lives, whereas 68 per cent of bottle-fed ones started crying then.

Twenty-six per cent of these mothers never breast-fed, 14 per cent stopped within one week of birth, 27 per cent stopped between 1 and 6 weeks, 10 per cent between 6 weeks and 3 months, and 12 per cent between 3 and 6 months. Thus, by the time these babies were 3 months old, less than a quarter were breast-fed – which for many of their mothers was a measure of the desperation they felt about their crying.

The most difficult criticism that the breast-feeding mother of a crying baby has to face is the accusation that she is being selfish if she continues to breast-feed against advice. Few of us are so self-assured that we can deny that we are selfish with certainty. Picking up the baby when he cries, having the baby in bed with us at night, feeding whenever the baby wants it – is it all sheer self-indulgence?

Professionals may suggest to a mother who is unwilling to give up breast-feeding that she is doing so because of her own unfulfilled emotional needs rather than through a genuine desire to do the best

for her baby. When she is already anxious that her milk may not be 'good enough' or that she is not producing sufficient, this makes her still more tense and anxious and may interfere with the milk-ejection reflex. If there is evidence that the milk supply is inadequate, she needs help in increasing it, and accusing her of being selfish and stubborn only makes matters worse.

Sharon, for example, told me that her baby was healthy, alert and gaining weight well, but cried a lot and regularly brought back milk. Though she knew there was nothing wrong with her baby and breast-feeding was going beautifully, she asked her health visitor if she thought anything was wrong: 'It was my birthday and I was covered in sick, the baby and her mattress smelt revolting, and it suddenly got me down.' The health visitor diagnosed colic and gave her a bottle of Merbentyl (dicyclamine) syrup with which to dose the baby before each feed. The baby quietened down, but Sharon then had the frightening experience of watching her become limp and comatose following administration of the drug. 'She was so distant that I was terrified she was dying.' Thoroughly scared, she stopped using the Merbentyl. At this point her doctor advised her to finish with breast-feeding and, 'after a struggle, the baby finally accepted a bottle', though Sharon continued to give two breast-feeds in the twenty-four hours. But things didn't really improve, and now there was an added problem – Sharon was depressed. 'I was desperately unhappy,' she told me, 'because I so much wanted to breast-feed but felt it would be irresponsible in the face of the doctor's advice.' The doctor then prescribed an antidepressant for her. 'Nobody could see I was depressed *because* I was not totally breast-feeding. I remember walking round and round the garden sobbing.' Rallying herself, she rang a National Childbirth Trust breast-feeding counsellor, who suggested that if she wanted to breast-feed she could do so, and Sharon began to put the baby to the breast more frequently. Within three days the baby was fully and satisfyingly breast-fed and Sharon's depression lifted. Now she felt she could cope, and with this the crying and the vomiting were also reduced. Yet she found she had forfeited professional sympathy: 'The health visitor seemed cross,' she comments, 'saying I was feeding for my own satisfaction and not the baby's.'

Coping with advice

Since every new mother is likely to be assailed by advice, and if her baby cries a lot it pours in from all sides, it pays to be prepared and think ahead to how you want to deal with it. You don't want to feel battered by it. On the other hand, you probably don't wish to be rude to people who are genuinely trying to help.

Many women who told me about their experiences had developed a strategy, but did so the hard way, after attempting to follow every bit of advice and discovering that much of it was useless. As one woman says:

For the first few weeks I let everyone boss me around: 'You feed him too often', 'Put him in another room when he cries and shut the door' or 'You're spoiling him', 'He's wise to it now. He knows you will pick him up when he cries. Babies are crafty.' All rubbish! But keep the peace, say 'Thank you for the advice' and then do your own thing.

One way to show that you are taking suggestions seriously, which can provide an interesting record of the advice you receive, is to keep a special notebook in which you jot it down. If they actually see you writing it, so much the better. Since women say three-quarters of the advice they get is unhelpful, it follows that somewhere among all this advice you have a one in four chance of learning something that will help.

I found that some women welcome advice even when it is conflicting because trying a different tactic to stop the baby crying gives them hope. If you feel like this, you can make a careful selection from your list of suggestions and experiment with them. Since plan A didn't work on Monday or Tuesday, you can switch to plan B on Wednesday and Thursday, note the results, and then perhaps, using your judgement of the situation, change back to a modified plan A for the next two or three days. When you have worked through advice in this way and adapted different combinations of advice to what you are observing about your individual baby, the baby will suddenly stop crying. This will probably occur sometime between 3 and 4 months. One day he was a screaming horror. The next day he is a cooing, gurgling, contented and adorable baby. You may be fairly certain that it was chance that your baby went through this magic transmutation when he did and that it had little to do with what you happened to be doing that day, or you may be convinced that some new method of handling the baby did the trick. But knowing that there were other things that you could try has kept you going during those awful three and a half months.

On the other hand, many women feel that trying one thing after another *doesn't* help and makes the whole experience more of an ordeal. They often say that when they gave up trying, the baby became more peaceful. Somehow the frantic struggle to make the baby quiet has contributed to the baby's misery. When a woman relaxes and accepts her baby as she is, crying and all, the tension snaps and she can begin to enjoy her baby. But a prerequisite for this is having someone else, with the same relaxed attitude, who will take over total care of the baby for some time during the twenty-four hours, even if it is only for a couple of hours. If a woman is incarcerated with her baby without any break and with no other adult to take responsibility, it may be emotionally impossible to accept the baby in that way. The crying is too destructive. So if this is your preferred plan of action, make sure there is someone else who understands that the vital element in your strategy is that he or she takes over completely for a set amount of time each day or night, and work out the hours that person should be 'on duty' in order to cover a peak crying time.

If anyone continues to offer advice you do not want, hand the baby over to them and say you are so glad they are there as you would like to pop out to the shops, take a bath, make a phone call, dig the garden, walk the dog, or whatever, and *leave them with the baby*. They may explain immediately that they have urgent business elsewhere. But you may get breathing space this way and it is just possible that they succeed in making the baby stop crying, which would be an added bonus.

If you have a partner, it is vital for you both to agree about how to handle advice. Read this section together and decide what you want to do. You may need a buffer between you and your mother or your partner's mother, for example, and it is best to discuss this frankly and devise a plan together.

Being told that you ought to stop breast-feeding, especially if that recommendation comes from a doctor, is the most difficult advice to handle because if you don't, it is obvious to those giving advice that you are continuing to ignore it. This is where you need strong emotional support from someone who is 100 per cent on your side and will back you up, too. It could be your partner or someone else – a really reliable 'confiding' friend.

You do not have to argue. You do not have to provide a long list of references about the advantages of breast-feeding. Just say that you have decided to continue because you like it and the baby likes it. Sometimes it helps to convince a doctor if you can show that the baby sucks well and contentedly at the breast, so instead of being drawn into theoretical discussions, put the baby to the breast in the doctor's presence.

In the same way, if you have decided to bottle-feed, you do not need to justify it. You are less likely to feel under pressure of advice about feeding than the woman who wants to go on breast-feeding, but people who are committed to breast-feeding may make you feel that you have somehow failed. You can make it clear that whether or not it was the best decision, you have made up your mind.

Though you may not feel confident inside, a little assertiveness goes a long way and is very effective in dealing with advice. Breathe out, drop shoulders and relax, make eye contact with whoever is offering advice, thank them for their help, jot the suggestions down and change the subject, or if the baby is crying too loudly for conversation, say goodbye and leave. Becoming confident about handling advice can help you grow in confidence in dealing with your baby, too.

CHAPTER 9

Drugged Babies

> *The mother had to work hard all day and got little rest at night, as the fifth child was weakly and ailing, and the neighbour who looked after the child during the day used to put gin in its milk to stop its crying, which it did till the effects of the gin had passed off. The poor mother, not knowing that gin was given to the child, would often, after a hard day's work, spend most of the night pacing the bedroom floor, trying to soothe the fretful child, and often had to go downstairs because the crying disturbed her husband. It was not until her sixth child came, the feeble-minded one, that the neighbour admitted giving it gin.*
> Margaret Llewelyn Davies (ed.), *Maternity: Letters from Working Women*, 1915[1]

Drugging babies to keep them from crying is certainly not a new idea. In Britain in the eighteenth century, for example, babies were often treated with opiates and gin to keep them quiet. In France it was laudanum, diacodion and eau-de-vie.[2] Babies often died from overdoses of special potions made up by pharmacists. Wet-nurses smeared their nipples with opiate drugs so that the baby would take them in with the milk. Many of these wet-nurses were not allowed to keep their own babies with them, so had to farm them out to foster parents, where they were kept heavily doped with gin and laudanum. For thousands of these babies it proved a death sentence.

By the nineteenth century 'teething powders' and other mixtures to dope babies were in common use. In a letter written in 1849, following the birth of her second child, Edward, Elizabeth Prentiss described how the 4-month-old baby had colic: 'Dear little Eddie has found life altogether unkind thus far, and I have had many hours of heartache on his account; but I hope he may weather the storm and come out safely yet . . . Instead of sleeping twelve hours out of the twenty-four, he sleeps but about seven and that by means of laudanum.'[3] A report in a British newspaper, the *Morning Chronicle*, for 15 November 1849 includes a comment from a pharmacist saying that on market days customers from the country came in to buy laudanum and opium for themselves and Godfrey's or Quietness for the children. He sold enormous quantities and supplied 700 families with an ounce (28 ml) of opium syrup every week.[4]

It was common practice for nurses in Europe and the United States to treat colicky babies, even into the twentieth century, with 'paregoric' – camphorated tincture of opium flavoured with aniseed and benzoic acid. A splendid instructional book for parents called *The Science of a New Life*, published in 1869, by Dr John Cowan, described how babies were stuffed with gruel and pounded biscuits, which produced indigestion, to treat which: 'Recourse is had to catmint [catnip] tea, aniseed tea, Godfrey's cordial, soothing syrup, paregoric, or some other palliative or nostrum, by which another source of gastric derangement and indigestion is brought into operation.[5] He advised that mothers who wanted their children to survive infancy 'should avoid and shun all manner of patent nostrums – such as paregoric, cordials, soothing syrups, etc., all of which contain opium'. He warned mothers that they should be vigilant about the way wet-nurses treated babies, claiming that nurses overfed them and dosed them with laudanum and paregoric so that they could get some rest. In Dr Joseph DeLee's *Obstetrics for Nurses*, published in 1904,[6] this famous obstetrician at the Chicago Lying-In Hospital criticized nurses who gave babies paregoric and whisky, and says that he had treated one baby who had become addicted to *crème de menthe*. In 1905 Charles Paddock, MD, in his book on child care entitled *Maternitas*,[7] warned against using paregoric, whisky or brandy: 'These "soothing syrups" are not necessary and are often positively injurious.'

As infant care became increasingly medicalized and a matter of 'expert opinion' and different 'management methods', women were rounded on by their doctors for their ignorance and laziness in sedating babies in these ways. Most books written by doctors for mothers warned them of the dangers of giving drugs and alcohol to their babies. (However, at least one recent American book for parents[8] recommends paregoric and 'your favourite liqueur' for colic. Paregoric is sold on prescription as Donnagel PG, Kaoparin, Parapectolin, Pomalin, Brown Mixture or opium tincture.) Women continued to dose their unsettled babies with alcohol mixed with dill syrup in Britain in the form of the ubiquitous gripe water. Many babies became mildly addicted to it and sometimes so did mothers themselves.

By the 1970s, however, proprietary tranquillizers had largely taken the place of paregoric and all the other mixtures. In 1974 it was revealed that 200,000 British children and babies under the age of 11 were being doped with doctor-prescribed tranquillizers.[9] In Australia it was reported in 1981 that half of all children under 5 were on regular medication, most of it Valium syrup and anti-histamines – over-the-counter drugs obtainable at any chemist's (drugstore).[10] Though the Illingworths in their book *Babies and Young*

Children[11] guardedly advised the use of chloral hydrate when the situation was desperate, it was not until John Cobb, a psychiatrist, published a book that, he claims, is from the mother's point of view[12] that it was taken for granted that sedatives and tranquillizers like Phenergan and Vallergan, be used for healthy babies.[13] Drugs were once more approved, but now they were doctor-prescribed and in some cases stronger than ever before.

When I asked women with crying babies about the kind of advice they were given and the different ways in which they had tried to stop the crying, many of them told me that their doctors had prescribed drugs for the baby and tranquillizers for them. As one woman says: 'My doctor told me I was over-anxious and causing the problem myself!' Doctors reach for the magic prescription pad because they cannot think of anything else to do when they see a woman obviously at the end of her tether. They prescribe 'colic' medicine or a sedative for the baby and often, on the basis that babies pick up any stress in their environment, tranquillizers or antidepressants for the mother as well. They may be well aware that in inner city areas, for example, many of these women are living in substandard and overcrowded housing, some virtually in slum conditions, some in boarding house accommodation where they are eight to a room. Walls are thin, uncarpeted rooms and stairwells echo with noise, and neighbours bang angrily on walls and ceilings when the baby cries.

Many doctors with jam-packed waiting rooms also feel under pressure to produce a prescription because they haven't time to give to listening to the mother. It is the quickest way to get a clinic visit over, the woman believes that she has been given something effective with which to cope with the problem and may be so desperate that she will try anything, and the doctor can switch attention to other patients with clearly defined physical symptoms.

A quarter of all babies have had sedative drugs by the time they are 18 months old, some for four months or longer. Many have had a succession of different drugs – not only sedatives, but also antihistamines (which have a sedative effect), antispasmodics, colic medicines and pain-relievers. Advertisements in British magazines for parents suggest the use of paracetamol, a non-aspirin analgesic (acetominophen), to 'soothe pain – 3 months to 6 years . . . If a cuddle alone isn't working to relieve your child of his little aches and pains, a dose of Paracetamol Pain-Relief Syrup will help' and promise 'sweet dreams for everyone . . .' Medised (another paracetamol syrup) 'restores sleep' and 'soothes away the pain that stops children getting a good night's sleep.'

In addition to these, babies are also often treated with over-the-counter teething preparations, which produce a slight, local anaesthetic effect. Some of these products are jellies that are rubbed on the gums. Others are in the form of syrup, drops or pastilles. They all contain large amounts of sugar (sucrose, lactose and glucose) and damage the baby teeth as they are just coming through the gums before the enamel is fully mineralized. Gripe water, widely used by British mothers, is 95 per cent glucose, and 5 per cent alcohol. A woman convicted of shoplifting pleaded in her defence that she was not responsible for her actions because she was addicted to gripe water, and drank twelve bottles a day.[14]

Until recently the drug used most frequently for colic was dicyclamine (dicyclomane in the USA), in the form of Merbentyl, Bentyl or Bentylol syrup or Ovol colic drops. In 1984, 74 million doses of these medicines were sold in Britain alone. Reports of breathing problems following administration of Merbentyl first came in to the pharmaceutical company Merrell Dow in 1981. In 1985 a letter went out from the British Committee on Safety of Medicines and the manufacturers warning doctors that a number of babies had stopped breathing for a while, had suffered convulsions or had gone into a coma after being given this drug. Some had died. A label was put on the package of Ovol drops saying that they should not be given to babies under 3 months, and shortly after the product was withdrawn. Merbentyl syrup is still on the market but now has a label on the bottle saying that it is not suitable for babies under 6 months, though Merrell Dow claims that 'events recorded may be chance associations'.[15]

The warnings about dicyclamine came as a shock to mothers who relied on regular dosing with this drug to keep their babies placid. One mother told me it was her 'liquid gold'. Another said she knew she was overdosing her baby but '*anything* to shut her up!' Many mothers who had found dicyclamine a life-saver told me that they had no idea how they would manage if they had another crying baby, and it was a very frightening prospect.

A major problem with dicyclamine is that it has to be given about a quarter of an hour before a feed. If a baby is fed on demand, it is very difficult to know exactly when the baby is about to want a feed and then, having wakened him, to keep him waiting while he is screaming with hunger. Mothers say they hate trying to keep a crying baby waiting for fifteen minutes before a feed is allowed. The manufacturer's advice is that it should be given before every feed, based on the assumption that there are four or five scheduled feeds a day. As a result breast-fed babies who are not on a rigid timetable have often been having much more than the recommended dose.

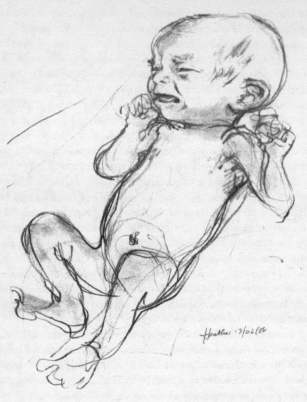

Some women described giving two or three times more than was prescribed.

With most colic medicines, which are central nervous system depressants, the baby becomes sedated, breathing slows down and the pulse may be affected. The trouble is that dicyclamine sometimes makes a restless baby even more uncomfortable because it causes a dry mouth, constipation, retention of urine and skin rashes. Some mothers also told me how this drug was over-prescribed by the doctor, with the result that their babies did not wake for feeds, had to be coaxed to suck and fell asleep before the feed was finished. Most of these babies were under 4 months old.

The effects of dicyclamine are also often increased by its combination with other drugs, such as tranquillizers or antihistamines, which have been prescribed previously, or when the doctor hopes that a powerful drug cocktail will succeed in soothing a relentlessly crying baby. This drug mixture may make the baby even more jumpy and irritable, one drug acting on the other to produce the opposite effect to that intended. Babies can have hangovers, too, and often being in a drunken stupor at night are desperately miserable the next day. Used in this way, drugs defeat their purpose.

Mothers sometimes described giving their babies a succession of drugs or drug mixtures. Vallergan (sold in the USA as Temaril), for example, is a powerful sedative that is used in low doses to control itching, but in higher doses is also used in psychiatry and as pre-medication for surgery. The manufacturers warn that it can potentiate symptoms of other drugs. A woman whose baby was on Merbentyl and Vallergan at the same time told me that she stopped giving the drugs because 'I couldn't bear to see him so dopey.'

I discovered that some babies are so heavily drugged that they no longer make eye contact with their mothers. When this happened, women got no pleasure from their babies and mothering became very unrewarding. This is another dominant theme in women's accounts: 'He didn't cry as much – but I couldn't enjoy him any more.' It has serious consequences for the mother-child relationship. When you lose all human contact, looking after a baby turns into drudgery.

Women told of frightening incidents when their babies stopped breathing for a while or became floppy, 'zombie-like' and comatose. These incidents lasted only about ten minutes and if a doctor saw the baby afterwards, there were no signs that anything untoward had occurred.

A typical account came from a woman who described to me what happened when giving dicyclamine to her 4-month-old baby. One evening, after he had had his bottle:

> He sank into a deep sleep on my lap. So deep, in fact, that he went quite limp, and even when I tickled his toes or raised his arms, they just fell with no reaction. I pushed back his eyelids to see if his eyes were rolling – nothing. He was almost waxy looking and I became extremely

alarmed. I held him away from me and shook him, but he was still limp. I rattled and shook him again, and as a last resort I put my fingers down his throat. He started to stir finally and was a little sick. Soon after, he was coughing. All this time I had been dialling the doctor with my free hand. Still shaking like a jelly myself and holding back the sob of relief, I told the doctor what had happened.

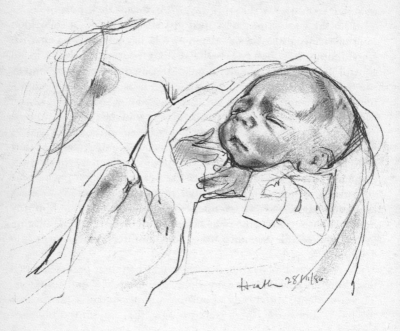

The doctor told her that the baby 'had gobbled his bottle too quickly and had an air bubble'. 'I was not convinced, but as he seemed OK, I thought I was just another hysterical mother.'

Since these drug-stupefied babies slept solidly, often had to be wakened for feeds, sucked feebly and then fell asleep during a feed, it is not surprising that some of them did not put on weight or that they actually lost weight and were admitted to hospital for 'failure to thrive'. This happened to a premature baby who started to cry at $3\frac{1}{2}$ weeks. The doctor prescribed six different drugs, including Phenergan, an antihistamine of high potency; Mazolon, which speeds up gastric action; chloral hydrate, a hypnotic that can cause gastric irritation; and Ovol colic drops. None of them worked, so the mother was advised to give solid food, which the baby didn't like. Soon after this the baby had to be admitted to hospital for failure to thrive.

Drugs are often prescribed when what the mother really needs is down-to-earth practical help with the sheer hard work of coping with a baby, emotional support with a new and frightening task, and help in building up her own self-confidence. A 20-year-old first-time mother was prescribed six different drugs for her baby by her doctor: Infacol, Merbentyl, Piptal, Dentinox, Eastrop and pheno-barbitone, and when the baby continued to be restless, she gave her gripe water and whisky as well. The problem, the woman explained to me, was that her baby cried for about one hour every day and she couldn't stand it. This mother needed help with her loneliness, anxiety and depression, and her resulting panic when the baby cried. But she never got that. Instead her baby was drugged to the eyeballs.

Whatever makes babies cry, drugs – even if they work – provide a very short-term answer. They can't tackle the fundamental problems. They may make the baby still more irritable. They can produce coma. Sometimes they kill a baby. There must be a better way.

SOME OF THE DRUGS THAT ARE GIVEN TO BABIES WHO CRY

DRUG NAME			WHAT IT IS	USED FOR	DANGERS
USA	*UK*	*OTHER*			
Bentyl	Merbentyl Ovol	Bentylol (Canada)	Dicyclomine-hydrochloride; a gastro-intestinal sedative and anti-spasmodic	Colic, in babies over 6 months only	Limpness, headache, dry mouth, hot dry skin, thirst, dizziness, dilated pupils, fits, coma
	Infant Gaviscon		Antispasmodic and antacid, consisting of alginic acid, magnesium trisilicate, aluminium hydroxide and bicarbonate of soda	Vomiting, from birth. Not suitable for premature babies or if baby has a fever	Dehydration
Mylicon			Anti-flatulent, containing simethicone	Colic	None stated in the sources
Tylenol, Tempra, Panadol drops	Calpol Infant Suspension		Paracetamol (UK) (acetaminophen in US)	Pain, in babies over 3 months only	Skin becomes pale, baby does not want to feed, may vomit. Prolonged treatment in high doses can cause damage to kidneys
Temaril	Vallergan Syrup	Vallergan Syrup (Australia, South Africa) Panectyl (Canada)	Antihistamine, a sedative and tranquillizer which, in strong doses, is used in psychiatry and pre-medication for surgery. A central nervous system depressant	Babies over 6 months only Pre-operative medication, relief of itching from rash	Baby gets very drowsy and 'out of touch'. Taken along with other drugs, makes their effects more marked
Phenergan Syrup	Phenergan Elixir		Promethazine, a long acting antihistamine of high potency, a sedative used also for pre-medication for surgery	Babies over 6 months only (American PDR warns not to use in children under 2 years of age)	Baby gets very drowsy, dizzy, or very excited and uncoordinated, hands writhing. Sometimes fits, coma. Taken along with other drugs, makes their effects more marked

Benadryl	Benadryl		antihistamine, anti-spasmodic and sedative	Adults, not children	Baby becomes very drowsy, is dizzy and has a dry mouth
Donnatal	Donnatal		Natural belladonna alkaloids plus phenobarbital. Gastro-intestinal sedative	Colic	Dry mouth, hot dry skin, dizziness, nausea and vomiting, blurred vision, difficulty-swallowing
Levsin or Levsin with Phenobarbital			Belladonna alkaloid (hyoscyamine) with or without sedative	Colic	Headache, nausea and vomiting, blurred vision, hot dry skin, dizziness, difficulty swallowing
	Asilone for Infants		Dimethicone, alum and sorbitol. An antacid	Indigestion and vomiting in babies over 1 month only	Sometimes disturbances in bowel function
Reglan Maxeran	Maxolon Paediatric Liquid		Metoclopramide hydrochloride, speeds gastric action	Indigestion and vomiting	Drowsiness, restlessness. Baby may have spasm of muscles in face and around eyes, and jaw may lock, may stick out tongue rhythmically, adopt peculiar positions of head and shoulders and rigidly arch back; this drug can mask symptoms of an underlying disorder
Noctec	Noctec	Noctec (Australia, Canada)	Chloral hydrate	Sedation. Children over 12 years only	Tummy ache, headache, skin rashes, addiction, damage to kidneys
Phenobarbital	Phenobarbitone	Phenobarbitone (Australia, South Africa, Canada)	Barbiturate	Sedation	Baby may become very drowsy, go into coma, can become addicted

The information in this chart is derived from *ABPI Data Sheet Compendium 1986–87: The Physicians' Desk Reference*, (PDR) 41st edition, 1987; *Drugs: Complete Guide to Prescription and Non-Prescription Drugs*, 3rd Edition, Griffith, H. W., HP Books, Tucson, 1987; *The Extra Pharmacopoeia*, 28th edition, Martindale, W. edited by J. E. F. Reynolds and A. B. Prasad, Pharmaceutical Press, London, 1982; and *The Essential Guide to Non-Prescription Drugs*, Zimmerman, D. R.; Harper and Row, NY, 1983. They are compilations of data about drugs produced by the pharmaceutical companies themselves.

CHAPTER 10

Lashing Out

I imagine all the ways I can kill you.
I can drown you in the bathtub,
I can smother you with a pillow.
I can bang your head on the floor: once, hard.
Last month I wept when I heard about a baby
dying. This month I do the killing. I kill – and
tremble in horror. Why such images? I'm enraged.
My life is gone. There is only 'us',
with you always first.

Phyllis Chesler, *With Child*

When you have a crying baby it feels as if the whole world revolves around that crying. It completely takes over your life and you feel obliterated as a person. Instead of being able to 'get back to normal' after carrying the child for nine months, you now exist only in relation to the child. It is important to allow yourself to focus on your own feelings instead of thinking about the baby all the time. Before you had the baby you may have expected these feelings would all be positive. Other people often take it for granted that the baby is so beautiful that you must be feeling wonderful. It seems mean, ugly and ungrateful to say, 'Actually, I feel awful. There are times when I hate the baby and could wring its neck. I can't go on like this. Something is going to have to change.' It may not only be impossible to admit that to other people, it is difficult to admit it to yourself.

For many of us these violent feelings are so dangerously ready to erupt, and we feel so ashamed of them, that it is hard to be honest about them even when with other women going through the same experience. In any group of mothers of under-2s the public, polite, coping self seems to take over, and social masks are carefully adjusted.

'Oh yes, he's a little monster!' one says – with a laugh. Everyone tacitly agrees to make a joke of it.

In her autobiographical account of birth and new motherhood, Jane Lazarre describes her search among other mothers for co-conspirators who also have babies who cry and who, like her, feel they are bad mothers. They meet with their babies and the expected questions come:

> 'How is yours doing, oh how is yours doing, sleep through the night?' 'Yes, oh yes' (she would say) and 'No, not yet' (I would have to report): and then, 'Cry much?' 'No, very contented baby it seems' (she said proudly) . . .
> 'How is yours doing, sleep through the night, and aren't they wonderful? . . .'
> 'No,' I said, short and clipped. 'No, he doesn't sleep through the night, no, it is not wonderful. Sometimes I wish I'd never had a baby.'
> The way she looked at me I had to renege a bit, cowardly rebel that I was.
> 'Oh, I love him and everything.'
> She relaxed. Angry at my compromise, I attacked again.
> 'But I could kill him sometimes.'
> The other woman can't stand this – or, perhaps, can't comprehend it – and quickly changes the subject. 'It's cold,' she said.[1]

Getting out and meeting other mothers can make you feel human again, but joining groups is usually of limited help in coming to terms with your own emotions. Most women who told me about their family experiences found that one good, confiding friend or a health visitor, doctor, counsellor or someone else to whom they could safely bare their souls gave most help as they groped their way through the tunnel.

Any woman with an inconsolably crying baby knows what it is to be very near breaking point. When reports appear in the media about parents who have harmed a child, there is usually someone who says, 'I can't understand how anyone could hurt a baby.' But anyone who has an inconsolably crying baby *can* understand how this is possible. One in ten of the women who told me about their experiences said she had smacked or shaken her baby violently or gripped it far too tightly. When Cry-sis, a British support group for parents of crying babies, analysed sixty-one accounts of women who sought help from them, they found that more than half the mothers admitted they came very close to hurting their babies.[2]

Any mother or father with a constantly crying baby is at risk of being violent to that child. Those who smack, hit or fling a baby on the floor are not monsters. They are human beings at the end of their tether. They have passed the point of endurance and lost control. The child is the victim, but they, too, are victims of a society that fails to support parents to help them cope adequately with the stresses of parenthood and to make provision for child care when it is desperately needed.

It is normal to want to escape from a baby whose crying is inconsolable, normal to feel angry, too, when a baby goes on and on and on, whatever you do, and for there to be times when you hate the baby for subjecting you to this sustained torture. Courts sometimes recognize this. A father who killed his 17-day-old son because he cried inconsolably was convicted of murder, but on appeal the conviction was quashed and one of manslaughter substituted. The judges said there was no evidence that he was 'other than a loving and affectionate father', and that 'the provocation was such as would make an ordinary and responsible person lose self-control.'[3] Most mothers have probably dumped the baby forcibly in his crib when they could endure it no longer, have screamed at the child or done something else that startles and frightens him. We are often unwilling to admit it because we are horrified that we could behave like this. The image of a mother is one of all-loving, all-giving, tenderness and self-sacrifice. It is an impossible, romanticized ideal. No wonder we feel failures!

As women talked to me about their feelings, many said things like: 'I came very near to doing *anything* to stop the crying' and 'Now I understand how easy it is to hurt a baby.' In fact, it is often the shock of realizing how close you are to child abuse that brings you up short and releases a flood of shame and remorse.

When a woman overcomes her reluctance to talk about these violent feelings, she rarely finds anyone who can fully accept her emotions in a non-judgemental way and offer practical opportunities for constructive action. Instead, attention tends to be directed to the horror of violence against the baby. Action may be taken to prevent the possibility of physical damage at the cost of completely separating the mother from her baby and treating her as a criminal.

A woman who said that her baby was crying continuously one day, only letting up for twenty-minute intervals, told me:

It was desperately hot. She wouldn't feed. She wouldn't drink. She just screamed. I thought perhaps it was the heat. The coolest room in the house was the toilet, so I sat there with my baby on my lap to try and feed her. It took me two hours to get her to take just an ounce and then she vomited it all back up. That was the last straw, I walked into our bedroom, laid her on the bed – she was screaming – and I was desperate, confused. I don't know how long I stood there, but in one split second I just grabbed at her and shook her. I felt upset. I couldn't think. But something made me rush downstairs, put the baby in the pram [baby carriage] and phone my health visitor. I was devastated by what followed. She marched into my home like the Gestapo, went straight to the baby and checked her over. She was fine and fast asleep, more than she had done all day. She phoned the doctor and asked him to come immediately, and told me that the baby would have to go to hospital and I could go if I wanted to. Of course I wanted to go, but I didn't understand why we had to go to hospital. She very coldly and carefully said that my daughter might be taken into the care of the hospital. All I could do was cry. My daughter was okay, it was me who needed some support. My doctor came, said all was well, and gave me a lecture on the seriousness of shaking a baby and said he had phoned an ambulance to take my baby to hospital. I couldn't even phone my husband, there was no time. When I got there, my daughter was taken from me and I was taken into another room. It was like being interrogated, worse than a nightmare. Without any knowledge to myself or my

husband my daughter was put under a place of safety
order for twenty-eight days and I was told if I tried to
remove her from the hospital I could face prison. We
were devastated. I didn't understand what they were
saying to me.

Subsequently the court put her under a supervision order for
three years. The baby was later discovered, three weeks after her
admission to hospital, to suffer from lactose intolerance. Once she
was put on soya milk, the crying ceased.

Media reporting of violence against children, vital though it
has been in alerting the public to the problem, has made social
workers, health visitors and other care-givers acutely aware that
they might inadvertently miss a case and fail to save a child who is
at risk of abuse. Yet they are for the most part without the resources
to offer parents the help they need and to provide a safe, nurturing environment.
    A woman who is living in one room with her baby, perhaps in
welfare housing or in a sleazy 'hotel' where whole families are packed

into every room, or on the seventeenth floor in a high-rise dwelling where the lift (elevator) is often broken, or anywhere where building standards are low, partitions thin and neighbours batter on the wall and floor, yelling at her to 'keep that bloody baby quiet!' is locked in a situation where she may find it impossible to defuse her emotions and where they can spill over into violence. If she cannot be re-housed, at least she needs time away from her baby – but there is usually no way she can get that.

A doctor who becomes aware of what is happening may decide to treat the mother's emotional condition with tranquillizers. The theory behind this seems to be that if she can calm down, the risk of child abuse will disappear. In fact, under the influence of tranquil-lizers, the opposite may happen, for powerful mood-changing drugs can remove inhibitions and prevent the woman taking avoiding action when she feels hostility towards the baby. Many women say that when they can't stand the baby any longer, they go into another room or run out into the street. Some lock themselves in the bath-room or go to someone else's house in order to protect the baby. They realize how close they are to violence and make safety-valves for themselves. A woman who is heavily tranquillized may be unable to do this and not even be aware of the consequences of her actions or the degree to which her anger is mounting, and just goes along with it. Her inner rage is reduced, but at the same time her self-control is lessened.

Women from all social classes have described to me the violent emotions they feel when their babies cry incessantly and how they find themselves shouting at the baby to stop, pummelling their fists against the table, crashing down a plate, throwing something across the room or screaming at someone else in the family. But for many of them there is an escape route, even though temporary. They say they go out of earshot or retreat into a hot bath while the baby 'cries it out'. Kate, for example, has become very clever at monitoring her own feelings and takes action before her anger snaps: 'If I get to shouting point, I shout – but not at the baby. I leave the room and have a good yell, cry, whatever relieves me. I don't shout at him. He won't realize what it's all about, it will only frighten him more. His own crying is frightening enough. I try very hard to think of it from my baby's point of view and stay on his side.' Elaine says: 'When I feel angry I bite a cushion or kick a chair to relieve the tension because I would never want to take it out on my children and I would never forgive myself if I hurt them.' Other women say they throw things or break china – anything rather than harm their babies.

Some women leave the baby in someone else's care while they go out or, since babies almost always drift off to sleep when in a moving car, put the baby in the back of the car and drive around. Many pick up the phone to talk with someone who is sympathetic, a relative, friend or member of a post-natal support group. For a woman living on welfare benefit or a low income who has no phone, no car, no garden and who may be completely socially isolated, retreat of this kind is impossible.

In Britain pregnant women and families with children represent three-quarters of all homeless households that are assisted by local authorities, and increasingly residents in welfare bed-and-breakfast accommodation are women with young children. Unemployment and poverty is highest among the young. It is hard to cope with the violent emotions triggered by a baby's crying when you are very young. Though older women who told me about their experiences felt anger and despair, they tended to express more compassion for their babies than did very young mothers. Those under 20 were much more likely to say there was 'no reason' for a baby's crying, and that it was 'playing up' or simply demanding attention.

Many of these young women were unsupported single mothers or were in an uneasy relationship with the father of the child. Few had support from other women and, stuck in one room with the baby, their lives were very different from those of their contemporaries who had jobs. As I listened to them, it seemed to me that they were crying out for love, but all they had was the never-ending thankless task of dealing with a baby who screamed or fretted on and on and on.

This bears out previous research that shows that mothers of battered babies tend to be younger than other mothers at the time of the birth of the first child, to be single and not living with the baby's biological father. Many of these women have themselves been victims of violence, often from a father, but sometimes from their mothers, in their own childhood.[4]

The lives of many teenage girls are infused with ideas of romance and fantasies about boys desiring them and sweeping them off their feet into the 'happily ever after'. The contrast between this and being stuck at home with a crying baby brings a shock of cold reality, is shattering to self-esteem and may plunge a mother into depression or goad her into anger against the baby who seems to be the cause of all the trouble.

In Sue Sharpe's perceptive book, *Falling for Love*, in which teenage mothers tell their own stories, one woman who became pregnant when she was 16 and married her 18-year-old boyfriend, whom she had known for only two months, says that before she was pregnant, 'I lived in dreamland.' When the baby was born they had to live in one room, Steve was unemployed and at home all day, but Marie says, 'He thought a man goes out to earn money and a wife stays at home . . . We got on each other's nerves. We didn't have enough money, so we couldn't go out in the evening either.' The baby cried all the time and this unnerved Steve, who then became violent and hit Marie, 'either over something petty, the TV or something, or nothing at all'. Then he started on the baby. Marie didn't want anyone to know about it. 'I felt ashamed. I thought it was my fault. It made me feel guilty.' As for the baby, she says: 'I couldn't love him at first . . . He was just . . . something to play with. Then when it came to the crying, I haven't got a lot of patience. I lost my temper easily . . . I haven't got any motherly instinct but I've got to look after him.' At one point she said: 'Sometimes I think, God I hate you.' Then she corrected herself: 'No, I love him really. Sometimes things just get on top of you.' And she adds: 'When I was going to have Jamie adopted, people said I was unloving and cruel, but now I wish I had done it . . . If you had money, a nice home and good future ahead of you, having children young is a lovely idea. But if you are single, you could be stuck in a bedsitter for years and no money. Trapped.'[5]

A woman may feel hostility to her baby from the very beginning because of the pain and suffering it has caused her and because she has not been adequately nurtured through the experience of childbirth. Some women are especially vulnerable because they were deprived of love in their own childhood. Having a baby triggers the anger they felt towards their mothers and a sense of deep personal deprivation. They are jealous of their own babies. Some feel as if they want to crawl back inside their mothers and are unable to give themselves to the baby because their own need for security and love is so great. Try as they may to love and care for their babies, crying may be the last straw. They want to run away and hide or to throw the baby out of the window. A single mother still in her teens, shocked by the experience of childbirth, and who felt her body had been mutilated by an episiotomy performed regardless of whether she wanted it or not, told me:

> I hated him [the baby] for ruining my body and I hated John [her boyfriend] for letting them do it. On the second day my mum was visiting me when one of the other mothers told me Alexander was crying. My mum and John said they would go. I was so upset that when I went into the ward, I pulled the curtain and I shook him very hard. I can't believe I did it, but I hated him. I just wanted him to die.

This anger is often linked with a sense that the baby does not really 'belong', and that it is an invader or is rejecting its mother. A woman whose father's funeral took place on the day she went into labour, and who suffered a post-partum psychosis and was under heavy sedation in a psychiatric hospital following the birth, didn't even see her baby for the first seven days. She told me: 'I felt cut off from the child, as if I'd bought him in a shop, and wondered if he wasn't mine and he'd got mixed up in the hospital. The baby didn't seem to like me at all. He cried every time I tried to cuddle him. I felt I had failed to win his love.'

A feeling of alienation from your own child is what psychologists and pediatricians mean when they talk about 'failure of bonding'. It is not just that you haven't yet fallen in love with your baby – that can take weeks – but that it might as well be a little Martian, an extraterrestrial visitor, with whom you have nothing in common. Yet you are required to go through the actions of caring for it. When this strange creature cries and cannot be stopped, the burden placed on a woman proves too great. Her temper snaps and she lashes out against the baby as if it were a domestic pet that had not yet been house-trained. At the time she may even think of it as 'discipline' or 'punishment', rather than abuse. If the baby lay passive and inert like a doll, she might be able to cope. As it is, she feels flayed alive by the child's screams.

In my study I found that women whose dominant emotion about their babies is one of anger tend to get less depressed than other mothers of crying babies. When most women lose self-control with their babies, they feel guilty and depressed afterwards. But angry women direct the anger outwards towards their babies and often feel justified in losing their tempers and hitting out at them. These mothers describe their babies as having 'a terrible temper', being 'demanding' and 'always seeking attention'. They smack them because they are 'naughty'.

In contrast, for most women anger is mixed with compassion: 'I hated her, yet at the same time I felt sorry for her.' Any outburst is quickly followed by horror at what they had done or been about to do: 'The baby would lie there screaming. This was when I felt I couldn't cope any more and I tried to smother him, but the fact that I loved him and knowing he was only a baby, stopped me.'

Roberta Israeloff, in *Coming to Terms*, her diary of the complex

143

emotions she experienced in pregnancy and after the baby was born, describes how, in the dead of night, trying to soothe her crying baby and suddenly overwhelmed by hatred for him, she became aware of similar emotions she had felt as a child when her baby sister was born, and realized she had not yet come to terms with those violent feelings. She had tried everything she knew to get the baby off to sleep but he cried and cried until he got hiccups:

> 'I'll throttle you' I thought, though all I did was pick him up and hold him away from me and give him a shake . . . But in the instant that I pulled him away from my body I was flooded with more intense shame and remorse than I had ever known . . . His cries crawled into my ears like snakes, reminding me of my sister's cries when she was an infant . . . I wasn't only angry at Ben but also at an early scenario, when my baby sister had shown up out of nowhere, crying and crying.[6]

Sometimes it is in the night that sudden insights come like this, and you realize that it isn't just your baby with whom you feel so angry, but that the cries have triggered violent emotions you first experienced when you were a child yourself – rage at a sibling who had replaced you and left you comfortless and in distress when you felt abandoned by your mother. A parent who realizes this – who can put it into words – is probably less likely to harm a child than one who is overcome by emotions that aren't understood and feels only blind, uncomprehending rage.

Some of the women who lash out against their babies are themselves being physically abused by male partners who become more violent when the baby cries. Realizing that the man is on a short fuse, a woman is then desperate to shut the baby up. There is often no way she could keep the baby out of earshot or away from the man in the conditions under which they are living.

Sometimes the baby becomes the target for assault by the man because it belongs to her and hurting the baby is hurting *her*. At other times the man treats the baby, along with the woman, as his property, with whom he feels he has a right to do whatever he likes.

The breaking point for men, and for women too, sometimes

comes when a baby cries at night. Most crying babies concentrate their crying during the day and are especially restless in the evening, but settle before midnight, waking in the night only to be fed. Some, however, cry much of the night too. Parents then find it much more difficult to cope during the day. Tempers become frayed and, with continued sleep deprivation, there are fewer rational controls on behaviour. Some women are saved by having partners who share the night-time ordeal: 'Nothing seemed to alleviate the crying. Our whole world was trying to soothe this screaming bundle. I cried almost as much as the baby. As soon as our evening meal was on the table she started crying and didn't stop until the early hours of the morning.' Other women have to cope with a baby alone at night in the realization that the man is getting bad-tempered and may turn violent because his sleep is being disturbed.

On the other hand, some point out that continuous lack of sleep means that they and their partners are in a zombie-like state and don't have the energy to lash out against the baby. They just go on doing things to try to stop the crying as if they are machines that have been switched to automatic. Hitting or shaking the baby is out of the question. They simply don't have the strength.

If there are already other children, a crying baby wakes the others at night. One woman told me how her older children would land up in bed with her, along with the baby, every night. In spite of approving of the idea of a 'family bed', she found it impossible to sleep. For weeks on end she only dozed fitfully. She had fantasies of different ways in which she could kill the lot of them and get some peace at last. She thought at the time that she was the only woman in the world who had these 'wicked thoughts'. Then she met another woman who was under similar strain and they managed to get out together regularly and 'spill the beans' to each other. Being able to be honest about her feelings enabled her to work out some new strategies for coping. Two things enabled her to pull through: she joined a preschool playgroup with the older children and she expressed breast milk so that she could alternate nights on duty with her partner.

When you have a new baby, the other children seem to become much older all of a sudden and you expect them to be reasonable, fairly independent and more grown up than they are. In a family where children are born close together and in which there is a crying baby, one of the others may bear the brunt of the mother's anger. What starts as a disciplinary smack turns into violence. Even if there are only two children, coping with one crying baby is very different from coping with a crying baby *and* a 2-year-old with temper tantrums. The rage a woman feels towards her constantly crying baby may be redirected onto the older child who is misbehaving. Many older children pretend to be babies after a sibling's birth in order to get the love that they see is given to the new baby. It is common for a child who was previously potty-trained to start making messes and need to go back into nappies (diapers) for a while, to play up about food, become 'whiney' and difficult to handle or to develop sleep problems.

This is what happened to one woman who described what she went through after the birth of her second baby, who was 'dreadful and demanding' and cried a lot, when her older child also became very difficult. There was one awful day when the elder girl was having a tantrum in the supermarket, which started the baby crying too, and she found herself with her hands round the little girl's throat screaming, 'Shut up, shut up, or I'll kill you!' Other shoppers took no notice, apart from one older woman, who remarked to another: 'That's the trouble with these young mothers. They spoil their children!' She got very run-down with recurring infections and constant headaches. Her doctor wrote prescriptions for pain-killers and antibiotics, and didn't realize how desperate she was. Fortunately she met someone who gave her time to talk, asked her the important question: 'What do *you* want?' and *listened* to her answers. There were bad times afterwards, but she began the long, painful process of building her own self-esteem. She joined several mother-and-toddler groups and then offered herself as a volunteer with Parents Anonymous, a support group for parents who have violent feelings about their children.

Confronting your anger

Acknowledging anger is the first step to being able to do something about it. Once you have admitted to yourself 'I sometimes hate my baby', you can see where the danger points are, the times when you

feel most desperate, and develop a strategy to deal with or avoid them. You know the emotional signals that mean that you must walk away – perhaps go out and close the door on the crying baby because you are near breaking point. A teenage single mother who became severely depressed when her baby was 10 weeks old told me: 'If he gets too much for me and I feel like hitting him, I leave him for a little while. It sounds callous, but it's better than getting so het up that I hit him.'

One of the best ways of coping with anger is to make it *all right to be angry* by redirecting your rage on to something inanimate. You can thump pillows with a clothes hanger and shout and scream. If you are worried about what other people might think, turn the radio or TV on loud first. You can even use this anger constructively.

You can tackle a task in the house or garden that involves whacking, thudding or breaking something up. Digging, bread-making or scrubbing could all be ways of letting your rage out.

The trouble is, though, that many women are so exhausted with their babies that they have no energy left to do these things. The anger stays like a poison inside them. When they begin to crack under strain, it erupts, like scalding lava. So it is very important that you are able to hand over the baby to someone else before this happens. It could be your partner, an understanding friend or someone whom you pay. Having a person like this is your first priority. Think about the periods in the twenty-four hours when you are likely to be under most stress and see if it is possible to have some time away from the baby regularly during that period. For many women it is in the evening, when they are tired and the baby tends to cry. This, of course, is the most difficult time in which to call on outside help, and for many women it is a counsel of perfection, because they have no one else reliable with whom they can trust the baby. But consider an older woman, one whose children have grown up and is living alone, perhaps, who lives nearby. If she is at home all day she may be rather lonely and welcome having the baby for a couple of hours each evening. You may be able to find someone like this through your church, doctor, health visitor or neighbourhood association. Get to know her first, of course, and be sure that you can trust her and that she and the baby will get on together.

Another thing you can do is to make a chart for yourself, based on a timetable that you keep over several days, which shows times during which the baby is least likely to be restless and crying. Even if you can find only half-hour gaps between crying, you can use these to make a little personal space for you to enjoy. Plan to do things then that you want to do, not those that you feel you ought to do. Soak in a bath, do your hair, relax and listen to music or play an instrument yourself, read, paint or draw, or do a jigsaw – anything but attend to the baby. These are your breathing spaces.

See if you can find some time each day in which you can relax. Advice is often given that you should sleep when your baby sleeps, however odd the times when you can do this. The problem is that you may feel numb and overtired so that you cannot settle into a restful sleep. You fall asleep in an uncomfortable position, sitting up with your clothes on, and wake fitfully, wondering where you are and what has happened. Or there are interruptions: somebody is knocking at the door, the phone rings or a TV programme suddenly gets noisy. So it helps to make a little oasis of peace to which you can retreat. Put a notice on the door saying 'Mother and baby resting' and take the phone off the hook. Choose some place where you are least likely to be interrupted and where you can draw the curtains, put your feet up and relax against pillows.

Use the relaxation you learned in childbirth classes now. Breathe out, drop shoulders and relax and then breathe slowly in through your nose and out through your mouth, listening to the wave-like rhythm of your own breathing. When you start to do this you may find that it is impossible to continue because tears well up. If you want to weep, do so – have a good cry. You will feel much better afterwards.

Consciously release one part of your body after another, using your breathing to help you, so that each time you breathe *out* you relax deeply. Visualize the anger flowing out from the core of you to the surface of your body and then flowing away from you with each complete breath out. Imagine a wide sweep of sky with soft, fluffy clouds. If any anger is still clinging to you, think of scooping it up and placing it on a cloud and watching it float away. Use as many clouds as you need in order to get rid of all the anger and hatred.

Once you have emptied yourself of the bad feelings, with each breath in, draw into yourself peace and fresh energy.

Even if you can do this for only ten minutes or so, it will enable you to have some space for yourself from which you come refreshed and with renewed energy.

- Get out of the house every day with the baby, even in bad weather. Make a trip to the shops or the local park, or go out for coffee with a friend. It breaks the intense relationship between you and your crying baby and protects you both, because you are very unlikely to give way to violent feelings if you are among other people.
- Arrange for a babysitter at least once a week, so that you can either get out or relax at home. If you can afford it, you may like the idea of a meal out. But there is no rule that you have to go out when your babysitter comes. Explain that you will probably be at home but need a break from the baby. One thing

you could do, for example, would be to take your evening meal to bed on a tray.

- Make contact with other women with young babies. Find, or start, a mother-and-baby group, meeting in each other's homes, the clinic, church hall, a community centre, the YWCA or other suitable place once a week.

- Buy a personal stereo and tapes you enjoy. It can be used in two ways. You can put on a disco dance for your baby, playing it and dancing or just gliding about with your baby in your arms, which is soothing for you both. Or it can be a music screen, when you wear the earphones to tone down the sound of crying so that you have something pleasant on which to focus while you deal with the baby. It won't cut you off from the baby, but by providing a sound waterfall, muffles the crying and enables you to be more relaxed.

- Have some physical exercise, even if it is only going for a brisk ten-minute walk. You may be able to find a mother-and-baby exercise class in your neighbourhood. If you possibly can, make a weekly break for yourself from the baby and get vigorous physical activity. Swim, play tennis, squash or badminton or go jogging or cycling.

- Share the way you are feeling with someone who understands. You may be able to seek help from your doctor or health visitor. A caring family doctor will often suggest half an hour a week to talk about yourself and your problems in a non-judgemental atmosphere. Or if there are problems between you and your partner, marital counselling may help. Such counselling sessions can be a lifeline. The health visitor may drop in more often for a chat, too. There may even be an offer of a home help – which can really make a difference! Parents' Anonymous is one organization that specializes in helping parents who feel on the edge of violence against a baby. They have drop-in centres and you can get to know someone whom you can ring when things are bad. There is sure to be a branch of the Samaritans in your area, who will also offer support and counselling. Addresses of organizations which can help are on pages 251–76.

- Whenever you feel you can't stand any more, put the baby down in a safe place and simply *go out of the room and close the door.*

CHAPTER II

The Pre-term and Low-birthweight Baby

She was seven weeks premature and had respiratory distress, apnoea attacks, jaundice, septicaemia and pneumonia. We both fluctuated from elation to depression, cheered up when she progressed from the ventilator to the oxygen head box, plunged into gloom when she developed infections which caused further breathing problems . . .

In hospital I only saw him at feeding times. We were allowed to go down to special care at any time, but I didn't like to bother them and he was asleep most of the time anyway. When I brought him home I didn't feel at all maternal.

Mothers talking about their babies

Some pre-term babies cry a lot, whereas others are very placid. Caring for them can be difficult even if they don't cry because they have a limited attention span, can't hold their heads up to make eye contact, and you don't have the rewarding 'conversations' that make it fun to care for full-term babies. They need a high degree of stimulation before they take any notice of you and have ways of screening you out when they are at risk of being over-stimulated by dropping off to sleep, crying irritably or, if you have managed to start an eye-to-eye conversation, looking away as if they were terribly bored with you.

Tiffany Field, a child development specialist who studies ways in which new-born babies interact with those looking after them, says that a mother with a pre-term baby has to walk a fine line: 'She may not provide enough stimulation to get the child to respond or she may be too stimulating. She's got to be really sensitive to the baby's signals.'[1]

In my own study I found that most of the pre-term babies cried no more than full-term babies. There is evidence, however, that a baby who is pre-term because the mother had very high blood pressure or pre-eclampsia – so that labour was induced – tends to cry more than usual. The same may happen if a pre-term baby had breathing difficulties after birth.[2] It looks as if babies who have had a particularly rough ride before, during or just after birth are also among those who are difficult to settle and cry more than usual. Their sleep disturbances may last a long time, sometimes well into the second year of life.[3]

Even babies who just happen to have been born too soon and have had an easy birth and started breathing straight away may take a long time to get accustomed to the rhythms of night and day. They are still tuned to time in the uterus and may continue to be so at least until after the time when they were due to be born. Although they do not cry any more than other babies, they do so at highly inconvenient times.

There are other reasons why pre-term babies may be jumpy and unsettled, even if they do not cry for prolonged periods. They have often spent days or weeks in the special-care nursery, separated from the comfort of their mothers' bodies, isolated in a plastic crib or incubator under bright fluorescent lights that are usually on night and day, with machines clicking and roaring in their ears, and surrounded by other babies who are disturbed and crying. They will almost certainly have suffered a number of painful investigations and treatments, which make them restless and irritable.

A study of babies' experiences in a special-care unit revealed that babies have, on average, 144 very unpleasant things done to them by the time they are 1 week old, compared with 38 if they are given routine care in the ordinary nursery.[4] These include having their breathing passages cleared by suction, being put on artificial ventilation, having tubes and catheters pushed down them for endotracheal or nasotracheal intubation and suction, lumbar puncture, having a chest drain inserted, being immobilized and blindfolded under phototherapy lights, having sticky tape pulled off, masks clamped over their faces, catheters pushed into and removed from the umbilicus, eyedrops that sting, X-rays, injections and their heels cut for blood tests. The researchers didn't watch what happened when babies were cared for by their mothers all the time. My guess is that few babies who stay with their mothers would have had more than two or three unpleasant experiences of this kind. They say:

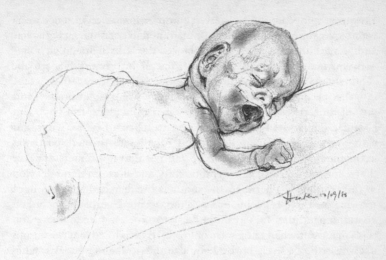

At an older age one might expect that such a prolonged unpleasant experience would be followed by emotional and behavioural disorders. Perhaps some of the difficulties which mothers experience with their babies on taking them home from the special-care baby unit represent 'neurotic behaviour' by the baby resulting from his traumatic, post-natal experiences.[5]

Whether or not you consider your baby 'neurotic', it is reasonable to think that when a baby has had all its senses assaulted by this kind of treatment – even though it may have been necessary and life-saving – and has been through a lot of pain, it may take some time to settle down and feel secure. All babies need to be with their mothers or with someone else with whom they can form an intimate bond, but babies who have been through horrible experiences like these especially need loving closeness and to know that they are safe. When they cry, perhaps part of the reason for it is that they are separated from this person who can make them feel that the world is a secure place.

Yet when a baby is pre-term, a woman is put under great stress. It is much harder to mother a tiny pre-term infant who looks like a red, splayed-out frog than a plump, responsive, full-term baby whom everyone tells you is beautiful. When experts have taken over and you feel that they are responsible for the baby being alive now – and enormously grateful to them – it can be very difficult to be confident about caring for the baby yourself. Even if you are welcome into the special-care unit at any time in the twenty-four hours – and not all nurseries adopt this system – it is difficult to feel confident about handling your baby when it is attached to tubes, wires and catheters and all you can do is to put your hands through portholes in the incubator. This stress can be so great that it is understandable that some mothers withdraw emotionally and that problems develop in the relationship between the mother and her child. It has been shown that there is an increase of 'mothering disorders', including abandonment, the 'vulnerable child syndrome', failure to thrive and cases of assault when babies are of low birthweight.[6] Generalizations like this are not likely to be helpful unless we understand exactly what it is that causes a woman's sense of dis-ease with her baby, acknowledge all the things that are intruding on and interfering with their relationship, and try to change them. We don't have to go any further than the special-care baby unit to realize that both the mother and her baby have suffered a great deal by the time the baby leaves hospital, and that this can affect them both for months – even, sometimes, years – afterwards.

The small-for-gestational-age baby

Sometimes the inconsolably crying baby is one who has not been nourished well in the uterus, because the placenta has not functioned completely in the last weeks of pregnancy. One in three low-birthweight babies is small because of not growing well in the uterus, not because of being born too soon. When fetal growth retardation is diagnosed, doctors get very concerned. They may urge the mother to eat more and rest more, take her into hospital for bed-rest and induce labour because the baby is 'small for dates' and there is evidence of placental malfunction.

Many women feel it must be their fault when a baby does not grow well in the uterus. The placenta is a complex organ that acts as life-support system, lungs and feeding mechanism for the baby. All nutrients in the mother's bloodstream are filtered through its fine membranes into the baby's bloodstream. (Usually the mother's and baby's blood never mix.) It is not always understood why a placenta does not work as well as it should, but it tends to happen when a woman's blood pressure is very high and if she develops symptoms of pre-eclampsia – protein in her urine, fluid retention and sudden large weight gain. Like any other physical organ, the placenta also has a life-span. It usually works well for forty to forty-two weeks. Some placentas age faster than others and we do not know why this is so. Good nutrition in pregnancy helps the placenta to function well. But sometimes a placenta which has not formed perfectly in early pregnancy fails to nourish the baby adequately. No end of 'eating for two' and stuffing yourself with protein can make up for that.

The new-born SGA (small-for-gestational-age) baby looks worried and has dry, peeling skin and tends to be slightly jaundiced. If you pick up the baby and talk to her, she looks even more worried, and when you cuddle or stroke her, she may not nestle into you like other babies, but becomes tense. In the days immediately following birth she seems to like being left alone, is undemanding if not disturbed and may have to be woken for feeds. If you play with her during or after a feed, she brings back milk and seems exhausted with her efforts to respond to you and cope with other people.

Over the next three weeks or so these babies suck well, gain weight quickly and fill out, but continue to look a bit anxious, and when handled and played with seem even more worried.

When they are about 3 weeks old they start to cry. From being quiet and sleeping a lot, they have long periods of screaming – sometimes for as long as eight hours in the twenty-four, usually starting in the early evening. They startle readily and seem to be about to jump out of their skin when a door bangs, the dog barks or a light is suddenly switched on. Whereas 'colicky' babies usually stop crying at about 3 months, these babies may go on to 5 months. And long after that they are intensely active, hypersensitive babies, easily stimulated to distress. A pediatrician explains the function of this kind of crying as being to shut out further stimulus and to discharge the disturbance resulting from a too sensitive, 'raw' nervous system.[7]

Any mother who has had a baby like this will tell you that he needs peace and quiet, firm, slow, gentle handling and to have everything in the environment and in people's behaviour around muted and low-key. These babies enjoy being swaddled and, like other babies, being carried in a sling against your body. They are often much more contented when they have a dummy (pacifier) to suck. It seems to have the effect of blotting out other stimuli. Though most babies cope well with the noise of other children and enjoy being part of the rough and tumble of life with siblings, these don't. As they grow older, they relish it for short periods, but soon become over-stimulated and cry.

It is easy to over-stimulate the SGA baby, trying one thing after another to stop the crying. This makes the baby more and more uptight, and though when startled he stops crying for a few moments from sheer shock, he starts up again even more vociferously than before.

If you recognize this as a portrait of your baby, you may like to try the low-key subdued approach. Tone down your reactions. Be slower in the way you handle the baby, making all your movements deliberate, like those of a much older person. Watch your grandmother or some other elderly woman with the baby. You may find that the baby quietens when with an assured older person. If so, this is an important clue to how your baby needs to be handled. 'When parents care a great deal,' Brazelton says, 'they can get locked into doing too much, into ignoring the very behaviours and reactions in the baby that may help explain what his cries are trying to say.'[8]

Your baby may be happiest when bundled up firmly. Lie her down on a large, soft, stretchy blanket or shawl. Fold one edge over the baby's shoulder and front, round her elbow on the other side, and tuck it snugly under her knees. Then pick up the other edge and fold it over the front of her body, pulling it taut so that you have a firm bundle, and tuck it either under her body or anchored under the mattress of the crib or basket.

Another thing you can do with a hypersensitive and easily over-stimulated baby is to try to get in tune with her and to adapt to her pace by sometimes just copying what she does. If she yawns, for example, yawn yourself. If she makes little, fussy, whimpering noises, do this too. If she cries, try imitating her crying. When she blinks, you blink. You may find that this helps you become more sensitive to what your baby is trying to tell you. It can also turn into a lovely game between you, a game in which the baby controls the pace. When your baby looks away, it is a signal for you to stop. She has had enough stimulation for the time being. She may fall asleep or, after a pause, may turn to you in order to start the game again. Take the cue from the baby.

Powerlessness

As I talked to women who had pre-term or low-birthweight babies I became aware that when a baby went to special care, those who maintained some feeling of still being in control over what happened, were consulted by staff about any treatment and shared with them in decision-making, and who were welcome at all times and able to help care for their babies were less likely to have babies who cried inconsolably several weeks later. For many women whose babies went to special care there was an overwhelming feeling of power-lessness. Other people had taken over responsibility for their babies. They were the experts and the mother felt helpless, ignorant and, at best, a clumsy pupil. When I examined in depth how women described their feelings when their babies went to special care, I found that three-quarters of them talked about a sense of powerlessness. Almost every one of these women had babies who cried excessively.

A woman who had been heavily tranquillized before birth and then had a Caesarean section said: 'I was depressed and worried about the baby. Pediatricians kept looking at him but wouldn't tell me anything, which added to my worry.' Her baby was at first very sleepy and had feeding problems, which were probably caused by the heavy doses of tranquillizers he had received from his mother's bloodstream, but began to cry inconsolably when a few weeks old right through the day for periods of up to two hours at a time. She said: 'I felt very isolated and guilty, and anxious that I couldn't do anything to stop the crying. My doctor told me I was over-anxious and causing the problem. I had been a very confident and capable person. I just couldn't cope, although I should have been able to.'

Another, whose baby was taken to the special-care baby unit

twice, where she was tube-fed and very jaundiced and sleepy, said: 'I felt that it was my fault. I felt a failure when I gave up breast-feeding. I felt the baby belonged to the hospital and not to me.'

A baby who had inhaled meconium during the birth was 'whisked away immediately' by a pediatrician: 'We were absolutely terrified that there was something wrong with him, as nobody had explained what they were going to do.'

Another baby, five weeks pre-term, was also taken straight to special care: 'No one bothered to explain what this meant to the child and how long he would take to adapt to the world.'

One woman considered suicide: 'I was very, very depressed. I seriously considered jumping from the balcony of my room [on the sixth floor]. My daughter was in an incubator. I felt it was all my fault. Each change of nurses gave new information, contradicting the previous shift.'

Over and over again women said they couldn't find out what was happening: 'I was totally ignored, my partner shooed off home and my baby taken to the special-care baby unit.' Later, not being able to get any information about her baby, 'I just walked out to find my baby, as no one bothered about telling me anything.' Her partner was very embarrassed by this and kept saying, 'They're doing their best, love.' She became depressed, largely because she was not allowed to breast-feed as she wished: 'When I removed the tube from his nose, he breast-fed beautifully, but because he would not take a feed from a bottle, they insisted the tube was put back. This made him uncomfortable at the breast, which made doctors and staff say he had to take a bottle before they would remove the feeding tube.' This woman had four children, two of whom had cried excessively as babies. Both had been in special care and she says that breast-feeding was restricted because on both occasions staff told her that 'It wasn't worth breast-feeding until my milk had come in.'

Some women do not even know why their babies have been taken to special care. One of these women, who says she was never told and didn't like to ask because everyone was so busy, had a baby who later cried excessively day and night and was admitted to the hospital for failure to thrive.

When other people take over completely, women often feel that the baby does not belong to them. One woman, who had a Caesarean section at thirty-three weeks because of pre-eclampsia, said her baby was 'whisked to special care' and she did not see him until thirty hours later. The baby was in an incubator attached to a heart monitor: 'It was hard to believe he was ours. We had no name chosen. It was as if I had lost him in some way, as I could no longer feel him kicking inside.' She became very depressed: 'The main reason was that we had no idea how long Darren would be in hospital. The staff would not give us any idea.'

Even when a baby does not go to the special-care nursery, if a mother is not kept informed and cannot share in decisions made about her and her baby, she often feels a similar sense of powerlessness, as did a woman who had a perfectly straightforward birth, but with a quick second stage. The baby cried very loudly at delivery – and continued. The doctor commented on the baby's crying, adding that it had been a 'traumatic birth'. The mother told me: 'I thought he wasn't normal. I thought he was brain-damaged and they weren't telling me', and she became depressed.

It is this feeling of powerlessness – of things being kept from you, your baby not needing you because other people can look after her better, of being out of touch with the little creature who you have produced from your body – that contributes to the loss of confidence that many women describe as preceding their baby's inconsolable crying. When a baby starts to cry, it adds to these feelings of helplessness and confirms the mother's sense of inadequacy.

Reaching out by touch

Slow, gentle touch is one way in which you may be able to soothe and give pleasure to your baby. Touching and stroking provides stimulation and can communicate that the world is a good and friendly place. In special-care nurseries very tiny and sick babies often 'forget' to breathe because they are under-stimulated. Nurses go round flicking the soles of their feet with their fingers when the alarm rings, in order to stimulate them to start breathing again. It seems sad that the only way a baby should be aroused to get back into the rhythms of life is by slapping its feet. There are other, more loving ways of giving stimulation.

In the 1950s Eva Reich developed a way of helping sick and low-birthweight babies when she was working in a hospital in Harlem, New York. It grew out of the 'orgone therapy' taught by her father, the psychoanalyst Wilhelm Reich. Using a butterfly stroke from the baby's head down to its tummy, she has also found a method of helping a baby screaming with colic to relax and says that touch can 'reconnect the broken segments of our life energy'. Because tension is always discharged from the centre outwards, movements should be made from the middle of the body flowing out towards the periphery.

Research involving stroking, cuddling and rocking of low-birthweight babies was started in the 1960s and showed that increased touch had a positive effect. These studies demonstrated that babies who are touched more cry less, gain weight faster, have better motor development and show more advanced behaviour.[9]

A massage, rocking and cuddling method called the Infant

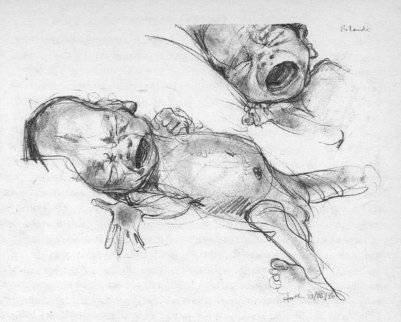

Sensory-Motor Stimulation Technique or, more simply, Loving Touch was developed by Ruth Rice.[10] She suggests lying the baby on her back and stroking from the crown of the head down and over the side of the head to the ear, and from the eyebrows out to the ears. Then circle the eyes and stroke down either side of the nose and out over the cheeks. This is followed by stroking down the chin and neck. Circling one arm at a time, stroke down the arm and over the hand, and then down either side of the chest and tummy. Encircle the upper leg and stroke down it and along the foot, and repeat the movement on the other leg.

With the baby on her front, stroke from the forehead back over the top of the head, then down either side of the spine from the top to bottom. With fingertip touch, make tiny circling movements down the little valley at either side of the spine. Then tuck the baby up firmly and rock and sing to her. A tiny baby may be over-stimulated and distressed by vigorous massage, but Elvedina Adamson-Macedo, a Brazilian developmental psychologist who researches the effects of stroking on pre-term babies, has developed a kind of touching she calls TIC TAC – short for 'touching and caressing, tender and caring' – which can be done while a baby is still in an incubator. It is different from massage in that it doesn't entail rubbing or any pressure on muscles. Instead, it stimulates nerve endings in the skin through very light stroking, sometimes involving only the fingertips.

Kangaroo babies

A very tiny baby is often more contented if nestled against your body day and night. At the San Juan de Dios hospital in Bogota, Colombia, the special-care baby unit is always overcrowded. It is full to overflowing with very-low-birthweight babies, many of whom have a poor chance of survival, and there is a great deal of cross-infection. Or that is how it was until some years ago. In 1979 a home care programme was started, and once babies are out of danger, they are now looked after at home, bound between their mother's breasts like baby kangaroos in a pouch.[11] It has been discovered that one-third of the babies admitted to the special-care unit can be sent home in this way, so freeing resources for better care of other babies who are too frail to be included in the programme. Before this form of care was introduced all babies weighing less than 2 lb 3 oz (1000 g) died. In the two-year period after the programme was set up some babies still died at or immediately after birth, but of those who lived, 72 per cent weighing between 1 lb 1½ oz and 2 lb 3 oz (501 and 1000 g) survived. Whereas previously the survival rate of babies weighing 2 lb 3 oz to 3 lb 5 oz (1001 to 1500 g) was only 27 per cent, now 89 per cent survived.

Something else happened, too. Parents living in dire poverty sometimes abandon their sick and low-birthweight babies because they feel they cannot possibly rear them and there is no hope. Before 'kangaroo care' began, thirty-four babies were abandoned in a two-year period; since then, only ten babies have been abandoned in the same length of time.

Conditions are very different in hospitals in more advanced and richer countries. Many more very-low-birthweight babies survive because of highly sophisticated intensive care facilities. But research is taking place at the Hammersmith Hospital, London, to discover whether there may not be other advantages in kangaroo care, especially to see if and how it affects the relationship between the mother and her baby.

It can be difficult to fall in love with a scrawny-looking, pathetic baby who ignores you or gets upset when you try to make contact. Having her baby literally in touch with her and nestled against her body not only helps a mother feel that her baby really belongs to her, and not to the hospital, but also makes it easier for her to get to know and understand her baby. This may herald a revolution in the care of very tiny babies that is no less important than the introduction of sophisticated technology.

If you want to try a kangaroo experiment with your own baby you will need loose clothing that opens at the front. Wear a baby carrier next to your skin under your clothes and pop the baby, naked except for a nappy (diaper), into it so that she is tucked in between your breasts. You can either not wear a bra at all if that is comfortable, or wear a nursing bra leaving the flaps open so that the baby can easily reach the nipple. Since you may leak some milk, cotton shirts are probably the most practical wear, since they can be washed and dried quickly.

Your baby is kept warm from your own body heat. The space between your breasts is especially warm. When you are breast-feeding, as you become aware that your baby is stirring and ready to feed, your breasts will become hotter still. In cold weather you will want to dress more warmly and your baby can wear a little cap, too. Because the baby's head is the largest organ in its body, most heat loss occurs from there. Premature babies need to be kept cosily warm at all times. If they get cold, they lose the energy they need for feeding.

Whatever has happened while you were in hospital, however much experts took over, having your baby nestled close against you like this enables you to feel that you are in control and that you and your baby have started out together in intimate, tender partnership. You won't have to wait for your baby to cry to know when she wants to be suckled, talked or sung to, to have her bottom gently patted with a steady beat or her back rubbed. Instead, you will be aware from tiny movements the baby makes that she is wanting reassurance and security. The baby will luxuriate in this intimacy, a loving continuation of life inside the uterus, and will enjoy being

quite naturally rocked by your body as you move around and change position, comforted by your smell, your warmth and your voice.

While you nurture your baby in this way you may discover that, mysteriously, your baby is also nurturing *you*.

CHAPTER 12

Bored and Lonely

The nurse must not allow the infant to get into bad habits –
for example, water tippling, peppermint
tippling, sucking on a nipple or the finger, water and whisky
tippling, sleeping with its mother or other
person, being taken up when it cries, held, rocked or
carried, etc.
By proper training the child may be taught to sleep
nearly the whole night through, to sleep between nursings,
and to cry only when hungry,
uncomfortable or sick.
Joseph D. DeLee, *Obstetrics for Nurses*, 1904

Imagine being stuck, helpless, inside a plastic box, unable to move much, to get food or a drink when you are hungry or thirsty, or do anything for yourself, and being expected to lie there, in solitary confinement, staring at the ceiling. The only thing you can do to change what happens round you is to make a very loud noise. *Then* there is some action!

Babies cry when they are lonely and bored. They like to know there are people around, exciting things happening – changing images, sounds and movements. As their nervous systems mature and they are capable of greater coordination – controlling the movement of the head, for example – they want a richer and more varied scene. They do not like being tucked up and put to bed while life is going on elsewhere.

Yet by the time the baby is about 1 month old many women are struggling desperately to 'get back to normal', develop a routine, plan some sort of timetable for the baby because they have to return to work outside the home or, even if they are home-based, to cook proper meals at last and get the housework done. They also often feel under pressure to show everyone that they can cope and, as we have seen in Chapter 7, may be under considerable pressure from a male partner to give time to attending to *his* needs rather than the baby's.

It is often at the same time that the baby starts crying constantly to be picked up. Many of us have been taught that babies should be controlled and not allowed to 'dictate to' or 'dominate' the family. It is part of the tradition of Nanny. Like any well-tended garden, order must prevail, and to 'give in' to a baby suggests that wildness and nature are taking over. Even if you do not feel the need 'to show the baby who is master', most books and magazine articles for parents stress that you should be consistent. Yet any mother of a crying baby knows that the first thing to go out of the window is consistency; for babies have not read these particular rule books. When they cry because they long for stimulus, loving arms to hold them, to feel secure and wanted, and to know they are part of our human community, they do not know our fear of losing control, our longing for order, our self-doubt and lack of confidence, our guilt about being inadequate mothers, our terror of chaos.

In the small contemporary family, when the only person at home all day tends to be the mother, the baby can get stimulus only from her. Many of the women who talked to me about their crying babies spend long hours alone with the baby, except, perhaps, at weekends. Forty per cent of those whose babies cry most had spent between eight and twelve hours completely alone the day before they answered my questionnaire, compared with 27 per cent of those whose babies do not cry much. When a woman is isolated she either notices the baby's crying more, or her baby actually does cry longer. Without being able to record the babies' actual crying time it is difficult to be sure of the amount of crying. But the important thing is how the mother *feels* about it, and it came over very clearly that mothers feel much more anxious and distressed about their babies crying when they are socially isolated.

Aidan MacFarlane, a community pediatrician, told me: 'Babies treated as if they were in cottonwool and put down in silent rooms, tend to cry more than those who experience the general hubbub of life and are included in all the socializing right from the word go. Yet, of course, when a woman is alone at home for many hours at a time, there is no hubbub of this kind. Or if it does exist, it takes place merely on the TV screen. There may be no other children to watch as they play; the father leaves in the morning and comes back in the evening, often expecting peace and quiet after a gruelling day. He does not usually bring craft work home, which could be interesting for the baby to watch, and if he does have to work, it tends to be paperwork or at a flickering computer screen, which demands concentration and silence.

Moreover, a woman who is at home alone all day, bearing total responsibility for a baby and cut off from other human contact, is – as we have seen already in Chapter 6 – vulnerable to depression. Sometimes one of the reasons she is alone is that she cannot work up the energy to go out to meet people because she is already depressed. Social isolation further feeds her depression.

A depressed mother may be unable to offer her baby adequate stimulation. Her face feels frozen or set in a mask. She moves slowly. Her voice is flat. There are times when she cannot respond to her baby at all, and the child soon learns that there is no point seeking her attention by meeting her eyes, turning towards her or making little noises that get her into conversation. The baby of a depressed mother may either give up and become passive, or discover that the only way to get her attention is to cry loudly. The crying makes the mother still more deeply depressed, and she feels even less able to escape from her solitary confinement and seek help. She may feel sucked into a vortex of despair.

Meanwhile a male partner often feels helpless to do anything about it. One reaction is to try to maintain a semblance of normality by cutting himself off from her. Already burdened by the responsibility of this new baby, he worries that his work is suffering because of the crying, even that he may lose his job. One woman, for example, told me how, 'absolutely exhausted' with her baby's crying, she and her husband both felt 'detached' from each other. She says he was concerned only about his work, while she concentrated on the baby and the 2-year-old, who was 'constantly whining and crying for some of the attention the baby's crying achieved'. She described how she and her husband felt 'completely cut off from each other' and as long as this continued, the baby went on crying. When this kind of thing happens, the only way to get a happier baby may be for the couple to get in touch with each other again, for the baby needs stimulation and a sense of security from belonging that comes from active relationships between human beings. And the baby is crying out – often literally crying out – to be welcomed into a relationship that is a going concern and not to be treated merely as an object of care.

Some women told me: 'My baby is only crying for attention' – and even added: 'So I ignore him.' One older mother told me: 'With both my children I found it was just attention they wanted, so I left them alone.' And another with a new-born baby, who was determined to take a tough line, advised: 'If a baby cries a lot, leave him to it. As long as it's been fed and changed and nothing appears to be wrong with it – then leave it in its cot [crib] and let it cry it out. They soon get the message to be quiet and that they are not going to get attention.'

The attention-seeking baby is a stimulus-seeking child, who is eager to learn. This stimulus can be very simple and does not entail expensive playthings or crib computers (one method by which parents in North America are urged by some electronic firms to produce brighter babies). Try branches waving in the breeze or washing on the line, Christmas tree ornaments attached to a clothes hanger, a mirror suspended over the crib, brightly painted cotton reels (thread spools) threaded on a cord, a beach-ball hanging from elastic or balloons to push and pat with hands and feet, tissue paper or newspapers to rustle, different textures to explore – sandpaper, wood, velvet, satin – or blow soap bubbles for your baby.

The attention-seeking baby is also a relationship-seeking child, who needs to be assured of being part of the rhythms of human community. An important way in which parents can reduce crying is to acknowledge a child's need to share in the excitement that comes from social interaction. When this happens, not only do we discover a more contented baby, but we are building a basis for all the communication skills that the child will develop later in life.

Communication is dependent on synchronization, and it is this that the baby learns in these early encounters – making eye contact and then, when the time is right, looking away to 'punctuate' the conversation, giving attention, being expressive, responding, eliciting response in the other person, mimicking and engaging in the whole give-and-take of social relationships.

Interactive play is one way in which adults enjoy relating to babies: games like pat-a-cake, peep-bo (peek-a-boo), 'I give you the rattle and then you give it to me', and 'round and round the garden' – walking fingers round the palm of the baby's hand and finishing with a tickle. These repetitive games are far less simple than they look. They involve amazingly complex social skills: participants sharing the same signal codes, understanding each other's vocabulary and non-verbal language by which such messages as 'it's fun – go on' and 'not yet – I haven't finished' are communicated. And on top of all this they have to synchronize what they are doing and integrate it in a harmonious flow.[1] This 'interpersonal synchrony' begins at birth with the interchange of gaze and the relation between this and sucking, swallowing and breathing. The mother and baby form, at least potentially, 'a dyadic unit'.

Babies only 3 days old can already imitate the expressions on their mothers' faces. In a study of babies' ability to mimic adults' expressions babies born a few days previously were held in a face-to-face position by someone who adopted a happy, sad or surprised-looking expression and who kept this up until the baby looked away. Then the adult did a couple of deep knee-bends and tongue clicks and made another face, until the baby looked away again. Meanwhile an observer who could see only the baby's face would guess, on the basis of the baby's expression, which expression the adult was modelling. It was not difficult to do this and guesses were correct for sad expression in 59 per cent of cases, a happy one in 58 per cent, and surprise, 76 per cent of the time.[2] (When you think of all the antics the adults were getting up to, it is understandable that the babies found no difficulty in looking surprised.)

Games-playing is a spontaneous outcome of the satisfying give-and-take between mother and baby. You do not have to think of games as educational experiences or be at all deliberate about them. Your baby's reaction indicates to you when the time is right for introducing play of this kind and also the times when the baby has had enough of them and does not want further stimulation. Some of this dramatic interplay you may immediately acknowledge as a game – when you bend your face close to the baby and say: 'I'm going to get you, I'm going to get you', and the baby smiles or laughs. Other kinds you may see more in terms of 'conversations', as when you say to the baby, 'Tell me all about it then' or 'you tell me a story', and the baby starts to coo and murmur while you listen and nod. Then you respond with words which interpret the rudimentary sounds that the baby is making, and may introduce an emotional component, interpreting what the baby is *feeling* about it all: 'And that was a very nice feed, wasn't it? You were saying your tummy is full up now', or 'You didn't like being left all alone. You wanted your mummy and now you're happy because I've come.' It may sound nonsense to other people, but it definitely is not nonsense to the baby, and as you communicate and synchronize with each other it is like joining in the intricate steps of a dance in which you both know the pattern, provide each other with cues and respond in a mutually satisfying way. And you don't need a degree in child psychology to do it! The chart on the following pages is a useful guide to what your baby can do and the things she finds stimulating at different ages.

WHAT YOUR BABY CAN DO AT DIFFERENT AGES

Babies develop at their own pace. Sometimes there seems no progress at all for a while. At other times there is a rush of achievement and they seem to be growing up very fast. When you do not see obvious progress, it does not mean that nothing is happening. Development is taking place, connections are being made, and the achievement will follow in its own time.

Being sensitive to your baby's needs entails careful observation so that you adapt yourself and the baby's environment to the phase of development she has reached, and she can grow in self-confidence. The ages given below are approximate ones and if your child reaches these 'milestones' earlier or later than the average, it is unlikely to mean that she is either intellectually brilliant or retarded; it is simply an expression of her personal pattern of growth.

AROUND 1 WEEK

The baby can use her neck muscles to hold up her head for several seconds at a time. Occasionally you may notice a beatific Buddha-like smile when she is in a state of inner contentment.

AROUND 4 WEEKS

She begins to experiment with a repertoire of different sounds. She starts to reach out with her eyes for the source of your voice and one day soon you will be rewarded with her first social smile when you are talking to her.

AROUND 5 WEEKS

She may discover her thumb or fingers to suck and starts to be able to soothe herself in this way.

AROUND 6 WEEKS

The baby recognizes and smiles at you even if you are not talking to her. When you smile and talk at the same time, she smiles back and kicks and gurgles with delight. She may open her hand, grasp one hand with the other, and play with the fingers by touch. She may enjoy holding a rattle, fascinated to discover that it makes a noise.

AROUND 8 WEEKS

When a rattle or ring is placed in her hands, she grasps it and waves it around. She may follow the sound with her eyes, turning her head from side to side and up and down. She can also focus on and follow an object placed 20 centimetres (8 inches) in front of her face. This is an important phase for learning the connection between what she can see,

171

hear and touch. She distinguishes between smiling and talking, smiling when you smile at her, and making noises back when you talk to her. When lying down she starts to uncurl from the fetal position. She likes to be propped up in a baby chair and will lift both head and shoulders in order to sit up more. She enjoys being naked and touching her body and getting to know it.

AROUND 9 WEEKS

If you put her down on her side, she may roll over on her back, and so start to select her own sleeping positions.

AROUND 10 WEEKS

The baby plays with her hands, watching them with fascination. She not only stares at an object placed so she can see it, but also may try to hit it. She often misses. She stares at her hand and at the object, and then has another go. A soft ball or toy that makes a noise when hit, suspended about 25 centimetres (10 inches) from her face, is a good plaything. She is learning that she has power to make things happen.

AROUND 3 MONTHS

The baby has uncurled from the fetal position. You will notice more control of head movement. When lying on her tummy, she can hold her head up for a long time and prop herself on her forearms so that she can see more. On her back, she can lift her head right up. By now she can roll from her back to her side. If held in an upright position or sat in a chair, she will gaze fascinated at any activity there is to watch. She likes to lie on her back and kick, wave her hands about and watch them, bringing them near her face for a closer look. She likes being pulled up into a sitting position, and will start to do it herself if you simply hold her hands, keeping her head in line with her body as she does so. She enjoys looking at and listening to people. She selects favourite people and smiles and coos more at them than those she does not know so well. She puts her hands, fingers and thumbs in her mouth, looks at them and then tries a different combination of fingers, thumbs and fist instead. Everything goes into her mouth to be explored, chewed and sucked. She pokes and picks up playthings and is getting better at assessing the distance between her hand and an object for which she is reaching, but needs time to work this out. Don't do everything for her. Let her explore and discover for herself. To develop eye coordination she needs fixed objects of different shapes, sizes and colours that she can touch. They should not bounce away when her hand meets them, as she wants to find out more about them. She gets bored if the objects around her are not changed. If she knows you are going to pick her up, she lifts her head in readiness. She can sit up for a while if she uses her hands for support. When lying on her front she can stretch out her arms and lift her head and shoulders and can roll over. She alternately lifts her head and shoulders and her bottom, humping up and down like the Loch Ness monster, and may creep with her tummy on the floor. She enjoys being in a supported standing position and using her leg muscles to bounce. Most sounds she makes are vowels, for example: 'aaah' and 'oooh'.

AROUND 4 MONTHS

The baby can pull her knees up and push with her feet, and can raise her shoulders to push with her hands, using muscles she will later need for crawling. She demonstrates that she is especially attached to you, poking, prodding, stroking and playing with your face, body and clothing, but is more restrained with strangers. She can focus over a wide visual range and can also grab things, shaping her hands to hold them easily. She holds large objects between both arms. She is a busy conversationalist. When you pause in talking to her, she babbles in answer. When alone, she talks to herself a lot.

AROUND 5 MONTHS

The muscles in her back are stronger and she can sit comfortably, provided she has support at the base of her spine.

AROUND 6 MONTHS

She gets excited if she hears the voice of someone she knows well who is outside the room. She may start to be suspicious of strangers. She laughs and chuckles a lot. She starts using her hands to explore different textures.

AROUND 7 MONTHS

The baby uses fingers and thumbs, not only her whole hand, for grasping and holding. She changes one syllable sounds into two syllable 'words' by repetition – for example, 'mama', 'baba' – and may use the same 'word' for different things and people, and different sound combinations for the same thing or person.

AROUND 8 MONTHS

The baby sits for lengthy periods without support and can lean over to pick up playthings. She can get up on all-fours and make all sorts of rolling, pushing and turning movements. She may start to crawl, lifting her tummy off the ground, or may prefer a bottom-shuffle. The great adventure has begun! This is the time for separation anxiety and many babies get 'clingy' if there is only one care-giver. Your baby may want to have you within sight every second of the day. She uses elbows and wrists, not only her whole lower arm, to gesticulate, and can wave 'bye-bye'. Exclamatory two syllable 'words' are added to her repertoire, and she will imitate words and actions.

—————————— AROUND 9 MONTHS ——————————

The baby pulls herself up using furniture for support. She can crawl or bottom-shuffle everywhere. She may at first be better at crawling backwards than forwards, and get cross as a desired plaything recedes farther and farther away. She can use her index finger to point and poke. She enjoys pulling a string to which a wheeled plaything is attached. She turns her head towards people as they talk to each other, 'joins in' conversations, and may shout for attention. 'Words' sometimes acquire three syllables – for example, 'choo choo choo' – and there are varied inflections so that her voice sounds questioning or demanding, as if she is speaking an exotic language you do not understand.

—————————— AROUND 10 MONTHS ——————————

The baby can take her whole weight when held in a standing position, but cannot yet balance. She can uncurl fingers to release an object at will, and enjoys practising dropping playthings, food and everything else. She may say her first real word, identifying an object or person, such as 'man', 'ball', 'shoe'.

—————————— AROUND 11 MONTHS ——————————

She pulls herself up to a standing position, and may get stuck standing.

—————————— AROUND 1 YEAR ——————————

The baby 'cruises' now, shuffling along holding onto furniture and anything that gives firm support. She starts to stand alone, and may take a few steps by herself. She can pick up tiny objects, such as crumbs or peas. She enjoys throwing things and filling and emptying boxes, saucepans and plastic containers. This is the time for a sturdy cart or baby walker with a low centre of gravity, which she can also load and unload with toys.

For a more detailed description of the behaviour and development of babies, see Penelope Leach's *Baby and Child*,[3] a superb book on baby care, and one that I have used in compiling this chart.

————————————————————————————————————

Under-stimulation is not always the result of depression or not knowing *how* to stimulate a baby. It can also come from deprived social conditions – the kind of poverty, for example, that means that the baby is dumped somewhere out of sight and earshot because otherwise there will be no food or money coming in.

In an isolated and impoverished mountain area of Guatemala people believe it is dangerous to bring babies outside the hut, so when their mothers have to go to market, they may be left alone in semi-darkness.[4] Even when adults are present they expect babies to be passive, and rarely speak to or play with them. These babies do not cry much because no one responds to their crying. By the time they are about 1 year old many of them are so passive that they are classified as mentally retarded. But when they can walk, they suddenly wake up to what life is all about and become active and inquiring. They then develop quickly and become adventurous, outgoing and bright children.

Research with babies who have some kind of facial disfigurement (hare lip, for example) shows that these babies, especially, may be deprived of stimulation.[5] Tiffany Field studied interaction between some of these babies and their mothers and found that though the mothers look at them as often, their faces are not as lively as those of other mothers, and there is reduced eye contact and less smiling, vocalization, imitation and reactivity between mother and baby. Dr Field is continuing this research, monitoring what happens after these babies have had corrective surgery. It may be especially important if a baby is disfigured to develop the kind of games and conversations that encourage social participation and responsiveness.

One of the earliest neurological systems to develop in the fetus is the vestibular system – concerned with balance and equilibrium. While still in the uterus the baby receives messages from the mother's movements as it is rocked in the bony cradle of her pelvis. Perhaps this is why babies can often be soothed by being rocked, and especially by a forward and backward, as compared with a side-to-side, rocking movement. In fact, the degree of rock most likely to be effective in comforting a baby corresponds to that produced by the mother's pelvis when she walks vigorously or dances. When movement exceeds 60 rocks a minute or a swing of $2\frac{3}{4}$ inches (7 cm) the baby may be disturbed rather than comforted, and less than this is not effective in soothing the baby.[6]

One of the best ways of giving a baby stimulation, together with the security that comes from closeness, is to use a baby carrier –

not only for walks and shopping trips, but every day around the house, and more or less whatever you are doing. The baby is bounced and rocked as you move, is in contact with the warmth and comfort of your body, sees people interacting with each other – talking, laughing, with their faces creasing, eyes shining, mouths changing shape, their cheeks plumping up and the angles of heads altering – and becomes aware of expressions and ways in which people relate to each other, so that he is in touch with the interplay of other people's emotions and the give-and-take of social life, and is part of our human community.

A trial of soft baby carriers was carried out in New York among low-income women attending a clinic, who were randomly assigned immediately after birth to three groups: one was given soft baby slings, one given nothing and another given plastic baby seats.[7] When the babies were 13 months old, the quality of attachment between mothers and babies was assessed blindly (that is, the researchers did not know which groups the mother had been in). By accident there were equal numbers of breast- and bottle-fed babies in each group, and the women who breast-fed did so for about the same length of time, so whether or not they were feeding their babies themselves could not have influenced the outcome. The results were conclusive: babies who were in soft carriers seemed to be more emotionally secure than those in the other two groups, and they fussed and cried less. This was true for babies of both sexes and those of different ethnic groups, whether or not it was a first baby, and whether or not the mother had social support. Eighty-three per cent of the babies who had 'contact comfort' from being carried around in a soft sling were assessed as feeling secure, but only 38 per cent of those who were in plastic seats.

A baby enjoys vestibular stimulation best and can probably make most use of it to learn about the world around her from the comfort and security of your body. Just to sit the baby where she can see what is going on is not enough. It is fun to watch people washing dishes, cooking and cleaning, banging nails into wood and digging the garden, but the child soon gets restless and may feel insecure. A baby needs human physical contact, and without that, stimulation may turn out to be irritating. Once soothed and in comfortable contact with the mother, she can be attentive and explore the surroundings and learn. Anneliese Korner demonstrated this first in the 1960s, showing that a crying baby who is picked up and held over the mother's shoulder is much more likely to stop crying than when simply propped up in a sitting position or left in the crib. A baby who is held over your shoulder tends not only to stop crying, but also to open his eyes and look about.[8] The comfort does not come only from being in close contact with you, but from your movement, and this is probably the most important element in it.[9]

Paradoxically, stimulation can be soothing. When calming external stimuli are provided, the baby, instead of being bombarded by internal stimuli, is free to turn attention to the outside world. Rudolph Schaffer expresses this succinctly when he says:

> Much of early mothering ... is a matter of modulating the baby's state, warding off stimulation as well as providing it, protecting against excessive doses as well as supplying extra stimuli. The interaction of mother and baby is often treated as a purely emotional affair, yet it appears that certain quite specific aspects also have cognitive – intellectual – implications, in that they enable the baby to attain a level of attentiveness at which he can begin to explore his surroundings and perceptually (later on also manipulatively) familiarize himself with the environment ... When caretakers do not have the time or sensitivity to help a baby to reach a state in which he can maximally profit from encounter with his world, even the richest environment will fail to 'get through'. In the end it is the personal attention involved in picking up rather than a great range of impersonal toys that speeds developmental progress.[10]

When you are choosing a baby carrier, make sure you get one that grows with the baby, that supports a sleeping baby's head and neck, is made of durable, washable fabric, has firm shoulder pads so that you are comfortable, and is easy to put on and take off. Questions to bear in mind are: Will I want to breast-feed the baby while she is in the carrier? Do I want the option of carrying the baby facing forward as well as snuggling into me? Would it be useful to have interliners that can be taken out and washed separately? If I am likely to be in a hot climate, is the fabric cool for the baby? Can the carrier be easily adjusted so that my partner can use it too?

Baby carriers can sometimes be obtained in kit form, and fabric is either included or you provide your own material. The advantage is that you can then add your personal touches. Or you can use a Mexican rebozo, a wide strip of cloth, Welsh shawl or any of the fabric carriers used by mothers in the Far East if you know someone who can show you the technique of folding the cloth and putting it on.

Some kinds of stimulation are so soothing that they actually enable the baby to drop to sleep. They, too, are part of an interactive pattern between mother and baby. Massage and touch, for example, can be arousing or comforting depending on how it is done. Sound – spoken words or music – can also lull a baby to sleep or signal alert attention. Movement, too, depending on the speed and rhythm, and whether the baby is being rocked or bounced, can soothe or excite. Mothers have a whole repertoire of skills like these and often use them without conscious thought. But they are not 'natural' or 'instinctive'. We learn them from our own mothers and by watching other people with babies, and they are part of our cultural heritage. When a woman has never been able to absorb these rhythmic actions, she is faced with the task of learning them for the first time, or inventing them for herself, when she has a baby.

The overtired baby, whose eyelids are flickering shut but who still refuses to go to sleep, the 'jumpy' baby who is crying irritably, unable to 'let go' and relax, is often helped by touch, sound and movement that offer not only stimulation but also calm and comfort.

Touch and massage

A baby's skin is especially sensitive not only because it quickly becomes chafed and sore when wet with urine, or dirty, or when overexposed to the sun, but also in terms of *feeling* and the messages that are received through touch. In many ways the baby learns through contact. This protective envelope of skin has multiple functions: differentiation between the internal and external worlds, the setting of a firm boundary for body image, linking the different parts of the body into one person, and a transmitter for communication. The skin envelope gives us identity as individuals and also is our point of contact with other human beings.[11]

By making skin contact in many different ways – holding firmly or lightly, stroking, rubbing, bouncing and so on – a mother conveys unspoken messages to her baby, who in turn reacts with changes in muscle tone, galvanic skin response, breathing, movement of the head, gestures, gaze, vocalization and sucking. It is an intensely

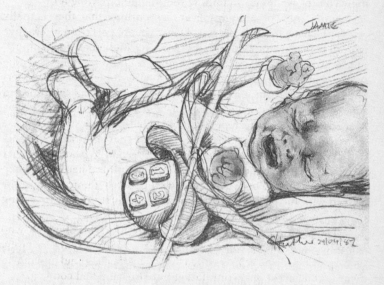

physical language of communication. Because this cannot be learned from books, only from your baby, it has often been overlooked.

Just as mothers can identify their own babies' crying among a host of others, in the same way a baby knows her mother's voice distinct from all others, and responds to it rhythmically, punctuating speech sounds with movements of lips, head, arms, legs and the whole body.[12]

Lullabies are an ancient way in which babies are comforted by rhythmic sounds. When singing, the parent often rocks or pats the child at the same time, thus providing vibration and vestibular stimulation in addition to the pleasure that comes from sound. You do not have to be musical or have a good singing voice to be able to comfort a baby with your own made-up lullabies or any songs that fit in with the mood of the moment. 'The importance of singing is not in the musicianship but in the communication.'[13]

Fragmented experience

There is something else – closely related to boredom and loneliness – that may make a baby distressed: it is difficult to describe, but we might call it 'unfinished business' or 'fragmented experience'. When you rush a baby, trying to complete a feed, for example, so as to switch attention to another task, you can be almost certain that the baby will become restless and cry just when you need to be free to do other things. Every mother knows what happens when she cannot help feeling impatient because she planned to go out in the evening or is having people round for a meal and wants to settle the baby first. This is the time when the baby, sensing her urgency or, perhaps, the way in which her thoughts are detached, seeks attention and refuses to be put down.

This occurs because a satisfying pattern of reciprocity has been disrupted and a harmonious sequence of activity cut short. It is as if the baby is left 'at a loose end'. In hurrying the way she handles the baby the mother has omitted something precious, even though this may be to her an almost inperceptible omission. It could be a pause that served as counterpoint to action, the eye contact that means so much to a baby or a special kind of lingering touch. Whatever it may be, for the baby it is part of the mutuality with the mother in the complex drama that is played out between them. When forgotten or hastened, it is like omitting a vital part of a game, rhyme or song, or leaving a tune incomplete. Winnicott was referring to this when he said:

> When you are in a hurry, or are harassed, you cannot allow for *total happenings*, and your baby is the poorer . . . Total happenings enable babies to catch hold of time.
>
> By allowing your baby time for total experiences and by taking part in them, you gradually lay a found-

ation for the child's ability to enjoy all sorts of experience without jumpiness.[14]

The example he gives of a *total happening* is of a 10-month-old baby boy sitting on his mother's lap while she is talking to Dr Winnicott. Dr Winnicott places a spoon on the table near the baby, who reaches out for it, then withdraws as if he had better think again whether his mother is happy for him to have it. So he turns away from it, but then turns back to and puts a tentative finger on it. Then he grasps it and looks at his mother to see the message in her eyes. It is clear that she does not disapprove, so he grabs it and 'begins to make it his own'. He is still tense because he is not certain what he wants to do and what will happen with this thing he desires.

There follows a process of discovery. His mouth becomes excited and saliva flows. His mouth wants the spoon and his gums long to bite it. He puts it in his mouth and bites on it 'in the ordinary aggressive way that belongs to lions and tigers, and babies, when they get hold of something good. He makes as if to eat it.'[15]

In place of wonder, doubt, lack of confidence, there is now supreme confidence as he makes the object his own. In his imagination he has devoured and incorporated it into himself. Having done that, he is free to *give* it. He will put it to his mother's mouth, and she will probably play at eating it and say, 'Yum, yum, that's good!' He knows she is not really eating it and that it is a game. The two are sharing in a play of imagination. Then he puts the spoon to the doctor's mouth and wants him to pretend he is eating it, too. If there is anyone else in the room he may want them to join in the game as well.

Then he slips it inside his mother's dress and finds it again, then under something on the desk – and plays the game of losing and rediscovering it, or perhaps he sees a bowl on the table and scoops imaginary food from it.

Simple as all this may seem to anyone watching, it is enormously enriching play that feeds the imagination, forms the stuff of dreams and builds the baby's self-confidence as a person.

Then the baby notices another object and drops the spoon. Someone picks it up and he takes it from them, but now the game is different. He drops it again. The adult retrieves it and hands it to him. He drops it again. This goes on, perhaps for several minutes until he really has finished with the spoon.

What has happened during this sequence is that the baby has become attached to an object, made it part of himself, used it imaginatively, incorporated it into transactions with other people, and then discarded it. There was a complete experience.

That baby was 10 months old. For a much younger baby a total happening is usually focused on feeding, digestion and excretion. The process cannot be rushed. And even as early as 3 months imagination may play a part in the pattern. The baby may stick her finger in her mother's mouth, for example, playing at feeding her while she is sucking at the breast. She may intersperse sucking the breast with sucking her fist or a finger. She may play with the nipple by licking or chewing it – catching the mother's eye to note her reaction – or stroke her breast, hair or the material of her dress.

It is important to allow space for this kind of play and to participate in it. For the baby to have a satisfying experience, there must be no unfinished business, no loose ends in the sequence.

Imagined monsters

The whole process of feeding, digestion and excretion is not only a total happening. It is also a momentous event for a baby. It can be disturbing and frightening. Intense sensations are produced: gnawing hunger, painful emptiness, passionate longing, rage, possession and triumph, and internal physiological states of pressure, fullness, spilling over, stretching, opening, together with intestinal contractions and rectal distension. All this can be an overwhelming experience for the baby, which we often over-simplify by describing it in terms of pain: 'he's got a tummy-ache', 'she's a colicky baby'. In fact, as we saw in Chapter 3, there is no evidence that what is happening in the stomach and gut of a screaming baby is any different from that which occurs in the stomach or gut of a contented, peaceful baby. The physiology is exactly the same. In a few months' time this same baby is likely to behave very differently, yet exactly the same processes of digestion and excretion are taking place inside her.

Though being able to attach the diagnosis of 'colic' to a baby, and thus account for the distress, often makes it easier for parents to cope with the emotions aroused by their baby's distress, this particular diagnosis really explains nothing.

Adults who are on fairly good terms with their bodies enjoy eating, feel comfortable while digestion takes place and have a satisfying feeling of completeness at the end of the process, when emptying the bowels. There are no hold-ups or interruptions in the sequence and everything takes place smoothly and harmoniously. But for a baby who is only a few weeks old the experience is full of surprises and it can be terrifying. He may feel gripped by powerful forces inside himself, which he is unable to control. 'When babies begin to feel hungry something is beginning to come alive in them which is ready to take possession of them.'[16] If you watch a baby who is not yet familiar and contented about all the sensations, you can often see restlessness, surprise, shock, fear and even panic. What I am describing is not so much *pain* as a psychosomatic state that the baby does not yet understand.

If a mother gets anxious and alarmed when her baby starts to wriggle, blink, stiffen and let out little mewing cries, and if she communicates this anxiety to the baby by the way she holds, looks at and speaks to him, this experience becomes even more threatening for the baby. A mother with a crying baby has learned the signals that presage distress and tends to get anxious and to convey this to the baby. It is as if the two are playing an elaborate, and painful, game together. This may be why the baby often quietens down when held in someone else's arms, especially if this person is a more experienced and confident mother who is not herself emotionally involved in the same way.

Taking in milk, digesting and excreting waste matter is, for a baby, an exciting process that has to become a *total happening* – undisturbed, harmonious, accepted by the baby and by those caring for her. It must not be hurried, fragmented or forced. It needs to occur in its own way and its own time, and it is vital that whoever is caring for the baby acknowledges and, as it were, validates what the baby is experiencing without getting tense or worried about it. She can make all these odd sensations *safe*. Then the baby feels that instead of being possessed by hunger and these other intense feelings, and at their mercy, he possesses them, and is in control. It may take as long as twelve weeks – sometimes even longer – for a baby to learn this and develop the inner confidence to handle hunger and the digestive process with *savoir faire*.

The baby who is abandoned to cope with all this alone – expected to lie contented till the next feed – or left to cry because other people and books say that she is just 'trying it on' and should not be picked up, may scream with terror and loneliness.

If you have tried to settle your baby and have resisted picking her up when she cried, you may have discovered that when, at last, you could not stand it any longer and went to pick her up and comfort her, she acted as if she did not know you. She may have arched her back and struggled and screamed. It is as if she was a wild animal. This is the typical situation in which the label of 'colic' gets attached to a baby.

Winnicott tells how the baby's stomach is a muscle-bag that automatically adapts itself to different conditions, unless disturbed by strong emotions such as fear, anxiety or over-excitement. There is always liquid in the stomach and air at the top. As milk goes into the stomach, digestive juices increase, the muscle wall relaxes and the stomach grows larger. It may take a little while for this flow of juices and release of muscles to occur, however. Meanwhile uncomfortable pressure builds up. When the baby burps, some of the air is released, thus reducing pressure, so the baby feels more comfortable. One who is held in an upright position – over your shoulder or sitting on your lap while you rub or pat her back – finds it easy to release this air. If you try to get it up with the baby half-lying down, she is likely to bring back milk as well as air. It is normal for milk to be curdled, for curdling is the first stage in digestion.

If the baby is tense, or the mother herself is tense and communicates this to the baby, the stomach muscle cannot adapt quickly. As increased pressure builds up with the intake of milk, the baby becomes more and more uncomfortable. Something else may happen, too: the milk is pushed through the intestines before it has gone through all the digestive changes that should take place inside the stomach, and it comes out green and watery at the other end.

A baby's intestines are approximately 12 feet (3·66 m) long, and they start to contract as soon as milk is taken into the mouth, so babies often have a bowel motion while feeding. Mothers sometimes say that 'as fast as the milk goes in at one end, it comes out the other' and believe the milk can't possibly be doing the baby any good. But this is all part of the intricately co-ordinated physiological process. The mother who knows that the baby is likely to dirty her nappy (diaper) while feeding has everything handy so that she does not need to disrupt the feed by leaping up to clean the baby.

The breast-fed baby's motion is often quite liquid and bright mustard yellow. Only with the introduction of other foods or modified cow's milk does it get harder. When the baby gets the sensation of a full rectum – especially if the motion is solid – it produces intense feelings, and the baby may cry out.

The mother who is sensitive to what the baby is experiencing, yet confident that all this is part of a natural process, and who is not herself bewildered or disturbed by it, gives security and communicates strength as the baby confronts these strong feelings. If she goes away and leaves the baby to cope alone, tries to rush her through the process or ignores these momentous happenings, the baby is left isolated and afraid. If she herself becomes agitated, still more frightening feelings are stirred up in the baby, and they become more difficult to endure because the muscles of the stomach and intestines contract with fear and anxiety and the whole process becomes painful.

One of the most important tasks in caring for a baby is simply to be there, helping to contain experience, and giving your strength and confidence to guard against monsters.

CHAPTER 13

Living with a Crying Baby

We went through fire and water almost in trying to procure for him a natural sleep. We swung him in blankets, wheeled him in little carts, walked the room with him by the hour, et cetera, et cetera, but it was wonderful how little sleep he obtained after all. He always looked wide awake and as if he did not need sleep.
G. L. Prentiss, *The Life and Letters of Elizabeth Prentiss*, 1822.

Anyone who lives with a wide awake baby, even one who does not cry inconsolably, needs to develop survival strategies. It is all very well being told by other people what you can and can't do, but, as we have seen in Chapter 8, advice is often irrelevant and sometimes disastrous.

I asked women what they had worked out as positive ways of coping with crying. Some of these tactics may be equally effective for you. They will suggest creative strategies for handling situations of overwhelming stress and for releasing tension – both yours and the baby's. Others will not meet your or your baby's needs. There are things you can do for the baby, things you can do for yourself and others that you can share. In practice, each of these categories overlaps: anything that you do to give yourself a bit of personal space helps the baby become more contented, and ways you discover of helping the baby settle make *you* feel better.

Shared sleeping

Many babies long for physical closeness and to be nestled against their mother's bodies. If your baby cries at night or is restless right through the evening, it will probably help to take him to bed with you. Sleeping alone in separate beds – for adults as well as children –

186

is a recent historical innovation. Traditionally, most families have lived in close proximity and it has been taken for granted that the baby at the breast sleeps alongside or in the same bed with his mother. In many countries of the world today poverty and over-crowded living conditions make any other arrangement unthinkable. When I worked in Jamaica, exploring what it was like to give birth and to be a mother in homes out in the bush and in slums in Kingston, I became used to seeing children tucked up in bed beside their mothers, the baby nearest and older children on the outside, at the foot of the bed and even lying under it. For hundreds of years it was much the same in Europe, except that when babies were nur-tured by a wet-nurse, the woman in whose bed the baby lay was not his biological mother.

Preachers and doctors in medieval Europe (all of them men) wrote books about how children should be brought up and the right conduct of family life, and repeatedly told mothers they should not sleep in the same bed as their breast-fed babies lest they overlay and smother them. 'But, since the poor could not afford even a separate cradle and bedding for the child,' a woman historian observes, 'it remained more common to share the bed of [wet] nurse or mother at least until it was weaned.' [1]

In eighteenth-century colonial America it was a general custom for nursing mothers to have their babies in bed with them. Writing in 1779, during the American War of Independence, to her husband who was a prisoner of the British, Rebecca Silliman talked about her sons, Sellek, who was 2 years old, and Benjamin, who was 4 months. She said the baby was 'a fine little fat fellow, as good as possible at night, and so in the daytime too, if properly attended to. His little brother is very fond of him: they both sleep with me, and both awake before sunrise, when I get up and leave them to play together.' [2] Lucy Lovell, writing sixty years later, described how she managed to persuade her little daughter, Laura, to sleep separately from her for the first time at the age of 18 months: 'In the course of the summer I got Laura so that she would go to sleep in her little crib. Sometimes I had some difficulty with her, but generally when she saw that I was decided, she would go quietly to sleep.' [3]

The switch to separate beds and rooms during the industrial revolution of the nineteenth century came about as a result of increased economic prosperity and a sudden change for much of the population from a subsistence and cottage-based economy to wage-earning and work away from home in factories. Simultaneously with this, the germ theory of disease was developed. In 1893 an advertisement for twin beds in *Scrivener's* magazine announced: 'Our English cousins are now sleeping in separate beds. The reason is: NEVER BREATHE THE BREATH OF ANOTHER.'[4] New psychological theories of child-rearing emerged, too. In wealthy and middle-class houses children were banished to the nursery and 'scientific' methods of child care expounded, which entailed strict regulation of the child's life, with no unnecessary cuddles or indulgence.

Then in the 1920s J. B. Watson invented behaviourist psychology, which taught that child-rearing was all a matter of good habits and systematic conditioning to independence. Dr Watson wrote about 'the dangers of too much mother love'; told women that if they stopped rocking their babies to sleep, they would have 'more time for household duties, gossiping, bridge and shopping'; warned them against 'mawkish sentimentality'; and advocated that babies should never be hugged or kissed. Ideally, they should have a different nurse every week. He added: 'I can't help wishing that it was possible to rotate the mothers, too.'[5] In Australia Dr Truby King, in the same vein, taught that babies should have strict timetables and that if a feed was not due, a baby should never be picked up, lest it learn that crying resulted in more attention. There was a whole generation of mothers who were frightened of indulging and spoiling their children, and who felt guilty about enjoying close physical contact unless it was justified as a consequence of manipulations entailed in feeding, bathing or nappy (diaper) -changing.

Though new psychological theories that focus on interaction and stimulation between mother and baby have taken the place of behaviourism, these principles of child-rearing die hard. It is clear from the way in which women describe their struggles to comfort crying babies that taking them into bed with them is often a solution discovered only after weeks – sometimes months – of trying one thing after another.

Sometimes the solution is suggested by someone else. When her baby was about 3 months old, Rebecca says that one night when she got angry because he cried inconsolably, 'I picked him up roughly, accidentally scratching his face. I got that upset and frustrated that eventually my mother-in-law (whom we lived with) took him into her bed, where he settled. If she hadn't, I don't know what I would have done.'

When at last a woman takes the baby into bed, so that instead of having to get up and attend to him at night, she can just cuddle up and let the baby suckle at will while they are both half asleep, she often wonders why she did not do this earlier.[6] Julie suffered from post-natal depression and told me she was seriously considering suicide, 'taking the baby with me. I was feeling emotionally dead, and desperate from lack of sleep and the baby's constant crying. The National Childbirth Trust advised me to take the baby in to my bed. I have found it very helpful in soothing and comforting her and relaxing me. Unrestricted feeding and as much body contact as possible were the solution.'

There is often a dramatic improvement once the baby can sleep close to her mother. 'I couldn't tell you how many feeds he had, or for how long. But I had a good night's sleep for the first night since he was born,' a mother of a 3-week-old baby said. 'I thought of doing it before but was worried about getting him into bad habits. But the bad habit is the crying and the general disturbance, and I reckon if I give him what he needs now so that there aren't these terrible crying sessions at night, he'll gradually grow out of needing feeding so often. After all, other babies do.'

Sometimes women are anxious that taking the baby into bed will interfere with a male partner's sleep, so it is not fair on him. One woman who resisted the idea for a long time told me:

I was worried about what it might do to my relationship with Tony [her husband]. I conceived on our honeymoon. It was too early really. We've only been together a year and there are things we still have to learn and understand about each other. I thought he might feel the baby was coming between us. And I suppose I was a bit frightened that once the baby came, the excitement would be lost, so I decided to put her in another room and we made a beautiful nursery and hoped we could shut the door and live our own lives as before. That's impossible, and it

189

only introduced more strain to try and pretend it is. I'm listening for Katy even when she *isn't* crying. And when she is, I can't let myself feel sexy because my thoughts are with her. So now she's moved in with us. Her carrycot [crib] is right by my side of the bed at the same level, so I just scoop her up when she starts to fuss, and I often wake in the night to find I've fallen asleep with her at the breast. We're all more relaxed now!

A woman with two babies under $2\frac{1}{2}$ was concerned that she and her partner would never have any sex life if the children were in bed with them, but says: 'Kevin and I creep downstairs, disentangling ourselves from nestling babies and make love in the living-room. We keep a spare duvet in the cupboard and some candles. It's rather like when we were teenagers. I suppose it's the thrill of doing it in secret!'

Frances has three children, and with the first two she says she tried to do it 'by the book' and have an orderly routine. She managed this, more or less, with the first baby, felt she was always in a muddle once the second was born, and made up her mind to organize things better when the third came along. But the first two started waking and whining for drinks of water and trips to the bathroom when the baby cried at night, and they all landed up in their parents' bed at about 4.30 a.m. after a very disturbed night:

I couldn't stand it any longer. I was going up the wall with it. So I reckoned peace at any price and took the baby into bed with me. The second one, who is only 2, wanders over and snuggles up as well, but now I've stopped worrying about it and accepted that he needs the comfort and cuddling because he's probably a bit jealous of the baby. It's working out well. I still feel rather ashamed admitting it to other people though.

It is certainly more difficult to see this as a solution if your partner is anxious that the relationship will be destroyed by the children. Ann is married to a man fifteen years older than she is, and it is his second marriage. He feels that since his first marriage failed, this one may also be at risk. His ex-wife managed their child in such a way that the baby's needs did not intrude on him, and he concentrated on his law career. Ann believed the baby's needs must come first, but this made him very uneasy:

> His attitude was 'Why can't you control that child? What's wrong with you?' He didn't actually say it, but I knew it's what he was thinking. So I chose a time when I was feeling more or less rested and not too fraught and said, 'Let's talk about this.' I told him I realized he felt threatened, I understood. He denied it at first, because he felt so uncomfortable about it that he couldn't face up to it, couldn't admit it. He wanted to be strong, not to have any emotions like that. I told him it was all right, that it was understandable, that any man would feel like that after his experience. Then we got on a new level of talking about feelings and I told him how I felt pulled in two directions, between the baby and him. We had to find a coming together for the three of us. The upshot was that we have the baby in our room now, where I can reach her without getting out of bed, and nights are far more peaceful. The result is we have more time together and he's enjoying the baby and doing things for her he didn't do before.

Women feel constrained to fit a pattern of mothering assumed to be 'normal' and right for everyone. Susan has an 8-month-old baby and says:

> I have learned not to try and pressure my baby to eat or sleep, and not to watch the clock. I always put her to bed when she is tired. That way I don't have her screaming for hours. People get disgusted with me and say she should be in bed at 6 p.m. She goes to bed at 9 p.m. But before, when I was trying to copy my friends, trying to force her to sleep at 6 p.m., she would scream until 12 p.m. or 1 a.m., and sometimes even 3 a.m.

When at last a woman has taken her baby into her bed, it has often followed a long battle to try to persuade the child to settle in her own crib and her own room because to have a baby in bed with you is seen as threatening to adult autonomy. Women try desperately to conform to standard child-rearing practices. Many of those relating to feeding and sleeping are derived from books about baby care written by pediatricians or psychologists. A good many of the authors are men. If these authors have children of their own, which is not always the case, they are by now grown up, so they tend to describe a culture of child-rearing that may have been appropriate twenty or thirty years ago, but that is no longer relevant in a fast-changing society.

There is a paradox in that though for most women a breakthrough comes when they take the baby into their own bed, for others it is the exact opposite and they find that the baby needs peace and quiet and her own space if she is to settle contentedly. One woman said: 'His crying stopped at 8 months when we moved and he had his own bedroom. I think he cried because he was tired and couldn't sleep with us in the same room.' When I talked to her I discovered that there was more to it than this. She and her husband were living with his parents in overcrowded conditions and both couples were feeling the strain of it. She was worried whenever the baby cried that they were disturbing the rest of the household and was anxious to show that she could cope with the baby and be a good mother. The result was that she was on tenterhooks all the time. There was no way she could avoid communicating her tension to the baby. When they moved to their own home she was at last able to relax. Having a room for the baby was only one element in a changed family situation that now enabled the younger couple to have their own space.

Sometimes, paradoxically again, a woman's realization that the baby needs to be physically close, but that she also needs time away from the baby, produces a dramatic reduction in crying. At night she cuddles up with the baby, who then becomes more contented, not only at night, but during the day, too. This brings freedom and the woman relaxes and begins to enjoy life, and the new spirit in her mothering is conveyed to the baby, who is able to relax as well.

When this happens, the urgent need to prove she is a capable mother gives way to pleasure. Part of this is a sensuous delight in the baby's sheer physical presence – seeing, touching, smelling and holding the baby. Part comes from the excitement of a living relationship – the pre-verbal communication involving eyes, facial expressions, movements and sounds. When she is struggling to organize her baby to a set timetable, to acquiesce in being put to bed when the rules say he should be, to suck fifteen minutes each side because some expert advises that this is how to breast-feed, she has little opportunity for simply enjoying her baby and for taking advantage of the quiet, alert phases in his activity cycle to join in this first kind of conversation. It is difficult to feel any pleasure in a baby if all the time you are engaged in a running battle to get him to conform to a schedule or grow up and start being independent. Once a woman has accepted her baby's spontaneous rhythms and enjoys being close, both of them feel much more contented and in tune with each other.

A baby carrier

For many women the use of a baby carrier dramatically improves the situation. They say they like knowing their babies are safe against their bodies. Many have not only become distressed listening to their babies crying, but are also anxious when they *stop* crying because they wonder whether they can be dead. If the baby is cuddled up against her breasts, a woman is at last free to think about and do other things. Housework, gardening and shopping are easier and she can go for a long walk or even on a hiking trip with her baby tucked against her. When she needs time away from the baby or has other work to do, the father or someone else can take over and carry the baby.

Kathy's baby cried inconsolably until at 6 weeks she put him in a baby sling. She uses it all the time now: 'Taking the dog to the park with Ben in his carrier where no one will hear him if he cries, I can sing at the top of my voice, and just to be out in the fresh air is bliss!'

A native American woman who is a healer and midwife to her people of the Onondage nation told me that one of her own babies cried and cried, and could only be comforted by being bound on his cradleboard and carried about. She recommends the cradleboard for inconsolably crying babies.

193

Having the baby close to you in some form of carrier or a shawl is an extension of the basic principle that babies are soothed when in contact with an adult's body. It has other benefits, too: the baby is upright rather than lying down. As we have seen in Chapter 12, research has shown that babies are more contented in carriers than when they are laid flat or in tilted baby chairs. A baby who is attached to someone else's body also gets all the stimulus that comes from that person's movements and, if against the front of the body, may be soothed by the regular sounds of the human heartbeat.

Soothing sounds

Professor Murooka of Japan put a miniature microphone inside a woman's uterus and recorded the sound. When this tape was played to crying babies they became quiet. He then tried other sounds, but the most effective turned out to be the intra-uterine sounds.[7] A midwife in an English hospital compared the effectiveness of a tape recording of intra-uterine sound with a music box (playing either 'Frère Jacques' or 'Rock-a-Bye-Baby') and with other methods of calming babies, such as talking to them and rocking and patting them. Most people quickly gave up on the music box because it didn't work. Intra-uterine sound was effective for 98·4 per cent of the time – and when it wasn't, the baby was due for a feed. The average time taken to calm a baby was ten minutes, but more than half the babies were quiet in less than five minutes.[8]

Many women say that when they put their babies to bed, they use a tape recorder with intra-uterine heart sounds. It is a method that is unlikely to be effective after 6 weeks of age, but can be very useful with babies younger than this. Some parents discover that other forms of sound are also effective. One tape that works with many babies is made up of rushing sounds that resulted from an error in a tape recorder when a father tried to record his baby's crying. When he played this back, the baby became quiet. Another reproduces the sound of rustling leaves and waterfalls. One woman told me: 'My mother bought me the [intra-uterine sound] cassette, which settled him after ten seconds. But the stereo is now broken, so we find a combination of hairdryer (low setting) and vacuum cleaner

plus dummy [pacifier] settles him.' Another woman advises: 'Always
have reasonable noise about in the house – the vacuum cleaner, TV,
radio, dog barking, people talking.' Another says of her baby daughter that 'a good ticking of a clock knocks her out.' In at least one
family the baby can be settled down only in the bathroom because
the most soothing sound proves to be the flushing of the toilet; while
one parent rocks and pats the baby, the other flushes the toilet over
and over again.

Babies often enjoy music, and their musical tastes vary widely.
Some prefer Bach while others enjoy lullabies, blues, pop music or
hard rock. One woman told me that her 4-month-old baby 'delights
in my daughter playing her guitar or recorder, or listening to the
piano'. Many parents sing to their babies and some find that their
babies are soothed most effectively by really loud music. One
woman, for example, found that very loud singing was about the
only thing that worked: 'One day I was horrified to find myself
yelling away in a totally silent house with my baby looking at me in
absolute amazement.' A father who is a drummer has discovered
that when he is practising, the baby usually drops off to sleep.

Mothers can make soothing songs out of almost anything, 'Casey Jones', hymns and cookery recipes included. Vietnamese women often sing lullabies that consist of cooking tips: 'To make a soup of fish and pumpkin add some pepper and chives to bring out the taste. Sleep soundly, my baby, so I can work to feed you.' To find the kind of music that suits your baby best you may need to experiment. If conventional lullabies don't seem right, you will probably find that any kind of music that helps *you* relax will help the baby relax, too. A mother of twins says she turns the radio on, has a cup of coffee and 'the music helps me relax and this passes through to the babies'.

If you don't feel like relaxing, but want instead to let out all the rage building up inside you as the baby cries, that is all right, too! Choose music or a song that gives vent to your feelings and you will entertain the baby *and* feel better afterwards yourself.

Lullabies and special songs for babies often give mothers 'permission' to express their consternation and anger. An old American lullaby epitomizes the ambivalent feelings that mothers have about their babies:

> *What'll I do with the baby-o?*
> *If she won't go to sleepy-o?*
> *Wrap her up in calico and send her off to her daddy-o.*
> *Wrap her up in the tablecloth and throw her in the old hayloft.*
> *Dance her north and dance her south*
> *Pour a little moonshine in her mouth.*
> *Pull her toes and tickle her chin, throw her in the old playpen.*
> *Eyes of blue and cheeks of red, lips as sweet as gingerbread.*[9]

You only have to think of a well-known rhyme like 'Rock-a-Bye Baby', which ends 'down will fall baby, cradle and all!', to realize that such lullabies, however sweetly sung, provide a socially sanctioned means of expressing violent emotions of hostility towards a crying baby that are stored just below the level of consciousness.

Comfort positions and movements

One of the things you will have learned is that your baby likes certain positions and changes of positions. Some babies are much more contented when placed on their tummies, for example. They like to lie firmly supported, face down, along your arm. Or they enjoy lying on their tummies across your lap while you pat their bottoms with a steady, regular beat. Or perhaps they are happiest propped against your shoulder and being bottom-patted in that position. Some babies get comfort from sitting on your lap supported by one hand and being gently rocked backwards and forwards by your other hand across their shoulders.

But all these positions are likely to work for only a few moments. Then the baby starts to fuss again and you have to use all your ingenuity to think what to do next. A really restless baby is never still except when fast asleep. There are little jerks and starts, fists punch out, feet clench and shove, back and tummy go rigid, and the baby twists and turns, arching her back, stiffening her shoulders, jumping and wriggling, grimacing and moaning as if you are subjecting her to prolonged torture.

All this uses a lot of energy, but it turns out that it is *your* strength that is being exhausted, not the baby's. That man with the haggard face and staring eyes driving round and round the block at midnight may not be a kerb-crawler after all; he may be a tired father with a baby on the back seat!

It is amazing how much energy this new-formed creature possesses. When you are weary and dropping from lack of sleep and constant attention to her needs, she is still going strong. It seems to be survival of the fittest – and looking at an energetic baby and then at her exhausted parents, it is quite clear who is the fittest!

Because this ceaseless activity demands so much output of energy, the baby is soon hungry and ready to feed again. She comes to the breast with alacrity. To the mother it may seem certain that each feed, rather than promising peace and content, tanks up this miniature power-packed dynamo so that she is able to continue the squirming, struggling, non-stop activity.

The essence of it all is *movement*. Babies like to move and to be moved. They like to explore a variety of movements of different kinds and tempo, and in this way they tone their muscles and increase their neuro-muscular coordination. At the same time they are discovering and testing their environment – the hardness, strength and resistance of solid objects and, above all, the actions and reactions of the people caring for them. It is like one big experiment to reveal all there is to know about the world and the human beings in it, a mighty effort to gatecrash human society, be acknowledged and recognized, succoured and sustained, and to assert the rights of this new person against all comers.

Movement is integral to all this action. Babies seem to be striving for movement. They like riding in fast cars, and cry when you stop at the traffic lights. They like to be trundled around in anything on wheels. They enjoy being carried, provided you don't pause for one moment. They like being patted, rubbed, massaged, swung, bounced and rocked.

Traditionally, babies have been rocked in cradles or in their mother's arms in rocking chairs. Vertical, rather than side-to-side, rocking is likely to be especially effective and resembles the up and down movement the baby felt when rocked inside the mother's pelvis before birth. The best speed for rocking has been shown to be from thirty to ninety rocks a minute.[10] Some women find that a vertical rocker suspended from a specially designed spring to maintain the rocking at this speed helps their babies to relax and sleep.

Babies like to initiate movement too, to stretch and curl up, twist and turn, and flex and extend their joints. Try putting your baby lying on a mattress on the floor in a warm room. Even newborn babies can move. They wriggle, press their heads up and make swimming-like motions with their arms and legs. Having the freedom of a mattress enables the baby to make all these exploratory movements without being hampered by clothing or blankets.

Getting in touch with your baby

People often suggest putting a crying baby out of earshot in a quiet, darkened room. Segregation and total lack of stimulation is the answer. Though this works for many babies, it is sad that the only way we should know to soothe a baby is to isolate him from all human contact and try to act as if he did not exist. In spite of it being sometimes necessary for the mother's sanity, as a general rule it is a counsel of despair: 'You can't do anything to calm your baby and get it contented, so leave it severely alone!' When mothers resist such advice, it may be because we know in our hearts that it seems to be confirmation that we are not getting in touch with our babies in the right way.

Women all over the world have communicated with babies through touch for thousands of years, usually without even thinking about it, together with all the rocking, crooning, ear-nibbling, bottom-kissing and baby talk that goes with it. Different systematic kinds of touching have been recommended in books since Greek and Roman times. A psychotherapist, Ian St John, has made an overview of some of these forms of massage.[11] In the second century AD Soranus of Ephesus advocated a vigorous moulding massage designed to shape the baby's body perfectly that he had observed nursemaids and mothers using with babies. First the baby was oiled all over and then the woman grasped an ankle and with the other hand stroked from one buttock upwards over the spine. Then she stroked from the shoulder blade down across the spine to the other thigh. After doing this oblique back massage, she massaged the spine, legs and head. The Greek idea of beauty was a perfectly shaped, athletic physique and, as with the modern Innuit, the aim of baby massage was to achieve a strong, straight, vigorous body. But it must have been fun, too – except, perhaps, for a baby who didn't want all that stimulation and preferred to be cosily nestled and only stroked very lightly.

Indian baby massage was introduced to the West by Leboyer in his book *Loving Hands*.[12] Variations on this have been developed in the United States, Australia and England,[13] and it is described and illustrated in a book of mine, *Woman's Experience of Sex*.[14] A major theme of this is that the baby is stroked in a continuous, flowing movement from head to foot, using light stroking and deeper massage.

A baby who enjoys being touched relaxes and is soft and floppy like a purring kitten, occasionally stretching and yawning. A baby who is startled throws up both hands in the Moro reflex – he flings his arms out and then brings them back when someone moves suddenly or there is an unexpected noise. Perhaps you are being too heavy-handed, or moving too fast, conveying your own anxiety through touch.

Watch to see the kind of touch your baby likes. You will find that once you have started massage, it is best to keep continuous contact. Always keep one hand or finger resting on the baby's skin as you change to a different part of the body. Touch gives security. Suddenly breaking it off can cause insecurity. On hairy parts of the baby's body stroke in the same direction as the hair grows. When you stroke the baby's head and forehead, the movement should be downwards, never up. Here are some other suggestions:

- Pour some warm oil in the palms of your hands, just enough for your hands to glide smoothly on your baby's skin.
- Gently cradle the baby's head from front to back in your hands, fingers touching at the centre of the crown of the head.
- Keeping one hand lightly on the crown of the baby's head, make small circular movements down over the forehead with your middle finger.
- Make little circular movements with your third finger between the baby's eyes.
- Starting at the bottom of both ears, with one finger of each hand trace their shape up and over, and round again to the lobe.
- Stroke down both arms and gently press the centre of the palms of the baby's hands with one finger for about ten seconds.
  For the next two kinds of stroking the baby should be naked.
- Stroke down both legs and finish by lightly pressing the middle of the soles of the baby's feet with one finger for ten seconds.
- With the baby lying on her front or side, still with one hand over her head, use two fingers to make gentle circular movements all the way down the spine from the nape of the neck to the buttocks. Experiment to see if your baby seems to relax more if you make the movements at either side of the spine rather than right over it.

Ian St John suggests that there are three basic approaches to care. The 'conventional' approach involves isolation of babies for long periods of time; massage may be given because cream is being applied, but not to get 'in touch'. With the 'integrated' approach the mother is aware of how artificial it is to isolate the baby from her and she wants somehow to compensate for this, so she uses touch and massage to communicate, to make up for something that is missing. The 'biological' approach entails continuous contact between mother and baby and another loving person to nurture them both. The mother keeps her small baby tucked inside her clothing and mother and baby are often massaged together 'in a relaxing mutual, emotional as well as physical, exchange . . . Each massage is original. There is no routine to follow; it is a very personal experience; what is important is generating a loving interaction as human beings.'[15] The woman can lie down with her baby at her side and snuggled up to her, or can have the baby resting on her body. Then another person massages them both, using stroking and pressing movements, and always following the 'hair streams'. The baby who is in skin contact with the mother, massaged and touched in this way as part of a shared experience, is 'body-reared, rather than hand-reared'.

Any calm, rhythmic touch that feels right at the time, may prove soothing for a baby. One woman, for example, has discovered that if she massages her baby's forehead, she can soothe him to sleep. Another says she takes off her baby's nappy and gently rubs his tummy. Though some babies hate being bathed, others stop crying when they are in warm water. 'Nothing helped at all, until I started bathing him,' one woman says, 'and that helped him relax.' Some women take the baby with them into a warm bath in a warm room so they can relax together.

Babies often seem to dislike being bathed because they are lain on their backs. They feel insecure in this position and fling up their arms and cry. Some of the Australian mothers in my study had learned a special method of bathing, which they found their babies enjoyed. This involves holding the baby under the chin and placing her on her tummy with her head turned to one side. You need to keep your knuckles raised from the water and your fingers spread apart so that water drains from your hands. Ann Burleigh of the Royal Hospital for Women in Sydney showed these mothers this way of bathing babies. She puts them in water that is $4\frac{1}{2}$ to 6 inches (12 to 15 cm) deep so that they can float and ensures that the water is really warm – about 100°F (38°C) – and she always bathes the baby on his front first and then, if he is happy, turns him over on his back later.[16] If your baby wakes at night and won't settle, you may find that it soothes and relaxes him to be bathed in this way, and after you have patted him dry, while his body is still warm from the bath, you may like to massage him with oil until he drops off to sleep. One woman said that giving her baby this kind of bath during her worst crying period enabled her to relax enough to feed contentedly and get to sleep.

Visual stimulation

One way of distracting and soothing crying babies, and even of preventing them crying, is to offer a great deal of varied visual stimulation. This should not be present all the time or the child gets accustomed to it. You need to present a display of objects providing visual excitement – perhaps using sound, too, in the form of a special '*son et lumière*' for babies.

Mothers invent all sorts of solutions to their babies' drive for visual stimulation: 'We put up home-made mobiles and picture books held open with large rubber bands'; 'There is a bird-table in the garden and we had a coconut hanging from the tree, and he loves to lie watching all the activity.' Babies like looking in mirrors, watching the play of light and shade on the wall, being shown big, brightly coloured books, and enjoy flags fluttering, and things that shine made of brass, copper and silver. They like candles, tinsel and bunting, flowers, peacock feathers, brilliantly coloured patchwork and intricate designs, rugs, wall hangings, Chinese paper lanterns and kites, puppets, masks and parasols, flames leaping in an open fire (with a good solid fire-screen of course), balloons bobbing, soap bubbles wafting past, lace curtains blowing in the breeze and the patterns formed by chinks of light through venetian or rattan blinds. By all means hang beads, balls and rattles made of multicoloured plastic over the crib, but they are not enough to keep a lively baby's attention for any length of time. Colours do not always have to be bright to fascinate a baby. Subtle distinctions can be appreciated too.

You will find that even a young baby can discriminate between shades of colour and shapes that are only slightly different from each other. If a mobile of graded shades and/or shapes is hung where she

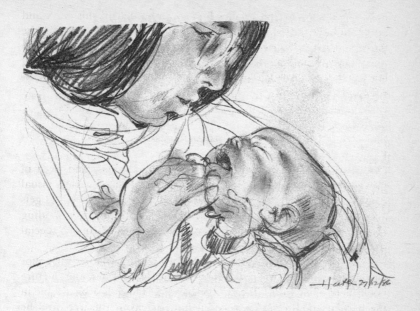

can easily see it, she may spend a long time concentrating on and
puzzling out the differences between the parts.

Other human beings, above all, provide the best visual stimulation around – people coming and going and taking notice of the
baby. A woman whose own childhood was spent in the Seychelles
says there is a great contrast between her own life as a small child
and her baby's day-to-day life in Wales, and she can understand
why he cries. She was the oldest of seven children and remembers
how the babies were put in front of the house where they could see
everything that was going on and were the centre of attention.
When I was doing anthropological field-work in Jamaica I often
saw children playing grandmother's footsteps or hopscotch with contented babies tied to their backs, and a favourite place to put the
baby was in a large pail on the clearing outside the hut – with
chickens scratching around, dogs chasing each other, birds swooping
from the mango tree, the families' goats or a donkey, and neighbours
preparing food or washing clothes together. No baby could get bored
given that lively scene!

Taking a break from the baby

A woman with her first baby often feels under pressure to conform to an ideal image of motherhood. It is one that has been superimposed by society and is a mixture of the Virgin Mary, Mrs Beeton and the Cosmo girl: perfect mother, perfect cook and housekeeper, perfect sexual playmate. No woman can be all these things at once. Some women go all out to fill one or other of these roles and find that even this is impossible to achieve. The most insidious demand that we make of ourselves may be that of being perfect mothers. Any woman who believes that she must be with her baby right through the twenty-four hours, feel only tenderness and love, and be completely selfless and nurturing, will find it very hard to accept the anger and hatred that a crying baby can provoke. In denying what she is feeling she is rejecting a part of herself, a part of her reality and her integrity as a person. Frustration and tension build up as she tries to hold the brake hard down on her emotions and resist acknowledging how she really feels, and the result, as we have seen in Chapter 10, can be disastrous. When, and if, at last someone in whom she can confide gives her permission to escape from her baby for a while, to reclaim herself and have a private space, the dreadful strain is eased. She can sleep, cry, listen to music, pummel the pillows, soak in a hot bath – do anything for an hour or so rather than try to be a perfect mother.

So whereas for some women with crying babies there is a major breakthrough when they acknowledge the baby's needs for close body contact and take the baby into bed, for others everything becomes simpler when they accept that they do not have to nurture their babies non-stop through the twenty-four hours, can resist pressure to conform to the image of an ideal mother, and make time for themselves.

This is quite different from the advice often given to 'put the baby out of earshot'. It is rather 'you have a right to create some space for yourself and not to be sucked entirely into motherhood.'

You may get a chance to have someone else take over the care of the baby for a while. If so, take it! Make a brief escape by going for a brisk walk or jog, doing some gardening out of earshot of the baby's crying, having a work-out in the local gym, going for a swim, or – sheer bliss – *sleeping*. Many women say that once they have had a good sleep, they have the energy to go on. Others say things like: 'I would be lost without my husband! I hand her over to him and then I go for a run to clear my head, and then I come back all refreshed and ready to start again.'

If you *both* have the opportunity for a break, grasp that too! As one woman who, fortunately, has someone else who can keep an eye on the baby puts it: 'We make sure we go out alone each day even if it is for half an hour. We need it. We have asked friends and neighbours for help and aren't ashamed about it.'

Though at first it is hard to feel that it can be right to take a break from the baby, because you are so obviously needed, and to shut the door on a crying child seems like the ultimate rejection – sometimes that is the only thing to do. It saves your sanity. And in interrupting the cycle of conflict between you and the baby it can help the baby be less troubled. One mother told me she had learned that 'a baby can have enough of your company.' She has found that her little girl is soothed now that she is put regularly in a darkened room for a daytime nap: 'I close her curtains, pop her in her crib, and she sees me walk out of the room and shut the door.' That may not work for everyone, but for this mother and baby it seems right. The baby settles down after a brief cry and the mother gains a little personal space.

Some women learn that their babies get irritable when they are longing to be left at peace, but because their own physiological rhythms of sleep and waking are interrupted to fit in with other people's schedules or because they are constantly stimulated by someone trying to soothe them, are unable to let go: 'My baby gets overtired if I have to keep waking him up to pick other children up from playschool or school or riding or Cubs or whatever. Then he cries excessively'; 'She cries hysterically when she is overtired and we have missed the moment at which she would fall asleep without a fuss'; 'We discovered that Philip [5 months] cried when he was overtired. We tried putting him down as soon as he got a bit whiney and things improved remarkably. I keep track of how long he's been awake during the day and make sure he goes to bed a bit earlier if he's had a very active day. He soon falls fast asleep and is in a much better mood when he awakes.'

Single mothers who must bear full responsibility, and women who have absentee or uninvolved partners, find it particularly difficult to get the help they need so that they can take a break from the baby. Caring for a baby is hard work. Mothers need practical help, not just sympathy. As one woman who became depressed puts it: 'I cracked up every day. I just screamed out loud. I felt out of control and very frightened. I hated myself for not being able to cope. I phoned Opus [a help-line] but just talking to someone didn't help. I needed *practical* help, someone to look after the baby for a couple of hours.'

As many women point out, the only thing that allows them to cope at all is occasionally 'getting away from it' and 'having someone else to hand him to when I can't take any more'. 'I ask a neighbour to take the baby from me,' one woman said. 'I find that if I give my son to someone else, I calm down. Then I am able to cope better afterwards. When he wouldn't stop crying, it was as if he was rejecting me. I found that very often I was unable to stop his crying, but someone else could. At the time I thought I must be a useless mother. I know better now.' One woman told me that the solution she found to her feeling of being overwhelmed was having a woman friend to take turns holding him. When someone else was holding her crying baby, she said, she no longer felt 'so drawn into the baby's fear and loneliness. I could be grown-up support for my baby.'

Women with close friends or relatives with young children sometimes manage by sharing baby-care so that each woman gets a break. Ann has three children. Her sister had a baby ten weeks before Ann's last one was born:

> If I minded her children [the baby and another of not quite 2 years], it gave her a rest or she could go shopping. She didn't want to leave her baby at first, as she is fully breast-fed, but I persuaded her that I could breast-feed her baby – and it worked well. She was going through a severe crying period, my sister was getting upset with her, and her 2-year-old was showing signs of jealousy. We both found that my feeding her [baby] relieved her tension with the crying baby.

Another woman suggests teaming up with a neighbour with older children and alternating baby-sitting: 'Older kids are great with babies and will spend hours rocking the pram [baby carriage] or playing with the baby.'

Sometimes the break needs to be more drastic, because a woman is at the risk of destroying herself and the baby. She simply cannot go on any longer. Amanda's baby son cried inconsolably for eight months. Then the health visitor suggested a residential nursery so that Amanda could have a rest. She did not like that idea, so explored other possibilities with her health visitor. The upshot of the discussion was that she decided to return to work outside the home and the baby went into a crèche (nursery) each day: 'In two weeks he had improved magically, slept better and was much happier. I missed him during the day, but I felt really pleased to see him when I did, and my son was pleased to see me. We got along a lot better.'

Mary's baby is now 5 months old and she says she has finally 'relented and let my Mum have her for the whole weekend. My guilt is gone, my mother is in her element and my husband spoilt and happy with some attention for himself for a change. If she offers

207

again, I shall accept with pleasure. I still feel sad about leaving her with someone else but it's the only way to survive.'

'Growing out of it'

Many women in my study described how crying stopped spontaneously, often within a period of two or three days – sometimes even overnight – between 10 and 16 weeks. The most usual time for sudden change like this to occur is in the thirteenth or fourteenth week. It seems to be part of the baby's developmental pattern, a new phase in which the baby does not *need* to cry. They related this to a particular aspect of neurological and motor development: the baby could grasp and hold playthings, roll over or be mobile. They felt their babies had been frustrated and bored.

One thing that helps some babies a great deal is finding their thumbs to suck. A baby may have such a strong sucking instinct that she really relaxes only when she has a breast or breast substitute, such as a dummy (pacifier) or an adult's finger, inside her mouth. There is an especially sensitive place just inside the upper gums that is packed with nerve-endings. New-born babies feel exquisite pleasure when something is pressed against it. Stimulation of this area excites a baby rather like stimulation of a woman's clitoris brings sensory pleasure. If you watch a baby sucking in a satisfying way, it can look as if it has all the passion and intensity of sexual experience. It involves the whole body, not just lips and mouth, but hands and feet, which curl and uncurl with delight. Then, as the baby continues sucking, she begins to relax and a pleasurable drowsiness steals over her. For some babies, sucking seems to be the only time when they can easily relax enough to fall asleep.

This is why being able to find his own hand on which to suck, which may occur at about 5 weeks, can be an important developmental step. The baby knows how to soothe himself. Some babies never do work out how to do this, however, and many women try dummies (pacifiers), often guiltily at first, since they think it is an unsavoury habit and don't like other people to see the baby with a dummy in its mouth, perhaps because it suggests that the baby is being neglected. Some babies take to their dummies with alacrity.

Others value a different kind of 'transitional object' – a piece of material, which represents for them the mother's love and the security she gives. A woman with a 5-month-old baby said: 'I give him a flannel [washcloth], which he screws up in his hand to go to sleep with or he snuggles his face or head in it. When in his cot [crib], his crying has been considerably reduced due to this and he goes to sleep quickly. He uses this as a plaything too.' Another told me: 'My child eventually settled at 8 to 9 months after being given a variety of silky petticoats and scarves.'

With other babies, the crying ceases when they develop sufficient neuro-muscular coordination to handle objects and begin to control their immediate environment by moving themselves and the things around them. Women say things like: 'It stopped at about 6 months of its own accord. He began crawling then, which helped, as some of it was frustration'; 'At about $2\frac{1}{2}$ months my baby became more settled, was less demanding for food and more able to amuse herself for short periods of time'; 'By the time he could sit on the floor and play with his toys he was extremely happy to entertain himself and things began to get a lot easier'; 'Once she was sitting on her own and could get up on her feet, she settled down. She seemed so desperate to move and do different things that frustration was the greatest problem.'

The wide variety of 'teething rings' and small objects designed to be put into the baby's mouth that have been produced by different cultures and in different historical periods is evidence that babies like to explore things with their mouths and to bite and chew: small gourds on sticks, silver and ivory rattles, wood, rattan, leather, shell, mother-of-pearl and coral whistles, beads and bells that tinkle, rattles of hemp and rope, corn and seed-filled gourds – they are the first objects a baby learns to manipulate and offer the satisfaction that comes from a new-found skill.

Our own emotions and expectations

The most important factor for many women in coping with crying is a change in their expectations and in their own emotional state, which leads to a change in their own behaviour.

When you have a crying baby, you lose all sense of time. It is difficult to think of anything else *but* the crying and do anything except to try to stop it. Women say that this distorts thinking processes so that they cannot believe that this noise will *ever* cease, and that the longer it goes on, the more it feels that the baby is out to get you! Yet when I talked to mothers who had been through this awful experience and come out the other side, they often said that it was important to keep a sense of perspective: 'Remember that a baby will not cry for ever and that it is too young to take anything personally. The baby does not "hate" you and is not purposely trying to upset you. There is something definite that it needs.' This woman said that she had to remind herself that the baby needed to feel her love, even if it was only by being changed or petted or rocked.

For a first-time mother a baby's crying can come as a dreadful shock. She may have expected her baby to go to sleep following a feed, feel utterly confused when he does not and believe that it is evidence that she is a bad mother. All her efforts may then be directed towards trying to get the baby to sleep and to fit some schedule advised in a book about baby care. Yet, as one woman explained: 'Once I stopped trying to get her to go to sleep after a feed and kept her up to play instead, practically all her crying stopped.'

Because a woman is trying to follow instructions in a book, rather than getting to know her baby, sometimes the crying proves to be a simple matter of hunger. Feeds have been cut short and the baby is crying for more milk. This is not, strictly speaking, 'inconsolable' crying, because the baby stops if put to the breast again, but because the mother feels that the baby should have had enough, it results in crying that she is powerless to stop. One woman, for instance, went on like this for six weeks because she had read that babies 'should' go three to four hours between feeds, and no one had told her that breast milk, in contrast to artificial milk, is often digested in two hours.

Sometimes a baby triggers a negative response in a mother, which intrudes on and interferes with her ability to respond sensitively to his needs, and it is only when she becomes aware of it and can cancel it out that the relationship between them improves. A woman who believed that her healthy, vigorous baby was attacking her breast approached each feed feeling under threat. 'I dreaded feeding times,' she told me. The baby cried for hours every evening and colic was diagnosed. 'Nothing would quieten him.' She was at breaking point and the baby was clearly at risk. She felt she could smash him against the wall. Her doctor arranged for the baby to be admitted to the hospital for forty-eight hours' observation. This was long enough for the mother, with counselling, to see what was happening, and her panic about being attacked by the baby passed. 'He came out of hospital colic-free and quiet, calm and relaxed. Naturally, so were we.'

A big, hefty baby may not elicit the tenderness a woman can feel towards a small, delicate one. A long, thin baby may not be for that particular mother as rewarding as a plump and sturdy one. She may not find it easy to respond to one with a strong drive towards independence – who always fights and struggles, for example – whereas she would enjoy a baby who moulded himself to her body and clung in satisfying dependence. Or, in contrast, she may dislike the baby's constant dependence and long for him to grow up and do things to amuse himself and demonstrate that he is attaining new phases of development. When a woman feels disappointed about her baby like this, it can be very difficult for the two of them to get into synchrony.

A mother and child can get locked in conflict when expectations do not match reality. It is as if the woman is unwilling to part with her fantasy baby – the dream baby of pregnancy – and as if the one she has is an interloper. The emotional journey towards acknowledging this can be a painful one. It entails facing up to longings that may have been hidden from the woman herself, yet were the basis of her expectations and assumptions about the kind of baby she would have. Monica admits: 'Because she is a girl I tend to feel less sympathetic than towards my son.' She feels that her daughter, like herself, should be able to handle life's problems and not complain. But there is more to it than that. In Monica's case there have been daunting problems. Her first child, a boy, was born with a severe handicap, and in coping with this she has needed all her self-discipline. She went on to tell me: 'My daughter is perfect, whereas my son is not, and I feel she shouldn't cry or demand attention.' It seemed unfair that this baby, who is well and strong, should make such a fuss when the older child had a better claim to be unhappy. So long as Monica felt like this her baby cried inconsolably. Then she realized how her own resistance and anger with the baby were causing the distress: 'The crying stopped when I managed to calm myself down and not blame her for my problems. I put them into perspective.'

Some women feel they have been on an emotional journey that, though painful at the time, ultimately is enriching. A single mother who did not want her baby and was very frightened of motherhood said that having a crying baby entailed learning a lot about herself, and she discovered a capacity for adaptation and for accepting responsibility that she did not realize she had. 'At first I had a terrible time adjusting. Now I know that I can give my child a happy, secure life. It's taken three months to reach this stage.' She says that as she grew more confident the baby cried less. She doesn't know whether this was cause and effect, or sheer chance.

Some women attribute the reduction in crying as a baby develops to an increased feeling of security. It is as if babies are afraid of all the changes that come with life outside the uterus. We have seen already that pre-term and low-birthweight babies may startle readily and look anxious. Other babies, too, often seem anxious. One woman described her baby in this way: 'The crying stopped spontaneously. It coincided with the introduction of a bedtime routine – bath, play, cuddle, feed, bed. We think she realized that going to sleep didn't mean parting from us for ever and she ceased to be afraid of the evenings. It was something she had to discover for herself. Nobody could learn it for her.' For her baby 'body contact' is of supreme importance – even more important than food.' She added: 'Babies can't bear loneliness and frustration in those early weeks. They are too frightened. Allowing my baby to express her sorrow and fear in the only way she could, by crying, while supporting her with my warm, soothing bodily presence was all I could do.'

Another woman said that at first she was afraid that she was spoiling her crying baby when she picked her up, but began to understand that if the baby stopped crying when she did this, it showed that she could respond to love – 'and that is nice. All the hard work you put in at first is worth it a thousand times over to have a good relationship with your baby.'

Breathe out and relax

Some women say that the breathing and relaxation they learned in antenatal classes comes in useful when mothering a crying baby – especially the instant release achieved by dropping shoulders, giving a long breath out and letting all tension disappear with it. Half a minute spent breathing right down your back and into your tummy is like a safety valve to prevent you hitting or shaking the baby. It gives a pause so that you can clear your head. And it breaks the spiral of stress building up between you and the baby. 'I think he could sense my anxiety,' one woman, who was feeling trapped and isolated, explained. 'As I became more relaxed, so did he.' Helen's baby was waking at three in the morning. She already felt worn out because 'I seemed to exist for everyone else and not at all for me in those first weeks.' The 3 a.m. crying was the last straw: 'Above all I tried to keep calm when I went to her. I took some deep breaths and remembered that I was the centre of her universe and that, in spite of everything, I still loved her.' Sandy's baby cried for most of her first year of life and she says that learning to breathe fully kept her going: 'The crying made me tense. This tension transmitted itself to the child, thus creating a vicious circle. I found that taking a few deep breaths made a tremendous difference.' Another woman told me: 'When things get bad I put the baby down anywhere safe and go out of earshot for a few minutes, take three deep breaths and start again.'

Breathing and relaxing is not a counsel of perfection. No one can stay relaxed all the time. But if you are in a situation of crisis, knowing how to use breathing to release your tension can be a life-saver.

Getting out in the fresh air

Going out with the baby, whatever the weather, provides a safety valve and refreshment for the mother, and the baby often becomes contented. 'Buy a dog and a pair of heavy walking shoes,' one woman advises. Others say: 'Things never sounded as bad in the open air. You may meet someone you know to cheer you up, and you will never get to the ultimate pitch of hurting the baby while you are out'; 'If the baby is playing up more than usual I leave the housework and get out. It's never as bad out of the house as it is in'; 'Get out of the house and do lots of walking. A baby crying in a buggy isn't half as bad as one glaring you in the face.'

Women told me how for cold weather they bought a greatcoat, large duffle coat or cape inside which they could tuck the baby in the carrier and then stride out regardless of rain, wind and snow, like pioneers forging a trail into new territory; or how with baby equipment, nappies (diapers), changing pad and cream in or under the pram (baby carriage), they started on an expedition bundled up like explorers in the Antarctic. They do this because they cannot tolerate being shut in at home with the baby one minute longer, feel that they are being driven mad, and – often – that they will smash the child against the wall unless they escape out of the prison of their homes and can switch their attention to something other than the constant, relentless crying.

They even do it after dark, too. Inconsolable crying at 2 a.m., as one woman put it, 'can seem like the end of the world'. She told me that she and her husband walked the streets at night, as he stopped crying only when in the pram.

Crying is most stressful when you feel *isolated* with it. That fact comes over clearly from everything women say when describing their experiences. Getting out enables you to make human contact with someone who may help, even if it is only a matter of telling you what a lovely baby you have and making you feel pleased with yourself. The combination of fresh air and meeting other adults sometimes brings a near-miraculous end to crying. A woman told me how her baby cried inconsolably until at $2\frac{1}{2}$ months they went on holiday (vacation) with six other people who 'gave me a break, and all the fresh air seemed to knock her out'. If there is no chance of a proper holiday, arranging to meet other women with babies of about the same age in a local park, going to the beach together or having a picnic in the countryside or a friend's garden can make you feel human again.

Human contact and loving support

Any woman with a baby, whether or not that baby cries excessively, needs to be in relationships with adults who enable her to function socially as someone other than a mother. She needs people with whom she can talk and relax, people who reinforce her sense of self, and who validate her in her role as an adult capable of taking on responsibility and making decisions for herself – others with whom she can share experience and feel part of a community. A loving, supportive partner who understands what she is going through and gives solid practical help, and who is able to be available when her need is urgent, can give her the strength to carry on. As one woman said, 'I was able to share the crying period with a very loving husband. We took turns to cuddle and comfort her, and consoled ourselves with the knowledge that it would stop in time.' Another, whose baby was a night-crier said: 'What helped most was being able to sit there, night after night, with my husband, each saying, "Shall we try so and so now?" As long as we were both there together things weren't quite so bad.'

Where there is another child, this genuine sharing of responsibility can save the family from disintegrating: 'We take it in turns twelve hours out of the twenty-four. I pace the floor at night and John deals with the toddler during the day while I give my attention to the baby.'

Couples who together face the anxiety triggered by an inconsolable crying baby may find that, even though it is an emotionally shattering experience, they are drawn closer: 'We used to drink coffee at nights and take hourly turns with Sara. I have never yet shouted, shaken or smacked her, and I doubt whether I could say that were it not for my husband (who is in a wheelchair). Those awful months united us even more than before.'

Yet many new mothers are socially isolated and terribly alone. Sometimes they feel ashamed to meet other people because they think the baby's crying will demonstrate what bad mothers they are. They are frightened of being branded as failures, like the woman who told me: 'I didn't seek help, as I didn't want anyone to think I could not cope.' But often there is just nobody there to whom they could reach out to talk about their frustration and despair. As one woman said: 'I never had anyone to talk to. I couldn't go to a mother and toddlers' group or a friend's house, as I got embarrassed with him crying so much. If I could have had a telephone number and got someone to talk to or to come round to take over, it would have saved lots of tears and mental anguish.'

Over and over again women say that meeting other mothers enables them to cope with their crying baby in a much more positive way, and one spin-off from these social contacts is that their babies seem actually to cry less. Somehow the strain is eased. One woman told me 'I think now that I was having jealousy problems with my other daughter and that emotionally I was beginning to crack up. Talking with people about it helped a lot, and most important for me was to be able to leave the baby with my husband or mother and go out on my own to see friends for a couple of hours.' Another said: 'When my baby cries for no apparent reason, other adult company seems to stop me from getting worked up – even if they know even less than I do about babies.'

On the other hand, it can be really difficult when a woman finds herself in a group of mothers all of whom seem to be coping well with their children – or at least give that impression – and she feels that she alone is a failure:

> Other mothers who hadn't had problems with their babies made me feel inadequate or somehow at fault. I felt very isolated with the problem, and guilty and anxious that I couldn't do anything to stop the crying. I tried every remedy anyone suggested: I had been a very confident and capable person and felt reduced to a nervous wreck, I just couldn't cope, although I should have been able to.

This is where special groups for new mothers are particularly helpful, since there is bound to be someone else who is facing a similar problem. Women say they gain moral support from joining a post-natal group or an organization that puts mothers in touch with each other. Those trying to cope alone say they have a lot of help from groups for single parents. Many continue friendships first made in their antenatal classes and form baby-sitting groups and arrange outings together. Others join classes for exercises, yoga, swimming and discussion. 'It helped if I talked to anyone, but not many people really understood. When I talked to other mothers who had similar problems with their children, I felt much relieved.'

For a woman with a crying baby support from other women – who share, listen in a non-judgemental way, give down-to-earth practical help, affirm each other, are open and honest, laugh and cry together – is the most effective strategy for survival. If a woman has that, she can be strong and know that, whatever the problems, she will overcome them in the end.

CHAPTER 14

Babies in Other Cultures

The mother carries the child on her back most of the
day and there is always a close physical
contact between them, such that it is rare to hear an African
child cry for want of a comforting touch, or
warm embrace.
Mirella Ricciardi, *Vanishing Africa*

All over the world babies have the same needs. They cry if they are uncomfortable, unhappy, over-excited, bored or in pain or distress of any kind. The odd thing is, however, that in many traditional cultures babies seem to cry very little. Travellers and anthropologists have noted it, and mothers themselves coming from other countries to the West – from West Africa, for example – are often surprised at how much our babies cry. What is it that makes their babies more contented?

Co-mothering

The first important factor is to do with the mother: she is not alone. She is surrounded by other women, many of whom also have babies or have had babies in the past, who give her emotional support and practical help. There may often be bickering and arguments. As anyone who has had sisters knows, there may be highly charged emotional encounters, and there is always someone who is not getting on with someone else. In India, for example, a great deal of time and energy is taken up with domestic conflict between sisters-in-law and mothers-in-law and all the other 'pent up womenfolk'.[1] But in a group of some ten or twenty women, or even more, there are always

218

some close friendships. Women feel a sense of unity, tackle challenges together and share each other's grief and joy. In matrilocal cultures, too (where a woman after marriage lives with her husband near her mother), sisters often share in caring for each other's babies and breast-feed for each other. The maternal grandmother may look after the baby when her daughter returns to work in the field. And in patrilocal societies a woman may have known her female in-laws ever since childhood, especially if cross-cousin marriage is the norm.

The Navajo of northern Arizona are a matrilocal society and sisters share responsibility for each other's children. Among the Comanche, maternal aunts are all called 'mother'. The same is true for the Hopi, where sisters often spend their whole lives together in the same large house.[2] When Margaret Mead first did her research in Samoa, she commented on the way in which babies were passed casually from one woman's arms to another. She believed that this taught a lesson of not setting high hopes on any one relationship and that it led to unattached sexual liaisons later in life, without possessiveness or jealousy. Whatever the long-term consequences of co-mothering, it takes the burden of complete responsibility from the biological mother. She learns by example how to handle her baby and is shepherded by other women into her new role.

But it is not just a question of co-mothers. Many of these traditional societies have classificatory kinship systems. The whole of society consists of individuals who are in relationships that simulate and are based on those of the blood tie. In peasant communities older men and women are frequently all addressed as 'mother' and 'father'. These people are fully aware that there is a difference between their biological parents and those whom they also call 'mother' and 'father', of course. But a classificatory system serves a useful purpose, since it extends the concept of parental responsibility and authority, and that of the obligations and rights of children throughout the community. A child is taught the appropriate behaviour towards each person he or she meets. There are special terms for distant relatives and others whom we should not consider related at all, and for all the people an individual is ever likely to encounter. To the small child, no one is simply a stranger or just someone who knows his father or mother. Each has a specific title that represents a potential for action.

The Latin American *compadre* bond and, to a lesser extent, the Western European provision of ceremonial 'godparents' indicate recognition of the social function of other adults in a parental relationship with children who are not biologically their own. There is an echo of the same kind of thing when we call our own adult friends whom a small child meets 'aunty' or 'uncle'. The same verbal signal of potential action is utilized deliberately in clubs and societies in industrialized societies when members address each other as 'brothers' or 'sisters'.

Thus in a traditional society the small child's universe is minutely stuctured and the larger social system is merely an extension, in ever widening circles, of the family group.

In traditional societies a first-time mother knows that there are willing hands to help and that she can always draw on some other woman's wisdom and experience. Her baby is not dependent on her as an individual in the same way as a baby in an industrialized country. Other laps, other comforting arms, even other lactating breasts are available if need be. Of course, it also means that she cannot decide to rear her child in an idiosyncratic and different style. She has to accept ways of doing things with babies that everyone else takes for granted, and that her mother and her mother before her probably also took for granted. Child-rearing is not done from books. It is not based on advice from a range of professionals. There are no conflicts and no puzzling theories. It is what it seems every mother always does.

When a baby *does* cry, there are culturally patterned ways of dealing with the problem in which empirical knowledge is often combined with powerful symbols relating to myth and religion. If a baby cries a great deal among the Seri of New Mexico, a woman performs a special curing ceremony. Twigs from the nest of a bird known as 'the bird who sleeps in the afternoon' are burned on small fires built on four heaps of sand placed around the baby. As the smoke rises, the curer sings and calls on the spirit of the bird whose nest is burning to cure the baby of his crying.[3] Women may explain and justify a baby's crying in religious terms. The baby is communicating with ancestor spirits, for example. The Ibo of West Africa believe that for some time following birth a baby remains in touch with unborn spirit children and that they are calling to their companion to come back to them. When a child's crying cannot be explained in other ways, it may be interpreted as part of the baby's communication with these unborn spirits.[4]

A woman starts to learn about how to care for babies when she is herself a small child, and there are always babies around, either siblings or cousins and other relatives. Older children care for babies. In Yucatan an older child, not necessarily a brother or sister, is asked to serve as the baby's *cuidadora*. The older child carries the baby around or sits with it, only leaving it in the hammock when it is asleep, and is quick to run and pick it up if it wakes and cries.[5] In Jamaica an older girl who is considered responsible enough to care for a baby may have the baby actually bound to her back so that she can continue playing and helping the older women while looking after the baby. I have seen babies almost as big as their little nurse-maids clinging limpet-like to their backs while they played an energetic game of hopscotch or a ring game. The baby seems to join in the movements of these games, bouncing happily and sharing in the other children's excitement, until falling asleep contentedly while still being tossed up and down in this manner.

When a woman has her first baby, she has seen a baby put to the breast in just that way hundreds and thousands of times from her own childhood on. She neither questions it, nor doubts that she can do it too. Though her behaviour may seem to her perfectly natural, it is in fact dictated by culture. Boat-women in one part of China, for example, feed their babies from one breast only, so that the right hand is free to continue with work. In fact, their clothing opens on one side only, so it would be impossible to give the other breast without first undressing. For them this style of breast-feeding is normal. In the Kalahari Desert there are tribes in which women carry their babies on their backs and feed them by slinging a breast over their shoulders, so that they can continue with whatever they are doing while the baby sucks contentedly. To do this, they have to lengthen their breasts. For them it is the natural way to care for a baby and nobody questions it.

Women spontaneously handle and hold babies in culturally patterned ways. An Indian mother sits on the ground, legs out-stretched, and lays her baby on her legs for an oil massage or to wash her, cradling the head against her feet. In Jamaica peasant women play with their babies' lips, suck bubbles from their mouths and fondle a baby boy's penis. This is a much more intimate and stimulating kind of touch than many mothers in industrial cultures would think was right.

Firmly held

Throughout European history, from Roman time on, babies spent long periods without being touched at all because they were firmly swaddled. The baby usually stayed in swaddling bands for about four months and was often so firmly bound that it was impossible for him or her to move head or limbs. When the mother or nurse was busy, the baby could be hung on a peg on the wall out of harm's way.

During the late eighteenth century swaddling started to go out of fashion in England and America, and in 1762 Rousseau remarked that the practice was 'almost obsolete' in England.[6] In 1784 a German visitor was astonished to note that babies wore light clothing that allowed them to move freely. One historian thinks swaddling was abandoned because social and political ideologies saw it as an infringement on human freedom. He points out that because it is impossible to stroke and cuddle a tightly swaddled baby there was a new tenderness and gentleness towards babies once their mothers or wet-nurses could feel their bodies and play with them easily. This led to changing attitudes towards children in general. No longer were they simply immature adults, but little people in their own right who needed a special kind of care and consideration.[7] Parents showed more affection to their children, until by the end of the eighteenth century books began to be published written by experts who accused parents of 'spoiling' their children.

Swaddling, or bundling up firmly, is still one practical way to help a restless baby become peaceful; we may be able to learn a lot from mothers in our own historical past as well as mothers in other cultures of today.

The cradleboard is a device that achieves much the same result as swaddling. The baby is firmly and securely held and has restricted movement. Mothers in many cultures who have to work in the fields

either attach the cradleboard to their backs or use it like a seat, putting it down beside them while they get on with laborious tasks like food preparation or washing clothes on stones at the riverside.

On the American north-west coast the native baby used to be bathed every day in a maple wood dish in which the water was heated by hot stones, was wrapped in soft shredded cedar bark and then was placed in a cradleboard made of wood and supple leather. The cradleboard was constructed by someone specifically significant in the child's life and was a highly valued gift.[8]

Once firmly packed in a cradleboard the baby could be passed round and be part of the social life of the family. An anthropologist observes that in a family gathering among the Seneca so many adults and children wanted a turn at holding the baby that eleven people held the baby in the space of fifty minutes.[9] Among some native American tribes the mother used to take her baby on horseback, hanging it in a cradleboard on the pommel of her saddle.[10]

Babies sometimes remained in the cradleboard for much of the first year of life, being taken out to be cleaned, for exercise and to have a soothing massage. When they became tired and miserable, they often cried to be tucked back in the cradleboard and settled down immediately they were replaced in it.

The cradleboard seems to have been a 'transitional object' for some little children and was like the old blanket or grubby soft toy animal to which many of our children become attached and which is a symbol of security. One anthropologist, writing about the Skagit tribe in Washington, says that some toddlers played and ran around while dragging their boards behind them.[11]

Nestling close and suckling freely

In most cultures a baby is attached to the mother's body in some way until it can sit up by itself for long periods, and often for the first year of life. It is as if the baby is still part of the mother, though now outside her body, rather like a kangaroo in its mother's pouch. The baby is fed whenever he nuzzles up to the breast. No record is kept of feeding times – their number, length or the interval between them – and babies are rarely, if ever, weighed. Breast-feeding is part of the close, intimate contact between mother and baby, and is done casually and with superb confidence. Just as animals have milk for their young, so it is taken for granted that a mother will make milk for her baby.

In many cultures the mother's clothing is well adapted to having a baby at the breast. Some Arab women in Israel may wear a special silk robe made up of many different strips of material, with embroidery on the breast and slits at each side through which a breast can be slipped to feed the baby. In parts of Tibet nomad mothers tuck their babies under their sheepskin coats against their bare skin. In Africa the !Kung baby cuddles against her mother's body day and night, carried in a sling on her hip or sleeping nestled close. Breast-fed whenever she wants for the first three years or so, she may come to the breast several times an hour until she is about 18 months old.[12]

There is a wide variety of devices to enable babies to be kept close to their mothers' bodies. The Japanese baby is strapped at waist level, inside a double sash that is tied in front.[13] The East African baby pouch is usually made of specially softened animal skin, from a calf, sheep or goat that has been sacrificed celebrating the birth and giving thanksgiving for the mother's health and strength. The leg pieces of the skin are often used as straps and a piece of skin or cotton may also serve to shade the baby's head from the tropical sun.

In South America the mother' wraps a blanket around her pelvis and shoulders and then lifts the baby over her head to slip it into the pouch in the small of her back. The Chinese pouch is constructed of bands of hemp cloth. First a stiffened pad of cloth that extends over the baby's head is fixed to its back. The mother then fastens the baby to her back with strips of cloth that go over her shoulders, cross at her breast, tuck round behind the baby to hold it securely and are tied in front at waist level. Another piece of cloth hangs from the top of the baby's stiffened pad, which can shade it from sun or prevent it from getting chilled.[14]

The Innuit mother has a large fur-lined hood attached to her parka and the baby nestles in this, either looking out from above the rim or, when it is very cold, protected inside the hood, which covers both its and the mother's head. An Innuit lullaby talks of the 'fat baby I feel in my hood . . . When I turn my head he smiles at me, my baby, hidden deep in my hood.'[15] In parts of Southern India the rural woman carries her baby under the top part of her sari, next to her skin. A writer describes how he has seen women with their babies clinging to their bodies in this way 'while working in the immense labour gangs recruited for the reconstruction of the great dams of India's national development projects, and suckling them from time to time'.[16]

THE CRYING BABY

Movement and stimulation

Even when the Indian mother does not have her baby under her
sari, she somehow manages to work one-handed while carrying her
naked child astride her hip, supporting its back with her free arm.
Mothers notice that babies sleep best when attached to their moving
bodies. In Tanzania the Barabaig woman who wishes to soothe a
baby who starts crying when she is not at work pretends to be
working and makes the movements and sounds of grinding maize.
She bends forward at the waist, straightens up, bends again and
makes the noises of grinding until the baby settles down.[17]

Mothers in cultures who do not wear clothing that forms a
pouch or sling for the baby often nestle their babies into some form
of container that holds them firmly and leaves the woman's hands
free. A Chinese mother working in the rice fields may cradle her
baby against her back in a deep wicker basket attached by straps
round her shoulders. Australian Aborigine babies are carried over
the mother's left shoulder in a basket made of palm leaf or grass, or
in a trough of wood or bark, leaving her right hand free to use her
digging stick. Sometimes when she is searching for food she puts the
baby on the ground close to her on a strip of soft bark under a
shelter of bark or leaves, shaded from the sun by a curved mat
screen.[18] In Thailand the cradle is first a shallow winnowing basket
and later a wooden or bamboo cradle, which is suspended from the
rafters while the mother is busy. In New Guinea it is a string bag,
which is also hung from the rafters or on a tree or post while the
mother gets on with her work,[19] and in Borneo the land-Dyak use a
hollowed-out tree trunk suspended by strings.

In Turkey the baby may be hung in a cotton bag from the
apex point formed by three long upright poles placed together as if
to form a tent frame while the mother works in the field. Older
children are there, too, helping to pick the cotton, and they run
from their work to swing the baby and play for a while under the
shade of the awning made of an old sack that is spread over the pole
frame. The mother comes over whenever the baby is ready for a feed
and sits under a tree breast-feeding. The baby can watch traffic
speeding along the road, birds swooping in the sky, the men with a
tractor or other agricultural machinery and the women weighing

cotton and stuffing it into big sacks. There is action everywhere and the baby has both visual and auditory stimulation and, whenever patted or swung in its sack, motor stimulation, too. At home there may be a ring or hook on the wall from which a carpet cushion cradle can be suspended so that the baby can be swung as everyone sits and talks or works together.

Much the same effect is achieved in Jamaica, though the baby is not bound in its personal container, by using a pail. The baby is sat upright in it on the ground among the chickens, lizards darting about and other animals. At ground level the baby has a grandstand

227

view of everything that is going on: branches moving in the breeze, big butterflies wafting between them, tropical birds squawking, the mule braying and chomping at its feed, siblings and cousins, aunts and uncles – who may be all about the same age – playing hopscotch or 'catch', the young men lounging in the doorway playing a transistor radio and gambling at cards, and the women shelling coffee beans, working a treadle sewing machine or pounding annatto.

In all these containers the baby is in a more or less upright position and can see everything that is going on around him. Instead of being segregated in another room or in a pram (baby carriage) with the hood up, and expected to go to sleep, the baby is in the middle of activity, part of the social scene, surrounded by adults and children doing interesting things – moving about, talking, shouting, singing, dancing and working.

Though cradles were used in medieval Europe, thus separating the baby from his mother's body, these were always placed in the centre of the house, where there was most bustle and activity – not in a separate room – and anyone on hand could rock the cradle.

Seclusion

This concentrated social life in which babies participate in non-Western cultures starts when the baby is about 6 weeks old, usually following a naming ceremony. Until that time the baby is usually in rather muted, dim surroundings, kept well away from contact with anyone who could cast the Evil Eye on the child or whose malice could make the baby ill. It is as if the child is on a bridge from the spirit world into becoming a person and therefore in a vulnerable and potentially dangerous state of being.

Traditionally the mother is supposed to be in seclusion with her baby in a separate room or hut for some weeks. A seclusion period of forty days occurs over and over again in different societies. In fact, it rarely works out in quite that way, usually because there is work to be done. When a woman is living in poverty or when the rest of the family depend on her labour, she cannot stay in seclusion; but it still remains the ideal. During this time she must eat certain foods and avoid others and keep away from harmful influences.

Other women in the extended family look after her. If it is a polygynous household the co-wives care for her. Among contemporary polygynous Mormons in Utah, for example, sister wives take over all the household tasks and the care of the other children. The mother is often given a special oil massage either by her female friends and relatives or by the midwife. In Yucatan the traditional midwife comes each day to massage her legs, back and abdomen. The baby, too, is massaged every day.

The mother is supposed to keep very warm and it is thought that she is particularly susceptible to being chilled. In Jamaica, where the mother and baby are in a darkened room for the first nine days – sometimes longer – the mother wears a turban to protect her from 'baby chill', and neighbours or relatives bring her porridge and other hot dishes they have prepared for her. She also burns incense in order to attract 'the good angels'.

In Yucatan the Mayan woman spends the first eight days after birth in the security of her hammock with her baby. The room is dark and Brigitte Jordan, an anthropologist with specialist knowledge of birth among Maya women, says that the mother and baby are oriented almost exclusively to each other through touch, movement, sounds and smells. She points out that it is a very good setting for establishing breast-feeding. The mother puts the baby to the breast whenever it stirs or makes a sound, and Dr Jordan has never seen or heard of breast-feeding failure under these conditions.[20]

A new mother living in the mountains of Ecuador observes the *dieta*, forty to forty-five days of seclusion (now often shortened to eight days) in which special dietary rules must be kept. All the cooking is done by the woman's own mother and sister-in-law, and she is cherished by the women members of her own and her husband's family and given special nourishing foods: chicken and chicken soup, noodles, rice, milk dishes, porridge and potato soup. She rests in bed, stays indoors to avoid bright sunlight and is free from sexual obligations.

For the first three days the woman is swaddled in a similar way to her baby, to help her bones 'realign'. Once free of the swaddling bands, she has a six-week holiday (vacation) – something that must be excitingly different from the usual constant hard toil of a peasant woman's life – and can concentrate exclusively on her baby. At the

229

end of the *dieta* the woman is bathed in water with herbs, perfume and milk and resumes her household and other duties.[21]

In many cultures 'the fire rest' is kept for anything from one to six weeks after childbirth, depending on the mother's health and whether it is a harsh winter. People believe that a woman must be kept warm after having a baby. In Melanesia and Polynesia the mother lies beside a coconut fire while her women friends massage her with coconut oil.

This fire rest used to be common practice among native Americans. In the south-west a pit was made and hot stones put in it. This was covered with sand or ashes on which the mother could lie. Whenever the woman felt she was not warm enough, some freshly heated stones were put under her. In some tribes the new mother lay with the whole trunk of her body submerged in warm sand, which was replaced when she wanted more heat. The Hopi sandwiched hot sand between cloths and lay sheepskin over it on which the mother could rest.

Whether or not it includes a fire rest, the practice of seclusion results in the mother having a prolonged time in a private and intimate setting in which to get to know her baby and to come to accept her new role as a mother. She has practical help and emotional support from a small group of other women and does not have to carry on her usual duties or to do anything for her husband. It is a time for being cherished.

This is the very opposite of the image that many Westerners have of childbirth in the Third World – a woman having her baby in the fields or at the side of the road, then picking it up, biting the umbilical cord and carrying on with her work. Though this happens in some societies, it is from necessity and the exigencies of dire poverty rather than design. All over the world it is common for the new mother to be cared for by other women, be released from her usual duties and have time in which to get to know her baby. This cherishing of the mother is probably one of the elements in traditional post-natal care that helps her cherish her baby. She has been personally enriched by becoming a mother and the community acknowledges her enhanced status, celebrates with her and gives warm approval and unstinted practical help. Even in poverty, children are seen as a family's riches, and a woman who has borne a child has produced a welcome harvest.

Human fertility may be seen as closely linked with the fertility of animals and of the earth itself. When a woman bears a child, she stimulates a similar ripeness and richness in the rest of nature, especially the things on which the society depends for its livelihood and sustenance. Plants grow better, there are bigger catches of fish, rice germinates, maize springs, men return from the hunt laden with meat. It is not just that the woman has had a baby; the whole community is regenerated.

This is expressed succinctly in graphic form in a piece of woven cloth from the island of Mindanao in the Philippines. Successive scenes are depicted rather in the manner of a comic strip, starting with a solitary figure and a barren garden and then going on to symbolize conception, fecundity and birth, with the rectangle that represents the garden plot becoming stuffed with plants, until by the time the baby is produced it is in a state of resplendent harvest. Human fertility and the productivity of land are interdependent, and when a woman gives birth, she stimulates the earth, too, to bear fruit. Childbearing is a religious and ritual event undertaken for the welfare of the whole society, and birth a sacred act.

Contrasts

For a woman in a northern industrialized country today having a baby is very different. It is a medical rather than a religious act. It takes place among strangers rather than among friends. And the ultimate authority about how it is conducted usually lies with a man – the senior obstetrician – rather than other experienced women. For the most part it also takes place on alien territory – a hospital instead of in the woman's or her mother's home, or the village seclusion hut.

Many women find the whole birth experience not only painful but traumatic. They feel out of control of a major event in their lives. One consequence of this can be that they start off motherhood with reduced confidence and self-esteem, often with a sense of guilt that they have not performed well, and feeling inadequate in the most essentially female function of all.

At a time when a woman needs most self-confidence and

assertiveness, she is expected to be a passive patient and behave like an obedient little girl. This can incapacitate her in her new role as a mother. Because she feels a failure even before she has really started, it is hardly surprising that when the baby cries, she responds with fear, self-doubt, confusion – and sometimes sheer panic.

In any industrialized society a woman also faces motherhood more or less alone. Unlike women in traditional societies, she may be socially isolated in the box of a high-rise flat (apartment) or suburban house where she does not know the neighbours. (As I write, the body of an elderly man living alone has been discovered when officials broke into his home to find out why the gas bill had not been paid. He had been dead for six months.) Help is not volunteered and it is very difficult to ask for it when there is no customary mutual support system. In fact, to do so seems to be an admission of weakness and inability to cope and to intrude on other people's busy lives. Sometimes a woman is anxious that if she seeks help, someone else will come in and take over. She worries that if it is discovered that she cannot manage, the social services will be mobilized and she may be 'locked up' or 'put away' and lose her baby.

A new mother may be starved of all human contact except with a partner who comes in from work expecting peace, hot food, comfort and sex. Instead he finds a crying baby, chaos and a woman in distress. The old days before the baby came seem a dream that has faded. And it looks as if the baby is personally responsible for their present unhappiness.

Another major difference between industrialized and traditional societies is that the independence that adults are supposed to demonstrate in our culture is also imposed on children from a very early age, even from babyhood. If a woman feeds whenever the baby wants to suckle, if the child sleeps in her bed or she continues breast-feeding after the baby is 9 months, she may be criticized for 'giving in' to her baby and warned that she is 'making a rod for her back'. People tell her that she will never manage to get the baby out of her bed, that the child will grow up 'clinging' and fearful and, in the case of a son, 'tied to her apron strings' – implying that he will be effeminate and unable to form heterosexual relationships. There is great insistence in our culture on the inculcation of independence in our children. It is perceived as a moral responsibility. Sleeping through the night, progressing to 'solids', being potty-trained, are not merely matters of parental convenience, but are signs of this development towards social independence – milestones on the journey.

It is the very opposite of the relationship between the peasant mother and her child, whom she snuggles inside her shawl or poncho, or binds next to her skin. Perhaps we should not be surprised when babies protest about being forcefully parted from the comforting smell, the firmness, softness and security of their mother's bodies, the sound of their voices and the steady beat of the maternal heart.

Mothers, too, may miss out on something in our culture. It is sure to be more difficult to know and enjoy your baby if your main purpose is to service the child, keep it fed and clean and then put it down to sleep. When the baby shows that it does not like this treatment, often it turns into a permanent battle of wills.

In place of the spontaneous stimulation provided by an action-packed environment in a traditional society, our culture provides learning materials designed and mass-produced by baby-equipment manufacturers: mobiles, squeakers, rattles, soft toys, teething rings and beads – inanimate objects in moulded plastic. The baby is supposed to be contented staring at these things and, when a little older, playing with them so that adults can get on with their work and with grown-up occupations.

Special crib computers are now on the market. They can be activated by the baby's voice so that systematic learning can start even before the child can focus or grasp, and without requiring parents to give up any time to this task. A 'cognition crib' is advertised in the United States. It has a tape recorder that starts running in response to a command from the baby's voice, and into its frame are built 'programmed play modules for sensory and physical practice', which the parents are instructed to change at stated times. These include plastic faces, mobiles, an aquarium and 'ego-building' mirrors. The implication is that once the baby is provided with this costly piece of learning equipment, parents can go off and get on with their lives while he automatically receives all the stimulation and learning required to be a top-grade citizen. A basic idea behind it is that it is even better than the stimulation parents can give because it is devised by psychologists and pediatricians, who, rather than parents, are the real experts about babies.

The organization of infant stimulation in this way is part of a system of behaviour in which time is compartmentalized. A woman believes that she should really have a 'routine'. Books still suggest that she should plan her day so that the housework does not fall behind and her husband can come home to a meal with an attractive wife who has taken the trouble to do her hair and put on make-up, while the baby sleeps peacefully. If her marriage falls apart because the house is a mess, the draining board is piled high with dirty dishes and there are unidentifiable furry objects in the refrigerator, she is warned that she has only herself to blame. She feels under tremendous pressure to get the baby into some sort of routine. The child then becomes another work task, and the goal, to complete that task within defined time limits. Unfortunately the baby has not read these books. The inevitable result is conflict.

In many ways, then, being a mother is easier in traditional cultures and babies are probably happier. They do not have to be slotted into life. They belong to the community and are its justification, its hope and its future. No woman is considered 'just a housewife', and motherhood brings a sense of self-enhancement, which is also acknowledged by everyone else.

Yet there are many things, of course, about traditional cultures that a woman in the industrial north could not tolerate: the rigidity of tradition, the power of the old who insist that nothing must change, family systems in which there is no privacy at all and almost everything you have must be shared with others, having all decisions made for you by your husband and others in the family, and never being able to act independently – and all this when you may be living in desperate poverty and are expected to go on bearing children until your health is sapped. Few of us would really want to go back to a peasant past, even if that were possible.

There is also a problem in selecting elements in peasant life and choosing them as if from a menu to add to our own complicated lives. It is incredibly difficult because for us they are artificial additives. If we try to do some of the things that mothers have traditionally done in rural cultures, we are forced to explain and defend ourselves. A determined woman who decides to breast-feed a child who enjoys sucking until the age of 3 or more, for example, a traditional practice for Australian Aborigines, or another who has her children sleeping with her in the family bed or lets them stay up till all hours, is sure to receive a great deal of criticism from other people and is likely to have many doubts about what she is doing. We discover, in fact, that we are as culture-bound as they were.

Yet there are many things we can learn from women in other societies. In discovering what they do when faced with similar challenges we begin to question attitudes of behaviour we took for granted. We see our problems more in perspective and may come up with unexpected solutions. Long before any books were written women all over the world knew how to care for babies and bring up children, and they go on doing it in the absence of psychologists, educationalists, pediatricians and other experts. There is a great sisterhood out there, women in many different cultures and in our own, with the knowledge that grows out of women's shared lives and practical experience. Every page of this book is a celebration of what women already know and can give to each other.

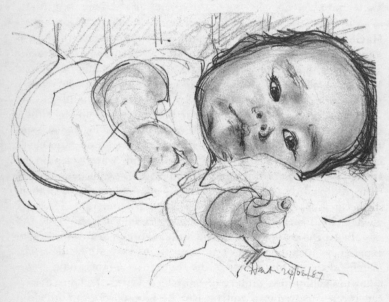

Postscript

Having a crying baby is often treated as if it were a private matter, something a woman has to sort out for herself. It is often also taken for granted that it is her *fault* in some way, and shows that she is inadequate as a mother. When help is offered, it is 'try this!' or 'try that!' or, if medical, it consists of drugs for her as well as the baby.

Listening to and learning from women, I see crying babies from a different point of view. Each inconsolably crying baby is evidence of how overwhelmingly difficult the transition to motherhood is for many women because we are isolated from each other. In fact, many remain socially isolated during the whole period until their children go to school. And when a woman becomes a mother, she becomes, in effect, a non-person – more or less invisible except as a wife to her husband and mother to her children.

Being the mother of a crying baby, like so many other female experiences, including biological processes such as menstruation and menopause, and physical problems such as vaginal thrush, pain following episiotomy, urinary incontinence, cystitis and breast cancer, is often treated as a guilty secret, to be confessed only to close friends, or a symptom for which a woman seeks professional advice in her doctor's office. Women find it hard to communicate about these things, both because we feel there must be something wrong with *us* and because there is often no language in which to talk about what is happening to us.

Because having a crying baby is a temporary phase of motherhood we tend also to push it into the background of our minds once the baby has stopped crying, and to refer to it merely as a bad patch in our lives. We see it as an aberration from the normal rather than as a direct reflection of the ordinary experience of being a woman and a mother in our society.

One of the things women have learned through feminism is that the personal is the political. When we confront enormous challenges in our lives, when we are overwhelmed with pain and suffering, we can be certain that other women are enduring the same stress, facing the same crises. As women come together and share what we know, we can create the words needed to describe female reality. We can validate each other's experiences. Instead of discarding and trivializing them as we struggle to conform to socially imposed images of ourselves as mothers – instead of feeling sick with guilt because we are not up to standard – we can use these shared experiences to develop new insights into the lives of women and to create a political, economic and social system that is empowering for women as mothers.

Appendix

The British questionnaire

A Parents Survey: Why do babies cry?

All babies cry at times, but some cry excessively. In this special survey we hope to find out why some babies cry more than others and about how parents cope. So if your baby is 9 months or younger, we'd like you to help us by filling in this questionnaire about his or her crying, whether excessive or not and even if it's stopped now.

Although we've asked for your name and address, your personal details will remain confidential. If you don't mind being interviewed, please give your telephone number as well.

Name ....

Address...........................

....

....

Telephone number ....

1. Your age when this baby was born

under 16 ☐

16–20 ☐

21–25 ☐

26–35 ☐

over 36 ☐

2. Is this your first baby? yes ☐ no ☐

3. If no, how many other children do you have?

1 ☐

2 ☐

3 ☐

4 ☐

5 ☐

more than 5 ☐

4. Are you living with your partner?

yes ☐ no ☐

5. How old is your baby?

up to 6 weeks ☐

6 weeks to 3 months ☐

3–6 months ☐

6–9 months ☐

6. What sex is your baby?
boy ☐
girl ☐

7. Where was your baby born?
in hospital ☐
at home ☐
other *(please specify)* ....

8. Did you attend antenatal classes?
yes ☐ no ☐

9. Was the subject of 'unsettled babies' discussed?
yes ☐ no ☐

10. Were you prepared for the fact that your baby might cry a lot?
yes ☐ no ☐

11. Was this a planned pregnancy?
yes ☐ no ☐

12. Did you enjoy your pregnancy?
yes ☐ no ☐

13. Did you have any of the following problems during your pregnancy? *(please tick)*
medical ☐
financial ☐
family ☐
work ☐
personal ☐
marital ☐
other ☐

14. Was your labour induced?
yes ☐ no ☐

15. If yes, how was it induced?
with a drip ☐
with pessaries ☐
by rupture of the membranes ☐
don't know ☐

other *(please specify)* ....

16. Was your labour speeded up?
yes ☐ no ☐

17. If yes, by what method?
drip ☐
rupture of the membranes ☐
other *(please specify)* ....

18. Did you have drugs for pain relief while you were in labour?
yes ☐ no ☐

19. If yes, which one(s)?
epidural ☐
pethidine ☐
gas and oxygen ☐
don't know ☐
other *(please specify)* ....

20. How long was your labour?
less than 2 hours ☐
between 2 and 8 hours ☐
between 8 and 12 hours ☐
longer than 12 hours ☐
no labour because planned Caesarean ☐

21. Was your delivery
normal? ☐
forceps? ☐
Caesarean? ☐
ventouse *(suction)*? ☐

22. Were you able to move around freely during labour?
yes ☐ no ☐

23. Were you able to give birth in a position of your choice?
yes ☐ no ☐

24. How did you feel about the way the staff treated you during your labour and delivery?
very happy ☐
quite happy ☐

unhappy ☐

25. Were the medical staff concerned about your baby's condition immediately after the birth *(for example, problems with breathing)*?
yes ☐ no ☐

26. In the first two weeks after your baby was born did he/she spend any time in a special-care unit?
yes ☐ no ☐

27. If yes, for how long?
up to 48 hours ☐
up to a week ☐
longer ☐

28. Have phototherapy *(under the lights)* for jaundice?
yes ☐ no ☐

29. Have feeding problems?
yes ☐ no ☐

30. Have any other problems?
yes ☐ no ☐

31. If your baby cried a lot as a new-born, did your post-natal medical advisers *(doctor, health visitor and so on)* help you with this?
yes ☐ no ☐

32. Do you think your baby cries more than is normal now?
yes ☐ no ☐

Even if your baby has now stopped crying a lot, please complete as many of the following questions as you can as if you were answering them when your baby was still crying excessively.

33. If your baby cries a lot, at what age did this start?
from birth onwards ☐
1–6 weeks old ☐

6 weeks–3 months old ☐
3–6 months old ☐
6–9 months old ☐

34. Was this crying mostly during the day (including evenings) or during the night *(the hours you usually sleep)*?
day ☐
night ☐

35. If your baby is still crying a lot, on how many occasions has he/she cried more or less continuously for more than an hour during the last 24 hours?
on one occasion ☐
on two occasions ☐
on three occasions ☐
on four occasions ☐
more than this ☐

36. When your baby won't stop crying, is it because he/she is
hungry? ☐
uncomfortable? ☐
in pain? ☐
unhappy? ☐
seeking attention? ☐
being naughty? ☐
spoilt? ☐
crying for no real reason? ☐
don't know ☐

37. When does your baby usually cry most?
morning ☐
afternoon ☐
evening ☐
during the night ☐
after a feed ☐
after a bath ☐

38. During the period that your baby usually cries most, for how long does he/she cry?
up to one hour ☐
1–2 hours ☐
2–4 hours ☐

over 4 hours ☐

39. If your baby's stopped crying excessively now, at what age did he/she stop?
0–6 weeks ☐
6 weeks–3 months ☐
3–6 months ☐
6–9 months ☐

40. Have you had to cope with excessive crying with another child?
yes ☐ no ☐

41. Is your baby breast-fed?
yes ☐ no ☐

42. If no, when did you stop breast-feeding?
never breast-fed ☐
within 1 week of birth ☐
between 1–6 weeks ☐
between 6 weeks–3 months ☐
between 3–6 months ☐
between 6–9 months ☐

43. Is your baby bottle-fed?
yes ☐ no ☐

44. Is your baby having mixed breast/bottle feeds?
yes ☐ no ☐

45. If yes, at what age did he/she start having bottle feeds?
within 1 week of birth ☐
between 1–6 weeks ☐
between 6 weeks–3 months ☐
between 3–6 months ☐
between 6–9 months ☐

46. Is your baby having any solid foods?
yes ☐ no ☐

47. If yes, when did he/she start having solids?
before he/she was

2 months old ☐
between 2–3 months ☐
between 3–4 months ☐
between 4–5 months ☐
between 5–6 months ☐
between 6–9 months ☐

48. If your baby cries a lot and you're breast-feeding, do you think anything you eat or drink may be affecting him/her?
yes ☐ no ☐

49. If yes, what?
fruit ☐
vegetables ☐
dairy foods ☐
alcohol ☐
tea and/or coffee ☐
highly flavoured foods ☐
drugs ☐
other *(please specify)* ....

50. If you're bottle-feeding, what milk are you giving your baby?
SMA ☐
Cow & Gate ☐
Ostermilk ☐
Milumil ☐
cow's milk ☐
soya milk ☐
other *(please specify)* ....

51. If your baby's having any solid foods, what are these?
gluten-free cereals ☐
other cereals ☐
dairy products ☐
egg yolk ☐
whole eggs ☐
fruit ☐
vegetables ☐
fish ☐
white meat ☐
red meat ☐
other *(please specify)* ....

52. Is your baby feeding well?
yes ☐   no ☐

53. Is your baby healthy and gaining weight normally?
yes ☐   no ☐

54. How many hours a day do you spend on housework (cooking, cleaning and so on)?
2 hours or less ☐
3–4 hours ☐
5–6 hours ☐
7–10 hours ☐
over 10 hours ☐

55. Do you feel you're coping with the housework and so on to your satisfaction?
yes ☐   no ☐

56. Do you go out to work (or do paid work from home)?
yes ☐   no ☐

57. If yes, for how many hours each week?
up to 10 hours ☐
10–20 hours ☐
21–30 hours ☐
over 31 hours ☐

58. Do you have any help with housework and/or baby-care?
yes ☐   no ☐

59. If yes, who helps you?
partner ☐
relative ☐
paid help ☐
friend ☐
council provided home
   help ☐

60. On weekdays, how long are you usually alone at home without another adult?
less than 2 hours ☐
2–4 hours ☐
4–8 hours ☐
8–12 hours ☐

12–24 hours ☐

61. How do you feel about this?
very happy ☐
quite happy ☐
unhappy ☐

62. How long did you spend at home without another adult yesterday?
less than 2 hours ☐
2–4 hours ☐
4–8 hours ☐
8–12 hours ☐
12–24 hours ☐

63. Have you felt any of the following when your baby wouldn't stop crying?
desperate to make him/her
   stop ☐
alone with your problem ☐
sorry for your baby ☐
that it's part of being
   a mother ☐
sorry for yourself ☐
depressed ☐
angry ☐
guilty ☐
that you must get away ☐
other (please specify) ....

64. What have you done when your baby wouldn't stop crying?
cuddled or rocked the
   baby ☐
fed the baby ☐
talked to the baby ☐
changed the baby's
   nappy ☐
asked someone else to
   take the baby ☐
given the baby a dummy ☐
left the baby alone ☐
taken the baby out ☐
taken the baby to
   bed with you ☐
talked to another adult ☐
tried one thing after

another ☐
other *(please specify)* ....

65. Have you ever felt like doing any of these things *(but not actually done them)* when you couldn't cope with your baby's crying any longer?
crying ☐
shouting ☐
trying to get away
  from the baby ☐
smacking the baby ☐
shaking or gripping
  the baby ☐
taking a tranquillizer
  or other drug ☐
having an alcoholic drink ☐
other *(please specify)* ....

66. Have you ever done any of these things when you couldn't cope with your baby's crying any longer?
sought someone else's
  company ☐
asked someone else
  to take the baby ☐
cried ☐
taken the baby out ☐
shouted ☐
tried to get away
  from the baby ☐
smacked the baby ☐
shaken or gripped
  the baby ☐
taken a tranquillizer
  or other drug ☐
had an alcoholic drink ☐

67. Have other people commented on your baby's crying?
yes ☐ no ☐

68. Have other people made you feel guilty about your baby's crying?
yes ☐ no ☐

69. Has your partner said that your baby cries (or cried) a lot?
yes ☐ no ☐

70. How has your partner usually reacted to your baby's crying?
felt sorry for you ☐
felt sorry for the baby ☐
didn't notice ☐
became angry ☐
blamed you ☐
became upset ☐
other *(please specify)* ....

71. How has your partner made you feel about your baby's crying?
that you have to
  cope with it together ☐
that he's worried ☐
that he's upset ☐
that it's your
  responsibility ☐
guilty ☐
angry ☐
other *(please specify)* ....

72. What has your partner usually done about your baby's crying?
picked up baby ☐
rocked baby ☐
ignored baby ☐
become angry ☐
comforted you ☐
gone out ☐
taken baby out ☐
other *(please specify)* ....

73. What has your partner done when he couldn't cope with the baby's crying any longer?
asked you to take
  the baby away ☐
got away from the baby ☐
had an alcoholic drink ☐
shouted ☐
hit the baby ☐

hit you ☐
taken a tranquillizer
  or other drug ☐
other *(please specify)* ....

74. If your baby cries a lot have you sought help about it?
        yes ☐ no ☐

75. If yes, from whom?
doctor ☐
health visitor ☐
relative ☐
support group ☐
friend ☐
other *(please specify)* ....

76. Did you find the advice helpful?
        yes ☐ no ☐

77. Did it actually stop your baby from crying so much?
        yes ☐ no ☐

78. If no, did it make you feel better to have talked about it anyway?
        yes ☐ no ☐

79. If you've sought medical advice about your baby's crying *(doctor, health visitor and so on)*, did you feel that they took your problem seriously?
        yes ☐ no ☐

It would be very helpful if you could answer the following questions but if you prefer not to, please feel free to leave them blank. All information will be treated in the strictest confidence.

80. If your partner is living with you, is he employed?
        yes ☐ no ☐

81. What is your family's gross *(before tax)* annual income?
under £5000 ☐
between £5000 and

£10,000 ☐
between £11,000 and £15,000 ☐
between £16,000 and £20,000 ☐
over £20,000 ☐

82. What kind of accommodation do you live in?
council rented ☐
private rented ☐
own home ☐
with relatives ☐
other *(please specify)* ....

83. How much space do you have?
bedsit ☐
one bedroom flat or house ☐
two bedroom flat or house ☐
three bedroom flat or house ☐
four bedroom flat or house ☐
other *(please specify)* ....

Here are some additional questions which need detailed answers. Please write your answers on a separate sheet *(or sheets)* of paper and attach it *(them)* to the questionnaire. Please write the number of the question beside each answer.

1. If you were under any stress, or had any problems, during your pregnancy, please give details.

2. How did you feel about yourself, your partner and the baby (for example, did you feel depressed and unhappy or ecstatic)?
a) in the seven days after the birth
b) one to six weeks after the birth

3. If you felt there was some concern about your baby's condition immediately after the birth, please describe what it was.

4. If this is not your first baby and you've had to cope with excessive crying with another child, please describe what happened with the other child.

5. If you've sought help about your baby's crying, please describe the advice you've been given and who it came from.

6. How much time did you or your partner spend attending to your baby's practical needs (feeding, changing and so on) during the last 24 hours?

7. How much time did you or your partner spend cuddling, playing with or talking to your baby during the last 24 hours?

8. If your baby cries (or cried) a lot, does (or did) your partner give you the support you need(ed) to cope with this and with your baby generally?

9. What do you enjoy most about your baby?

10. If your baby cries (or cried) a lot, is (or was) there anything else about him/her, apart from the crying, that upsets you?

11. If the excessive crying has stopped, did you find a solution or did it stop spontaneously? Please describe what happened.

12. During your baby's excessive crying what has helped you to cope the most?

13. What advice would you give to other parents whose babies cry a lot?

The Australian questionnaire

Crying baby survey

We'd like you to tell us how you feel and what you do when your baby cries.

1. Your baby's age in months please ☐ ☐

2. Was the labour . . . *(please tick one)*
- induced (waters broken, no drip) ☐
- induced with drip (oxytocinon) ☐
- spontaneous (with pain relief) ☐
- spontaneous (without pain relief) ☐
- Caesarean section under epidural anaesthetic ☐
- Caesarean section under general anaesthetic ☐

3. How many hours does your baby usually cry?
- in the daytime ☐ ☐ hours
- in the night time ☐ ☐ hours

4. Why do you think your baby cries (the most common reason)? *(tick one)*
- hunger ☐
- not feeding properly ☐
- cold ☐
- wet or dirty nappy ☐
- too much light and/or noise ☐
- bored or lonely ☐
- colic ☐
- lost thumb or dummy ☐
- other. *(Explain)* .... ☐

5. Is your baby . . . *(tick one)*
- breast-fed ☐

- bottle-fed ☐
- mixed breast/bottle-fed ☐
- starting solids with breast ☐
- starting solids with bottle ☐
- eating family foods ☐

6. Is this your first baby? yes ☐ no ☐
If no, ages of other children *(in months please)*
- second child ☐ ☐
- third child ☐ ☐
- fourth child ☐ ☐
- fifth child ☐ ☐

7. Have you had to cope with a crying problem with a previous child? yes ☐ no ☐
If yes, describe what happened
....
....
....

8. Here is how some women describe their feelings when the baby cries. Tick the *one* that *most* expresses how you feel.
- helpless ☐
- depressed ☐
- angry ☐
- frustrated ☐
- guilty ☐
- that you must escape ☐
- other. *(Explain)* ....
....
.... ☐

9. What do you *usually* do when your baby cries *(tick one only)*
- feed the baby ☐

247

leave the baby alone ☐
change the baby's nappy ☐
cuddle, rock and talk to the baby ☐
wrap the baby up tightly and check he's comfortable ☐
phone mother or a friend ☐
one thing after another ☐
Add your comments here: ....
....
....
....

10. **Here are some things parents say they do, or feel like doing when they can't cope any longer. What about you?** *(Tick your usual reaction – one only)*

shake the baby, or grip the baby tightly ☐
smack the baby ☐
throw baby down or throw something at baby ☐
shout (at baby, partner, or other children) ☐
smoke ☐
have an alcoholic drink or take a tranquillizer ☐
eat ☐
try to get away from baby ☐
other. *(Please explain)* ....
....
.... ☐

11. **What does your partner usually do when the baby cries?**

go out ☐
ignore the baby ☐
take over and help out ☐
shut himself/herself in another room ☐
shout at you ☐
offer advice ☐
other. *(Please explain)* ....
....
.... ☐

12. **What does your partner do when he/she feels he/she can't cope with baby's crying any longer?**

shakes the baby, grips baby tightly or smacks baby ☐
throws baby down or throws something at baby ☐
shouts (at baby, you or other children) ☐
smokes ☐
goes out ☐
has a drink or takes a tranquillizer ☐
other. *(Please explain)* ....
....
.... ☐

13. **Do you take your baby into bed with you?**

always ☐
often ☐
sometimes ☐
never ☐

14. **Do you feel happy about this?**

yes ☐
no ☐
not sure ☐

15. **Does your partner feel happy about this?**

yes ☐
no ☐
not sure ☐

16. **How much time did you spend attending to your baby's practical needs (e.g. changing/feeding etc.) yesterday?**
about ☐ ☐ hours

18. **How much time did you spend cuddling/playing with/talking to your baby yesterday?**
about ☐ ☐ hours

19. **How much time did your partner spend**

248

cuddling/playing with/talking to your baby yesterday?

about ☐ ☐ hours

20. Do you have any help with the housework?

yes ☐ no ☐

If yes is it mainly *(tick one only please)*

your husband ☐
mother ☐
other relative ☐
friend/s ☐
paid help ☐
council help ☐
other. *(Please specify)* ....
....
.... ☐

21. Do you have any help with the baby?

yes ☐ no ☐

If yes is it . . .
your husband ☐
mother ☐
other relative ☐
friend/s ☐
paid babysitter ☐
crèche ☐
occasional care centre ☐
other. *(Please state)* ....
....
.... ☐ 9

22. On weekdays how long are you usually alone during the day without another adult?

hours ☐ ☐
Are you happy about this?
yes ☐ no ☐

23. When your partner comes home from work does he/she help with the baby?

yes ☐ no ☐
sometimes ☐

24. Does he/she help in the house?

yes ☐ no ☐
sometimes ☐

25. Do you or could you go out without the baby?

never ☐
sometimes ☐
when I need to ☐
once a week ☐

26. What do you enjoy the most about your baby?

watching him develop ☐
feeding him ☐
playing with him ☐
taking him out ☐
caring for him ☐
other. *(Please state)* ....
....
.... ☐ 6

27. Is there anything apart from crying which you really dislike about your baby?

yes ☐ no ☐

If yes, please state ....
....

28. If you have sought help, who has this been from?

clinic sister ☐
mother and baby home e.g.
  Tresillian ☐
family doctor ☐
pediatrician or specialist ☐
counsellor ☐
parent support group e.g.
  NMAA ☐
friend ☐
mother or mother-in-law ☐
other. *(Please explain)* ....
....
.... ☐

29. What advice were you given *(tick one)*?

change to bottle-feeding ☐
change to mixed bottle-feeding
  and breast-feeding
  (i.e. give 'complements') ☐
start solids ☐

wrap up tightly, make sure he's comfortable ☐

breast-feeding advice e.g. feed more often ☐

feed 'on demand' – when baby wants to ☐

play with baby ☐

give dummy ☐

other. *(Please explain)* ....
....
.... ☐

30. Did you follow this advice?
yes ☐ no ☐

31. Has it worked?
yes ☐ no ☐
sometimes ☐

32. What advice would you give to other parents? *(Tick one)*
seek help (from doctor, clinic sister, counsellor, state which)
.... ☐

attend to the baby whenever he cries ☐

ignore the baby if he cries 'too much' ☐

change to bottle-feeding ☐

ignore advice and follow your instincts and baby's cries ☐

join a parent support group, such as Nursing Mothers Association ☐

take the baby out at least once a day ☐

other. *(Please explain)* ....
....
.... ☐

If you would *like* to give it – you don't have to –

Your name ....
address ....
....
postcode .... **phone number** ....
Thank you

Helpful Addresses

Addresses for some of the smaller organizations listed below change yearly because officers hold honorary positions and there is no official headquarters, but it is worth contacting the individual listed to find the most up-to-date address. There are also many more organizations than those included in this list, and each one may be able to put you in touch with others.

Britain

Allergy

Allergy Support Service
Little Porters
64a Marshalls Drive
St Albans
Hertfordshire
Tel: 0727-58705

National Eczema Society
Tavistock House
North Tavistock Square
London WC1H 9SR
Tel: 01-388-4097

Asian Woman

Asian Women's Resource Centre (ASHA)
27 Santley Street
London SW4
Tel: 01-274-8854

Breast-feeding

Association of Breast-feeding Mothers
131 Mayow Road
London SE26 4HZ
Tel: 01-778-4769

La Leche League (Great Britain)
BM 3424
London WC1V 6XX
Tel: 01-404-5011

Counselling

Family Welfare Association
501–505 Kingsland Road
Dalston
London E8 4AU
Tel: 01-254-6251

Mainly London-based social work agency offering counselling help for families with personal and relationship difficulties.

Institute of Family Therapists
43 Cavendish Street
London W1M 7RG
Tel: 01-935-1651

Institute of Marital Studies
Tavistock Centre
120 Belsize Lane
London NW3 5BA
Tel: 01-435-7111

Parents Anonymous
6 Manor Gardens
London N7 6LA
Tel: 01-263-8918

A 24-hour telephone answering service for parents who feel they cannot cope or who feel they might abuse their children. Parents Anonymous Helpline is operated by about fifty volunteers, all of whom have access to an experienced adviser.

Relate
Herbert Gray College
Little Church Street
Rugby CV21 3AP
Tel: 0788-73241

Provides a confidential counselling service for people with relationship problems of any kind. To find your local branch, look under Marriage Guidance in the telephone directory or contact the above address.

Disability

Disabled Living Foundation
380–384 Harrow Road
London W9
Tel: 01-289-6111

Drugs

Life without Tranquillizers
Dr Vernon Coleman
Midhills
Lynmouth
Devon EX35 6EE

Helps anyone who is hooked on tranquillizers and campaigns for their control.

Tranx
17 Peel Road
Wealdstone
Harrow HA3 7QX
Tel: 01-427-2065

Help with Crying Babies

Crying Clinic
Department of Psychological Medicine
Great Ormond Street Hospital

For babies between 3 and 12 months via a general practitioner or health visitor

Cry-sis
BM Box Cry-sis
London WC1N 3XX
Tel: 01-404-5011

Network of local support groups for parents of crying babies.

National Association for Parents of Sleepless Children
Sally Baines (Secretary)
P.O. Box 38
Prestwood
Great Missenden
Buckinghamshire HP1 0SZ

Aims to offer support and advice to parents of sleepless children via quarterly newsletter and local groups. Write for more information and for details of your local group.

Homeopathy

British Homeopathic Association
27a Devonshire Street
London W1
Tel: 01-935-2163

Addresses of homeopathic hospitals can be obtained by sending an s.a.e. to the above address.

Liverpool Clinic
Department of Homeopathic Medicine
1 Myrtle Street
London L7 7DE
Tel: 01-709-5475

Royal Homeopathic Hospital
Great Ormond Street
London WC1
Tel: 01-837-3091

Society of Homeopathics
2a Bedford Place
Southampton SO1 2BY
Tel: 0703-222364

Meeting other Mothers

MAMA: The Meet-a-Mum Association
Kate Goodyear
3 Woodside Avenue
London SE25 5DW
Tel: 01-654-3137

Support available through social gatherings and on a mother-to-mother basis with volunteers who have themselves experienced post-natal problems. To find local MAMA group, write enclosing an s.a.e.

National Childbirth Trust
Alexandra House
Oldham Terrace
Acton
London W3 6NH
Tel: 01-992-8637

Childbirth classes, breast-feeding advice and post-natal support. Write or phone for information and details of your nearest branch.

OPUS
Lorna Jones (Secretary)
106 Godstone Road
Whyteleafe
Croydon CR3 0EB
Tel: 01-645-0469

National network of support
groups and day centres for
parents under stress.

Natural Healing

**British Naturopathic &
Osteopathic Association**
6 Weatherall Gardens
London NW3 5RR
Tel: 01-435-8728

For a list of 250 practitioners
enclose an s.a.e. and £1.00.

**International Institute of
Medical Herbalists**
41 Hatherlay Road
Winchester SO22 6RE

Enclose an s.a.e. for
practitioners' list.

Pre-term Babies

**NIPPERS: National
Information for Parents of
Prematures – Education,
Resources and Support**
Pauline Orpin
28 Swyncombe Avenue
London W5
Tel: 01-847-4721

Single Parents

Gingerbread
35 Wellington Street
London WC2E 7BN
Tel: 01-240-0953

Self-help association for one-
parent families. A network of
local groups offers mutual
support, information, and
practical help.

**Help
(Holidays Endeavour for
Lone Parents)**
59 Ridge Balk Lane
Woodlands
Doncaster
Yorkshire DN6 7NR
Tel: 0302-725315

Organization that arranges
holidays in Britain for single
parents, run by volunteers.

**National Council for One-
Parent Families**
235 Kentish Town Road
London NW5 2LX
Tel: 01-267-1361

For free and confidential advice
on matters relating to pregnancy,
housing, social security, taxation,
maintenance and housing
problems.

Twins and More

Twins and Multiple Births Association
20 Redcar Close
Lillington
Leamington Spa
Warwickshire CV32 7SU
Tel: 0926-22688

Send an s.a.e. for local contacts.

Other Sources of Help

Dial UK
Dial House
117 High Street
Clay Cross
Near Chesterfield
Derbyshire S45 9DZ
Tel: 0246-864498

National network providing information about professional and voluntary sources of help.

Hyperactive Children's Support Group
Mrs Sally Bunday
59 Meadowside
Angmering
West Sussex BN16 4BW

Pre-School Playgroups Association
61–63 Kings Cross Road
London WC1X NLL
Tel: 01-833-0991

Association of mother and toddler groups, playgroups and families of under-5s. Can give advice on setting up a nursery or playgroup, and provides help and support through a network covering England and Wales.

Women's Health Concern
17 Earl's Terrace
London W8 6LP

Send an s.a.e. for details.

United States

Babies in Hospital

Children in Hospitals Inc.
31 Wilshire Park
Needhan, Massachusetts 02190

Information about importance of close contact between parents and children in hospital; encourages hospitals to adopt policies of flexible visiting and rooming-in; publications.

Parents Concerned for Hospitalized Children Inc.
176 North Villa Avenue
Villa Park, Illinois 60181

Supports family-oriented pediatric care; offers support for parents with children in hospital.

Babies with Handicaps

American Cleft Palate Educational Foundation Inc.
331 Salk Hall
University of Pittsburgh
Pittsburgh, Pennsylvania
15261

Cleft Lip and Palate Group of CEA
129 Fayett East Street
Conshohocken,
Pennsylvania 19428
Tel: 215-828-0131

Down's Syndrome Congress
529 South Kenilworth
Oak Park, Illinois 60304
1640 West Roosevelt Road
Room 156-E
Chicago, Illinois 60608
Tel: 312-226-0416

Spina-bifida Association of America
343 South Dearborn 319
Chicago, Illinois 60604
Tel: 312-663-1562

United Cerebral Palsy Associations Inc.
66 East 34th Street
New York, New York 10016
Tel: 212-481-6300

Baby Carriers

Andrea's Babypack
2441 Hilyard Street
Eugene, Oregon 97405

Baby Carrier Kit
Chicks
PO Box 222
Sonora, California 95370

Baby Carrier Packet
La Leche League Order
Department
9616 Minneapolis Avenue
Franklyn Park, Illinois 60131

Information about different baby carriers.

Baby, too
A and B House
Box 166
Gilbertsville, New York 13776

Happy Baby Carriers
Happy Family Products
12300 Venice Boulevard
Los Angeles, California 90066

Pushka Front Baby Carrier
Cheralan Products
PO Box 1018
Greeley, Colorado 80631

Snugli Soft Baby Carrier
Snugli Inc.
1212 Kerr Gulch Road
Evergreen, Colorado 80439

Some Counselling Groups Specifically for Women

Berkeley Women's Health Collective
2908 Ellsworth Street
Berkeley, California 94705
Tel: 415-843-1437

Boston Psychological Center for Women
376 Boylston Suite 603
Boston, Massachusetts 02116
Tel: 617-266-0136

Crossroads Counseling Center
665 Deacon Street
Boston, Massachusetts 02215
Tel: 617-266-7805

Full Cycle Parents Network
PO Box 685
Capitola, California 95010
Tel: 408-475-6866

Help with household chores, workshops and publications.

Holistic Birth and Family Center
PO Box 421
Midwood Station
Brooklyn, New York 11230
Tel: 212-693-9230

Offers humanistic counselling and help with breast-feeding.

Sagaris: Women's Therapy Collective
2619 Garfield Avenue South
Minneapolis, Minnesota 55408
Tel: 612-825-7338

Womankind
5001 Olson Memorial Highway
Minneapolis, Minnesota 55422
Tel: 612-546-5001

Women Associates
402 West Mount Airy Avenue
Philadelphia,
Pennsylvania 19119
Tel: 215-248-4916

Women's Institute and Health Center Inc.
7151 West Manchester Avenue
Suite 1, Los Angeles,
California 90045
Tel: 213-641-2911

Women's Mental Health Collective Inc.
326 Somerville Avenue
Somerville,
Massachusetts 02143
Tel: 617-625-2729

Creating Self-help Groups

National Health-Help Clearinghouse
Graduate School and
University Center
CUNY
33 West 42nd Street
Room 1227
New York, New York 10036
Tel: 212-840-7606

Fathers

FAMLEE – Father and Mothers' Learning through Education and Experience
PO Box 15
Telford, Pennsylvania 18969

The Fatherhood Project
Bank Street College
610 West 112 Street
New York, New York 10025

Grieving

The Compassionate Friends Inc.
PO Box 1347
Oakbrook, Illinois 60521
Tel: 313-323-5010

Self-help organization for those who have lost someone they loved.

Nursing

BASE: Boston Association for Childbirth Education
Nursing Mothers' Council
184 Savin Hill Avenue
Dorchester,
Massachusetts 02125
Tel: 617-244-5102

Childbirth Education Association of Greater Philadelphia
Nursing Mothers'
Support Groups
5 East Second Avenue
Conshohocken,
Pennsylvania 19428
Tel: 215-828-0131

Human Lactation Center
666 Sturgess Highway
Westport, Connecticut 06880
Tel: 203-259-5995

Lactation Consultant Association
PO Box 4031
University of Virginia Station
Charlottesville,
Virginia 22903

La Leche League
9616 Minneapolis Avenue
Franklyn Park,
Illinois 60131
Tel: 312-455-7730

Offers mother-to-mother breast-feeding information.

Nursing Mothers' Council
PO Box 50063
Palo Alto, California 94303
Tel: 408-272-1448

Post-natal Support

Center for Family Growth
555 Highland Avenue
Cotati, California 94928
Tel: 707-795-5155

**COPE (Coping with the
Overall Pregnancy
Parenting Experience)**
37 Clarendon Street
Boston, Massachusetts 02116
Tel: 617-357-5588

Full Cycle Parents' Network
PO Box 685
Capitola, California 95010
Tel: 408-475-6866

Mother and Child Center
YM-YWCA
175 Memorial Highway
New Rochelle,
New York 10801

The Mothers' Center
United Methodist Church
Old Country Road and
Nelson Avenue
Hicksville, New York 11801
Tel: 516-822-4539

**Mothers' Center of
Central New Jersey**
YWCA
220 Clark Street
Westfield, New Jersey 17090
Tel: 201-233-2833

Mothers' Center of Queens
Bayside YMCA
214–11 35th Avenue
Bayside, New York 11361
Tel: 212-229-5972

Mothers' Center of Suffolk
PO Box 92
Holbrook, New York 11741
Tel: 516-585-5587

**Mothers' Center of
St Louis**
516 Laughbrough
St Louis, Missouri 63111
Tel: 314-353-1558

Pre-term Babies

Parents of Prematures
13613 North East 26th Place
Bellevue, Washington 98005
Tel: 206-883-6040

Single Mothers

**Parents without Partners
Inc.**
80 Fifth Street
New York, New York 10011

Twins

National Organization of Mothers of Twins Club
5402 Amberwood Lane
Rockville, Maryland 20853
Tel: 301-460-910

Other likely sources of help may be found through your local church, synagogue, women's health center or group and through chapters of ICEA.

ICEA
PO Box 20048
Minneapolis,
Minnesota 55420-0048

Canada

Babies with Handicaps

These addresses are the national headquarters of each organization. Each organization also has a provincial and/or a municipal representative. For information, write to the address below or your local representative.

About Face: The Cranio Facial Family Association
170 Elizabeth Street
Toronto, Ontario M5G 1E5
Tel: 416-593-1448

Asthma Society of Canada
PO Box 213, Station 'K'
Toronto, Ontario M4P 2G5
Tel: 416-977-9684

Canadian Association of the Deaf
271 Spadina Road
Toronto, Ontario M5R 2V3
Tel: 416-928-9137

Canadian National Institute for the Blind
1931 Bayview Avenue
Toronto, Ontario M4G 4C8
Tel: 416-480-7580

Cerebral Palsy Association of Canada
55 Bloor Street East
Toronto, Ontario M4W 1A9
Tel: 416-923-2932

Cleft Lip and Palate Family Association
175 Elizabeth Street
Toronto, Ontario M5G 2G3
Tel: 416-598-2311

Cystic Fibrosis Foundation, Canada
221 Yonge Street
Suite 601
Toronto, Ontario M4S 2B4
Tel: 416-485-9149

Down's Syndrome Association of Metro Toronto
120 Courcelette
Toronto, Ontario M1N 2T2
Tel: 416-690-2503

G.A. Roeher Institute/ National Institute for the Mentally Retarded
4700 Keele Street
York University
The Kinsmen Building
Downsview, Ontario M3J 1P3
Tel: 416-661-9611

Spina Bifida and Hydrocephalus Association of Canada
633 Wellington Crescent
Winnipeg,
Manitoba R3M OA8
Tel: 416-364-1871

Bereavement

Bereaved Families of Ontario
214 Merton Street
Suite 305
Toronto, Ontario M4S 1A6
Tel: 416-440-0290

Multiple Births

Winnipeg Parents of Twins and Triplets Organization
Winnipeg, Manitoba
Tel: 204-488-3732

Single Parents

One Parent Family Association of Canada
6979 Yonge Street
Toronto, Ontario M2M 3X9
Tel: 416-226-0062

Parents Without Partners, Canada
205 Yonge Street
Toronto, Ontario M5B 1N2
Tel: 416-363-0960

Zonta Centre for Young Single Parents
346 Murray Street
Ottawa, Ontario K1N 5N4
Tel: 613-235-0368

Other Organizations for Parents

Aid for New Mothers
994 Bathurst Street
Toronto, Ontario M5R 3G7
Tel: 416-535-2368

British Columbia Parents in Crisis Society
13-250 Willingdon (Burnaby)
Vancouver, BC V5C 5E9
Tel: 604-299-0521

Canadian Counsel for Co-Parenting
PO Box 555, Stn 'A'
Ottawa, Ontario K1N 9H1
Tel: 613-233-0273

Childcare Information
256 King Edward Avenue
Ottawa, Ontario K1N 7M1
Tel: 613-235-7256

Family Service Bureau
1801 Toronto Street
Regina,
Saskatchewan S4P 1M7
Tel: 306-757-6675

**Mother and Unborn
Childcare**
7-3580 Moncton Rmd
Vancouver, BC V7E 3A4
Tel: 604-272-0126

Parent Aide Program
Second Floor
611 Wellington Crescent
Winnipeg, Manitoba
R3M 0A7
Tel: 204-284-1657

Parent Child Centre
425 Elgin Street
Winnipeg,
Manitoba R3A 0K8
Tel: 204-947-6825

**Parent Information
Network of
Northern Alberta**
8530-101 Street
Edmonton, Alberta T6A 0K9
Tel: 403-433-0969

Parent Participation
540 Range Road
Whitehorse, Yukon Y1A 4N3

Organizations for Women

Montreal Women's Centre
3585 St Urbain
Montreal, PQ H2X 2N6
Tel: 514-482-1069

**Native Women's
Association of the
North West Territories**
Box 2321
Yellowknife, NWT X1A 2P7
Tel: 403-873-5509

Women in Transition
143 Spadina Road
Toronto, Ontario M5R 2T1
Tel: 416-967-5227

Women's Centre
83 Military Road
St John's,
Newfoundland A1C 2C8
Tel: 709-753-0220

Women's Centre
219-1810 Smith Street
Regina,
Saskatchewan S4P 2N3
Tel: 306-522-2777

Women's Centre
103-302 Steele Street
Whitehorse, Yukon Y1A 2C5
Tel: 403-667-2693

**Women's Counselling &
Referral Centre**
525 Bloor Street West
Toronto, Ontario M5S 1Y4
Tel: 416-534-7501

Women's Emergency Accommodation Centre
10007-105A Avenue
Edmonton, Alberta T5H 0M5
Tel: 403-423-5302

Women's Network
180 Richmond Street
Charlottetown, PEI C1A 1J2
Tel: 902-894-8024

Women's Place
1-1349 Johnson
West Rock
Vancouver, BC V6H 3R9
Tel: 604-536-9611

Australia

Babies in Hospital

Association for the Welfare of Children in Hospital
80 Phillip Street
Parramatta, NSW 2150
Tel: 02-635-4785

PO Box 2101
Southport, QLD 4215
Tel: 07-378-1701

Room 9, Florence
Knight Building
Adelaide Children's Hospital
72 King William Road
North Adelaide, SA 5006
Tel: 08-267-7000

51 Hill Street
West Hobart, TAS 7000
Tel: 002-34-4625

70 Sydney Street
Footscray, VIC 3011
Tel: 03-63-2864

1186 Hay Street
West Perth, WA 605
Tel: 09-321-4821

Babies with Handicaps

Association of Intellectual Disability
Block E
Acton House
Edinburgh Avenue
Canberra City, ACT 2601
Tel: 062-47-6022

Association of Relatives and Friends of the Emotionally and Mentally Ill (ARAFEMI) Victoria, Inc.
615 Camberwell Road
Camberwell, VIC 3124
Tel: 03-29-3733/1777

Association of Relatives and Friends of the Mentally Ill
165 Blues Point Road
McMahons Point, NSW 2060
Tel: 02-698-8216

35 Fullarton Road
Kent Town, SA 5067
Tel: 08-42-6772

2 Nicholson Road
Subiaco, WA 6008
Tel: 009-381-4747

Cerebral Palsy Association
31 Fitzmaurice Street
Kaleen, ACT 2617
Tel: 062-41-5652

Cerebral Palsy Self-Help Group of South Australia
1-3 Old Treasury Lane
Adelaide, SA 5000
Tel: 08-232-0407

Cleft Palate and Lip Society
7 Ernest Street
Sunshine, VIC 3020
Tel: 03-311-7893

Down's Syndrome Association
31 O'Connell Street
Parramatta, NSW 2150
Tel: 02-683-4333

10 Witherden Street
Nakara, NT 5792
Tel: 089-27-9408

101 Highgate Street
Cooper Plains, QLD 4108
Tel: 07-275-1947

PO Box 65
Burnside, SA 5066
Tel: 08-275-5326

55 Victoria Parade
Collingwood, VIC 3066
Tel: 03-419-1653

110 Bessell Avenue
Como, WA 6152
Tel: 09-443-3628

Grow (Queensland) Community Mental Health
43 Crown Street
Holland Park, QLD 4121
Tel: 07-394-4344

Queensland Spastic Welfare League
Spastic Centre
55 Oxlade Drive
New Farm, QLD 4005
Tel: 07-358-3011

Retarded Citizens' Welfare Association
11–13 Morrison Street
Hobart, TAS 7000
Tel: 002-23-6644

The Spastic Centre of New South Wales
6 Queen Street
Mosman, NSW 2088
Tel: 02-969-1666

Spastic Society of Victoria
135 Inkerman Street
St Kilda, VIC 3182
Tel: 03-537-2611

Spastic Welfare Association of Western Australia Inc.
106 Bradford Street
Coolbinia, WA 6050
Tel: 09-443-0211

Spina Bifida Association
14–20 Station Street
Harris Park, NSW 2150
Tel: 02-633-1311

387 Old Cleveland Road
Coorparoo, QLD 4151
Tel: 07-394-3822

GPO Box 349
Adelaide, SA 5000
Tel: 08-337-4066

82 Hampden Road
Battery Point, TAS 7000
Tel: 002-23-4537

52 Thistlethwaite Street
South Melbourne, VIC 3205
Tel: 03-698-5222

364 Cambridge Street
Wembley, WA 6014
Tel: 09-387-3431

Tasmanian Spastics Association
47 Sandy Bay Road
Sandy Bay, TAS 7005
Tel: 002-31-0466

Bereavement

Compassionate Friends
New South Wales
Tel: 02-267-6962

Australia Capital Territory
Tel: 062-81-2236

Queensland
Tel: 07-359-1897

Victoria
Tel: 03-232-8222

Southern Australia
Tel: 08-439-205

Western Australia
Tel: 09-474-1060

Tasmania
Tel: 002-552-145

Grieving
Victoria
Tel: 03-509-7722

PO Box 41482
Casuarina, NT 5792

South Australia
Tel: 08-336-8727

Western Australia
Tel: 09-451-4607

SIDA (Sudden Infant Death Association)
New South Wales
Tel: 02-639-6969
Australia Capital Territory
Tel: 062-54-2795

Queensland
Tel: 07-370-1311

Help with Babies

Hyperactivity Association
29 Bertram Street
Chatswood, NSW 2067
Tel: 02-411-2186

480 Ipswich Road
Annerley, QLD 4103
Tel: 07-848-2321

18 King William Road
North Adelaide, SA 5006
Tel: 08-267-5551

PO Box 17
East Doncaster, VIC 3108
Tel: 08-842-6428

77 Fernhurst Crescent
Balga, WA 6061
Tel: 09-446-1718

Marriage Guidance

Family Life Movement
41 The Boulevarde
Lewisham, NSW 2049
Tel: 02-560-3377

**Marriage Guidance Council
of Queensland**
Tel: 07-831-2005 for nearest
counsellor

**Marriage Guidance Council
of Victoria**
46 Princess Street
Kew, VIC 3101
Tel: 03-861-8512

Nursing

**Childbirth Education
Association**
127 Forest Road
Hurstville, NSW 2220
Tel: 02-574-927

**Nursing Mothers'
Association of Australia
Headquarters**
PO Box 231
Nunawading, VIC 3131
Tel: 03-877-5011
See your local telephone
directory for nearest counsellors.

**Women's Community
Health Centre**
6 Mary Street
Hindmarsh, SA 5006
Tel: 08-46-6521

**Women's Health Care
House**
92 Thomas Street
West Perth, WA 6005
Tel: 09-321-2383

Women's Health Collective
GPO Box 1053
Hobart, TAS 7000

**Women's Health
Information Services**
Royal Women's Hospital
132 Grattan Street
Carlton, VIC 3053
Tel: 03-344-2007

Post-natal Depression

Family Support Cottage
23 Victor Road
Brookvale, NSW 2100
Tel: 02-93-5600

PANDA
93 Booran Road
Glenhuntly, VIC 3163
Tel: 03-572-1559

**Post-Natal Depression
Support Group**
10 Wakelin Cres.
Weston, ACT 2611
Tel: 062-88-8337

**Post-Natal Support Group
of Western Australia**
Tel: 09-342-4560

Pre-term Babies

POPI (Parents of Premature Infants)
PO Box 225
Nedlands, WA 6009

**Premature Birth Support
Association**
Queensland
Tel: 07-245-4894

New South Wales
Tel: 02-670-2541

South Australia
Tel: 08-270-3821

Victoria
Tel: 03-221-2001

Single or Lone Parents

**Lone Parents Family
Support Service**
121 Pitt Street
Sydney, NSW 2000
Tel: 02-232-6455

Parents without Partners
PO Box 377
Granville, NSW 2142
Tel: 02-682-6677

PO Box 465
Dixon, ACT 2601
Tel: 062-48-6333

PO Box 464
Brisbane, South QLD 4101
Tel: 07-844-8567

PO Box 21
Canterbury, VIC 3126
Tel: 03-836-3211

PO Box 4290
Darwin, NT 5794
Tel: 089-81-8503

26 Currie Street
Adelaide, SA 5000
Tel: 08-51-6660

267

251-2257 Hay Street
Perth, WA 6000
Tel: 09-325-4575

Twins

**Australian Multiple Birth
Association**
1 Chedley Place
Marayong, NSW 2148
Tel: 02-621-2424

5 McGill Street
Evatt, ACT 2617
Tel: 062-58-7925

73 Glenview Road
Pullenvale, QLD 4069
Tel: 07-202-6557

71 Valley Road
Park Orchards, VIC 3114
Tel: 03-876-4188

38 Borella Circuit
Jingili, NT 5792
Tel: 089-85-5786

101 Elizabeth Street
Banksia Park, SA 5091
Tel: 08-264-5930

9 View Street
Blackmans Bay, TAS 7152
Tel: 002-29-5070

**The Twins Plus Club of
Western Australia Inc.**
PO Box 410
West Perth, WA 6005
Tel: 09-447-8034

New Zealand

Allergy

**Allergy Awareness
Association (Inc.)**
PO Box 12-701
Penrose, Auckland
Tel: 435-378
(Mrs Carolyn Sutherland)

To promote awareness of allergies
and their widespread effects on
health. To offer support and
encourage research.

Babies with Handicaps

**Arthritis & Rheumatism
Foundation of New Zealand
(Inc.)**
PO Box 10-020
Wellington

To provide contact among
parents of children with arthritis.

**Asthma Foundation of New
Zealand (Inc.)**
PO Box 1459
Wellington

Organizes educational meetings,
alleviates social distress, finances
medical research.

Brittle Bone Association
PO Box 76-145
Manukau City
Tel: AK275-5609
(Mrs Goulstone)

To provide a support group and
share experiences.

Cerebral Palsy Society
PO Box 24-042
Royal Oak, Auckland 3
Tel: 603-190

**Cleft Lip and Palate
Support Group**
16 Glenorchy Street
Glen Eden, Auckland
Tel: 818-3880

To help parents who have a baby
born with a cleft lip and palate.

**Coeliac Society of
New Zealand (Inc.)**
Head office
c/o Lynn Davies
15 Stenness Avenue
Christchurch 2
Tel: 37-793 (home)
Mrs H. Pentreath
4 Springfield Street
Auckland 10
Tel: 467-153

To support families, provide
information on diets, products
and recipes.

**Cystic Fibrosis Association
of New Zealand**
PO Box 1755
Wellington

PO Box 6460
Wellesley Street
Auckland 1
Tel: 298-4594

Down's Association
PO Box 4142
Auckland 1
Tel: 867-803

Emphasis on family support.

**New Zealand Crippled
Children Society**
PO Box 6349
Te Aro, Wellington
Tel: 845-677
(Mrs L. Outtrim)

Provides access to specialist
facilities, coordinates care and
aims to increase independence.

**New Zealand Diabetes
Association (Inc.)**
Mr M. Jones
PO Box 54, Oamaru
Tel: Oamaru 47-267

Aims to aid, educate and
support; provides camps for
diabetic children.

New Zealand Epilepsy Association
PO Box 190
Dunedin
Tel: 024-771-751

PO Box 5714
Wellesley Street
Auckland
Tel: 687-639

New Zealand Federation for Deaf Children
PO Box 2914
Wellington
Mrs M. Cooper
51a View Road
Henderson
Tel: 836-9863

New Zealand Paraplegic and Physically Disabled Federation
PO Box 610
Hamilton
Tel: 493-125

New Zealand Society for the Intellectually Handicapped
PO Box 4155
Wellington

Offers advice, help, medical services and social gatherings for parents and intellectually handicapped children.

New Zealand Spina Bifida Trust
PO Box 68-454
Newton

R. Vickery
104 Cobham Crescent
Auckland 7
Tel: 818-6300 (home),
735-026 (business)

Royal New Zealand Foundation for the Blind
Private Bag
Newmarket, Auckland
Tel: 774-389

Bereavement

Bereaved Parents Group
Mrs H. French
45 John Sims Drive
Wellington 4

PO Box 4267
Auckland 1
Tel: 586-562, 555-283

Help and understanding for parents who have suffered child bereavement. No religious affiliations.

Cot Death Division of the National Children's Health Research Foundation
PO Box 28-177
Remuera, Auckland 5
Tel: 548-597 (Dr S. Tonkin)

Supports parents and families who have lost a child due to cot death. Supports parents of babies considered to be at risk of cot death. Funds and initiates research.

Breast-feeding

La Leche League (NZ)
PO Box 2307
Christchurch
Tel: Christchurch 793-938
Wellington 785-213
Auckland 266-7387

To give help, encouragement and information, primarily through personal instruction, to mothers who want to breast-feed their babies.

Counselling Groups for Women

New Zealand Home Birth Association
PO Box 7093
Wellesley Street
Auckland

Promotes home birth and assists women wishing to have their babies at home.

Porirua Women's Health Group
PO Box 53055
215 Bedford Street
Cannons Creek
Tel: 376-135

Refer to the local Citizens' Advice Bureau or telephone book (under 'Women') for counselling groups in your area.

Pregnancy Counselling Service
PO Box 4278
Christchurch
Tel: 68-650

Pregnancy Help
National Secretary
PO Box 13-012
Johnsonville, Wellington

Hope Gibbons Building
Corner of Dixon and
Taranaki Streets
Wellington
Tel: 847-979

PO Box 28019
Thorrington,
Christchurch
Tel: Ch 63-355

30 His Majesty's Arcade
Auckland 1
Tel: 732-599

The Health Alternative for Women (THAW)
Corner Peterborough and
Montreal Streets
Christchurch

PO Box 884
Christchurch
Tel: 796-970

Offers pregnancy advice.

Women with Children Support Group
Tel: New Plymouth 896-965

Women's Health Collective
PO Box 9172
10 Kensington Street
Wellington

63 Ponsonby Road
Ponsonby, Auckland
Tel: 764-506

PO Box 47-090
Auckland

Offers workshops, counselling, crisis support.

Other Counselling Services

Federation of New Zealand Parents Centres
National Secretary
PO Box 11-310
Wellington

Pregnancy, childbirth and family education, antenatal classes. Opportunity to meet other new parents. See 'Parents Centre' in telephone book.

Little People of New Zealand
Jan Froger
4 Marr Road
Manurewa, Auckland
Tel: 266-6825

E.W. Gray
Tel: 04-786-459

To provide information and support for Little People and their families. To inform public of the equal rights of Little People.

National Marriage Guidance Council of New Zealand
PO Box 2728
Wellington
Tel: 04-728-798

New Zealand Family Planning Association
National Office
PO Box 68-200
Newton, Auckland

Assistance and advice on sex, contraception and family planning.

New Zealand Federation of Home & Family Societies
Secretary: Miss M. Nyhon
3 Shore Street
Dunedin
Tel: 024-43-448

Parent Help-New Zealand Child Abuse Prevention Society (Inc.)
PO Box 37-577
Parnell, Auckland
Tel: 601-052, 689-411

Telephone counselling service.

Presbyterian Support Services
PO Box 27-095
Wellington

Corner Khyber Pass Road
and Nugent Street
Auckland

Offers child and family
counselling from birth to school-
leaving age.

Society for the Protection of Home and Family (Inc.)
PO Box 6894
Auckland 1
Tel: 32-155

Telephone counselling and face-
to-face counselling for individuals,
couples, families.

Maori Women

Awhia Wahine
C/o Tris Roberts
Community Volunteers
12c Kensington Avenue
Wellington

Mana Wahine
PO Box 3128
Auckland

Maori Women's Centre
PO Box 1560
Hamilton
Tel: 80656

Maori Women's Group
PO Box 330
Whakatane
Tel: 22192

Maori Women's Welfare League
PO Box 12072
Thorndon, Wellington

Tautoko Wahine
26 Resolution Road
Tauranga
Tel: 441001

Tautoko Wahine Maori
PO Box 5097
Flaxmere, Hastings
Tel: 796282
(Deborah Petrowski)

Te Roopu Wahine Aroha
PO Box 86
Taihape

Natural Healing

New Zealand Homeopathic Society (Inc.)
PO Box 2939
Auckland
Tel: 726-310
(Mrs E. Boghurst, home)

Post-natal Support

New Mother Support Groups
PO Box 39-074
Auckland West
Tel: 788-627
(Mrs H. Pointon)
893-027 (Hilary Eason)

To provide an opportunity for women to come together and share their feelings about themselves, their needs and their resources.

Public Health Nurses
Listed in front of telephone book under Health Department; work with Plunket nurses to help families.

Royal New Zealand Plunket Society
Head Office
PO Box 6042
Dunedin North
Tel: DN 770-110

Provides home visits for first three months after baby's birth, then appointments at local Plunket clinic; help in caring for your baby; Plunket-Karitane Family Support Units for extra help.

Pre-term Babies

Parents of Prems
Tel: AK861-621
(Natalie Hick)
AK764-989 (Marie Vitali)
AK543-331 (Susan Callander)

Help and advice for parents of special-care infants from parents with prem babies.

Single Parents

Birthright
PO Box 6302
Te Aro, Wellington

Town Hall
Queen Street
Auckland
Tel: 797-740

Practical help and advice to families where one parent is permanently or temporarily absent. Budgeting, emergency accommodation.

Council for the Single Mother and Her Child
PO Box 47-090
Ponsonby, Auckland 2
Tel: 760-476; 769-363
(Ms C. Duggan, home)

Auckland based; offers information on legal matters, benefits available, refuges, general support. Provides individual and group counselling.

Solo Parents (NZ) Inc.
PO Box 30-970
Lower Hutt
Tel: 04-636-233

Twins and More

New Zealand Multiple Birth Association
PO Box 1258
Wellington
Tel: 766-003
(Ms D. Walton, home)

New Zealand Triplet Plus Club
Ms L. Bryson
RD3 Whakarane

A. Bailey
PO Box 86004
Mangere East

Twins Club
PO Box 69068
Glendene, Auckland
Tel: 818-4319
(Ms R. Jacobs, home)

Other Sources of Help

Barnardo's New Zealand
National Director:
PO Box 6434
Wellington
Tel: AK693-249
(Northern Region)

To provide quality child care in private homes and to give ongoing support to the parents, children and care-givers.

Hyperactivity Association
PO Box 36-099
Auckland 9

91 South Karori Road
Wellington

PO Box 292
Greymouth

New Zealand Childcare Association (Inc.)
PO Box 3402
Wellington
Tel: 04-846-947

New Zealand Playcentre Federation
PO Box 651
Pukekohe

References

Why I Wrote This Book

1. Pat Gray, *Crying Baby: How to Cope*, Chatham, Wisebuy, 1987.

CHAPTER I
The Impact of a Crying Baby

Epigraph: Semming, *A Father's Dairy*, quoted in Milicent Washburn Shimm, *The Biography of a Baby*, 1900.
1. John Todd, *John Todd: The Story of His Life*, London, Sampson, Law and Company, 1876.
2. Ibid.

CHAPTER 2
Why Do Babies Cry?

1. T. Berry Brazelton, 'Crying in infancy – is it really necessary', *Redbook*, April 1978.
2. Ibid.
3. Joy L. Paradise, 'Maternal and other factors in the etiology of infantile colic', *Journal of the American Medical Association*, 197, 1966, pp. 123–31.
4. R. Schnall *et al.*, 'Infant colic', *Australian Pediatric Journal*, December 1979.
5. D. W. Winnicott, *The Maturational Processes and the Facilitating Environment*, London, Hogarth Press, 1965.

6. B. A. Shaver, 'Maternal personality and early adaptation as related to infantile colic', in P. M. Shereshefsky and L. J. Yarrow (eds.), *Psychological Aspects of a First Pregnancy and Early Postnatal Adaptation*, New York, Raven Press, 1974, pp. 209–15.

7. S. Jorup, 'Colonic hyperperistalsis in neurolabile infants', *Acta Paediatrica Uppsala*, Supplement 85, 1982, pp. 1–92; R. S. Illingworth, 'Three months' colic', *Archives of Diseases of Childhood*, 29, 1954, pp. 165–74; *idem*, 'Crying in infants and children', *British Medical Journal*, 1, 1955, pp. 75–8.

8. M. A. Wessell *et al.*, 'Paroxysmal fussing in infancy, sometimes called "colic"', *Pediatrics*, 14, 1965, p. 421–34.

9. T. Berry Brazelton, 'Application of cry research to clinical perspectives', in Barry M. Lester and C. F. Zachariah Boukydis (eds), *Infant Crying*, New York, Plenum, 1985, pp. 325–40.

10. R. S. Illingworth, 'Three months' colic', *Archives of Diseases of Childhood*, 29, 1954, pp. 165–74; *idem*, 'Crying in infants and children, *British Medical Journal*, 1, 1955, pp. 75–8.

11. Ibid.

12. Marc Weissbluth, *Crybabies: Coping with Colic*, Priam Books, 1984, pp. 16–17.

13. T. J. C. Boulton and M. P. Rowley, 'Nutritional studies during childhood: incidental observations of temperament, habits and experiences of ill-health', *Australian Pediatric Journal*, 15, 1979, pp. 87–90.

14. Illingworth, op. cit.

15. Paradise, op. cit.

16. Illingworth, op. cit.; W. C. Taylor, 'A study of infantile colic', *Canadian Medical Association Journal*, 76, 1957, pp. 458–61.

17. Paradise, op. cit.; Illingworth, op. cit.

18. Wessell, op. cit.

19. M. Weissbluth, A. F. Davis and J. Poncher, 'Night waking and infantile colic', *Clinical Research*, 30, 1982, p. 793A.

20. Illingworth, op. cit.

21. I. Jakobsson and T. Lindberg, 'Cow's milk proteins cause infantile colic in breast-fed infants: a double-blind crossover study', *Pediatrics*, 71, 1983, pp. 268–71.

22. A. J. Cant *et al.*, 'Effects of maternal dietary exclusion on breast-

fed infants with eczema: two controlled studies', *British Medical Journal*, 293, 1986, pp. 231–3.
23. Cant *et al.*, op. cit.
24. J. N. H. Du, 'Colic as the sole symptom of urinary tract infection in infants', *Journal of Canadian Medical Association*, 115, 1976, pp. 334–7.
25. Aiden MacFarlane, 'Screening for congenital dislocation of the hips', *British Medical Journal*, 294, 1987, p. 1047.
26. G. Elander, 'Breast-feeding of infants diagnosed as having congenital hip joint dislocation and treated in the von Rosen splint', *Midwifery*, 2, 1986, pp. 147–51; Laurence Berman and Leslie Klenerman, 'Ultrasound screening for hip abnormalities: preliminary findings in 1001 neonates', *British Medical Journal*, 293, 1986, pp. 719–22.

CHAPTER 3
Is It Hunger?

Epigraph: Roberta Isaeloff, *Coming to Terms*, London, Corgi, 1987.
1. C. J. Bacon, 'Overheating in infancy – an avoidable cause of cot death?', *Update*, 15 February 1986, pp. 277–85.
2. Sheila Kitzinger, *The Experience of Breastfeeding*, London, Penguin, 1987.
3. Dana Raphael, *The Tender Gift: Breastfeeding*, New York, Prentice Hall, 1973.

CHAPTER 4
Stress in Pregnancy

1. W. A. Brown, *Psychological Care During Pregnancy and the Post-natal Period*, New York, Raven Press, 1979.
2. Jean A. Ball, *Reactions to Motherhood: The Role of Post-natal Care*, Cambridge, Cambridge University Press, 1987.
3. G. Caplan, *Principles of Preventive Psychiatry*, London, Tavistock Publications, 1964; *idem*, *An Approach to Community Mental Health*, London, Tavistock Publications, 1969.

4. R. W. Newton *et al.*, 'Psychosocial stress in pregnancy and its relation to the onset of premature labour', *British Medical Journal*, 2, 1979, pp. 411–13.
5. R. W. Newton and L. P. Hunt, 'Psychosocial stress in pregnancy and its relation to low birth weight', *British Medical Journal*, 288, 1984, pp. 1191–3.
6. H. A. Fox, 'The effects of catecholamines and drug treatment on the fetus and newborn', *Birth and the Family Journal*, 6, 1979, pp. 157–165.
7. James Pennebaker, paper given at the conference of the American Psychological Association, 1986.

CHAPTER 5
The Birth

1. J. Bernal, 'Night waking in infants during the first 14 months', *Developmental Medicine and Child Neurology*, 15, 1973, pp. 760–9.
2. N. Blurton-Jones *et al.*, 'The association between perinatal factors and later night waking', *Developmental Medicine and Child Neurology*, 20, 1978, pp. 427–34; Naomi Richman, 'A community survey of characteristics of 1- to 2-year-olds with sleep disruption', *American Academy of Child Psychiatry*, 10, 1981, pp. 281–91.
3. Rudolph Schaffer, *Mothering*, London, Fontana, 1977.
4. T. Berry Brazelton, 'Psychophysiologic reaction in the neonate II: the effects of maternal medication on the neonate and his behavior', *Journal of Pediatrics*, 58, 1961, pp. 513–18.
5. E. Tronick *et al.*, 'Regional obstetric anesthesia and newborn behavior: effect over the first ten days of life', *Journal of Pediatrics*, 58, 1976, pp. 94–100; E. M. Belsey *et al.*, 'The influence of maternal analgesia on neonatal behaviour I: pethidine', *British Journal of Obstetrics and Gynaecology*, 88, 1981, pp. 398–406.
6. Carol Sepkoski, 'Maternal obstetric medication and newborn behavior', in J. W. Scanlon (ed.), *Perinatal Anesthesia*, Oxford, Blackwell, 1985, pp. 131–74.
7. D. R. Rosenblatt *et al.*, 'The influence of maternal analgesia on neonatal behaviour II: epidural bupivicaine', *British Journal of Obstetrics and Gynaecology*, 88, 1981, pp. 407–13.

8. Carol Sepkoski, 'A 5-year follow-up study of obstetric medication effects: bupivicaine epidural anesthesia', paper presented at the Third World Congress on Infant Psychiatry and Allied Disciplines, Stockholm, 1986.
9. A. D. Murray *et al.*, 'Effects of epidural anesthesia on newborns and their mothers', *Child Development*, 52, 1981, pp. 71–82.
10. Ibid.
11. Tronick *et al.*, op. cit.
12. Rosenblatt *et al.*, op. cit.; Murray *et al.*, op. cit.; Tronick *et al.*, op. cit.
13. Murray *et al.*, op. cit.
14. N. Klaus and J. Kennel, *Parent-Infant Bonding*, 2nd edn, St Louis, C. V. Mosby Co., 1982.
15. Sheila Kitzinger, *The New Good Birth Guide*, London, Penguin, 1983.
16. Patrizia Romito, 'The humanising of childbirth: the response of medical institutions to women's demands for change', *Midwifery*, 2, 1986, pp. 135–40.
17. Ibid.

CHAPTER 6
Down from the Mountain

Epigraph: Jane Lazarre, *Mother Knot*, London, Virago, 1987.
1. Ann Oakley, *Women Confined*, Oxford, Martin Robertson, 1980.
2. *The Independent*, 24 March 1987.
3. Sheila Kitzinger, *Birth Over Thirty*, London, Sheldon Press, 1982.
4. Brice Pitt, ' "Atypical" depression following childbirth', *British Journal of Psychiatry*, 114, 1968, pp. 1325–35.
5. L. Chertok, *Motherhood and Personality*, London, Tavistock Publications, 1969; A. Nilsson, 'Parental emotional adjustment', in N. Morris (ed.), *Psychosomatic Medicine in Obstetrics and Gynaecology*, New York, Wiley, 1972.
6. T. F. Main, 'A fragment on mothering', in Elizabeth Barnes (ed.), *Psychosexual Nursing*, London, Tavistock Publications, 1968.
7. Sylvia Markham, 'A comparison of psychotic and normal postpartum reactions based on psychological tests', in L. Chertok

(ed.), *Médecine Psychosomatique et Maternité*, Paris, Gautier-Villers, 1965, pp. 499–503.

8. Jean A. Ball, *Reactions of Motherhood: The Role of Post-natal Care*, Cambridge, Cambridge University Press, 1987.

9. I. Al-Issa, *The Psychopathology of Woman*, Englewood Cliffs, NJ, Prentice Hall, 1980.

10. E. Haavio-Mannila, 'Inequalities in health and gender', *Social Science and Medicine*, 22(2), 1986, pp. 141–9; G. W. Brown and T. Harris (eds.), *Culture and Psychopathology*, Baltimore, Baltimore University, Park Press, 1982.

11. Central Statistical Office, *Social Trends*, London, HMSO, 1986.

12. Jane Price, personal communication.

13. Hansy Josovic, personal communication.

14. Mary Douglas, *Purity and Danger: An Analysis of Concepts of Pollution and Taboo*, London, Routledge & Kegan Paul, 1966.

CHAPTER 7
The Father of the Crying Baby

1. J. Martin, *Infant Feeding 1975: Attitudes and Practices in England and Wales*, London, HMSO/OPCS, 1978; M. R. Hally *et al.*, *A Study of Infant Feeding: Factors Influencing Choice of Method*, Newcastle, Health Care Research Unit, University of Newcastle, 1981; D. A. Jones, R. R. West and R. G. Newcombe, 'Maternal characteristics associated with the duration of breastfeeding', *Midwifery*, 2, 1986, pp. 141–6.

2. Jonathan Rutherford, 'I want something that we men have no language to describe, to look after a baby at home, not like a mother, but as a man', *Woman's Journal*, May 1987.

3. P. Shereshefsky and L. Yarrow, *Psychological Aspects of a First Pregnancy and Early Post-natal Adaptation*, New York, Raven Press, 1973; M. Richards, J. Dunn and B. Antonis, 'Caretaking in the first year of life', *Child Care, Health and Development*, 1977, pp. 23–6; Ann Oakley, *Becoming a Mother*, Oxford, Martin Robertson, 1979.

4. Association of Market Research Organizations, *Men and Domestic Work*, London, 1987.

5. Charlie Lewis and Margaret O'Brien (eds.), *Reassessing Fatherhood:*

New Observations on Fathers and the Modern Family, London, Sage Publications, 1987.

6. Charlie Lewis, *Becoming a Father*, Milton Keynes, Open University Press, 1986.

7. Jerrold Lee Shapiro, 'The expectant father', *Psychology Today*, January 1987, pp. 36–42.

8. 'Fathers '86', *Parents* (Australia), August/September 1986, pp. 47–59.

9. Claude Levi-Strauss, *The Raw and the Cooked: Introduction to a Science of Mythology*, London, Cape, 1970.

10. Marianne Glastonbury, 'Fathers-in-flight', *Women's Review*, 13, November 1986, p. 6.

11. *Parents* (Australia), op. cit.

12. Jonathan Rutherford, op. cit.

CHAPTER 8

Target for Advice

Epigraph: Morton Schatzman, *Soul Muder: Persecution in the Family*, London, Penguin, 1973.

Jean Liedloff, *The Continuum Concept*, London, Duckworth, 1975. Revised edition, London, Penguin, 1986.

1. Sheila Kitzinger, *The Good Birth Guide*, London, Fontana, 1979; *idem*, *The New Good Birth Guide*, London, Penguin, 1983.

2. Sheila Kitzinger, *The New Good Birth Guide*, London, Penguin, 1983.

CHAPTER 9

Drugged Babies

1. The letters from working women written to the Women's Co-operative Guild were first published in 1915. In the letter from which this extract is taken the problems faced by a mother with thirteen children are described.

2. Elisabeth Badinter, *The Myth of Motherhood: An Historical View of the Maternal Instinct*, London, Souvenir Press, 1981.

3. G. L. Prentiss, *The Life and Letters of Elizabeth Prentiss*, London, Hodder & Stoughton, 1982.

REFERENCES

4. Mary Chamberlain, *Old Wives' Tales: Their Histories, Remedies and Spells*, London, Virago, 1981; Christina Hardyment, *Dream Babies: Child Care from Locke to Spock*, Oxford, Oxford University Press, 1984.

5. John Cowan, *The Science of a New Life*, London, Hammond and Company, 1869.

6. D. Joseph DeLee, *Obstetrics for Nurses*, Philadelphia, W. B. Saunders, 1904.

7. Charles Paddock, MD, *Maternitas*, Chicago, Lloyd J. Head and Co., 1905.

8. Jack G. Shiller, *Childhood Illness: A Common Sense Approach*, New York, Stein and Day, 1978.

9. F. B. Smith, *The Peoples' Health, 1830–1910*, Canberra, ANU Press, 1979, pp. 93–9, quoted in Maureen Minchin, *Breastfeeding Matters*, Sydney, Alma Publications and Allen and Unwin, 1985, p. 210.

10. A. Schlebaum, 'From zygotes to zombies – a critical look at our children's brave new world of chemical abuse', in *Man, Drugs and Society*, pp. 181–7, referred to in Minchin, op. cit.

11. R. S. and C. M. Illingworth, *Babies and Young Children*, London, Churchill, 1954.

12. John Cobb, *Babyshock: A Mother's First Five Years*, London, Hutchinson, 1980.

13. Hardyment, op. cit.

14. Shirley Goodwin, 'Have you hugged our kid today?', *Nursing Mirror*, 5 January 1983, p. 49.

15. The Medical Director in a letter to me dated 4 April 1985.

CHAPTER 10
Lashing Out

Epigraph: Phyllis Chesler, *With Child: A Diary of Motherhood*, Wisconsin, T. W. Crowell, 1979.

1. Jane Lazarre, *The Mother Knot*, New York, Dell Publishing, 1976.

2. Pat Gray, *Crying Baby: How to Cope*, London, Wisebuy, 1987.

3. *Guardian*, 24 May 1986.

4. C. H. Kempe and R. E. Helfer, *Helping the Battered Child and His Family*, Philadelphia, Lippincott, 1972.

5. Sue Sharpe, *Falling for Love*, London, Virago Upstarts, 1987.

6. Roberta Israeloff, *Coming to Terms*, New York, Knopf, 1984.

CHAPTER 11
The Pre-term and Low-birthweight Baby

1. Quoted in Robert J. Trotter, 'The play's the thing', *Psychology Today*, January 1987.
2. J. W. Crawford, 'Mother-infant interaction in premature and full-term infants', *Child Development*, 53, 1982, pp. 957–62.
3. N. Blurton-Jones *et al.*, 'The association between perinatal factors and later night waking', *Developmental Medicine and Child Neurology*, 20, 1978, pp. 427–34; Naomi Richman, 'A community survey of characteristics of 1- to 2-year-olds with sleep disruptions', *American Academy of Child Psychiatry*, 20, 1981, pp. 281–91.
4. J. D. Baum and P. Howat, 'The family and neonatal intensive care', in Sheila Kitzinger and John A. Davis, *The Place of Birth*, Oxford, Oxford University Press, 1978.
5. Ibid.
6. M. Klein and L. Stern, 'Low birthweight and the battered child syndrome', *American Journal of the Diseases of Children*, 122, 1971, pp. 15–18.
7. T. Berry Brazelton, 'Crying in infancy – is it really necessary?', *Redbook*, April 1978; *idem*, 'Application of cry research for clinical perspectives', in Barry M. Lester and C. F. Zachariah Boukydis (eds.), *Infant Crying*, New York, Plenum, 1985, pp. 325–40.
8. T. Berry Brazelton, 'Crying in infancy – is it really necessary?', *Redbook*, April 1978.
9. E. G. Hasselmeyer, 'The premature neonate's response to handling', *Journal of the American Nursing Association*, 1, 1964, pp. 15–24; Norman Solkoff *et al.*, 'Effects of handling on the subsequent development of premature infants', *Developmental Psychology*, 1(6), 1969, pp. 765–8; Louisa Feldman Powell, 'The effect of extra stimulation and maternal involvement on the development of low-birthweight infants and on maternal behaviour', *Child Development*, 45, 1974, pp. 106–13; Norman Solkoff and Diane Matuszak, 'Tactile stimulation and behavioral development among low-birthweight infants', *Child Psychiatry and Human Development*, 6(1), 1975, pp. 33–7; Jerry L. White and Richard C. Labarba, 'The effects of tactile and kinesthetic stimulation on neonatal development in the premature infant', *Developmental Psychobiology*, 9(6), 1976, pp. 569–77.

10. Ruth Dianne Rice, 'Neurophysiological development in premature infants following stimulation', *Developmental Psychology*, 13(1), 1977, pp. 69–76.

11. Andrew Whitelaw and Katherine Sleath, 'Myth of the marsupial mother: home care of very low-birthweight babies in Bogota, Colombia', *Lancet*, 1, 25, 1985, pp. 1206–8.

CHAPTER 12
Bored and Lonely

Epigraph: Joseph D. DeLee, *Obstetrics for Nurses*, Philadelphia, W. B. Saunders, 1904.

1. Rudolph Schaffer, *Mothering*, London, Fontana, 1977, pp. 66–84.

2. Robert J. Trotter, 'The play's the thing', *Psychology Today*, January 1987.

3. Penelope Leach, *Baby and Child*, London, Michael Joseph, 1977.

4. Jerome Kagan and Robert Klein, 'Cross-cultural perspectives on early development', *American Psychologist*, 28, 1973, pp. 947–61.

5. Trotter, op. cit.

6. J. A. Ambrose, *Stimulation in Early Infancy*, New York, Academic Press, 1965.

7. U. A. Hunziger and R. G. Barr, 'Increased carrying reduces infant crying: a randomized control trial', *Pediatrics*, 77, 1986, pp. 641–8.

8. A. F. Korner and R. Grobstein, 'Visual alertness as related to soothing in neonates: implications for maternal stimulation and early deprivation', *Child Development*, 37, 1966, pp. 867–76.

9. A. F. Korner and E. B. Thoman, 'Visual alertness in neonates as evoked by maternal care', *Journal of Experimental Psychology*, 10, 1970, pp. 67–8.

10. Schaffer, op. cit.

11. Anne Bouchart-Godard, 'Une peau sensible', in Etienne Herbinet and Marie-Claire Bushel (eds.), *L'aube des Sens*, Paris, Stock, 1981.

12. O. Wasz-Hockert, *The Infant Cry*, London, Spastics Internal Medical Publications, Heinemann, 1968.

13. John Lind and Carol B. Hardgrove, 'Lullaby Bonding', *Keeping Abreast, Journal of Human Nurturing*, 3, 1978, pp. 184–9.

14. D. J. Winnicott, *The Child, the Family and the Outside World*, London, Penguin, 1964.
15. Ibid.
16. Ibid.

CHAPTER 13
Living with a Crying Baby

Epigraph: G. L. Prentiss, *The Life and Letters of Elizabeth Prentiss*, 1822.
1. Valerie Fildes, *Breast, Bottles and Babies*, Edinburgh, Edinburgh University Press, 1986.
2. George P. Fisher, *Life with Benjamin Silliman, LL.DD.*, vol. 1, New York, Scribner and Co., 1866, p. 10.
3. Malcolm Lovell (ed.), *Two Quaker Sisters*, New York, Liveright, 1937, pp. 57–8.
4. J. Luce and Julius Segal, *Insomnia*, New York, Doubleday, 1969, p. 153.
5. J. B. Watson, *Psychological Care of Infant and Child*, New York, W. W. Norton and Co., 1928, pp. 69–87.
6. Tine Thevenin, *The Family Bed*, PO Box 16004, Minneapolis, MN 55416, Tine Thevenin, 1977.
7. A. Tsutoma *et al.*, 'Induction of rest and sleep on the neonates by the rhythm of the maternal blood flow', *Journal of Nippon Medical School*, 42, 3, 1975, pp. 77–9.
8. Patricia M. Callis, 'The testing and comparison of the intra-uterine sound against other methods of calming babies', *Midwives' Chronicle*, October 1984, p. 336–8.
9. Sung by The Mothersong Choir of Santa Cruz, California.
10. J. A. Ambrose (ed.), *Stimulation in Early Infancy*, London and New York, Academic Press, 1970.
11. Ian St John, 'Motherbaby Massage', *Studies in Bioanalysis*, Bioinstitute Publications, Addlestone, 1984.
12. Frederick Leboyer, *Loving Hands: The Traditional Indian Art of Baby Massage*, London, Fontana, 1977.
13. Jacqui Showell, 'Touching babies', *Interface*, 3(6), 1977; Amelia D. Auckett, 'Baby massage: An alternative to drugs', *The Australia*

Nurses' Journal, 9(5), 1979, pp. 24–7; *idem, Baby Massage*, Wellingborough, Northamptonshire, Thorsons, 1982; Tina Heinl, *The Baby Massage Book*, London, Coventure, 1983.

14. Sheila Kitzinger, *Woman's Experience of Sex*, London, Penguin, 1986.
15. St John, op. cit.
16. 'Bathing babies without tears', *Parents* (Australia), August/September 1987, pp. 44–5.

CHAPTER 14
Babies in Other Cultures

Epigraph: Mirelle Riciardi, *Vanishing Africa*, London, Collins, 1974.
1. Richard Lannoy, *The Speaking Tree: A Study of Indian Culture and Society*, Oxford, Oxford University Press, 1971.
2. Carolyn Niethammer, *Daughters of the Earth: The Lives and Legends of American Indian Women*, London, Collier Macmillan, 1977.
3. Mary Beck Moser, 'Seri: conception through infancy', in Margaret Artschwager Kay (ed.), *Anthropology of Human Birth*, Philadelphia, F. A. Davis, 1982, p. 230.
4. Helen K. Henderson and Richard N. Henderson, 'Traditional Onitsha Ibo maternity beliefs and practices', in Kay, op. cit., pp. 190–91.
5. Brigitte Jordan, personal communication.
6. Laurence Stone, *The Family, Sex and Marriage in England 1500–1800*, London, Penguin, 1979.
7. Ibid.
8. Beverley Horn, 'Northwest coast Indians: the Muckleshoot', in Kay, op. cit., p. 374.
9. Veronic Evaneshko, 'Tonawanda Seneca childbearing culture', in Kay, op. cit., p. 411.
10. Virginia Cole Trenholm, *The Arapahoes, Our People*, Norman, Oklahoma, Oklahoma University Press, 1970.
11. June M. Collins, *Valley of the Spirits: The Skagit Indians West of Washington*, Seattle, University of Washington Press, 1974.
12. Marjorie Shostak, 'Earliest memories: growing up among the !Kung', in Anna R. Cohn and Lucinda A. Leach, *Generations*,

New York, Pantheon with Smithsonian Institution Travelling Exhibition Service, 1987, pp. 201–3.

13. Ruth Benedict, *The Chrysanthemum and the Sword*, Boston, Houghton Mifflin, 1946.

14. George J. Klima, *The Barabaig: East African Cattle-herders*, New York, Holt Rinehart and Winston, 1970.

15. Margaret Micky, 'The Cowrie Shell Miao of Keweichow', *Papers of the Peabody Museum of American Archeology and Ethnology*, 32, 1, 1947.

16. Lannoy, op. cit.

17. Anna R. Kohn and Lucinda A. Leach, op. cit., p. 155.

18. Donald Thompson, *Children of the Wilderness*, Melbourne, Currey O'Neill, 1983.

19. H. N. Hogbin, *Kinship and Marriage in a New Guinea Village*, London, Methuen, 1963.

20. Brigitte Jordan, personal communication.

21. Lauris McKee, 'Los Cuerpos Tiernos: Simbolismo y Magia en las Practicas Post-Parto en Ecuador', *America Indigena*, 62, no. 4, 1984, pp. 615–28. An English version of this paper is in Kohn and Leach, op. cit.

Index

INDEX

stress, 80–87
  see also tension; violence
  acknowledgement of, 54–5
  hormones, and, 43
  in pregnancy, 41–55
stroking see touch
sucking
  enjoyment of, 29–33
  epidural, after, 60–61
  soothing effect of, 171
  technique of, 36–40
  thumbs, 208
suckling see breast-feeding
support, xiii, 5, 39, 40, 42, 61, 80, 84, 86, 149–
  50, 204–8, 215–17, 218–20, 229–30
swaddling, 222–4, 229
sweating, 31
Sweden, 20
synchronization of babies, 168
syntometrine, 58

Tanzania, 226
teething rings, 209
Temaril (Vallergan), 129
temperature, 31
tension
  of babies, 19
  of mothers, 6, 10, 25, 33, 188–93: com-
    municating to babies, 26; flow of milk,
    36, 118; result, not cause, of crying, xiv,
    5, 10–11; release of, 55, 213, 204–8, 217
  see also stress; violence
Thailand, 226
theories about crying, 8–16
Third World practices see peasant communities
thirst, 30–31
thrush (candida), 26
thumb-sucking, 208
Tibet, 224–5
TIC TAC, 161–2
Todd, John, 1

total happenings, 180–84
touching babies, 8, 11, 160–64, 178–180,
  198–202, 233–4
  see also massage
tranquillizers, 25–6, 48, 58, 61, 78, 81–2, 139,
  146, 157
  for babies, 125–8
  see also drugs
Turkey, 226

ultrasound, 27
underfed babies, 14

vacations see holidays
Valium, 125
Vallergan (Temaril), 129
violence
  from partner, 45, 47, 48, 77, 100, 144
  to babies, 2, 67, 80, 90, 134–50: actual, 5,
    136; control of, 5, 139, 146–50; tempta-
    tion of, 67, 73, 114, 141–4
visual stimulation, 202–8
  see also eye contact

Wasz-Hockert, O., 180
Watson, J. B., 188
weaning, 233
weight of babies
  birth, 43: low, 154
  increase of, 14, 31–2, 155
  small-for-gestational-age, 50, 154–7
well-women clinics, 85
Wells, H. G., 100
wet-nurses, 187
whooping cough vaccine, 28
Winnicott, D. W., 11, 17, 180–82, 183–5
Women's Experience of Sex (Kitzinger), 199
women's health centres, 85
working (paid) mothers, 42

young mothers, 140–41
Yucatan (Mexico), 221, 229

FOR THE BEST IN PAPERBACKS, LOOK FOR THE

In every corner of the world, on every subject under the sun, Penguin represents quality and variety – the very best in publishing today.

For complete information about books available from Penguin – including Pelicans, Puffins, Peregrines and Penguin Classics – and how to order them, write to us at the appropriate address below. Please note that for copyright reasons the selection of books varies from country to country.

In the United Kingdom: Please write to *Dept E.P., Penguin Books Ltd, Harmondsworth, Middlesex, UB7 0DA*

If you have any difficulty in obtaining a title, please send your order with the correct money, plus ten per cent for postage and packaging, to *PO Box No 11, West Drayton, Middlesex*

In the United States: Please write to *Dept BA, Penguin, 299 Murray Hill Parkway, East Rutherford, New Jersey 07073*

In Canada: Please write to *Penguin Books Canada Ltd, 2801 John Street, Markham, Ontario L3R 1B4*

In Australia: Please write to the *Marketing Department, Penguin Books Australia Ltd, P.O. Box 257, Ringwood, Victoria 3134*

In New Zealand: Please write to the *Marketing Department, Penguin Books (NZ) Ltd, Private Bag, Takapuna, Auckland 9*

In India: Please write to *Penguin Overseas Ltd, 706 Eros Apartments, 56 Nehru Place, New Delhi, 110019*

In Holland: Please write to *Penguin Books Nederland B.V., Postbus 195, NL–1380AD Weesp, Netherlands*

In Germany: Please write to *Penguin Books Ltd, Friedrichstrasse 10–12, D–6000 Frankfurt Main 1, Federal Republic of Germany*

In Spain: Please write to *Longman Penguin España, Calle San Nicolas 15, E–28013 Madrid, Spain*

In France: Please write to *Penguin Books Ltd, 39 Rue de Montmorency, F-75003, Paris, France*

In Japan: Please write to *Longman Penguin Japan Co Ltd, Yamaguchi Building, 2–12–9 Kanda Jimbocho, Chiyoda-Ku, Tokyo 101, Japan*

FOR THE BEST IN PAPERBACKS, LOOK FOR THE 🐧

COOKERY IN PENGUINS

Fast Food for Vegetarians Janette Marshall

Packed with ideas for healthy, delicious dishes from Caribbean vegetables to rose-water baklava, this stimulating book proves that fast food does not have to mean junk food.

More Easy Cooking for One or Two Louise Davies

This charming book, full of ideas and easy recipes, offers even the novice cook good wholesome food with the minimum of effort.

The Cuisine of the Rose Mireille Johnston

Classic French cooking from Burgundy and Lyonnais, including the most succulent dishes of meat and fish bathed in pungent sauces of wine and herbs.

Good Food from Your Freezer Helge Rubinstein and Sheila Bush

Using a freezer saves endless time and trouble and cuts your food bills dramatically; this book will enable you to cook just as well – perhaps even better – with a freezer as without.

Roy Ackerman's Recipe Collection

Here is a treasure-trove of recipes that have been created by some of the top chefs in the very best restaurants in the British Isles. Handwritten and beautifully illustrated, it is a stunning selection of their favourite dishes, gathered together to recreate memories of a special experience.

Budget Gourmet Geraldene Holt

Plan carefully, shop wisely and cook well to produce first-rate food at minimal expense. It's as easy as pie!

FOR THE BEST IN PAPERBACKS, LOOK FOR THE

COOKERY IN PENGUINS

Simple French Food   Richard Olney

'There is no other book about food that is anything like it . . . essential and exciting reading for cooks, of course, but it is also a book for eaters . . . its pages brim over with invention' – Paul Levy in the *Observer*

The Vegetarian Epicure   Anna Thomas

Mouthwatering recipes for soups, breads, vegetable dishes, salads and desserts that any meat-eater or vegetarian will find hard to resist.

A Book of Latin American Cooking   Elisabeth Lambert Ortiz

Anyone who thinks Latin American food offers nothing but *tacos* and *tortillas* will enjoy the subtle marriages of texture and flavour celebrated in this marvellous guide to one of the world's most colourful *cuisines*.

Quick Cook   Beryl Downing

For victims of the twentieth century, this book provides some astonishing gourmet meals – all cooked in under thirty minutes.

Josceline Dimbleby's Book of Puddings, Desserts and Savouries

'Full of the most delicious and novel ideas for every type of pudding' – *Lady*

Chinese Food   Kenneth Lo

A popular step-by-step guide to the whole range of delights offered by Chinese cookery and the fascinating philosophy behind it.

PENGUIN HEALTH

Audrey Eyton's F-Plus   Audrey Eyton

'Your short cut to the most sensational diet of the century' – *Daily Express*

Baby and Child   Penelope Leach

A beautifully illustrated and comprehensive handbook on the first five years of life. 'It stands head and shoulders above anything else available at the moment' – Mary Kenny in the *Spectator*

Woman's Experience of Sex   Sheila Kitzinger

Fully illustrated with photographs and line drawings, this book explores the riches of women's sexuality at every stage of life. 'A book which any mother could confidently pass on to her daughter – and her partner too' – *Sunday Times*

Food Additives   Erik Millstone

Eat, drink and be worried? Erik Millstone's hard-hitting book contains powerful evidence about the massive risks being taken with the health of the consumer. It takes the lid off the food we have and the food industry.

Living with Allergies   Dr John McKenzie

At least 20% of the population suffer from an allergic disorder at some point in their lives and this invaluable book provides accurate and up-to-date information about the condition, where to go for help, diagnosis and cure – and what we can do to help ourselves.

Living with Stress   Cary L. Cooper, Rachel D. Cooper and Lynn H. Eaker

Stress leads to more stress, and the authors of this helpful book show why low levels of stress are desirable and how best we can achieve them in today's world. Looking at those most vulnerable, they demonstrate ways of breaking the vicious circle that can ruin lives.

BY THE SAME AUTHOR

Pregnancy and Childbirth

Written by the foremost childbirth educator of our time, *Pregnancy and Childbirth* is a complete, up-to-date manual of physical and emotional preparation for expectant parents. With openness and sympathetic understanding of the psychology of the whole birth experience, Sheila Kitzinger discusses every phase of pregnancy and birth, from conception and the early physical changes through to the first few days of the baby's life.

'A good book which answers all the questions parents expecting their first baby are likely to ask' – *New Scientist*

'Lucid and reassuring' – *Guardian*

The Experience of Childbirth

Since Sheila Kitzinger wrote the first version of this classic text on pregnancy and birth in 1962, after the birth of her fourth baby, *The Experience of Childbirth* has influenced thousands of families. The book has gone through numerous changes as she shared with and learned from women throughout the world.

Sheila Kitzinger explores the psychology and physiology of pregnancy and birth and explains how it can be a profound psycho-sexual experience and a powerful affirmation of self. Subjects such as the development of the foetus, different approaches to childbirth education, modern obstetric procedures and drugs used in childbirth, and sex before and after the baby comes, are all described in detail. Above all, the book concentrates on feelings, preparing both parents in a positive and joyful way for the challenges of becoming a family.

and

Birth Over Thirty
The Experience of Breast Feeding
Woman's Experience of Sex